FAITH & FIRE

BANE OF HERETICS and traitors, the Adepta Sororitas is a zealous, all-female army that enforces the will of the holy Ecclesiarchy. Trained in all forms of combat, indoctrinated in the fanatical Imperial faith, Sister of Battle Miriya has been shaped and forged to be the ultimate warrior.

When a dangerous psyker named Torris Vaun escapes from her custody, Miriya is shamed and humiliated in the eyes of her superiors. To regain her honour, and the respect of her commander, she must track down and recapture Vaun. Accompanied by the Sister Hospitaller Verity, Miriya and her fellow Sisters set off on the trail of the heretic.

The planet Neva holds many dark secrets, and Miriya uncovers a terrible plot that could threaten the safety of the whole Imperium. When the forces of darkness step out of the shadows, will faith be enough to save Miriya and Verity?

A WARHAMMER 40,000 NOVEL

FAITH & FIRE

James Swallow

For Mandy; my faith and my fire.

A BLACK LIBRARY PUBLICATION

First published in Great Britain in 2006 by
BL Publishing,
Games Workshop Ltd.,
Willow Road, Nottingham, NG7 2WS, UK.

10 9 8 7 6 5 4 3 2 1

Cover illustration by Karl Kopinski.

A CIP record for this book is available from the British Library.

ISBN 13: 978-1-84416-289-5
ISBN 10: 1-84416-289-3

Distributed in the US by Simon & Schuster
1230 Avenue of the Americas, New York, NY 10020, US.

Printed and bound in Great Britain by
Bookmarque, Surrey, UK.

See the Black Library on the Internet at
www.blacklibrary.com

Find out more about Games Workshop
and the world of Warhammer 40,000 at
www.games-workshop.com

IT IS THE 41st millennium. For more than a hundred centuries the Emperor has sat immobile on the Golden Throne of Earth. He is the master of mankind by the will of the gods, and master of a million worlds by the might of his inexhaustible armies. He is a rotting carcass writhing invisibly with power from the Dark Age of Technology. He is the Carrion Lord of the Imperium for whom a thousand souls are sacrificed every day, so that he may never truly die.

YET EVEN IN his deathless state, the Emperor continues his eternal vigilance. Mighty battlefleets cross the daemon-infested miasma of the warp, the only route between distant stars, their way lit by the Astronomican, the psychic manifestation of the Emperor's will. Vast armies give battle in his name on uncounted worlds. Greatest amongst his soldiers are the Adeptus Astartes, the Space Marines, bio-engineered super-warriors. Their comrades in arms are legion: the Imperial Guard and countless planetary defence forces, the ever-vigilant Inquisition and the tech-priests of the Adeptus Mechanicus to name only a few. But for all their multitudes, they are barely enough to hold off the ever-present threat from aliens, heretics, mutants – and worse.

TO BE A man in such times is to be one amongst untold billions. It is to live in the cruellest and most bloody regime imaginable. These are the tales of those times. Forget the power of technology and science, for so much has been forgotten, never to be re-learned. Forget the promise of progress and understanding, for in the grim dark future there is only war. There is no peace amongst the stars, only an eternity of carnage and slaughter, and the laughter of thirsting gods.

CHAPTER ONE

FROM HIS HIGH vantage point, the Emperor of Mankind looked down upon Miriya where she knelt. His unchanging gaze took in all of her, the woman's bowed form shrouded in blood-coloured robes. In places, armour dark as obsidian emerged from the folds of the crimson cloth. It framed her against the tan stonework of the chapel floor. She was defined by the light that reflected upon her from the Emperor's eternal visage; all that she was, she was only by His decree.

Miriya's lips moved in whispers. The Litany of Divine Guidance spilled from her in a cascading hush. The words were such a part of her that they came as quickly and effortlessly as breathing. As the climax of the declaration came, she felt a warm core of righteousness establish itself in her heart, as it always did, as it always had since the day she had discarded her noviciate cloak and taken the oath.

She allowed herself to look up at Him. Miriya granted herself this small gesture as a reward. Her gaze travelled up the altar, drinking in the majesty of the towering golden idol. The Emperor watched her over folded arms, across the inverted hilt of a great burning sword. At His left shoulder stood Saint Celestine, her hands cupped to hold two stone doves as if she were offering them up. At His right was Saint Katherine, the Daughter of the Emperor who had founded the order that Miriya now served.

She lingered on Katherine's face for a moment: the statue's hair fell down over her temple and across the fleur-de-lys carved beneath her left eye. Miriya unconsciously brushed her black tresses back over her ear, revealing her own fleur tattoo in dark red ink.

The armour the stone saint wore differed from Miriya's in form but not function. Katherine was clad in an ancient type of wargear, and she bore the symbol of a burning heart where Miriya wore a holy cross crested with a skull. When the saint had been mistress of her sect, they had been known as the Order of the Fiery Heart – but that had been decades before Katherine's brutal ending on Mnestteus. Since that date, for over two millennia they had called themselves the Order of our Martyred Lady. It was part of a legacy of duty to the Emperor that Sister Miriya of the Adepta Sororitas had been fortunate to continue.

With that thought, she looked upon the effigy of Him. She met the stone eyes and imagined that on far distant Terra, the Lord of Humanity was granting her some infinitely small fraction of His divine attention, willing her to carry out her latest mission with His blessing. Miriya's hands came to her chest and crossed one another, making the sign of the Imperial aquila.

'In Your name,' she said aloud. 'In service to Your Light, grant me guidance and strength. Let me know the witch and the heretic, show them to me.' She bowed once again. 'Let me do Your bidding and rid the galaxy of man's foe.'

Miriya drew herself up from where she knelt and moved to the font servitor, presenting the slave-thing with her ornate plasma pistol. The hybrid produced a brass cup apparatus in place of a hand and let a brief mist of holy water sprinkle over the weapon. Tapes of sanctified parchment stuttered from its lipless mouth with metallic ticks of sound.

She turned away, and there in the shadows was Sister Iona. Silent, morose Iona, the patterned hood of her red robe forever deepening the hollows of her eyes. Some of the Battle Sisters disliked the woman. Iona rarely showed emotion, never allowed herself to cry out in pain when combat brought her wounds, never raised her voice in joyous elation during the daily hymnals. Many considered her flawed, her mind so cold that it was little more than the demi-machine inside the skull of the servitor at the font. Miriya had once sent two novice girls to chastisement for daring to voice such thoughts aloud. But those who said these things did not know Iona's true worth. She was as devout a Sororitas as any other, and if her manner made some Sister Superiors reluctant to have her in their units, then so be it. Their loss was Miriya's gain.

'Iona,' she said, approaching. 'Speak to me.'

'It is time, Sister,' said the other woman, her milk-pale face set in a frown. 'The witch ship comes.'

In spite of herself, Miriya's hand tensed around the grip of her plasma pistol. She nodded. 'I am prepared.'

Iona returned the gesture. 'As are we all.' The Sister clasped a small fetish in her gloved grip, a sliver icon of the Convent Sanctorum's Hallowed Spire on Ophelia VII. The small tell was enough to let Miriya know the woman was concerned.

'I am as troubled as you,' she admitted as they crossed the chancel back towards the steel hatch in the chapel wall.

Iona opened it and they stepped through, emerging into the echoing corridor beyond. Where the stone of the church ended, the iron bones of the starship around it began. Once, the chapel had been earthbound, built into a hill on a world in the Vitus system, now it existed as a strange transplanted organ inside the metal body of the Imperial Naval frigate *Mercutio*.

'This vexes me, Sister Superior,' said Iona, her frown deepening beneath her hood. 'What is our cause if not to take the psyker to task for his witchery, to show the Emperor's displeasure?' She looked as if she wanted to spit. 'That we are called upon to… to *associate* with this mutant is enough to make my stomach turn. There is a part of me that wants to contact the captain and order him to take that abomination from the Emperor's sky.'

Miriya gave her a sharp look. 'Have a care, Sister. You and I may detest these creatures, but in their wisdom, the servants of the Throne see fit to use these pitiful wretches in His name. As much as that may sicken us, we cannot refuse a command that comes from the highest levels of the Ecclesiarchy.'

The answer was not nearly enough to satisfy Iona's disquiet. 'How can such things go on, I ask you? The psyker is our mortal enemy–'

Iona's commander silenced her with a raised hand. 'The *witch* is our enemy, Sister. The psyker is a *tool*. Only the untrained and the wild are a threat to the Imperium.' Miriya's eyes narrowed. 'You have never served as I have, Iona. For two full years I was a warden aboard one of those blighted vessels. On the darkest nights, the things I saw there still haunt me so…' She forced the memories away. 'This is how the God-Emperor tests the faithful, Sister. He shows us our greatest fears and has us overcome them.'

They walked in silence for a few moments before Iona spoke again. 'We are taught in the earliest days of our indoctrination that those cursed with the psychic mark in their blood are living gateways to Chaos. All of them, Sister Superior, not just the ones who eschew the worship of the Golden Throne. One single slip and even the most devout will fall, and open the way to the warp!'

Miriya raised an eyebrow. It was perhaps the most passion she had ever seen the dour woman display. 'That is why we are here. Since the Age of Apostasy, we and all our Sister Sororitas have stood at the gates to hell and barred the witchkin. As the mutant falls, so does the traitor, so does the witch.' She placed a hand on Iona's shoulder. 'Ask yourself this, Sister. Who else could be called forth to accomplish what we shall do today?' Miriya's face split in a wry smile. 'The men of the Imperial Navy or the Guard? They would be dead in moments from the shock. The Adeptus Astartes? Those abhumans willingly welcome psykers into their own ranks.' She shook her head ruefully. 'No, Iona, only we, the Sisters of Battle, can stand sentinel here.' The woman patted her pistol holster. 'And mark me well, if but one of those misbegotten wretches steps out of line, then we will show them the burning purity of our censure.'

The sound of her voice drew the attention of Miriya's squad as she approached. They did not exchange the curt bows or salutes that were mandatory in other Sororitas units. Sister Miriya kept a relaxed hand on her warriors, preferring to keep them sharp in matters of battle prowess rather than parade ground niceties.

'Report,' she demanded.

Her second-in-command Sister Lethe cleared her throat. 'We are ready, Sister Superior, as per your command.'

'Good,' Miriya snapped, forestalling any questions about their orders before they could be uttered.

'This will be a simple matter of boarding the ship and securing the prisoner.'

Lethe threw a look at the other members of the Celestian squad. Usually deployed for front line combat operations, the Celestians were known as the elite troops of the Adepta Sororitas and such a simple duty as a prisoner escort could easily be considered beneath them. Celestians were used to fighting at the heart of heretic confrontations and mutant uprisings, not acting like mere line officer enforcer.

Miriya saw these thoughts in the eyes of Lethe and the other Sisters. She knew the misgivings well, as they had been her own after the orders had first been delivered by astropathic transfer from Canoness Galatea's adjutant. 'Any duty in the Emperor's name is glorious,' she told them, a stern edge to her words, 'and we would do well to remember that.'

'Of course,' said Lethe, her expression contrite. 'We obey.'

'I share your concern.' Miriya admitted, her voice lowered. 'Our squad has never been the most favoured of units–' and with that the other women shared a moment of grim amusement, '–but we will do as we must.'

'There,' Sister Cassandra called, observing through one of the crystalline portholes in the corridor wall. 'I see it!'

Miriya drew closer and peered through the thick lens. For a moment, she thought her Battle Sister had been mistaken, but then she realised that the darkness she saw beyond the hull of the *Mercutio* was not the void of interstellar space at all, but the flank of another craft. It gave off no light, showed no signals or pennants. Only the faint glow of the frigate's own portholes and beacons illuminated it – and then, not the whole vessel but only thin slivers of it caught in the radiance.

'A Black Ship,' breathed Iona. 'Emperor protect us.'

IN TWO BY two overwatch formation, their bolters at the ready, Miriya's squad made their way up the corded flex-tube that had extended itself from one of the *Mercutio*'s outer airlocks. At their head, the Sister Superior walked with her own weapon holstered, but her open hand lay flat atop the knurled wood grip. The memories spiked her thoughts again, taking her back to the first time she had stepped into the dark iron heart of an Adeptus Telepathica vessel.

No one knew how many craft there were in the fleets of the Black Ships. Some spoke of a secret base on Terra, sending out droves of ebon vessels to scour the galaxy for psykers. Others said that the ships worked in isolation from one another, venturing back and forth under psychic directives sent by the Emperor himself. Miriya did not know the truth, and she did not want to.

Whenever a potent psyker was discovered, the Black Ships would come for them. Some, those with pure hearts and wills strong enough to survive the tests the adepts forced upon them, might live to become servants to the Inquisition or the astropathic colleges. Most would be put to death in one manner or another, or granted in sacrifice to the Emperor so that he might keep alight the great psychic beacon of the Astronomicon.

The Battle Sisters entered an elliptical reception chamber carved from iron and whorled with hexa-grammic wards. Strips of biolume cast weak yellow light into the centre of the space and hooded figures lingered at the edges, orbiting the room with silent footsteps. Lethe and the others automatically fell into a combat wheel formation, guns covering every possible angle of attack. Miriya watched the shrouded shapes moving around them. The Adeptus Telepathica had their own operatives but by Imper-ial edict they were not allowed to serve as warders upon their own vessels; it was too easy for a malig-nant psyker to coerce another telepath. Instead, Sisters of Battle or Inquisitorial Storm Troopers served in the role of custodian aboard the Black Ships, their adamantine faith protecting them from the predations of the mind-witches they guarded.

Footsteps approached from the gloomy perimeter of the chamber. Her eyes had grown accustomed to the dimness now, and she quickly picked out the fig-ures filing from an iris hatch on the far wall. Two of them were Sister Retributors, armed with heavy multi-meltas, and another a Celestian like herself. The other Battle Sisters wore gunmetal silver armour and white robes, with the sigil of a haloed black skull on their shoulder pauldrons. There were more behind them, but they remained in the shadows for now.

The Celestian saluted Miriya and she returned the gesture. 'Miriya of the Order of our Martyred Lady. Well met, Sister.'

'Dione of the Order of the Argent Shroud,' said the other woman. 'Well met, Sister.' Miriya was instantly struck by the look of fatigue on Dione's face, the tension etched into the lines about her eyes. Her fellow Sororitas met her gaze and a moment of silent communication passed between them. 'The prisoner is ready. It is my pleasure to have rid of him.' She beckoned forward hooded men and the two Retributors turned their guns to draw a bead on them.

The adepts brought a rack in the shape of a skeletal cube, within which sat a large drum made of green glass. There was a man inside it, naked and pale in the yellow illumination. His head was concealed beneath a metal mask festooned with spikes and probes. 'Torris Vaun,' Miriya said his name, and the masked man twitched a little as if he had heard her. 'A fine catch, Sister Dione.'

'He did not go easily, of that you can be sure. He killed six of my kith before we were able to subdue him.'

'And yet he still draws breath.' Miriya studied the huge jar, aware that the man inside was scrutinising her just as intently with other, preternatural senses. 'Had the choice been mine, this witch would have been shot into the heart of a star.'

Dione managed a stiff nod. 'We are in agreement, Sister. Alas, we must obey the Ministorum's orders. You are to deliver this criminal to Lord Viktor

LaHayn at the Noroc Lunar Cathedral on the planet Neva.' A hobbling servitor approached clutching a roll of parchment and a waxy stick of data-sealant. Dione took the paper and made her mark upon it. 'So ordered this day, by the authority of the Ecclesiarchy.'

Miriya followed suit, using the sealant to press her squad commander signet into the document. From behind her, she heard Lethe think aloud.

'He seems such a frail thing. What crime could a man like this commit that would warrant our stewardship?'

Dione took a sharp breath. Clearly she did not allow her troops to speak without permission as Miriya did. 'The six he murdered were only the latest victims of his violence. This man has sown terror and mayhem on a dozen worlds across this sector, all in the name of sating his base appetites. Vaun is an animal, Sister, a ruthless opportunist and a pirate. To him, cruelty is its own reward.' Her face soured. 'It disgusts me to share a room with such an aberrance.'

Miriya shot Lethe a look. 'Your candour is appreciated, Sister Dione. We will ensure the criminal reaches Neva without delay.'

More servitors took up the confinement capsule and marched into the tunnel back to the *Mercutio*. As Vaun was taken away, Dione relaxed a little. 'Lord LaHayn was most insistent that this witch be brought to his court for execution. It is my understanding the honoured deacon called in several favours with the Adeptus Terra to ensure it was so.'

Miriya nodded, recalling the message from Galatea. The Canoness would be waiting in Noroc City for their arrival with the criminal. 'Vaun is a Nevan himself, correct? One might consider it just that he be put to the sword on the soil of his birthworld, given that he created so much anarchy there.' She threw a glance at Lethe, and her second marshalled the rest of the Celestians to flank the prisoner as he vanished into the docking tube. Miriya turned to follow. 'Ave Imperator, Sister.'

Dione's armoured gauntlet clasped Miriya's wrist and held her for a moment. 'Don't underestimate him,' she hissed, her eyes glittering in the murkiness. 'I did, and six good women paid the price.'

'Of course.'

Dione released her grip and faded back into the blackness.

FROM THE RENDEZVOUS point, the *Mercutio* came about and made space for the Neva system. The Black Ship vanished from her sensorium screen like a lost dream, so quickly and so completely that it seemed as if the dark vessel had never been there.

The frigate's entry to the empyrean went poorly, and a momentary spasm in the warship's Geller Field killed a handful of deckhands on the gunnery platforms. The crew spoke in hushed tones behind guarded expressions, never within earshot of the Battle Sisters. None of them knew what it was that Miriya's squad had brought back from the Black Ship, but all of them were afraid of it.

Over the days that followed, prayer meetings in the frigate's sparse chapel had a sudden increase in attendance and there were more hymns being played over the vox nets on the lower decks. Most of the crew had never seen Battle Sisters in the flesh before. In dozens of ports across the sector they had heard the stories about them, just like every other Navy swab. There were things that men of low character would think of women such as these, thoughts that ran the spectrum from lustful fantasy to violent distrust. Some said they lived off the flesh of the males they killed, like a jungle mantis. Others swore they were as much concubines as they were soldiers, able to bring pleasure and damnation to the unwary in equal measure. The crewmen were as scared by the Sororitas as they were fascinated by them, but there were some who watched the women wherever they went, compelled by something deeper and darker.

LETHE GLANCED UP as Miriya entered the cargo bay, stepping past the two gun servitors at the hatch to where she and Cassandra stood on guard by the glass capsule.

'Sister Superior,' she nodded. 'What word from the captain?'

Miriya's frown was answer enough. 'He tells me the Navigator is troubled. The way through the warp is turbulent, but he hopes we will arrive at Neva in a day or so.'

Lethe glanced at the capsule and saw that Cassandra was doing the same.

'The prisoner cannot be the cause,' Miriya answered the unspoken question. 'I was assured the nullifying mask prevents any exercise of witchery.' She tapped her finger on the thick glass wall.

Sister Lethe fingered the silver rosary chain she habitually wore around her neck. She was not convinced. 'All the same, the sooner this voyage concludes, the better. This inaction chafes at my spirit.'

Miriya found her head bobbing in agreement. She and Lethe had served together for the longest span among this squad and often the younger woman was of one mind with her unit's commander. 'We have endured worse, have we not? The ork raids on Jacob's Tower? The Starleaf purge?'

'Aye, but all the same, the waiting gnaws at me.' Lethe looked away. 'Sister Dione was correct. Being in the presence of this criminal makes my very soul feel soiled. I shall need to bathe in sanctified waters after this mission is at an end.'

Cassandra tensed suddenly, and the reaction brought the other women to attention. 'What is it?' Miriya demanded.

The Battle Sister stalked towards a mess of metal girders heaped in one corner of the cargo bay. 'Something…' Cassandra's hand shot out and she dragged a wriggling shape out of the darkness. 'Intruder!'

The gun servitors reacted, weapons humming up to firing position. Miriya sneered as Cassandra hauled the protesting form of a deckhand into the centre of the bay. 'What in the Emperor's name are you?' she demanded.

'M-Midshipman. Uh. Vorgo. Ma'am.' The man blinked wet, beady eyes. 'Please don't devour me.'

Lethe and Cassandra exchanged glances. 'Devour you?'

Miriya waved them into silence. 'What are you doing here, Midshipman Vorgo? Who sent you?'

'No one!' He became frantic. 'Myself! I just… just wanted to see…' Vorgo extended a finger toward the glass capsule and just barely touched its surface.

The Sister Superior slapped his hand away and he hissed in pain. 'Idiot. I am within my rights to have you thrown into the void for this trespass.'

'I'm sorry. I'm sorry!' Vorgo fell to his knees and made the sign of the aquila. 'Came in through the vent… By the Throne, I was only curious–'

'That will get you killed,' said Lethe, her bolter hovering close to his head.

Miriya stepped away and made a terse wave of her hand. 'Get this fool out of here, then have the engineseers send a helot to seal any vents in this chamber.'

Cassandra hauled the man to his feet and propelled him out of the cargo bay, his protests bubbling up as he went. Lethe followed, hesitating on the cusp of the hatch. 'Sister Superior, shall I remain?'

'No. Have Isabel join me here forthwith.' Vorgo's protesting form between them, the Battle Sisters closed the hatch behind them.

The cargo bay fell quiet. Miriya listened to the faint, irregular tick of metal flexing under the power of the frigate's drives, the humming motors of the servitors, the murmur of bubbles in the tank. A nerve in her jaw twitched. She smelt a thick, greasy tang in the air.

'Alone at last.'

For a moment, she thought she had imagined it. Miriya turned in place, eyeing the two gun slaves. Had one of them spoken? Both of them peered back at her with blank stares and dull, doll-like sensor apertures, lines of drool emerging from their sewn lips. Impossible: whatever intelligence they might have once possessed, the machine-slaves were nothing but automatons now, incapable of such discourse.

'Who addresses me?'

'Here.' The voice was heavy with effort. 'Come here.'

She spun in place. There before her was the capsule, the ebony metal frame about it and the spidery, hooded man-shape adrift within. The Battle Sister drew her pistol and thumbed the activation rune, taking aim at the glass tank. 'Vaun. How dare you touch me with your witchery!'

'Have a care, Sister. It would go badly for you to injure me.' The words came from the air itself, as if the psyker was forcing the atmosphere in the chamber to vibrate like a vox diaphragm.

Miriya's face twisted in revulsion. 'You have made a foolish mistake, criminal. You have tipped your hand.' She crossed to a pod of arcane dials and switches connected to the flank of the glass container. Rods and levers were set at indents indicating the amounts of sense-deadening liquids and contrapsychic drugs filling Vaun's cell. The Battle Sister was no tech-priest, but she had seen confinement frames of this design before. She knew how they worked, pumping neuropathic philtres into the lungs and pores of particularly virulent psykers to stifle their mutant powers. She adjusted the rods and fresh splashes of murky fluid entered the tank. 'This will quiet you.'

'Wait. Stop.' Vaun's body jerked inside the capsule, a pallid hand pressing on the inside of the thick glass. 'You do not understand. I only wanted... to talk.'

Another dial turned and darts of electricity swam into the liquid. 'No one here wants to listen, deviant.'

The words became vague, laboured, fading. 'You... mistaken... will regret...'

Miriya rested the barrel of her plasma weapon on the glass. 'Heed me. If one breath more of speech comes from that cesspool you call a mind before I deliver you to Neva, I will boil you in there like a piece of rotten meat.'

There was no reply. Torris Vaun hung suspended in the foggy solution, slack and waxy.

With a shudder, Sister Miriya muttered the Prayer of Virtue and fingered the purity seals on her armour.

MERCUTIO FELL FROM the grip of the warp and pushed into the Neva system at full burn, as if the ship itself were desperate to deposit the cargo it carried. As the capital planet orbiting fourth from its yellow-white star swelled in the frigate's hololiths, a small and quiet insurrection began on *Mercutio's* lower decks.

Men from the labourer gang on the torpedo racks came to the brig where Midshipman Vorgo was confined, and in near silence they murdered the armsmen guarding him. When they freed Vorgo, he didn't thank them. In fact, he said hardly anything but a few clipped sentences, mostly to explain where the gun servitors were placed in the cargo bay, and how the Battle Sisters had behaved toward him.

Vorgo's liberators were not his friends. Some of them were men who had actively disliked him in the past, picking on him in dark corridors and shaking him down for scrip. There was a common denominator between them all, but not one of the men could have spoken of it. Instead, they went their separate ways, each moving with the same hushed purpose and blank expression.

In the generarium where the *Mercutio's* reactor-spirits coiled inside their cores and bled out their power to the vessel's systems, some of the quiet men walked up to the service gantries over the vast cogwheels of the coolant arrays. They waited for a count of ten decimals from the turning discs and then leapt in groups of three, directly into the teeth of the mechanism. Of course, they were crushed between the cogs, but the pulpy mess of their corpses made the workings slip and seize. In moments, vital flows of chilling fluid were denied to the reactors and alarms began to wail.

Vorgo and the rest of the men went to the cargo decks, meeting more of their number along the way. The new arrivals had cans of chemical unguent taken from the stores of the tech-priests who ministered to the lascannons. Applied in a vacuum, the sluggish fluid could be used to keep the wide glassy lenses of the guns free from micro-meteor scarring and other damage, but on contact with air, the unguent had a far more violent reaction.

AFTER THE INCIDENT with the midshipman, Sister Miriya had demanded and been given a third gun servitor from the ship's complement to guard the prisoner. Miriya made sure that no member of her squad was ever alone again with Vaun, pairs of the Celestians watching him around the clock in shifts.

Lethe and Iona were holding that duty when the hatch exploded inward. The machine-slaves stumbled about, their autosenses confused by the deafening report of the blast. The muzzles of weapons dallied, unable to find substantial targets to lock on to.

The Battle Sisters had no such limitations. The men that pushed their way in through the ragged hole in the wall, heedless of the burns the hot metal gave them, were met with bolter fire. Lethe's Godwyn-De'az pattern weapon chattered in her gloved grip. The gun's fine tooling of filigree and etching caught the light, catechisms of castigation aglow upon its barrel and breech. Iona's hand flamer growled as puffs of orange fire jetted across the bay, licking at the invaders and immolating them, but there were many, clasping crude clubs and metal cans. She spied Vorgo among them, throwing a jar of thick fluid at a servitor. The glass shattered on the helot's chest and the contents flashed magnesium-white. Plumes of acrid grey smoke spat forth as acids chewed up flesh and implanted machinery alike.

'Sisters, to arms!' Lethe shouted into the vox pickup on her armour's neck ring, but her voice was drowned out by the keening wail of the *Mercutio*'s general quarters klaxon. She couldn't know it from here, deep inside the hull, but the frigate was starting to list as the heat build-up in the drives baffled the ship's cogitator systems.

A scrum of deckhands piled atop another gun servitor, forcing it down, choking the muzzles of its guns with their chests and hands, muffling shotgun discharges with the meat of their bodies. Lethe's face wrinkled in grim disgust and it was then she noticed that the men did not speak, did not cry out, did not howl in frenzy. Doe-eyed and noiseless, they let themselves die in order to suffocate the prisoner's guardians.

Another chemical detonation signalled the destruction of the last servitor and then the attackers surged forward over the bodies of their crewmates, ten or twenty men moving in one great mass. Sister Lethe saw Iona reel backwards, choking and strangling on clouds of foul air from the makeshift acid bombs. The bleak woman's face sported chemical burns and her eyes were swollen. Unlike the superhuman warriors of the Adeptus

Astartes, the Sororitas did not possess the altered
physiognomies that could shrug off such assaults.

Lethe's lungs gave up metallic, coppery breaths as
the bitter smoke scarred her inside. The silent mob
moved to her, letting the Battle Sister waste her
ammunition on them. When the magazine in her
bolter clicked empty, they pounced and beat her to
the ground, the sheer weight of them forcing her to
her knees.

Time blurred in stinking lurches of pungent
fumes, fogging her brain. The toxic smoke made
thinking difficult. Through cracked and seared lips,
Lethe mouthed the Litany of Divine Guidance, calling to the Emperor to kindle the faith in her heart.

She forced herself up from the decking. Her gun
was missing from her grip and she tried to push the
recollection of where it had gone to the front of her
mind but the smoke made everything harsh and
rough, each breath like razorwool in her throat,
each thought as heavy and slow as a glacier.

She focussed. Vorgo had loops of cable and odd
metal implements in his hands, all of them still wet
with greenish liquid where they had been immersed
in the tank. He was struggling to breathe, but the
midshipman's eyes were distant and watery. Behind
the portly deckhand, a naked man was clothing
himself in a dirty coverall, running a scarred hand
through a fuzz of greying hair. He seemed to sense
Lethe's scrutiny and turned about to face her.

'Vaun,' she choked. His reply was a cold smile and
a nod at the broken capsule, thick neurochemical
soup lapping out of the crack in its flank. Lethe's

eyes were gritty and inflamed, making it hard to blink. 'Free...'

'Yes,' His voice was cool and metered. Under the right circumstances, it would have been playful, even seductive. He patted Vorgo on the shoulder and gestured towards the torn doorway. 'Well done.'

'Traitor,' Lethe managed.

Vaun gave a slow shake of the head. 'Be kind, Sister. He doesn't know what he's doing.' A brief smile danced on his lips. 'None of them do.'

'The others will be here soon. You will die.'

'I'll be long gone. These matters were prepared for, Sister.' The psyker crossed to Iona, where the injured woman lay gasping in shallow breaths. Lethe tried to get to her feet and stop him from whatever it was he was doing, but the deckhands punched and kicked her back to the floor, boots ringing off her armour.

Vaun whispered things in Iona's ear, brushing his hands over her blonde hair, and the Battle Sister began to weep brokenly. Vaun stood up and rubbed his hands together, amused with himself.

'You can't escape,' Lethe said thickly. 'It will take more than this to stop us. My Sisters are loyal. They will never let you get away from this vessel!'

He nodded. 'Yes, they are loyal. I saw that.' The criminal took a barbed knife from one of his erstwhile rescuers and came closer. Vorgo and the others held Lethe down in anticipation. 'That kind of loyalty breeds passion. It makes one emotional, prone to recklessness.' He turned the blade in his hand, letting light glint off it. 'Something that I intend to use to my advantage.'

Lethe tried to say something else, but Vaun tipped back her head with one hand, and used the other to bury the knife in her throat.

CHAPTER TWO

THE COROLUS WAS a starship in only the very loosest sense of the word. It didn't possess warp drives, it was incapable of navigating across the vast interstellar distances as its larger brethren could. And where the majority of vessels in service to humankind had some degree of artistry, however brutal, to their design, *Corolus* was little more than an agglomeration of spent fuel tanks from sub-orbital landers, lashed together with pipework and luck. Fitted with a simple reaction drive and a bitter old enginarium from a larger vessel now centuries dead, the cargo scow plied the sub-light routes across the Neva system from the core worlds to the outer manufactory satellites with loads of chemicals and vital breathing gases. The ship was slow and fragile and utterly unprepared for the fury that had suddenly been turned upon it.

There was a matter of communication that had not been acted on quickly enough, then thunderous flares of laser fire from an Imperial frigate had set *Corolus* dead in space while razor-edged boarding pods slashed into her hull spaces.

If the ship had a captain, it was Finton. He owned *Corolus*, after a fashion, along with most of the crew thanks to a network of honour-debts and punitive indenture contracts. He floundered around the cramped, musty bridge space, his hand constantly straying to and from the ballistic pistol on his hip. Over the intercom he kept hearing little snatches of activity – panic, mostly, along with bursts of screaming and the heavy rattle of bolt-fire. Piece by piece, his ship was slipping out of his grasp and into the hands of the Navy.

He'd dealt with Naval types a hundred times before. They were never this fast, never this good. Finton was entertaining a new emotion inside his oily, calculating mind. He was *afraid*, and when the bridge door went orange and melted off its hinges, he very nearly lost control of his bodily functions.

Figures in black armour came into the chamber, iron boots clanging off the patched and rusty deck plates. They wore dark helmets bannered with white faceplates, eyes of deep night-blue crystal that searched every shadowed corner of the bridge. Movement for them was graceful and deadly, not a single gesture or motion wasted. One of them noticed him for the first time and Finton saw a dif-ference: this one had a brass shape on the front of its helmet, a dagger-shaped leaf.

'Oh, Blood's sake,' whispered the captain, and he fumbled at his belt. The next sound on the bridge was the thud of Finton's holster and weapon hitting the deck. He bent his knees, hesitated, and then raised his hands, unsure if he should kneel or not.

As one, the invaders threw back their heads and the helmets snapped open. Their short, bobbed hair, framed eyes that were hard and flinty. The leader came forward to Finton in two quick steps and gripped him by a fistful of his jacket.

'Where is he?' growled Miriya, lifting the man off the deck.

Finton licked his lips. 'Sister, please! What have I done to displease the Sororitas?'

'Search this tier,' she shouted over her shoulder. 'Leave no compartment unchecked. Vent the atmosphere if you have to!'

'No, please–' said the captain. 'Sister, what–'

Miriya let him drop to the deck and kicked him hard in the gut. 'Don't play games with me, worm. You measure your life in ticks of the clock.' The Sister Superior carefully placed her armoured boot on Finton's right leg and broke it.

Behind her, Sister Isabel directed the other women to their tasks, then began a search of the bridge's control pits, pushing her way past doddering servitors and aged cogitator panels. 'As before, there is nothing here.'

'Keep searching.' Miriya presented her plasma gun to Finton's face, the neon glow of the energy coils atop it washing him with pale illumination. 'Where is Vaun, little man?' she spat. '*Answer me!*'

'Who?' The word was drawn out like a moan.

'You are testing my patience,' snapped the Sister Superior. 'Half your crew is dead already from resisting us. Unless you wish to join them, tell me where the heretic hides!'

In spite of his pain, Finton shook his head in confusion. 'But... but, no. We left the commerce station... You came after us, fired on us. Our communications were faulty.' He waved feebly at a jury-rigged console across the chamber. 'We couldn't reply...'

'Liar!' Miriya's face twisted in anger and she released a shot from the plasma weapon into a support stanchion near Finton's head. The captain screamed and shoved himself away from the corona of white-hot vapour, dragging his twisted leg behind him. Miriya tracked him across the floor with the gun muzzle.

Finton tried to make the sign of the aquila. 'Please don't kill me. It was just some smuggling, nothing more, a few tau artefacts. But that was months ago, and they were all fake anyway.'

'I don't care about your petty crimes, maggot.' Miriya advanced on him. 'I want Torris Vaun. The *Corolus* was the only interplanetary ship to leave Neva's orbital commerce platform.' She bit out each word, as if she were explaining something to a particularly backward child. 'If Vaun was not on the station, then here is the only place he could be.'

'I don't know any Vaun,' screamed Finton.

'*Lies!*' The Battle Sister fired again, striking a dormant servitor and killing it instantly.

Finton coiled into a ball, sobbing. 'No, no, no...'

'Sister Superior,' began Isabel, a warning tone in her voice.

Miriya did not choose to hear it. Instead, she knelt next to the freighter captain and let the hot metal of the plasma gun hover near his face. The heat radiating from the muzzle was enough to sear his skin.

'For the last time,' said the woman, 'where have you hidden Torris Vaun?'

'He's not here.'

Miriya blinked and looked up. It was Isabel who had spoken.

'Vaun was never aboard this vessel, Sister Miriya. These cogitator records show the manifest.' She held a spool of parchment in her grip. 'They match the dockmaster's datum for the *Corolus*.'

'The datum is wrong,' Miriya retorted. 'Would you have me believe that Vaun used his witchery to simply teleport himself to safety, Sister? Did he beg the gods of the warp to give him safe passage somewhere else?'

Isabel coloured, afraid to challenge her squad commander when her ire was so high. 'I have no answer to give you, Sister Superior, save that this wretch does not lie. Torris Vaun never set foot on this trampship.'

'No,' Miriya growled, 'that will not stand. He must not escape us–'

A hollow chime sounded from the vox bead in the Battle Sister's armour. 'Message relay from *Mercutio*,' began the flat, monotone voice. 'By direct order of Her Eminence Canoness Galatea, you are ordered to cease all operations and make planetfall at Noroc City immediately. Ave Imperator.'

'Ave Imperator,' repeated the women.

With effort, Miriya holstered her pistol and turned away, her head bowed and eyes distant. The rage she displayed moments earlier had drained away.

'Sister,' said Isabel. 'What shall we do? With him, with this ship?'

Miriya threw a cold glance at Finton and then looked away. 'Turn this wreck over to the planetary defence force. This crew are criminals, even if they are not the ones we seek.'

At the hatch stood Sister Portia and Sister Cassandra. Their expressions confirmed that they too had found nothing of the escaped psyker in their search.

Portia spoke. 'We heard the recall from Neva. What does it mean? Have they found him?'

Miriya shook her head. 'I think not. Our failure is now compounded, my Sisters. Blame... must be apportioned.'

THERE HAD BEEN Adepta Sororitas on Neva for almost as long as there had been Adepta Sororitas. A world of stunning natural beauty, the planet's history vanished into the forgotten past of the Age of Strife, into the dark times when the turbulent warp had isolated worlds across the galactic plane, but unlike those colonies of man that had embraced the alien or fallen into barbarism, Neva had never given up its civilisation. Throughout the millennia, it had been a place where art and culture, theology and learning had been ingrained in the very bones of the planet. From a military or economic standpoint, Neva had little to offer – all her industry existed on the outer worlds of the system, on dusty, dead moons laced with ores and mineral deposits – but she remained rich in the currency of thought and ideas. Grand museum-cities that were said to rival the temples of Terra reached towards the clouds, and in the streets of Noroc, Neva's coastal capital, every street was blessed with its own murals drawn from the annals of Imperial Earth and Nevan chronicles spanning ten thousand years of history.

There had been a time, after the confusion wrought by the Horus Heresy, when Neva had become lost once again to the Imperium at large. Warp storms the like of which had not been seen for generations cut the system off from human contact and the Nevans feared a second Age of Strife would follow, but this was not to be their fate. When the day came that the storms lifted, as silently as they had first arrived, Neva's sky held a new star – a mighty vessel that had lost its way crossing the void.

Aboard that ship were the Sisters of Battle, and with them came the Living Saint Celestine. Golden and magnificent in her heraldry, Celestine and her cohorts had embarked on a War of Faith to chastise the heretical Felis Salutas sect, but fate had brought them here by the whim of the empyrean. It was said by some that Celestine remained only long enough to allow her Navigators to establish a fresh course before leaving Neva behind, but for the planet it was deliverance from a servant of the Emperor Himself.

Internecine conflicts and the wars of assassination that had riven Neva's theocratic barony during the isolation years were instantly nulled. Chapels and courts and universities dedicated to the Imperial Cult flourished as never before. New purpose came to the planet, and that purpose was pilgrimage.

THE ORDER OF our Martyred Lady was not the only Chapter of the Adepta Sororitas to have a convent on Neva, but theirs was the largest and by far the most elaborate. The tower was cut from stone of a hue found only in Neva's equatorial desert, a honeyed yellow that made the building glow when the rays of the sunset crossed it. From the highest levels of the convent, an observer could look down along the graceful curve of Noroc City's bay, following the lines of the snow-white sand that mirrored the bowed streets and boulevards.

On any other day, the beauty of it might have struck a chord in Sister Miriya, but at this moment her heart was immune to the sight. From the battlements, she stared out over Noroc's cathedrals and habitat clutches without really seeing them, watching the day dissipate, observing nothing but the moments fading away from her in the march of shadows over the city's giant sundial.

A grim smile rose and fell on her lips as she recalled her words to the trampship's captain. *You measure your life in ticks of the clock.* Perhaps she had meant that as much to herself as to him. The time fast approached when she would be called to the Canoness and made to answer for her errors.

Miriya's gaze dropped to the plaza beyond the convent's gates. There were penitents there, robed in hair shirts and cloaks of fishhook barbs. Some of them moaned and growled their way through verses of Imperial dogma, while others took to picking out hapless members of the public who tarried too long, for shouted condemnation and censure. There were flagellators who whipped at children wearing the wrong kinds of hood, and men bearing spears that ended in festoons of candles.

She frowned. Parts of the rites at play down there were known to her. The Battle Sister recognised the Commemoration of the Second Sacrifice of the Colchans, the Litany Against Fear and one of the Lesser Prayers to Saint Sabbat – but there were other cantos that seemed strange and hard against her ears. The iconography the penitents bore brimmed with images of wine-dark blood, and unbidden the stark, lifeless face of Lethe rose to the surface of her thoughts, the dead woman's throat open like a second raw mouth.

'They do things differently here,' Cassandra's voice drifted to her on the evening breeze as she approached. The woman threw a nod at the people in the plaza. 'I've not seen the like on other worlds.'

Miriya made an effort to shake off her black mood. 'Nor I. Like you, this is my first venture to Neva. But each planet beneath the Emperor's light embraces Him in its own way.'

'Indeed.' Cassandra joined her at the balcony's edge. 'But some embrace with more fervour than others.'

The Sister Superior eyed her. 'Do I detect a note of disquiet in your tone?'

From a different squad leader, such a comment might have been a caution but from Miriya it was an invitation. Cassandra's commander demanded and respected honesty in the women who served the church with her. 'It troubles me to hear, but I have been told that in some of Noroc's less... civilised districts, there are women who will mutilate and murder their third child if it is revealed to be a female whilst still unborn. This is done in the name of some aged, arcane idolatry.'

'It is not our place to question their ways,' said Miriya. 'The Ecclesiarchy works to ensure that the veneration of the God-Emperor meshes with the doctrine of each and every planet. Some distasteful anomalies of belief are inevitable.'

'Fortunate then that our order is here to show the Nevans the way.'

'I have never believed in fortune,' Miriya said distantly. 'Faith is enough.'

'Not enough to find Vaun,' replied Cassandra in a morose voice. 'He tricked us, played us for fools.'

Miriya looked at her squadmate. 'Aye. But do not punish yourself, Sister. Canoness Galatea will wish to reserve that pleasure.'

'You know her of old, yes?'

A nod. 'She was once my Sister Superior as I am yours. An unparalleled warrior and a true credit to the legacy of Saint Katherine, but perhaps a touch too inflexible for my liking. We would often disagree on matters of our credo.'

Cassandra could not keep the fear from her voice. 'What do you think will become of us?'

'There will be a cost for our lapse, of that you may have no doubt.' Inwardly, Miriya was already rehearsing the plea she would enter, offering to fall on her sword and take all the blame for Vaun's escape rather than drag Cassandra, Portia, Isabel and poor Iona down with her.

Her Sister gripped the edge of the stone battlements tightly, as if she could squeeze an answer from them. 'This apostate torments me, Sister Superior. By the Throne, how could he have simply vanished into thin air? The escape pod Vaun stole from the *Mercutio* was found on the commerce station, witnesses saw him there. But the only ship he could have been on was that rattletrap scow we boarded.' She shook her head. 'Perhaps... perhaps he hides still on the orbital platform? Waiting for a warp-capable craft to leave?'

'No.' Miriya pointed at the ground. 'Sub-orbital craft are plentiful on the station. Vaun took one and made planetfall. He came *here*. It is the only explanation.'

'To Neva? But that makes no sense. The man is a fugitive, his face is infamous on every world in this system. Any rational person would find the first route out of this sub-sector as fast as possible.'

'It makes sense to Vaun, Sister. The witch's arrogance is so towering that he believes he can hide in plain sight. Mark me well, I tell you that Torris Vaun never had any intention of escaping from Neva. He wanted to come here.'

Cassandra shook her head. 'Why? Why take such a risk of discovery?'

The sun dropped away behind the Shield Mountains and Miriya turned from the balcony. 'When we learn the answer to that, we will find him.' She beckoned her Battle Sister. 'Come. The Canoness will be waiting.'

THE BOAT RODE in the swell, making good speed across the narrows, the lights of Noroc long since vanished over the stern. The first mate rose into the untidy flying bridge and gave the sailor on watch a jut of the chin, like a nod.

'Asleep,' he whispered, and the sailor knew who he meant. 'Fast asleep but still I'm adrift around him.'

The sailor licked his dry lips, chancing a look back through the open hatch at the shape beyond, hidden under the rough-hewn blankets. The atmosphere on the little fishing cutter had turned stale and leaden the moment they'd taken the passenger aboard. 'Wish I could sleep,' he muttered. 'Men been getting bad dreams since we left port, is what they say. Seeing things. Reckon he's a witchkin, I do.'

The first mate blinked owlishly. He was tired too. 'Don't you be saying what you're thinking. Keep a course and stay silent, lad. Better that way. Get us there quick-like, all be gone and over.'

'Oh aye–' The words died in the sailor's parched throat. Out of the windscreen, across the bow of the cutter, there was a dark shape rising from the ocean.

A razormaw, ugly as Chaos and twice as hungry. He'd never seen a fish so large, not even a deader like in the docker pubs where big stuffed heads and jawbones decorated the walls.

The sailor threw the wheel about in a panic, turning the boat on a hard arc away from the razormaw's grinning mouth. Ice water pooled in his gut. The thing was going to swallow them whole.

'You wastrel throwback, what are ye doing?' The first mate smacked him hard about the temple and shoved him away from the helm. 'Trying to capsize us?'

'But the razor–' he began, stabbing his finger at the sea. 'Do you not see it?'

'See what? There's nothing out there but ocean, boy.'

The sailor pressed his face to the window. No razormaw floated, arch-backed and ready to chew the boat apart. There were only the waves, rising and falling. He spun about, glaring at the sleeping man alone on the cot. For a moment, he thought he heard soft, mocking laughter.

'Witchkin,' repeated the sailor.

As THE RITUALS demanded, each of them surrendered their weapons to a grey-robed novice before they entered the chapel. The noviciates were just girls, barely out of the schola progenium on Ophelia VII, and they sagged beneath the weight of the heavy firearms. As Celestians, and with that rank, privileged, Sister Miriya and her unit were gifted with superior, master-crafted guns that resembled a votive icon more than a battlefield weapon, but as with all elements of the Adepta Sororitas's equipment, from the power armour that protected them to their chainswords and Exorcist tanks, every piece of the order's machinery was as much a holy shrine as the place in which they now stood.

The convent's chapel was high and wide, encompassing several floors of the building's shell keep design. Up above, where the pipes of the organ ended and biolume pods hovered on suspensors, cherubim moved in lazy circuits, handing notes to one another as they passed, the sapphire of their optic implants glittering in the lamplight.

The four women advanced across the chancel to where their seniors awaited them, falling as one into a kneeling position before the vast stone cross-and-skull that dominated the chapel altar.

'In the name of Katherine and the Golden Throne,' they intoned, 'we are the willing daughters of the God-Emperor. Command us to do His bidding.'

It was customary for the senior Battle Sister present to let the new arrivals stand after the ritual invocation, but Galatea did not. Instead, she stepped forward from the pulpit and took up a place before the altar. Her dark eyes flashed amid the frame of her auburn hair. 'Sister Superior Miriya. When Prioress Lydia informed me that it would be your Celestians bringing the witch to us, I confess I was surprised. Surprised that so sensitive a prisoner be given to a woman of your reputation.'

Miriya spoke without looking up. 'Sister Lydia showed great faith in me.'

'She did,' Galatea let the breach of protocol go unmentioned. 'How shameful for her now, given your unforgivable lapse of judgement aboard the *Mercutio.*'

'I...' Miriya took a shuddering breath. 'There is no excuse. The culpability is mine alone to shoulder, Canoness. I had the opportunity to terminate the psyker Vaun and I chose not to. His escape falls to me.'

'It does.' Galatea's cold, strong voice echoed in the chapel's heavy air. 'You have lived a charmed life, Sister Miriya. Circumstances have always conspired to save you from the small transgressions you have made in the past, minor as they were. But this... I ask you, Sister. What would you do, if you were me?'

After a moment she replied. 'I would not presume to have the wisdom for such a thing, Canoness.'

Galatea showed her teeth in an icy smile. 'How very well said, Miriya. And now I find myself on the horns of a dilemma. A dangerous warlock is loose on this world and I need every able-bodied Battle Sister I can field to corral him yet the more severe interpretations of our doctrines would seem to insist that you be made to atone. Perhaps in the most *final* of ways.'

Miriya looked up, defiant. 'If the Emperor wills.'

The Canoness leaned forward and her voice dropped to a whisper. 'You do presume, Miriya. You always have.'

'Then kill me for it, but spare my Sisters.'

Galatea gave a grim smile. 'I'm not going to make you a martyr. That would excuse you, and I am not in a forgiving mood...'

THE REST OF the Canoness's words were lost in a sudden crash of sound as the chapel doors slammed open. A commotion spilled into the room as a troop of armsmen and clerics marched through. At their head was a tall rail of a man, draped in fine silks and priestly regalia. Red and white purity seals hung off him like the medals of a soldier, and the rage on his face matched the crimson of his robes. In one fist he clasped a heavy tome bound in rosaries, in the other there was the clattering blade of a gunmetal chainsword, the adamantine teeth spinning and ready.

'Which of them is the one?' he bellowed, pointing across the book at Miriya's squad. 'Which of these wenches is the fool who lost me my prize?'

Galatea held out a hand to stop him, her face tight with annoyance. 'Lord LaHayn, you forget yourself. This is a place of worship. Shoulder your weapon!'

'You dare defy me?' The high priest's colour darkened, the mitre on his head bobbing.

'Aye,' Galatea shot back. 'This place is the sacred house of Saint Katherine and the God-Emperor. I should not need to remind you of that!'

There was a moment when LaHayn's wiry muscles bunched around the sword, as if he were preparing to strike but in the next the anger dropped from him and he stiffly forced the blade into the hands of a subordinate dean at his side. 'Yes, yes,' he said, after a long silence. 'Forgive me, Canoness. I allowed my baser instincts to overrule the better angels of my nature.' He gave a low bow that was echoed by all of his retinue. When he came up, he was looking into Galatea's eyes with a piercing, steely gaze. 'My question, however, still stands. You will answer it.'

'Vaun's escape is not so simple a matter that it can be laid at the feet of these women,' said the Canoness, each word carefully balanced and without weight. 'An investigation must take place.'

'The enforcers have begun an analysis,' noted the dean.

Galatea ignored him, concentrating on LaHayn. 'This cannot be left to the enforcers or the Imperial Navy. Torris Vaun was the responsibility of the Adepta Sororitas, and we will find him.'

The priest-lord's gaze drifted to Miriya and her troops. 'Unsatisfactory. While I applaud your determination to amend the oversights of your Battle Sisters, necessity demands consequences.' He took a step forward. 'In all things. Did not Celestine's arrival teach us that?' LaHayn smoothly shifted into a mode of speech better suited to a church mass with the common folk. 'This is a universe of laws. Actions beget reactions. For all things, there are costs and penalties.' His lined, hard face loomed over Galatea. 'There must be reciprocity.'

'Lord deacon, I would ask that you speak plainly.' The Canoness did not flinch from his gaze.

LaHayn showed a thin smile. 'The few survivors of the witch's escape, the man Vorgo and the others, they are to be taken to the excruciators to become object lessons. It occurs to me that perhaps a contrite Battle Sister should join them, as an example of your order's devotion.'

'One of my kinswomen has already perished in the unfolding of this sorry matter,' snapped Galatea. 'You would ask me to give you another?'

'The dead one... Sister Lethe, yes? She is the most blameless of all, falling in honourable conflict to the heretic. Her sacrifice is not enough.'

Miriya began to rise to her feet. 'I shall—'

'*You will kneel, Sister!*' The voice of the Canoness hammered about the chamber like a cannon shot, and by sheer force it pushed Miriya to her knees once more. Galatea's expression hardened. 'My Sisters are the most precious resource of my order, and I will not squander them to appease your displeasure, my lord priest.'

'Then what will you do, Sister Galatea?' He demanded.

Finally, the Canoness looked away. 'I will give you your sacrifice.' She gestured to her aide, a veteran Sororitas. 'Sister Reiko. Summon Sister Iona.'

A GASP OF surprise slipped from Portia's lips and Miriya shot her a look to silence her, but in truth, the Sister Superior was just as shocked to hear their errant squadmate's name spoken. From the dim shade of a sub-chancel, the woman called Reiko returned with Iona following behind. Her pale face looked down at the floor, her hair lank and unkempt. She seemed like a faint ghost of her former self, a faded copy worn thin through age and neglect.

In the aftermath of Vaun's escape, it was Isabel who had found Iona alone in the cargo decks of the *Mercutio*. Her eyes were faraway and vacant, and the cool, intense will she had always shown in the Emperor's service was gone. Iona's physical injuries were slight, but her mental state... That was a raw, gaping wound, ragged and bleeding where the psyker had pillaged her mind to exercise his powers. It was not until much later that Miriya had understood what the witch had been doing when he casually despoiled Iona's psyche. Vaun had used her to test the gallows, and left her alive as a warning.

None of them had expected to see Iona again. Her bouts of uncontrolled weeping and self-mutilation marked her as irreparably broken. Yet here she stood, still clad in her wargear.

'What is this?' LaHayn asked.

'Tell him,' said Galatea.

Iona looked up and blinked. 'I... I am far from absolution. Lost to any exculpation. I offer myself to repentance.'

'*No...*' Miriya was surprised by the denial that fell from her mouth. At her side, Portia's hand flew to her lips. Only Cassandra dared to whisper the terrible truth that all of them suddenly realised.

'She is invoking the Oath of the Penitent...'

Iona shrugged off her red robe and let it drop to the stone floor in a heap. Behind her, Sister Reiko silently gathered it up, never once looking upon the other woman as she trembled.

'Before the Emperor I have sinned.' Iona's voice found a brittle strength and swelled to fill the

chapel. 'Beyond forgiveness. Beyond forbearance.'
She blinked back tears. 'Beyond mercy.'

Miriya looked to the Canoness, a pleading expression on her face. Galatea gave her a tiny nod and the Celestians came to their feet, moving to surround Iona. All of them knew the pattern of the ritual by heart.

Miriya, Portia, Cassandra and Isabel each took an item of Iona's wargear and armour, detaching it and casting it aside. As one they spoke the next verse of the catechism. 'We turn our backs upon you. We cast off your armour and your arms.'

'I leave this company of my own free will,' Iona continued, 'and by my will shall I return.' Behind her, Reiko used a rough-hewn blade to rip the Sister's discarded robe into strips that Portia and Isabel tied over Iona's bare arms and legs. Cassandra strung barbed expiation chains across her torso and pressed seals bearing the words of the oath into her stripped tunic. 'I shall seek the Emperor's forgiveness in the darkest places of the night,' intoned the woman.

Sister Reiko bent forward with the knife and reached for a hank of Iona's hair, but Miriya took the blade from her with a stony countenance. The Sister Superior leaned close and whispered in her friend's ear.

'You do not have to do this.'

Iona looked back at her. 'I must. With just one touch he hollowed me out, did such horrific things... I cannot rest until I cleanse myself.'

Miriya nodded once and said the next stanza aloud. 'When forgiveness is yours, we shall welcome you back.' With sharp, hard motions, she cut off Iona's straw-coloured tresses until her scalp was bare and dashed with shallow scratches. 'Until such time you are nameless to us.'

With that, the oath was sealed, and the Battle Sisters took two steps back before turning away from her. Miriya was the last to do so, gripping the paring knife in her hand.

'See me and do not see,' Iona sighed, speaking the final verse. 'Know me and know fear, for I have no face today but this one. I stand before you a Sister Repentia, until absolution finds me once more.'

'So shall it be.' Galatea bowed her head, and all others in the chapel did the same. Iona walked past them all, into the stewardship of a lone Battle Mistress at the chapel doors. The Mistress carried a pair of matched neural whips that crackled and hummed with deadly power. In her hand she held a ragged red hood. Iona donned it, and then they were gone.

LaHayn broke the silence with a grunt of contentment. 'Not quite the price I would have demanded, but it will do.' He gave a shallow bow and snapped his fingers to summon the dean. 'Until the Blessing, then, Canoness?'

Galatea returned his bow. 'Until then, lord deacon. His light be with you.'

'And you.' The priest's delegation filed out, leaving the Battle Sisters alone again.

The Canoness made a dismissive gesture. 'Leave me now. I will deal with your dispensation later.'

The rest of the Celestians did as they were commanded, but Miriya remained, still kneading the grip of the knife. 'Iona was unfit to take the oath,' she said without preamble. 'It is a death sentence for her.'

Galatea snatched the blade from her grip. 'Fool! She saved your life with her sacrifice, woman. You and all your unit.'

'It is not right.'

'It was her choice. Willingly taking up the mantle of the Repentia is a rarity, you know that. Even Lord LaHayn could not deny the piety and strength of zeal Iona showed today. Her gesture casts away any doubt on the devoutness of your squad and our order...' Galatea looked away. 'And what other path was open to her? After suffering so terribly at the hands of that monster... Honourable death was her only option.'

'What did Vaun do to her?' Miriya swallowed hard. Even thinking about such a thing made her feel ill. 'What horrors must he have conjured to breach her shield of faith?'

'The witch's way sees into the very core of a human soul. It finds the flaws that all of us hide and cracks them wide open. Pity your Sister, Miriya, and pray to Katherine that you never have to face what she did.'

When she was alone, Miriya knelt before the altar and offered up an entreaty to the Saints and the God-Emperor to keep Iona safe. To become a Sister Repentia was to throw away all thought of survival and fight possessed by a righteous passion. Ushered into battle by the whips of the harsh Mistress, the Repentia were the fiercest and most brutal of the Battle Sisters. Enemies lived in dread of their fearless assaults as their mighty eviscerator chainblades blazed through heretic lines, and only in death or forgiveness would their duty to the Emperor end. Some said that they lived in a state of grace that all aspired to reach, yet few had the purity of heart to attain. Each day, each breath for these women was an act of self-punishment and penance in honour of the Golden Throne – and they turned their right-eousness into a weapon as keen as their killing swords.

Miriya had seen the Repentia on the field of battle in the past, but she had never expected to count one of her own among them. The purity of Iona's sacri-fice stabbed at her heart; it would take much to prove herself worthy of it. The Sister Superior resolved then and there that Torris Vaun would be brought to justice, or she would forfeit her life in the attempt.

CHAPTER THREE

THE HATCH FELL open like a drawbridge, allowing a perfumed gust of Neva's pre-dawn air to sweep in and scour the transport's cargo bay. The shuttle pilot eyed the three women standing on the lip of the hatch and rubbed at his face. He was wondering if there was some sort of special dispensation he could get from the Blessing for carrying Adepta Sororitas down from orbit. There had to be a little value to it, he reasoned. They were holy women, after all. That had to count for something towards his yearly tithes.

The tallest of the three, the ebony-skinned one with the curly hair, gave him a warning glance with her dark eyes. The pilot was smart enough to read it and pretended to make himself busy with a cargo web that was hanging loose. Better to let them

complete their business without interfering. When
she turned away again, the pilot stole another look
at the trio. They had kept to themselves all the way
down, talking in hushed voices at the back of the
compartment while he had navigated the flight
corridors to Noroc's port complex. Now and then,
the winsome-looking one with the brown hair
would sob a little, and the other one, tawny of face
and elegant – by his lights, the prettiest of the three
– would comfort her with whispers.

He would never have even dared to stay in the same
room with them had they been Battle Sisters, but the
Adepta Sororitas had many faces to it, and these three
were just nurses. Sister Hospitallers, they called themselves. The pilot amused himself thinking of how he
might like them to comfort him in bed one night.

As if she smelled the notion in his brain, the tall
woman broke away and came over to him. 'Could
you give us a few moments, please? In private.'

'Uh, well.' He stalled. 'The thing is, you said this
would be quick. I've got a perishable load waiting on
the dock up at the commerce station, bound for the
epicurias in Metis City.' The pilot gave a vague wave
in the direction of the ocean. 'I can't spare the time.'

'No,' said the woman firmly, 'you can. And you will.
I am a servant of the Divine Imperial Church. Do you
know what that means?'

'That… I have to… do what you say?'

'I'm glad we understand each other.' She turned her
back on him and returned to her Sisters, who were
walking out on to the starport apron.

* * *

'ARE YOU SURE you don't want Sister Zoë or me to go with you? You do not have to bear this sorrow alone, Verity.'

The girl swallowed hard, watching the first rays of sunlight cresting the mountains in the distance. She could smell the salt of the sea in the cool air. 'Inara, no. You have already done enough.' Verity forced a weak smile. 'This is something that I must attend to myself. It is a matter of family.'

'We are all family,' Zoë said gently. 'All Sisters by duty if not by blood.'

Verity shook her head. 'I thank you both for accompanying me, but our order's work on the outer moons is more important. The Palatine might bear to lose me for a time, but not you two as well.' She took up her bag from Zoë and gave them both a curt bow. 'Ave Imperator, Sisters.' With finality, the Hospitaller withdrew a black mourning shawl from her pocket and tied it about her neck.

Inara said her farewell with a light touch on her arm. 'We will pray for her,' she promised, 'and for you.'

'Ave Imperator,' said Zoë, as the hatch began to rise up again.

Verity made her way down from the landing pad, turning back just once to see the cargo shuttle throw itself up into the lightening sky on plumes of dirty smoke. She brushed dirt from the ruby hem of her robes and set off across the port, a fistful of papers and consent seals in her hand.

SHE FOUND A stand of cable-carriages outside the port proper, where the hooded drivers congregated in clusters under clouds of tabac smoke. Verity had Imperial scrip with which to pay, but none of them would even meet her gaze. Instead, the driver at the head of the group pulled a mesh veil down over his eyes and beckoned her towards his vehicle. With a rattle of gears, he worked the lever on the carriage's open cockpit and the boxy vehicle moved off along the wide, curved boulevard.

Trenches set into the surface of the roadway criss-crossed every major artery in the city, through which lines of cable rolled on endless loops. The carriages had spiked cogs in their wheel wells that bit into the cables and locked, allowing the vehicles to move about with no power source of their own. It kept the city's air clean of combustion fumes and engine noise, replacing it with the constant hiss and clatter of cabs jumping slots and passing over points. The metal landaus that travelled Noroc's streets varied in size from small taxis to large flatbed haulers and triple-decker omnibuses. Only the wealthy and the church had their own.

Verity understood from her indoctrination assemblies that Neva's laws forbade everyone but the agents of the Emperor himself – and by that they meant the Arbites, Imperial Guard and Ecclesiarchy – the use of a vehicle with any true freedom of movement.

She had never been on Neva Prime before. In all the months that the Order of Serenity had been in service to the poor and wretched of the outer moons, Verity had never once come to the world those innocents served. The moons were desolate places, each and every one of them. Whole plane-toids given over to open cast mines or deep-bore geothermal power taps, riven with sickness from the polluting industry that controlled them. It was no wonder that Neva itself was such a jewel of a world, she reflected, when every iota of its effluent and engineering had been transplanted to the satellite globes about it.

She caught reflections of her face in the windows of shops as they trundled through the vendor district. Her flawless skin and amber hair did nothing to hide the distance in her eyes; what beauty she had was ruined by the sadness lurking there. Stallholders were already erecting their pitches, piling high stacks of fat votive candles, cloth penitent hoods, paper offerings and icons cast out of resin. Once or twice there was the crack of a whip on the wind, but that might have just been the cables. The cable-carriage clanked past a flatbed piled high with what seemed to be hessian corpse sacks, there and then gone. At an interchange, a train of teenagers, ashen, shaven-headed and sexless, were led across the avenue by priests in bright regalia. Then the cab was moving again, the driver plucking at the wires in the road to steer it.

Verity sighed, and it felt like knives in her chest. Gloom crowded her. She was hollow and echoing within, as if everything that had made her who she was had been scooped out and destroyed. Once again, tears prickled at her eyes and she gasped, trying to hold them back and failing.

Through the gauzy muslin curtains across the carriage she saw the Convent of Saint Katherine emerging in the distance, and presently the woman surrendered herself to the grief that churned within her, muffling her sobs in the folds of her black shawl.

THEY BURIED SISTER Lethe in the memorial garden, a space of light and greenery on the southern face of the convent. It grew out of the side of the building in a flat disc-shaped terrace, emerging from the wide portal doors of the chapel. The garden was dominated by a statue of Saint Katherine, dressed in the armour of a Sister Seraphim. She stood as if ready to leap off her plinth and take to the air, carved coils of flame and smoke licking from the jump pack on her back.

In keeping with her new status and penances, Iona was not permitted to attend the funeral. Instead, Cassandra walked ahead of the pallbearer helots in their white robes, a censer of votive oils burning as she swung it back and forth like a pendulum. Miriya, Isabel and Portia followed the cloaked body, their black Celestian armour polished to a mirror-bright sheen. In accordance with the rites of the order, cloths of red silk were tied across the barrels of their guns to signify the silence of the weapons in this moment of reflection.

Reiko, the veteran Sister Superior who served Canoness Galatea as her aide, conducted the ceremony in a correct but not heartfelt manner. A scattering of other Battle Sisters, women that Miriya

did not know by sight – most likely members of the
Convent's garrison – paid their respects as they were
wont to do. Yet, not one of them had known Lethe,
none of them had fought alongside her against traitors and xenos, none of them had bled red for the
same patches of accursed ground.

Miriya grimaced. She had lost women under her
command before, in circumstances much worse
than this one, and yet the simple and utterly brutal
manner of Lethe's murder weighed her down with
guilt. It was all the Sister Superior could do to hold
back the tirade of inner voices that would willingly
blame her for her error aboard the *Mercutio*.

In her mind's eye she saw herself again, in that
moment when she placed the plasma pistol against
Vaun's capsule and threatened to kill him. *Why
didn't I do it? Then Lethe would still be alive, Iona
would still be one of us…* But to do so would have
been to disobey a direct command from her church.
Miriya had often been called to account for her fre-
quently 'creative' interpretations of instructions
from her seniors, but she had never defied a superior; such an idea was anathema to a Sororitas. Her
gaze dropped to the stone path beneath her feet. Sister Dione had warned her not be complacent, and
she had not fully heeded that warning until it was
too late. *I will make those responsible pay*, she vowed.

An oval slot in the stony path of the garden was
open to the air, revealing a vertical silo a few metres
deep. Reiko brought the Litany of Remembrance to
a close, and the white-clad servitors tipped Lethe's
body into the space and filled it with earth. As the

Nevans did with all their dead, they buried her
standing up with her face tilted back toward the sky.
It was for the deceased to see the way back to Terra,
and to the path that led them to the right hand of
the Emperor, so their clerics said.

'In His name, and by the sanction of Our Martyred Lady, we commit our Sister Lethe Catena to
the earth. There to rest until the Divine One calls
upon His fallen to rise once more.' Reiko bowed her
head, and the others did the same. Miriya hesitated
for a second, catching the eye of a young Sister wearing the robes of a different order. She gave the
Celestian a look loaded with pain and anger.

'Praise the Emperor, for in our resolve we only
reflect His purpose of will,' intoned Reiko. 'So shall
it be.'

'So shall it be,' they chorused.

DRAWN INEXORABLY TO the place where Lethe lay,
Miriya approached the woman kneeling there even
though part of her knew only ill could come of it.
Closer, and she recognised the unbroken circle symbol on the girl's robes, the mark of the Order of
Serenity. Like the Order of our Martyred Lady, the
Sister Hospitallers who served in the name of Serenity came from the Convent Sanctorum on Ophelia
VII. Hospitaller orders were, by Imperial law, non-
militant, but that by no means meant their ranks
were filled with weaklings. These women were
chirurgeons and nurses of expert skill and great
compassion, serving the warriors of the Imperial
military machine on countless thousands of worlds.

They were also full trained in the arts martial, and were fully able to take action if circumstances demanded it. No planet that dared to consider itself civilised was without a hospice or valetudinarium staffed by such Sisters.

The woman stood and met Miriya's gaze. She seemed on the verge of tears, but her hands were balled into fists. 'You... You are Lethe's commander. Sister Miriya.'

'I had that honour,' Miriya replied carefully.

The words seemed to pain the girl. 'You. Let her die.'

'Lethe ended her life as she lived it, in battle against the heretic and the witchkin.' Miriya replied, taken aback by the young woman's grief.

'I want to know how it happened,' snapped the Hospitaller. 'You must tell me.'

Miriya gave a slow shake of the head. 'That is a matter for the Orders Militant, not for you.'

'You have no right to keep it from me.' Tears streaked the woman's face. 'I am her sister!'

Miriya's gesture took in the whole of the convent. 'We are all her Sisters.'

The Hospitaller pulled at her collar and tugged out a length of intricate silver chain: a rosary, the like of which Miriya had only ever seen worn by one other person. 'Where did you get that?'

'I am Sister Verity Catena of the Order of Serenity,' said the girl. 'Sibling to Sister Lethe of the Order of our Martyred Lady, orphan of the same mother.' She grabbed Miriya's wrist. 'Now you will tell me how my only blood kin was killed, or by the Golden Throne I'll claw it from you!'

She saw it instantly: the same curve of the nose, the eyes and the determination burning behind them. The moment stretched taut in the silence, Verity's anger breaking against the cold dejection that cloaked Miriya.

'Very well,' said the Celestian, after a long silence. 'Sit with me, Sister Verity, and I will tell you the hard and unforgiving truth.'

THE SKINNY YOUTH rolled the lit candle between his fingers, playing with the soft tallow, tipping it so the rivulets of molten wax made coiled tracks around its length.

'Nervous?' asked Rink, balancing on the edge of the table.

Ignis glanced up at the other man. 'Are you asking me or telling me?' Rink hadn't been able to sit still for five minutes since they arrived in the saloon, and even now in this secluded back room, he was constantly in motion. As if to illustrate the point, Rink fingered the tin cup of recaf on the table and licked his lips.

'I'm not nervous.' The large guy said it with such bland innocence that it made Ignis smirk. 'I just... don't like this place.'

'You'll get no argument from me,' said the youth, teasing the flame along the candle's wick. He shook his head. 'Ach. I can't believe we're even here.'

'My point,' retorted Rink, putting the cup down again. 'Maybe we should just give this up as a bad job and–'

'And what?' A hooded figure pushed open the bead curtain cordoning off the room from the rest of the saloon. 'Whistle down a starship to come get you?'

Rink gaped like a fish and Ignis got to his feet, a grin springing to life on his lips. 'By all that's holy, is it you?'

Torris Vaun returned the smile. 'Oh yes, it's me. In the flesh.' He patted both of the men on their shoulders. 'Bet you never thought you'd see this face again, eh?'

'Well, uh, no, to be honest,' admitted Rink. 'After them nuns took you in the nets on Groombridge, we reckoned that was it. All over.'

'*Some* of us did,' Ignis added, with a pointed look.

'They were a bit rough with me, but nothing I wasn't ready for.' Vaun helped himself to a cup of recaf and sweetened it generously with the brandy bottle on the table. 'Got a smoke?' he asked, off-handedly. 'I'm gasping.'

Rink nodded and fished out a packet of tabac sticks. Vaun made a face at the label – it was a cheap local brand that smelled like burning sewage – but he took one just the same. 'Your hand is shaking, Rink,' noted the criminal. 'You're not happy to see me?'

'I'm... uh...'

'He's nervous,' explained Ignis. 'Honestly, Vaun, I'm in there with him on that. Coming here... Well, there's been talk it was a mistake.'

'Mistake?' Vaun repeated. He tapped the end of the cigarillo with the flat of his finger and it puffed alight. 'Who has been saying that?'

The two other men exchanged glances. 'Some people. They didn't come.'

'Like?'

'Gibbin and Rox. Jefter, too.' Rink sniffed.

Vaun made a dismissive gesture. 'Ah, the warp take them. Those bottom-feeders never had the eye for a big score, anyway.' He smiled. 'But you boys came, didn't you? That warms my heart.' The tip of the tabac stick glowed orange.

'The others are scattered about. Lying low,' noted Ignis. 'But we all came.'

'Even though you didn't want to,' Vaun voiced the unspoken part of the sentence. 'Because you're asking yourself, what in Hades made Torris Vaun think he could get free from the Adepta Sororitas?'

'Yeah,' said Rink, 'and the message. Didn't even know the twerp who brought it, some moneyed little fig with his hands all high.'

'You still came, though. That's good. Even though LaHayn's dogs and every city watch on Neva will be sniffing for us, you still came.' He exhaled sweet smoke. 'You won't regret it.'

Ignis blinked. 'We're not staying here... Vaun, tell me we're not gonna stay on this churchy prayer-pit one second longer.' His voice went up at the end of the sentence.

'Watch it,' said Vaun, amused. 'This is my homeworld you're disparaging. But yes, we're staying. There's a big prize here, Ig. Bigger than you can imagine. With the help of my, ah, moneyed friends, we're going to have it, and more besides.'

'More?' asked Rink. 'What like?'

'Like revenge, Rink. Bloody revenge.' Vaun's eyes glittered with violence.

Ignis looked away. He toyed with the candle some more, making the flame change shape. 'Who are these friends of yours, then? Highborns and top caste lackwits? Why do we need them?'

'For what they can give us, boy. You know the way it is, rich folk only want to be richer. They don't know what it's like to be poor and powerless, and they're terrified of falling to it. Makes them predictable, and fat for the gutting.'

The youth frowned. 'I don't like the way the people around about look at me. Like they see the mark on me. Every time I'm walking down the street, I think I see folks on the vox to the ordos, calling out… "Come and get him. Witchboy!" I don't want to stay here.' The candle burned brightly, licking his fingers. Ignis seemed not to notice.

Vaun took a long draw on the tabac. 'How about you, Rink? You have a complaint, too?'

'Don't like the priests,' said the big man at length. 'They beat me when I was a nipper.'

A slow smile crossed Vaun's face. 'Aren't we all the wounded little birds? Listen to me, lads, when I tell you there's no man alive who hates Neva more than I do. But I have unfinished business here, and with the good grace of the Sisters of Our Martyred Lady, I am now delivered back to my place of birth to conclude it.' He waved the cigarillo in a circle. 'For starters, we're going to light some fires back in Noroc and give the goodly lord deacon the hiding he so richly deserves. Then we'll move on to the main event.' A smile crossed his lips. 'When we're done, this entire damned planet will be burning.'

Ignis perked up at those words. 'I'd like that.'

'Wait and see,' promised Vaun. 'Just you wait and see.'

THE PRISON WAS a monument to deterrence. There were no windows of any kind along its outer facia, nothing but the thin slits where cogitator-controlled autoguns peeked out at the open plaza around it. The brassy weapons hummed and clicked as people passed beneath their sights, ever prepared to unleash hails of bullets into escapees or trouble-makers.

There was never any of either, of course. Noroc's central district was a model of pious and lawful behaviour, and had it not been for the less salubri-ous activities of the commoners in the outer zones of the city, the local enforcers precinct would have had little to do but polish their power mauls and take part in parades. Part of the strength that kept the citizenry quiet came from buildings like the prison. One only had to raise one's head and look to see the cone-shaped construction, with the relief of brutal carvings that covered its every surface.

The reformatory, as it was known, was a propa-gandist artwork on a massive scale. Each level showed sculptures of the Emperor's agents – Arbites, Space Marines, inquisitors, Battle Sisters and more – killing and purging those who broke Imperial law and doctrine. Crimes as base as rape and child-murder were there, along with petty theft, lying and tardiness. Each and every perpetrator was shown in the moment of their guilt, suffering the full weight of retribution upon them. At the very top of the conical construct, loud hailers broadcast stern hymns and blunt sermons on the nature of crime. Everything about the building was a threat to those who would entertain thoughts of malfeasance.

Sister Miriya approached the prison across the plaza, with Cassandra at her side and the Hospitaller Verity a step or two behind.

'Is her presence really necessary, Sister Superior?' Cassandra asked from the side of her mouth.

'Another pair of eyes is always useful,' replied Miriya, but in truth that was a poor justification. Had she wanted another observer, it would have been a simple matter for her to summon Isabel or Portia to accompany them. She was conflicted by Verity, pressured by a sense of obligation to her comrade Lethe. In some way Miriya felt as if she owed the Hospitaller a debt of closure. *Or is it my own guilt she reflects back upon me?* The Sister Superior shook the thought away. Verity wanted to see the men who had aided Vaun in murdering her sibling, and Miriya could think of no good reason to refuse her.

An enforcer with veteran sergeant chevrons on his duty armour was waiting for them at the gate, and with grim purpose the enforcer ushered the three of them in through the prison's layers of security. Other enforcers stopped what they were doing to watch the Sisters passing by. They did not look at them with reverence or respect; the lawmen half-hid smirks or sneers and muttered among themselves, quietly mocking the women who had so publicly lost the notorious psyker.

Cassandra's lip curled and Miriya knew she was on the verge of snapping out an angry retort, but the Sister Superior silenced such thoughts in her with a brief shake of the head. They had more serious concerns than the opinions of a few common police troopers.

'We've got them segregated,' said the enforcer sergeant. 'A couple have died since we got them here.'

'How?' piped Verity.

He gave her an arch look. 'Wounds, I imagine. Fell down the stairs.'

'Have you interrogated them?' Miriya studied the line of cell doors as they passed into the holding quadrant.

'Couldn't get much sense out of them,' admitted the enforcer. 'Crying for their wives and kids, mostly.' He grimaced. 'Big men, some wetting their britches and wailing like newborns. Pathetic.'

'They know the price they will pay for turning on the Emperor's benificence,' said Cassandra. 'They have nothing to look forward to but death.'

The sergeant nodded. 'You want to see them all, or what? You won't learn anything of use, I'll warrant.' He handed a fan of punch cards to Miriya and signalled another enforcer trooper to open the heavy steel door to an interrogation chamber.

She scanned the names. 'This one,' said Miriya after a moment, tapping her finger on a worn card. 'Bring him to us.'

* * *

THE SERGEANT AND the trooper returned with Midshipman Vorgo strung between them like a side of meat. The sailor's face was all pallid skin and fresh bruising, but even a swollen-shut eye was not enough to hide the look of abject terror that appeared when he saw the Battle Sisters. Vorgo made weak mewling noises as the enforcer shackled him into the stained bronze restraint harness, above the drainage grate in the centre of the room.

Miriya gave Verity a sideways look. The Sister Hospitaller's expression was conflicted, compassion at the wretched man's mien warring with anger at his misdeeds. The Sister Superior stepped closer, into the circle of light cast by the biolumes overhead. 'You remember my face, don't you?'

Vorgo gave a jerky nod.

'Let me explain what is going to happen to you. There will be no court of law, no appeals, no due process.' She took in the lawmen and the prison with a wave of her hand. 'You will not be heard by the enforcers judges, you will not submit to a captain's mast aboard the *Mercutio*.' Miriya studied him gravely. 'You have aided and abetted in the murder of a Sororitas, colluded in the escape of a terrorist witch. You belong to the Sisters of Battle for us to persecute as we see fit. You have no rights, no voice, and no recourse. All that remains to be decided is how you will perish.'

Vorgo emitted a whimper and said something unintelligible.

'Have you ever seen an arco-flagellant, Vorgo?' Miriya signalled to Cassandra and the other Battle

Sister dropped her bolter into a ready stance. 'Let me tell you about them.' Her voice took on a cold, steely quality. 'As the Emperor wills, those who are found guilty of heresy and crimes of similar gravity are taken into the service of we who hunt the witchkin. Chirurgeons and Hospitallers adapt them to this new life with surgery and conditioning, implanting pacifier helms and lobotomaic taps in their brains.'

For emphasis, she tapped Vorgo's forehead with a finger. 'Imagine that. Your limbs removed, replaced with spark-whips and nests of claws. Eyes bored from your skull and stained glass in their places. Your heart and organs fixed with stimm injectors and neuropathic glands. And then, proud in your new body, what remains of your drooling waste of a mind will be turned to the good of the Imperium. With a word of my command, you'll willingly fling yourself into the jaws of hell, a berserk flesh-machine bound for a long, long death.' When she threw Cassandra a nod, the Battle Sister took aim at Vorgo's head. 'There is a cleaner, quicker way... but only for the repentant.' Miriya paused in front of the restraint rig. 'I will give you that gift if you tell me who you were working for. What compelled you to free Torris Vaun?'

'Who?' said Vorgo, pushing the word out of his mouth. 'I don't know any Vaun.'

'Are you playing games with me?' Miriya growled. 'There are others I can offer my mercy to. Now answer me, why did you free Vaun?'

'Don't know Vaun.' The sailor shouted suddenly. 'My daughter. What have you done to my daughter, you bitch?'

'What is he talking about?' asked Verity.

The enforcer sergeant shifted and frowned. 'This again. Like I said, crying for his family, like all of them. Can't get a proper answer from any of these wastrels.'

Verity took the punch card that showed Vorgo's record and held it up to the light. 'The Imperial census notation here shows this man has no family. No daughter.'

'You can read the machine dialect?' asked Cassandra.

The Hospitaller nodded. 'A little. I have worked closely with Sisters of the Orders Dialogous in the past. Some of their skills are known to me.'

'I love my daughter.' spat the sailor, desperation making him lunge at the manacles. 'And you took her and put her in that glass jar. You black-hearted whores–'

Miriya slapped him with the flat of her ceramite gauntlet, knocking out a couple of teeth and silencing him for the moment. 'He thinks our prisoner was his daughter? What idiocy is this?'

'Why in Terra's name would he think we had his non-existent child as our prisoner?' Cassandra shook her head. 'This man was *there*. He saw the capsule's occupant first hand. He freed Vaun from the pskyer hood himself.'

Miriya cupped the prisoner's chin in her hand. 'Who was in the capsule, Vorgo?'

'My daughter…' He sobbed. 'My beautiful daughter.'

'What is her name?' asked Verity, the question cutting through the air. 'What does she look like?'

Something went dark behind the sailor's eyes. 'Wh-what?' His face became slack and pasty.

'Her name, Vorgo,' repeated the Hospitaller. 'Tell us your daughter's name, and we'll bring her back to you.'

'I… I don't… remember…'

'Just tell us, and we'll let you go free.' Verity took a step closer. 'You *do* know the name of your own daughter, don't you?'

'I… I…' From nowhere, the midshipman let out a piercing scream of agony, throwing his head from side to side. Vorgo wailed and his eyes rolled back in their sockets, blood streaming from his nose and ears. Verity ran to him as the man went limp against the rack.

After a moment she shook her head. 'Dead. A rupture within his brain, I believe.'

'The psyker did that to him?' asked the enforcer with disgust.

'Impossible,' Miriya shook her head. 'Vaun's witchery is all brute strength and violence. He lacks the subtlety for something like this.'

'He would not have been able to control this man's mind from inside the capsule,' added Cassandra, 'and certainly not the minds of a dozen men.'

Verity looked at the sergeant. 'The others from the *Mercutio* who helped Vaun escape, you say they are all calling for their loved ones?'

A nod. 'Like lost children.'

The Hospitaller turned to face Miriya. 'Sister Superior, your prisoner did not escape of his own accord. Someone freed him, someone who used these weak men like regicide pawns. They were compelled to believe that a person they cared for deeply was in your custody.'

The sergeant snorted. 'You're an inquisitor now as well as a nurse, then, Sister?' He snapped his fingers at the dead man and the trooper at his side took the corpse away. 'Please excuse me if I don't take the word of a dozen lying traitors as to why they took it into their heads to free a mass-murderer. These men are bilge-scum, plain as nightfall. They reckoned they might earn some gratitude from Vaun, so they busted him out. There's no witch-play or magic about it, pardon me for my impertinence!' He said the last words in a way that clearly showed he didn't mean them.

'The simplest explanation is usually the right one,' admitted Cassandra, and Verity looked at the floor, crestfallen.

'When one deals with witches, nothing is simple,' commented the Sister Superior.

CHAPTER FOUR

THE CANONESS DID a poor job of hiding her dismay as Miriya entered her chambers, frowning deeply over the pict-slate in her hand. The Sister Superior gave a contrite bow.

'Your eminence. I would speak with you.'

Galatea did not offer her the room's only vacant chair. Instead, she placed the slate on her wide wooden desk and rolled back the sleeves of her day robe. 'I knew, Miriya. I knew it, somewhere deep in my marrow, from the moment the astropaths brought me the message from Prioress Lydia. When I saw your name on the document, I knew this day would not run smoothly.' She gave a bitter laugh. 'I was in error, it seems. I underestimated considerably.'

Miriya scowled. 'You and I have always read from different pages of the Emperor's book, but you understand me, Sister. We have fought the foe and prayed together afterwards a hundred times. You know I am not so lax that I would have let this happen–'

'But you did,' Galatea insisted, 'through your fault or not, Vaun's escape was on your watch and so you bear responsibility. And as our order's prime representative on this planet, by extension so do I. You have brought disgrace to Saint Katherine's name.'

'Don't you think I am aware of that?' Miriya snapped angrily. 'Don't you think I would take my own life here and now if that could undo what happened? I lost two comrades to that monster, one buried, one broken.'

The Canoness nodded. 'And more will die before Vaun is made to answer for his crimes, that much is certain.' She turned to study the view through the room's stained glassteel window. 'You have given me a bloody mess to clean up, Miriya.'

'Let me do something about it.' The Celestian took a step forward. 'No one on this world wants Vaun to pay more than I do. I want your permission to pursue my investigation of the fugitive.'

'He will be found. Neva is sealed tight. Vaun will never make it offworld alive.' Galatea shook her head. 'His arrogance in coming home will be his undoing.'

'Vaun's not going to leave,' insisted Miriya. 'Not until he gets what he wants.'

'Oh?' The Canoness threw an arch look at her. 'Suddenly you are an expert on this man? You have some inner knowledge of his thoughts and desires? Pray tell, Sister, of your belated insight.'

She ignored the thinly veiled sarcasm. 'He's a brute, a thief and a corsair drawn only to what makes him richer or more powerful. He came to Neva because he wants something that is here.'

'Vaun came to Neva because he was captured, not of his own will.'

'Did he?' It was Miriya's turn to sneer. 'Or perhaps he allowed himself to be caught, knowing full well he would be freed.'

Galatea returned to her pict-slate, her attention fading with every moment. 'Oh, this is the theory advanced by the Hospitaller, yes? What is her name? Verana?'

'Sister Verity,' corrected Miriya, 'of the Order of Serenity.'

'An order not known for its expertise in martial matters,' commented Galatea, dryly.

Miriya suppressed a snarl. 'She may not be a Battle Sister, but she has a keen mind and a strong heart. Her skills could prove useful to us.'

'Indeed? Or is it merely that you feel an obligation for letting her sibling perish?'

She looked away. 'There is some truth in that, I will not deny it. But still I stand by what I have said. I… I trust her.' The admission surprised her as much as it did the Canoness.

Galatea shook her head again. 'Be that as it may, Sister Verity has no place here. Her dispensation to visit Neva extended only to the duration of Lethe's funerary service. The Order of Serenity has its works to perform on the outer moons with the sick and the diseased. It is my understanding that the workers there suffer in their service to the Imperium…'

'You outrank the Palatine leading the mission on the moons,' noted Miriya. 'You would be within your remit to order Verity to linger here, if you wished it.'

'*If* I wished it,' repeated Galatea. 'I'm not convinced there is any value to having her remain. It's enough that you, a senior Battle Sister, have allowed your emotions to cloud your judgement on this matter. What can I expect of a mere medicae like Verity, a woman unused to the violence and trials that we will be facing?'

'The same as any one of us,' Miriya said grimly, 'that we embrace the passion and do the Emperor's will.' She advanced as close as she could and laid her hands flat upon the Canoness's desk. 'Give me this, Galatea. I will ask you for nothing else, but give me this chance to make amends.'

The weight and intensity behind the Sister Superior's words gave her pause, and the two women studied each other for a long moment, measuring each other's resolve. Finally, Galatea broke the stalemate and gathered up a fresh data-slate and an electro-quill. 'Despite what you may think of me, Miriya, I have always considered you to be an exemplary warrior. Because of that, and that alone, I'll grant you the freedom to pursue this.' She scratched out a line of words, the glassy plate turning her flowing script into precise letters as she wrote. 'But understand, you have no margin for error. If you do not bring Vaun to book, it will be the end for you –

and you will drag the Hospitaller down as well.' The slate gave a soft, melodic chime as the messenger program within came to an end.

Miriya gave a low bow. 'Thank you, Sister Canoness. I promise you, we will see the witch burn for his transgressions.'

Galatea smiled a crooked smile. 'It is not me that you need to convince, Sister Superior. The esteemed Deacon Lord LaHayn is watching our convent like a hawk. I'm certain he will want to know every detail of how you plan to locate the psyker.'

'I do not understand.'

'You shall. The Blessing of the Wound begins at eight-bell today, and tradition requires that our order be in attendance at the fête of observance in the Lunar Cathedral.' She made a dismissive gesture with her hand. 'You will accompany my party. Dress robes and full honours, Sister. Inform your squad.'

IN THE STREETS, children who were too young to understand the true nature of an adult's penance ran alongside the flagellatory wagons and threw loose cobbles at the moaning, soiled people inside. Drawn down in cattle-shuttles from the penitentiary mines and work camps on the moons, the remorseful were brought to Neva by the promise of time deducted from their indentures or sentences, should they survive the great games of the festival. The ones who were already broken in will were of no use; those were kept on the moons to work until they died. Only the men and women who still held a living spark of inner strength were allowed to sacrifice themselves to the machine of the church in this great annual celebration.

So the priests and clerics in the chapels told it, everyone was remorseful. To be human was to be born that way, already alive only at the sufferance of the Emperor, but hard graft and piety were a good salve, and only the truly low were irredeemable. Criminals and heretics, dissidents and slaves, only they had no voice in the church – and as such, they were the best sacrifices for the Blessing of the Wound. Persistent rumours said that they would be joined by innocents who spoke too loudly about the church's severe rule or the flaccid, ineffectual regime of the planetary governor; the festival was always a good time to rid the city of unmutual thinkers.

On other Imperial worlds, there would be harvest celebrations and burnt offerings, great hymnal concerts, sometimes fasting or dancing. A million planets and billions of people celebrated the greatness of the Master of Mankind in their own sanctioned ways, and here, on this world of theologians and rigid dogma, there was no dividing line between zealous penance and devout worship.

This year Noroc was alive with chatter on the streets and in the pulpits, even among the youths spilling out of the seminaries and schola. The lord deacon had promised the death of a witch to cap the festival's commencement this year, not a make-believe one using fireworks and lightning guns like they'd seen before, but a real live psyker. Now that was not going to come to pass, and rumours ran about the city like mice in the walls.

The barony and the moneyed castes looked on at the commoners and pretended they knew what was to be done instead, but they were just as ignorant – save for the knowledge that Lord LaHayn and Governor Emmel would have to collude to create something of equal spectacle to placate the people. All across the metropolis, individuals donned their ritual wear or chose their costumes if they were lucky enough to have received a blood red summons paper. The icon sellers filled their stalls and emptied them, filled and emptied them again, taking in fists of Imperial scrip and church-certified tithe beads.

This year, it was the new cotton shirts adorned with a gold-thread aquila that were the must-have item, and the enforcers had already broken up a minor fracas in the linen quarter after stock had sold out. Elsewhere, devotional parades where local girls painted themselves sun-yellow and wore wings, celebrated the passing of Celestine. In other districts there were gleeful, impromptu stonings for those whose petty crimes had gone unpunished by the judges. The mood was a strange, potent mix of the buoyant and the fierce, with the lust for hard violence hovering just beneath the surface. You could see it in the eyes of the running children, on the faces of their parents, reflected in the fervour of the city's thousands of clerics.

The carriages jumped cables and fell down the gentle incline towards the grandest of Noroc's basilicas, the lofty pinnacle of the Lunar Cathedral. From a distance, the cathedral resembled a tall cone with geometric scoops cut from its flanks. In fact, these carefully assembled voids were aligned with the complex orbital paths of Neva's many moons, and during midnight mass it was often possible for parishioners inside to see the pinprick lights of fusion furnaces on the surfaces of the distant, blackened spheres.

Below the church was the oval ring of the amphitheatre from which LaHayn himself sometimes held sermons. The ancient power of the great hololithic projectors ringing the edges turned him into a glowing ghost ten storeys tall, the ornate brass horns of a thousand vox-casters throwing his voice across the city. For now, the arena was quiet, but that would soon change. Already, the shapes of elaborate scenery flats and large sections of stage set were coming together, casting alien shadows beneath the crackling yellow floodlights that hung from gas balloons. Once the carriages disgorged their cargoes of conscript actors, once the guns were charged and the mesh-weave costumes donned, the great performances of the day would begin in earnest.

VERITY'S FIRST GLIMPSE of the Lunar Cathedral's great chamber came over the shoulder of Sister Miriya's power armour, the high vault of the white stone ceiling rising away from her. The rock had a peculiar glitter about it where flecks of bright mica were caught in its matrix. Lights seemed to dance and play in the heights, and it was a far cry from the close, introspective feel of the convent. The

Hospitaller had never seen so much gold in one place. It was on every surface, worked in lines across the mosaics on the floor, climbing up the columns in coils of High Gothic script, fanning in thick cables like a vast, honeyed web.

The people here were just as gilded as the cathedral interior. She passed by women with arch expressions and a sense of disdain that seemed so deeply ingrained that it must have been bred into them. Their clothes mimicked the cut of Inquisitorial robes or, among the more daring, the garb of living saints. They fanned themselves with tessen, semicircles of thin jade that could double as an edged weapon in a fight.

Verity doubted that any of these perfumed noble ladies would ever do anything so base, though. There were troupes of elaborate servitors hovering about each of them, some peeling grapes, some tasting wines for their mistresses. Each of the helots was probably armed with all manner of discreet – but lethal – firepower. She watched the machine-slaves drift to and fro, and observed the way the women edited their servants from their world: they never looked directly at them, never spoke to them. They ignored their very existence, and yet depended entirely upon it.

One of the more audacious of the ladies said something whispered behind her fan and set a clutch of her friends giggling. Verity, the smallest and plainest thing for what must have been kilometres around, instantly knew the insult was directed at her.

At her side, the Battle Sister called Cassandra caught the ripple of spiteful amusement and made a show of sniffing, before turning a soldier's eye on the servitors. 'A passable combat construct,' she noted to no one in particular, 'but I imagine any attacker would be turned back before these slaves could be called to arms.'

'How so?' asked Sister Portia.

'Even a Space Marine would find those fragrances an irritant,' she replied, her voice low – but not *that* low. 'I suspect a crop-duster was used to apply them.'

Verity couldn't help but snatch a look back at the noblewomen, and the pink blushes colouring their faces.

They walked on, the rolling murmur of the fête rising and falling as merchants and theologians made their small talk in drifting shoals of conversation. The Hospitaller kept in line with Miriya and her unit, as Miriya in turn followed the Canoness Galatea and her adjutant Sister Reiko. Verity saw dozens of priests of ranks too numerous to tally, all in various cuts of crimson and white. A very few wore gold and black, and the men in red congregated around them, pups before pack leaders. Verity bowed whenever one of them crossed the orbit of the Adepta Sororitas contingent, but she suspected that her presence was not even noticed. She allowed herself to survey the edges of the gathering as they crossed beneath a great silver glow-globe hanging on suspensors in the chancel. There were a few Sisters from other orders here, representatives of the

Orders Famulous and Dialogous. She shared looks with those women, curt nods that carried a dozen subtle signals.

The mix of the pious and the laity was about even. The cream of Neva's magnate class preened in their copious robes, and something of the arrogance of it made Verity uncomfortable. This was, after all, a place of the Emperor's worship, not a ballroom for foppish merchants. The men – they were almost all male – proudly displayed the sigils of their noble houses on medallions, tabards and tunics. The Hospitaller reflected: the last time she had seen many of those symbols, they had been rendered as livid brands burnt into the flesh of indentured workers, or carved across the smoke-belching stacks of manufactories, as an undisciplined child might daub their name on a wall.

Their procession stopped with such abruptness that Verity was jolted from her thoughts and almost walked into the back of Sister Isabel. She recovered quickly, frowning at her lack of focus.

It took a moment for Verity to recognise the man that Galatea stood before, a stiff salute in her pose. She had seen his placid, patrician face on billboards out at the port, and on some of the moons, on posters drawn over with rude graffiti.

'Governor Emmel, are you well?' asked the Canoness.

He presented an expression of theatrical sadness. 'As well as can be expected, my dear lady. It has been explained to me that my festival's star attraction will not be appearing.' Verity could tell from his tone of voice that Emmel was more distressed about the prospect of throwing a poor festival than he was that Torris Vaun was at large among his people.

'The Adepta Sororitas will ensure that your distress will be short-lived,' Galatea replied smoothly. 'The matter is in hand.'

That seemed to be enough to satisfy the planetary ruler, his gaze already wandering to the perfumed women congregating at the wine fountain. 'Ah, good. I know I can place my trust in the Daughters of the Emperor…'

From the edge of her vision came a cluster of other aristocrats, buoyed up on drink and sweet tabac smoke. 'With all due respect, that may not be an entirely good idea.' This new arrival was of the same stock as Emmel, but he had the look about him of a hunting dog. He was lean and spare, and hungry with it. The analytical part of Verity's mind automatically noticed the telltale yellowing around the edges of his eyelids common to those who smoked kyxa. The plant extract from worlds in the Ultima Segmentum was a mild narcotic and aphrodisiac, far too costly for the common folk.

Governor Emmel gave a shallow bow. 'My honoured Baron Sherring, your counsel is welcome at all times. There is an issue you wish to bring to my attention?'

Sherring glanced at Galatea and the assembled Sisters, then away again. 'I would not be so bold as to cast doubt on the dedication of these fine women, but voices are raised in chambers, governor. My fellow barons wonder if our personal guards might not take up the hunt for this Vaun fellow.'

Miriya spoke for the first time since they had entered the room. At first she seemed apologetic. 'Begging the baron's pardon, but you overlook a matter of some importance.'

'Does he?' piped Emmel, drawing a goblet from a passing cherubim. 'Do tell.'

'Torris Vaun was loose on this planet for a full two solar years before he ventured offworld to further his criminal career. In that time, the soldiers of your noble houses utterly failed to effect the witch's capture.' She laid a cool eye on Sherring. 'But forgive me. I am not party to the radical, sweeping changes in combat doctrine that you must have instilled in your guards since then.'

Sherring covered his annoyance with a puff from a tabac stick, and Emmel tapped his lips thoughtfully. 'I don't recall any changes,' he said aloud. 'Perhaps there were and I was not informed?'

The baron bowed and made to leave. 'As I said, it was a suggestion, nothing more. Clearly the Battle Sisters have everything in hand.' Sherring retreated back into the gathering, bidding farewell with a plastic smile.

Emmel found Verity watching him and he threw her a slightly boozy wink. 'Good old Holt. Stout fellow, if a bit ambitious.' He glanced at Miriya. 'Sister, your forthrightness is refreshing. A good trait for a warrior.' The governor leaned closer to her, and in that moment his mask of affable geniality slipped. 'But I will be disappointed if that is the only arrow in your quiver.' Then the smirk was back and he was drifting away, draining the goblet to the dregs.

In his place appeared an officer of the planetary guard garrison, bearded and furrow-browed. The man wore the local uniform of grass green and black, dotted with highly polished decorations of many kinds. At his waist was a ceremonial lasgun made of glass and a scimitar. 'The lord deacon asks that you attend him on the tier.' His voice was flat.

'I would be glad to do so, Colonel Braun,' began Galatea, but the officer gave a slow shake of the head.

'Lord LaHayn wishes to address Sister Miriya.' Braun looked at Verity. 'And the Hospitaller as well.'

The Canoness covered a twitch of annoyance. 'Of course.' She nodded, but the colonel was already walking.

Verity felt her throat go dry as she fell into step with Miriya. It took her a moment to find her voice. 'What do I tell him?'

Miriya's expression remained rigid. Her distaste for these people was more potent than the perfumes. 'Whatever he wants to hear.'

THE TIER OF Greatest Piety extended out like a jutted lip from the cathedral tower at its thickest point, high up over the teeming masses below. While white noise generators kept the genteel music inside the chapel, out here on the crescent-shaped terrace the night seemed to float on waves of cheering and hymnals. There were ranks of illuminators everywhere, but none of them were operating at the moment. The only light came from below, from the floodlamps and the uncountable numbers of electro-candles in the hands of the amphitheatre audience. Braun guided them between busy lines of servitors preparing hololith lenses and nets of vox cabling. At the raised edge of the terrace, the great Lord Deacon of Neva, Viktor LaHayn, sat atop a stone battlement watching the crowd, apparently unaffected by the dizzying view.

He had to raise his voice a little to be heard. 'They can't see us up here yet,' began the priest-lord. 'We are dark. Anyone who looks up will miss the words and that would be unforgivable.'

Miriya saw down below where vast turning boards made of small painted shutters flapped and clacked into words in High Gothic. The lyrics to the hymns rolled over them for the massive crowd to see. 'Surely, lord, they should know the words by heart?'

LaHayn threw an amused look to the dean at his side. 'Spoken like a true Sororitas, eh Venik?'

The other man just nodded, and then gestured to Braun. Without words, the colonel gave a shallow bow and retreated into the company of a dozen armsmen near the chapel door. It became clear to Miriya that the deacon was waiting for the soldiers to be out of earshot.

'Those who cannot read, learn by rote,' said LaHayn. 'In this way, the word of the God-Emperor is never lost to us. It remains unalterable, inviolate, eternal.'

'Ave Imperator.' The ritual coda slipped from her mouth without conscious thought.

'Indeed,' said the priest-lord, and he smiled again. 'Sisters Miriya and Verity, I hope you will not think ill of me for my display in the convent. Understand that the zeal the Emperor imbues me with is sometimes more than an old man may conduct. In the matter of the criminal Vaun, I am most ardent.'

'His light touches all of us in its own way,' piped Verity, keeping her eyes lowered.

'And you share my passion for this mission, yes?' LaHayn's voice was casual, level, but aimed like a laser at the Sister Superior.

'How could I not?' she replied. 'The man took the life of one of my most trusted comrades, a decorated Sister who devoted her entire existence to our church, and for that alone he should die a hundred deaths.' She kept her voice steady with effort. 'His violation of Sister Iona's mind blackens him further still. If it is in my power, I should like to present the wastrel to her so that she might be the one to strike his head from his neck.'

Dean Venik raised an eyebrow, but LaHayn's expression did not alter. 'It pleases me to hear you say those words. I prayed for Sister Iona's soul today at my private mass. I hope that in the grace of the Condicio Repentia she might find the solace she seeks.'

A nerve jumped in Miriya's jaw. Iona might never have taken the terrible exile of the repentant had it not been for LaHayn's demands for contrition. That simple fact seemed to escape the priest-lord.

'Honoured Sisters, I require you to keep the dean appraised of your investigations at all times. I'm sure you understand that Governor Emmel and the planetary congress have their issues with your continued involvement, but I have ensured that you may progress without undue censure.'

'His lordship has instructed me to open my office to you during your hunt for the criminal,' added Venik. 'You may petition me directly on any matters that fall outside your purview.'

'You are most generous,' added Verity.

'Tell me,' the priest-lord said in a confidential tone. 'I understand you conducted an interrogation at the reformatory. What did you discover?'

'I have no conclusions to offer at this stage, lord,' Miriya spoke quickly, pre-empting anything that Verity might say. 'But I fear that the orchestration of Vaun's escape was not mere opportunism. There is a plan at work here.'

'Indeed? We must consider that carefully.' Something below in the arena made the crowd cry out in awe and it caught LaHayn's attention for a moment. He studied Miriya. 'Vaun is no easy prey, Sister. He is elusive and deadly, but brilliant with it.'

'He's a thug,' she grated, a growing sense of irritation building in her.

The priest seemed not to notice. 'Only on the outside. I've met him face to face, my dear, and he can be charming when he wants to be.'

'If you were close enough to look him in the eye, why is he not dead?' Venik inhaled sharply and shot her a warning glare, but Miriya ignored it. 'I find myself wondering why a creature such as he was not gathered up as a youth for the harvest of the Black Ships.'

'Torris Vaun is wily,' noted LaHayn. 'Compassion and love are absent from his heart. He burns cold, Sister.'

Verity studied his face as he spoke. 'You sound as if you admire him, lord.'

The priest snorted lightly. 'Only as one might admire the function of a boltgun or the virulence of a disease. Believe me, there is no one on Neva who will be more content than I when Vaun meets the end I have planned for him.'

The dean made to dismiss them, but Miriya stood her ground. 'If it pleases the deacon, you have not answered my questions.'

LaHayn stood, brushing a speck of dust from the rich crimson and gold fabric of his robes. 'Sometimes, death alone is not enough to satisfy the Emperor's decree.' He was terse now, each word sharp and hard. 'As to the inner workings of the Adeptus Telepathica, that is something that I am pleased to be untouched by.' The priest-lord gave the two women a long, calculating look. 'Let me ask you something. Do you fear the witch?'

'The psyker is the gate through which Chaos enters. Only by sacrament and denial can those cursed with the witch-sight hope to live and serve Terra.' Verity repeated the words from the Liturgy of Retribution.

'Well said, but now it is *you* who does not answer *my* question.' He stared at Miriya. 'Answer me, Sister. Do you fear the witch?'

She didn't hesitate to respond. 'Of course I do. Verity is right in what she says, the witchkin would destroy mankind if left unchecked. They are as great a foe as the mutant and the heretic, the alien and daemon. Our fear makes us strong. It is the spur that takes us to destroy these monsters. If I had no fear of these things, I would have nothing to fight for.'

'Just so,' LaHayn nodded. 'If there were any doubts in my mind that you are the one to catch this pestilent, they have fled.' He bowed to them. 'Now, forgive me, but the bell comes close to ringing and I have a sermon to deliver.' The priest-lord took in the crowds below with a sweep of his arms.

As Venik ushered them away, Miriya halted and turned back to face LaHayn. 'Begging your pardon, deacon. There is one other question I wish to pose to you.'

'If you are quick about it.'

She bowed again. 'While we have focussed on the incidence of Vaun's escape, a single factor eludes me. The criminal had the chance to go where he wanted, to strike out for a hundred worlds other than this one. Why, in the Emperor's name, did he elect to return to a planet where his face and his villainy are so well known? What possible bounty could exist on Neva that he would risk all for it?' Miriya became aware that Verity was watching both of them very closely.

LaHayn's face became very still. 'Who can fathom the mind of a madman, Sister? I confess I have no answer for you.'

Miriya bowed once more and let Venik hand them off to Colonel Braun, who in turn led them down a few levels to the viewing galleries. Verity was quiet, her face pale and her gaze turned inward.

'What say you?' she asked.

Verity took her time answering. 'I... am mistaken,' said the Hospitaller, the words difficult for her to give voice to. 'For a moment, I thought... the dilation of his eyes, the blush response...'

Miriya leaned in close, so that only the two of them could hear one another. 'Say it.'

'No.' Verity shook her head. 'I am in error.'

'*Say it*,' repeated the Battle Sister. 'Tell me so I know I am not alone in my thoughts.'

Verity met her gaze. 'When you asked him about Vaun's reasons... he lied to us.'

'Just so,' said Miriya. 'But to what end?'

WHEN THE LAMPS illuminated him, LaHayn felt as if he were being projected upward into the stars, cutting free of the confines of his human meat and becoming something greater and more ephemeral – something linked directly to the bright supernova that was the Light of the God-Emperor. It never failed to elate him.

There was an old saying on Neva, that all men born there had the calling. Indeed, every male child was required to take a term in the seminary to see if they were suitable for the planet's massive caste of clerics. It had been under such simple circumstances that Viktor LaHayn had come into the orbit of the Church of Terra, and in those gloomy cloisters, among the grim-faced adepts and the priests alight with brimstone oratory, he had truly found his first vocation. The mere thought of those days brought a smile to his face. Those were less complicated times, when the word and deed of persecution were all that occupied his mind, when all he needed was the chainsword in his strong right hand and the Book of the Fated in his left.

The roaring crowd filled his senses and he welcomed them in, raising his hands in the age-old sign of the aquila, the divine two-headed eagle. Blind and yet not blind, forward looking yet knowing the past, wings unfurled to shield humanity.

In moments of introspection like this one, LaHayn wondered what he would say if he were able to step back into the past and meet his younger self in those lost days. What would he have told him? Could he have stood to whisper the secrets that would later be revealed to him? How could he, when to do so would deny that callow youth the shattering, soul-blazing revelation that his later years brought?

LaHayn watched his hololithic image grow to giant proportions and drank in the awe of his congregation. If his first calling had taken him to a vast, new world in the Emperor's service, then his second had pressed him to the very foot of the Golden Throne. None of them down there in the amphitheatre could see it, but they sensed it in the words he spoke, in the touch he laid on them. They knew, in their hearts, just as he did, never doubting, unflinching in his righteousness.

The final pieces were coming together. Lord Viktor LaHayn was the hand of the God-Emperor, and His will would be done. Nothing would be allowed to prevent it.

CHAPTER FIVE

THE IMPERIAL CHURCH was an engine fuelled by devotion, a machine lubricated by the blood of its faithful, and across a hundred thousand stars, the temples and spires of the God-Emperor's spirit cast long shadows. As each planet and populace was distinctive, so each society took the worship of the Lord of Mankind and made it their own. On feral planets like Miral, the primitive natives saw Him as a great animal stalking the stygian depths of their forests. The forge world Telemachus revered Him as the Great Blacksmith, the Moulder of All Things, and the people of Limnus Epsilon believed He lived in their sun, breathing radiance down upon them.

The church had learned in the days of the Great Crusade that enforcing its will on worlds by eradicating their belief systems and starting from scratch was a lengthy and troublesome process. Instead, the Ecclesiarchy worked by coercion and change, turning native religions to face Holy Terra and showing them the great truth of the universe – that all gods were the God-Emperor of Man in one guise or another.

On a world such as Neva, where dogma and creed were irreversibly threaded through every single aspect of its civilisation, wars had been fought over single verses in holy tracts, over the smallest points in the reading of prayers. Barons and city-lords had put each other to the sword when interpretations of credo boiled into violent discord. On such a planet, where every man, woman and child prayed to Terra in fear of their immortal souls, there was friction and dangerous strife over the meaning and the matter of the church's word.

To end such disharmony, Neva required a miracle, and by the grace of the God-Emperor, it received one. The people called it the Blessing of the Wound.

LORD LAHAYN DID not speak or gesture for the crowds to become silent. He merely watched and waited, his aspect neutral and his hands clasped behind his back. The tall hololithic ghost projection glittered beneath him, hovering over the stage sets mounted in the amphitheatre's dirt arena. He allowed his visage to turn gently this way and that, the image's eyes scanning the people with a cool, unwavering stare. LaHayn had long ago mastered the ability to address a crowd and have each person in it think that it was only they to whom he was speaking.

When they were quiet, he gave them a shallow bow. 'Sons and daughters of Neva. We are blessed.' The priest-lord felt the gaze of thousands upon him, thousands of breaths held in tight throats. 'The path towards a better tomorrow stretches out before us, towards a future that is golden and eternal, but our journey together must cross a wilderness of hardship and struggle.'

He bowed his head. 'Each year we gather here and ask for the Blessing, and we are granted it. Why? Because we are humanity. Because we are the children of the God-Emperor, the most supreme man that ever drew breath. Through His servants, we know Him and we know His words. We understand what is expected of us. Our duties, to be strong, to never weaken, to purge the xenos, the mutant, the heretic from our ranks.' The priest looked up again. 'We know that the price of all things is not gold, not uranium, not diamonds. It is *faith unfailing*. And that price is paid with blood.'

WHEN SAINT CELESTINE's warfleet had appeared in Neva's orbit to herald the passing of the warp storm that had isolated the system, the churches across the planet were filled to bursting. Lives were lost in some places when chapels, overflowing with worshippers, collapsed under their own weight. According to some records from that time, the living saint herself made planetfall at the Discus Rock some kilometres from Noroc – although log-tapes from the warrior's flagship never fully corroborated this incident, leading some historians on other worlds to doubt the words of the Nevan priests. But true or not, the saint's passage under Neva's sun changed the planet forever. The monks living in the monastery that stood at Discus now guarded the spot. Ringed with brass electro-fences there was a shallow imprint in the flat stone, allegedly marking the place where Celestine's golden boot first touched the surface of Neva. The very richest and most favoured of the planet's noble castes were allowed to kneel there and kiss the mark. Some would ritually cut themselves and offer a few drops of blood to the footprint, if they were highborn enough.

Saint Celestine, the Hieromartyr of the Palatine Crusade, was second only to the Emperor in the number of Nevan chapels dedicated to her name. Her face adorned coins, icons and devotional artworks, and in every one, the man who had come to be known as Ivar of the Wound attended at her feet.

THE PRIEST GATHERED the people in with his open arms. 'I am humbled by the magnificent example that you, my congregation, have set. The workers and artisans among you who toil and ask not for acclaim, but accept the honour of our noble Governor Emmel. The soldiers and warriors who burn with cold fire and unyielding resolve, never flinching before the threat of the heretical and unmutual. The pastors and clerics who hold the very soul of our people in their hands, shielding it from the lies of the treacherous and disloyal. You seek reward in service alone.' He made the sign of the aquila once

more. 'I am forever in awe of you.' After a long
moment, he spoke again, but now the warmth in
his voice was bleeding out, changing to something
cold and hard. 'The greatest pride of the Nevan people is order and yet there are those among us who
seek only chaos and destruction. As a chirurgeon
might sever a limb to excise a lethal cancer, we must
do the same. Our society offers so much to those
who follow the rule of law, and yet these criminals
want only discord and anarchy. To be pious is to be
strong and never yield to such offenders. Remember! The stalwart will inherit tomorrow; the weak
will be buried today. We must protect our children
and our nation from the malignancy of rebellion. In
Ivar's name, they must know the cost. They must
know it!'

IVAR'S STORY WAS famous to every Nevan, taught in
crèches and re-told to them again and again
throughout their lives. There were books of his life,
heavy with garish illustrations and few words for
the simple-minded and the young, or dense with
layers of interpretation for the thinker. Each year the
church had the public vox networks produce a lav-
ish viddy-drama biography. He was celebrated in
song and his patrician profile adorned murals
across the planet.

  An ordinary soldier in Noroc's city guard, Ivar had
witnessed first-hand the arrival of Celestine in those
turbulent days, and when the shadow of her starship quieted the assassin-wars and dismissed the
warp storm, he was so moved by the event that he

gathered a legion of warriors and followed the saint on her War of Faith. He called it a payment in return for Celestine's rescue of his homeworld, and so in the months that ensued Ivar and his men pledged themselves as militia in the service of the Adepta Sororitas. Ivar's soldiers fought with the passion of true zealots, their numbers thinning through attrition until at last only Ivar himself was still alive.

Finally, on the battlefields of the Kodiak Cluster where Celestine's force had engaged an eldar conclave, the living saint was drawn into close combat with an alien warlord. Ivar, attempting to prove his devotion, tried and failed to strangle the warlord with his bare hands, and instead found himself taken as a human shield by the xenos creature. Confronting Celestine, the alien believed that she would never willingly kill a member of her own species in cold blood but Ivar called out for the saint to sacrifice him in order to destroy the eldar commander. Celestine plunged the burning tip of her Ardent Blade through Ivar's chest, running him through and cleaving the heart of the alien behind him, but when the sword was withdrawn, by some miracle Ivar still lived.

'ZEAL. PURITY. DUTY. The pillars of the church are the platform on which we stand, unbreakable and unending. We look to the future that only we can achieve. As Ivar showed us, history does not long entrust the care of freedom to the weak or the timid.' LaHayn gently returned to the smooth, careful cadence of his earlier words. 'Each of you shares in the greatest glory of them all – you are the truly virtuous. We, who are ruthless to those who oppose our vision, masters of those we defeat, unflinching in the face of adversity. I pity all those who are not born beneath our skies, for they will never know the touch of righteousness as we do.'

The crowd roared its approval, and LaHayn gave it a fatherly smile. 'The path we have chosen is not an easy one. Struggle is the parent of all things and true virtue lies in bloodshed. But we will not tire, we will not falter, we will not fail. In the blood of our children comes the price we must pay. Blood alone moves the wheels of history, and we will be resolute, we will fear no sacrifice, and surmount every difficulty to win our just destiny. Redemption is within your grasp. The Emperor rewards His children who show courage and fidelity, just as He rejects those without it!' The amphitheatre exploded with sound, cheers pealing off the walls and booming across the city in waves of sound. Across Noroc and across the planet, the priest-lord's sermon reached the ears of Neva's faithful and they loved him for it.

THE SWORD CUT in Ivar's chest never healed. In honour of his great courage, Saint Celestine released him from his obligation to her and bid him return to Neva, there to serve the will of the God-Emperor among his people. From that day until the end of his life, Ivar's holy wound never closed, and despite the constant agony it brought him, he wore it as a badge of honour. It was said that those anointed with a drop of blood from Ivar's cut were blessed, and the bandages with which he wrapped it were held to this day as sacred relics. Ivar rose to the rank of lord deacon and founded the construction of the great Lunar Cathedral. His legacy of willing sacrifice, penitence, bloodshed and pain became the foundations on which the Nevan sect of the Imperial Church stood – and with his guidance, the Blessing of the Wound took its place as the most important religious ceremony in the planet's calendar.

MIRIYA AND VERITY stood at the lip of the gallery's fluted balcony, watching the riot of activity at the edges of the arena. LaHayn's hololithic image bowed and faded into the evening, a great cry rising from the audience as it went. Below, figures in all kinds of gaudy costumes were streaming out of hidden gates, forming up into ragged skirmish lines or gadding about in peculiar, directionless dances. Just beneath the level of the observation galleries, there were catwalks and gantries made of thin steel, painted in neutral shades so as not to stand out beneath the floodlamps. The Celestian and the Hospitaller could see people in grey coveralls working feverishly at cables and pulleys, making parts of the wooden sets below shift and move in time to the building hum of choral chants.

Verity blinked at the figures in the ampitheatre. 'Those are... They are just children.'

Miriya followed her gaze towards a group of youngsters and her brow furrowed. They were clad in crude approximations of Adepta Sororitas wargear, but made from simple cloth and cardboard

instead of ceramite and flexsteel. One of the
teenagers stumbled, clutching at her head to hold a
wig of straw-like white hair that mimicked the tra-
ditional cut of the Battle Sisters.

'I… I saw those youths in the street, when I was travelling to the convent. Is this some sort of game?'

Miriya gave a nod. 'The Games of Penance, as they
are known. A reconstruction of great events from
Saint Celestine's Wars of Faith. I have never seen them
myself…'

'Look, there,' Verity pointed. 'Do you see those players on the stage? What are they supposed to be?'

'Eldar,' Miriya observed, recognising the rudimen-
tary capes and plumes adorning the fake armour of
the actors. 'They are playing at the battle for Kodiak
Prime, or something like it.' She failed to keep a grimace from her face. The whole performance was a
caricature, a ridiculous spectacle that might have been
comic if she had not found it so offensive. Miriya had
faced the xenos in battle, and the eldar she had fought
were terrifying, deadly killers full of powerful grace
and unstoppable speed – these moronic mimics in
the ampitheatre were blundering jesters in comparison, exaggerated and simplistic parodies of the real
thing.

The crowd did not share her low opinion, however.
The locals were chanting and whooping, spinning cel-
ebratory banners over their heads or letting off small
screamer fireworks. Over the loud hailers in the stadium the opening bars of the Palatine March issued
forth, and the two sides in the imitation battle rushed
at one another, screaming incoherent war cries.

'This is a mockery,' growled Miriya.

'It is… disturbing,' admitted Verity, 'but not to the Nevans. This is their way of honouring the living saint.'

The Battle Sister's rejoinder was silenced as a clatter of gunfire rose up from the ampitheatre. Miriya's gauntleted hands tensed automatically at the sound of a hundred ballistic stubbers going off in ragged succession. All of the participants in the ersatz skirmish were firing on one another, but where she had expected them to knock each other down with paint shells and powder rounds, there was the flat crackle of bullets.

'They are using live weapons…' As the Sister Superior watched, one of the youths dressed as a Sororitas inexpertly discharged a salvo of shots into a boy on stubby stilts, the heavy rounds ripping through the wood and cloth imitations of eldar armour. Blood was already pooling on the arena's sands where figures from both sides had been cut down.

'Holy Terra!' gasped Verity, her hand flying to her mouth in shock.

Close by, one of the merchantmen from the cathedral clapped and let out a guffaw. 'What a magnificent effort this year. This Blessing will be one for the ages.'

Miriya rounded on him. 'They're killing each other.'

The portly man's expression shattered under the Battle Sister's leaden stare. 'But… But of course they are. That's how it is done…' He forced a smile. 'Ah, of course. Forgive me. You must both be off-worlders, yes? You are both new to Neva and the festival?'

'What kind of blessing demands you force your people to kill one another?' challenged Miriya.

'F-force?' said the merchant. 'No one is forced, honoured Sister.' He fumbled in the folds of his robes and recovered a fold of long papers from a hidden pocket. 'The participants in the reconstruction are all willing... Well, except for a few irredeemables from the reformatory and some asylum inmates.' One of the papers was a dark crimson, and he peeled it from the pack to wave it at her. 'Every citizen who received one of these dockets in the clerical lottery knows they are obligated to take part in the great re-enactment. We are all more than ready to do our part in penance!'

Miriya snatched the red paper from him. 'Then tell me, sir, why are you here and not down there?' She jerked a thumb at the melee below them.

The merchant's face coloured. 'I... I was happy to present the church with a substantial forfeit donation in my stead!'

'You bought your way out with coin? How lucky for you that your coffers are deep enough,' she sneered. 'If only others were so fortunate!'

'Now see here,' the noble retorted, attempting to maintain a level of superiority. 'Those who endure the Blessing are praised and rewarded. Our finest chirurgeons attend them in the aftermath, and those whose fortitude is lesser are buried with honours!'

Barely able to contain her anger, Miriya turned away, her hand dropping unconsciously to the grip of her holstered plasma pistol. The sound and fury of the confrontation set her teeth on edge, triggering old, ingrained battle instincts.

'Celestine. *Celestine*!' The cry came from one of the merchant's retinue, and the name was picked up and repeated by the crowd.

From a hidden hatch in the walls of the cathedral, a winged figure in gold emerged to fly over the ampitheatre, swooping like a bird of prey.

VERITY WATCHED THE girl garbed as the living saint race over the blood-stained sands, a fat set of pulley-wheels in the small of her back connected by glassy cables to a rig on the suspended catwalks. The grey-suited workers pulled at levers and tugged spindles to work her like a puppet, and in turn her wings of paper feathers fluttered and snapped through the air. A heavy brass halo hung about her head, decorated with yellowish biolumes, and she had an oversized replica of the Celestine's blessed weapon, the Ardent Blade, secured to one hand by tethers.

A dispenser tucked under her waist spat out a stream of paper slips, each one printed with a devotional message and a tithe voucher. People in the crowds tussled and snatched at the air trying to pull them from the night winds.

The psuedo-saint fell low and her sword clipped the heads and torsos of a dozen men in eldar costume. The blade was just for show and too blunt to sever a limb; those it struck were concussed or reeled away with broken bones.

Verity watched, and she felt queasy. It was not that she was frail or unused to the sight of spilt blood, but the malicious theatre with which this spectacle was unfolding made her uncomfortable. On the moons where she served in the wards of the hospices, there had been stories of the things done in the Emperor's name on Neva – but there were always such stories on the outer worlds, and Sister Verity was never one to place too much credence in rumour and insinuation. She wished now that she had paid greater mind. The wanton disregard for human life at play here jarred with the very core of Verity's vow to the Order of Serenity and her life's work as a Sister Hospitaller. The oath she had sworn the day she entered the Sisterhood returned to her: *First, do no harm to the Emperor's subjects. Take pain from those who revere Him, inflict it only on those who stand against His Light.*

'This is a harsh universe,' she heard the merchant remark to one of his cronies. 'It is not by chance that our church and our festival reflect the truth of that. After all, if no blood were shed this day, in what possible way could we hope to show the Emperor our devotion?'

A flurry of motion drew her eye. On the gantry a few metres below, the men in grey were panicking. Aged, overworked metal snapped with a percussive crash and cables whipped free, slashing one man across the chest and throwing another over the catwalk's rail and down to his death. The girl playing

Celestine was suddenly jerked out of her pattern of
flight and reeled upward like a hooked fish. The
sword dangled from her fingers, and in horror, Verity saw where the glass cables looped about her
head and neck. If the crowds in the stands understood or even cared what had happened, the
Hospitaller had no idea but she saw clear as day the
face of the costumed girl in abject terror as she
started to choke.

Sister Verity reacted without conscious thought,
and vaulted over the edge of the balcony. Boots
scraping on stone, she slipped down the sheer face
of the cathedral and landed on the catwalk. She was
running to the trapped girl before she was even
aware of Miriya calling after her.

THE MERCHANT AND his troupe of perfumed dandies
actually broke out in laughter when the Hospitaller
jumped, and it took much of Miriya's self-control
not to toss one of them after her. Shooting them an
iron-hard glare, she followed the woman down to
the gantry, shouting her name, but Verity did not
seem to hear her, intent instead on the luckless girl
caught up in the wires beneath the catwalk.

The workers who had not been struck insensate or
dead by the broken cables were of little use, and she
forced them aside. The catwalk squealed and com-
plained beneath her every footfall, flecks of dust
trickling off ancient joints. The shattered pulley
mechanism lowed like a dying animal, and Miriya's
hand shot out to grab a support as the decking began
to tilt. The framework was rife with rust and decay.

'Verity! We are not safe here.'

The Hospitaller was already pulling the girl up. She was ashen-faced as she worked to unwind the cabling from the youth's pale, bruised neck. 'I think she may still live…'

In reply, the catwalk let out a shriek of buckling steel and listed sharply. All at once, the costumed girl fell away from Verity's grip and Miriya bounded forward to snag the Sister Hospitaller before she went along with her. Their hands met, the Battle Sister clutching a handful of Verity's robes and then the gantry broke apart.

It was centuries old, and maintained as well as it could have been, but artisans and technicians were not the most favoured of castes on Neva and even in the ampitheatre of the Lunar Cathedral, there were never enough skilled hands to service all of the church's machinery. Steel and bodies fell through the air and crashed into the wood and fibre of the false eldar domes, straight into the middle of the arena.

GALATEA'S KNUCKLES TURNED white where she gripped the stone balustrade. 'In Katherine's name, what is she doing?'

At her side, Sister Reiko peered through a small monocular. 'An accident, Canoness? I do not think this was intentional–'

'Now, this is an interesting development.' Governor Emmel's words cut off Reiko's speech as he approached, his retinue trailing behind him and the lord deacon at his side. 'My dear Canoness, if your

Battle Sister wished to take part in the games, she had only to ask.'

'Governor, I fear that a mistake has been made,' Galatea spoke quickly. 'Perhaps if you would consider a pause in the proceedings?'

Emmel made a face. 'Ah, that would not be prudent. The rules of the fête are quite clear on these matters. The re-enactment must be played out to its conclusion without interruption. There would be much discord if I tried to halt it.'

'Perhaps even a riot,' ventured Dean Venik.

The governor cupped his ear. 'Listen, Canoness. Do you hear? The people are enraptured. They must think this is some surprise performance in lieu of the witch they were promised.'

'Perhaps not a mistake after all,' added LaHayn. 'The God-Emperor moves in mysterious ways.'

Emmel nodded and clapped his hands. 'Oh, yes, yes. You may be right!' His eyes sparkled with the idea of it. 'I wonder, an actual Sister of Battle on the field? What a game that will be!'

'With respect, governor, Sister Miriya may be injured, and she was not alone. Sister Verity is a Hospitaller, not used to combat.' Galatea's words were intense.

LaHayn accepted this with a dismissive nod. 'I am sure the Emperor will extend to her the protection her vocation merits.'

MIRIYA HAULED HERSELF out of the ruins of the wooden set and winced in pain: her right arm was dislocated. Gritting her teeth, she gripped her right wrist with her left hand and yanked. A sickening snap and a moment of sharp agony resonated through the Battle Sister's frame. She shook off the pain and coughed out metallic spittle.

A groan drew her to where Verity lay. The Hospitaller was uninjured but dazed, and Miriya pulled her unsteadily to her feet.

'The… the girl…' began Verity, but she fell silent when the other woman pointed a gloved finger at the wreckage. The teenager dressed as Celestine had broken the Hospitaller's fall and rested there in an untidy heap. Sightless, dull eyes looked up into the night sky. Verity knelt and closed the dead girl's eyelids, whispering a verse of funerary rites over her body.

The roaring of the audience crashed around them, loud as ocean breakers on a storm-tossed shore. In among the players fighting the mock battle, several of the imitation eldar had been startled by the sudden cacophony of metal that had dropped from the air, and they milled about, unsure of themselves. This close to them, Miriya could see that the weapons they bore were actually common projectile rifles and shotguns disguised to resemble the alien shuriken projectors. The Battle Sister knew the look in their eyes all too well. She had seen it before on the faces of heretic vassals and slave-troopers, on cultists whipped into frenzy by their demagogues.

'Stay close to me,' she hissed to Verity. 'They're going to fire on us.'

The Hospitaller shook her head. 'But why?'

Miriya ignored her and advanced, stepping off the pile of wreckage and holding up one hand, palm flat in a warding gesture. 'We have no part in your games,' she said aloud, in a clear, level voice. 'Stand aside.'

The costumed men were all dressed in the same warped outfits, so it was unclear if there were any ranks or hierarchy among them. They shot nervous glances at the women and at each other. Miriya saw a path she could take, up and behind the wreckage of the stage to where the gates in the arena walls would lead to safety.

'Don't run,' she whispered. 'If we run, they'll attack.'

'They're just ordinary people,' insisted Verity.

Miriya made eye contact with one of the alien-attired men, catching sight of his gaze through the triangular slits in his plumed helmet. 'That doesn't matter.'

She saw the thought forming in his mind before the man was even aware of it, her hand tearing away the peace-bond ribbon wrapped around her pistol holster. A dozen camouflaged weapons came about to bear on them and Miriya shoved Verity out of the firing line, her gun clearing its leather as shot and shell spat into the air.

'Death to the humans!' The call exploded from the lips of the false eldar, and the crowd watching them roared once again.

Automatic training born from decades of hard, unswerving service in the name of the Emperor took over. Miriya's gun barked, the ear-splitting shriek of supeheated plasma bolts drowning out the dull rattle of lead shot. It became a rout, every trigger-pull marking a critical hit, no single charge from the energy pistol wasted as the costumed men screamed and died. Paper and cloth in garish oranges and greens were stained with dark arterial crimson. Helmets made out of softwood splintered and broke.

The Battle Sister heard the pellets clattering off her power armour, as ineffectual as hailstones against the black ceramite sheath. A chance ricochet nicked a line of stinging pain across her cheek and she ignored it, turning and firing again in a single fluid motion.

When all the assailants lay dead or bleeding their last into the dust, Miriya closed her eyes and prayed for silence but she was denied it, the air about her filled to overflowing with the deafening adulation of the congregation.

Verity grabbed at her arm and turned her about. The Hospitaller was furious. 'You didn't need to kill them!' she shouted, her voice barely audible above the crowd. 'Why did you do that?'

The other players in the reconstruction were gathering to them, pathetic remnants in their tattered and bloody costumes. Some dragged injured comrades with them, others limped and showed wounds that were wet and ragged. Miriya shook off Verity's grip with an angry snarl and jerked her chin at the penitents. 'Help them.'

The Hospitaller left her there and took to ripping bandages from torn robes. Miriya surveyed the dead arranged around her, Verity's question ringing in her mind. What madness was this, that these people would force her to end their lives, all in the name of a brutal game? There were other ways to show devotion to the Golden Throne that did not require such a wasteful sacrifice. Was life valued so little on Neva?

The vox speakers struck up again with a fresh barrage of song, beginning with a stern rendition of the grand hymnal from Enoch's Castigations. Miriya cast her gaze upward, searching the dark sky for some sign, some explanation. Her thoughts were a churn of confusion, a state that was unacceptable for a Sister of Battle. Her skin crawled, and she found that all she wanted at this moment was to purify herself with a purgatory oil and take prayer in the convent's chapel. What cursed luck has brought me to this madhouse, she asked herself?

A handful of bright dots crossed the night above the ampitheatre, moving with purpose and great speed towards the towering Lunar Cathedral. Just as it had moments before when she locked gazes with the gunmen, Miriya's honed combat sense rang a warning in her mind. 'Aircraft,' she said aloud, 'in attack formation.'

As if they had been waiting for her to voice her thoughts, the flyers suddenly split apart and swept away in pairs towards different points of the compass. The closest duo dipped low and came into the nimbus of the floating lamp-blimps. They were coleopters, vessels with a ring-shaped fuselage enclosing a large spinning fan that kept them airborne. The unmistakable shapes of boxy weapons pods hung on stubby winglets.

No alarm cry would have warned the people in the crowds, and they watched the flyers with disbelief, perhaps believing them to be yet another surprise addition to the Games of Penance. In the next second panic and terror rose up in a wave as fountains of firebombs spat from the coleopters and fell in orange trails towards the stadium. Everywhere they landed, great balls of black smoke and yellow flame bloomed, immolating hundreds. The aircraft wove through the mayhem they seeded, strafing the panicked people, while above them another lone ship dropped out of sight on the Tier of Greatest Piety. Whoever these killers were, they were landing men on the upper levels of the church tower.

Lasers lanced out of the observation galleries, questing after the darting ships and missing. Miriya assumed the shots were being fired by the gun servitors she had seen serving the nobles earlier. She swore a gutter oath recalled from her childhood. How in Terra's name had such a thing been allowed to happen? Were the planetary defence forces stationed in Noroc so lax that any terrorist could idle into the city's airspace unchallenged?

Unbidden, another, darker thought rose to the surface of her mind. Was this some other part of Neva's dogma of atonement and suffering, a random attack thrown at the innocent as some kind of penance? She shook the idea away and sprinted towards the arena's edge, where elevator cages would carry her back up to the galleries of the cathedral.

Verity came after her. 'Where are you going?'

'To fight a real enemy,' she retorted. 'You may join me, if you can stomach it!'

CHAPTER SIX

THE MEN OF the Noroc city watch would later report that the terrorist coleopters had come from the south and the west, flying in the nap of the earth along valleys or over the scudding white tops of shallow waves. Too low to the ground for detection by conventional sensors, hulls daubed with black paint and running lights blinded, the aircraft threaded into the air over Noroc and went about their business. In the throes of the festival, where sacramental wines were flowing freely and hymns were blotting out the sound of everything else, not many eyes turned from their devotions to maintain watchfulness. In the days that followed, the enforcers would have their hands full, in both matters of arrest and punishment as well as purging its own officers guilty of inattention.

A good percentage of the men in the flyers had previously visited Noroc, some had even been born there. All of them were chosen because they knew the city well enough to wound it. Torris Vaun had gathered them all in the hold of a chilly, echoing transport barge as they crossed the coastal waters, goading them into readiness. Some of these men brought their own codes and morals to the fight, with big talk of striking against the moneyed theocrats in the name of the people, but most of them, like Vaun himself, were in the game for the fire and the havoc. They wanted anarchy for the sport of it, because they thrived on it.

The rockets dropped from the coleopters were stolen from Imperial Guard regiments, elderly area denial munitions pilfered from bunkers where they waited for rebellions and uprisings that never came... until now. The warheads broke open in bright plumes that made miniature daybreaks wherever they struck, and where people did not die from smoke and flame, they smothered each other in panic.

THE AIR INSIDE the Lunar Cathedral was hot with terror. Many of the nobles had fled to the lower levels to find their carriages and draymen destroyed by explosion and firestorm, and they milled about and became frantic, some of them starting small scuffles as their frustrations boiled over. On the higher levels, in the vaulted space of the chapel proper and the galleries that ranged above it, barons and upper echelon priests took to gathering in small, terrified

packs with their gun servitors surrounding them,
bleakly waiting for invasion, destruction or salva-
tion.

The flyer that approached the Tier of the Greatest
Piety executed a running touch-and-go, its wheels
barely kissing the careworn granite for ten seconds
before it took off again, thrusting away to enter a
wide, lazy orbit of the conical tower. It left behind a
squad of rag-tag men with no single uniform or
look to them. All that united these killers was a callous, predatory anticipation, that and the absolute
loyalty they showed to their leader.

Vaun dropped a pair of battered night vision gog-
gles from his eyes and pointed with both hands.
'Get in there, and make some trouble.'

The men obeyed with harsh laughter and ready
violence.

Rink jogged to keep up with him. 'We gonna kill
them here, then?'

'Patience,' replied the other man. 'It's a nice
evening. We'll see how things play out.'

The big thug's eyes glittered. 'I wanna do the
priest.'

Vaun shot him a hard look. 'Oh no. That one's for
me. I *owe* him.' The criminal's hand strayed to an
old, hateful scar beneath his right ear. 'But don't
worry, I've got something in mind for you.'

THE RATTLING CAGE was little more than a basket of
steel mesh, but it clambered doggedly up the stone
wall of the cathedral, cogged teeth picking their way
past oval service hatches cast from fans of brassy

leaves. Oil and sparks spat at them as the elevator slowed and halted, presenting them to the observation level. Miriya came through the hatch leading with her pistol, and Verity was close behind, virtually throwing herself out of the lift. The clattering machine seemed to have unnerved the Hostpitaller – and after the accident with the falling catwalk, it was perhaps no surprise that she was newly afraid of Neva's ill-maintained mechanisms.

There were bodies. Mostly they were servitors, and by the pattern of the kill shots they had been targeted by weapons aimed from a moving platform beyond the balconies. Miriya recognised the distinctive wound patterns of shells from Navy-issue heavy bolters. The bodyguards had died under the guns of the coleopter as it strafed the tower with random cascades of fire. With a degree of delicacy that seemed out of place among the carnage, Verity stepped lightly over the bodies of a few aristocrats, giving each a murmured prayer verse.

The Celestian saw one of the perfumed women they had crossed earlier in the evening, her only bouquet now the copper of spilt blood.

'Sister, how many times have you given last rites?' The question came from nowhere.

Verity gave her an odd look. 'There was once a time when I kept a count. I decided to stop when the number brought me to tears.'

'Take comfort then that those you attended are at the Emperor's side now.'

The Hospitaller gestured to the dead servitors. 'But not all.'

'No,' agreed Miriya. 'Not all.'

From the inner halls of the gallery at the back of the platform a figure approached, a sharp-edged shadow where the dying glow of broken biolumes struck it. 'Stand and be recognised!' called a voice.

Miriya returned a nod. 'Sister Isabel, is that you?'

Isabel emerged into the flickering light cast from the fires down in the amphitheatre, throwing the screaming crowds a cursory look. 'Sister Superior, it's good to see you're still with us. The Canoness bid me to scout this tier for any fresh threats, but these cloisters are like a maze…'

'Where are the other Battle Sisters?'

'Below in the chapel. It is pandemonium in there. The cathedral has been compromised. Invaders are abroad.'

'I saw their aircraft land,' said Miriya. 'Not a large ship. Less than ten men, I'd warrant.'

'Very likely, but we have barely that number of able fighters here–' A crashing salvo of bolt fire from the floors below them cut into Isabel's words and her eyes went wide.

The Sister Superior spoke into the vox pickup on her armour's neck ring. 'This is Sister Miriya, report. Who is firing?'

'He's here,' Galatea snarled in her ear bead speaker. 'Vaun. Warp curse him, the witch is here!'

ACROSS THE MOSAIC floor of the chapel the fleeing, shrieking nobles fled back and forth, clouding Galatea's line of sight and that of every other Battle Sister in the chamber. Fallen braziers knocked askew in the panic had set light to tapestries as old as the city itself, filling the vaulted chamber with thick, choking smoke. The Canoness wished that she had ordered her women to bring their helmets: the optical matrix of Sabbat-pattern Sororitas head-gear had a full-spectrum capacity that would render the darkest clouds transparent. But then, they had not expected to face a terrorist attack on this, the most sacred of Neva's holidays, and by the order of the High Ecclesiarch they had only been allowed to carry token weapons into the house of the God-Emperor.

She glimpsed Vaun and his killers as they moved and fired. They had no need to pick their targets, discharging streams of stubber rounds into silk-clad torsos, firing without aiming. Behind her, the floating illuminator that dominated the centre of the chapel took a shot in the heart and exploded, showering her with glass fragments and curls of hot brass.

'The governor,' she snapped. 'Where is he?' It did not occur to her to ask after the ecclesiarch. Lord LaHayn was more able to defend himself than the fragile politician ever could be. Years in service to the church had taught LaHayn how to fight against the enemies of order. But Emmel... He was another case entirely. Born of Neva's best noble stock, he fancied himself a man of action, but the reality was far less flattering. He was a peacock among pea-cocks, as much as he played at being a hawk, and was certainly no match for a killer of Torris Vaun's calibre.

Sister Portia was close by, clearing a fouled cartridge from her bolter. The ritual cloth of ceremony that chapel law required she wrap about her gun had tangled in the mechanism, stopping her from shooting back at the attackers. 'I last saw the governor in the company of Baron Sherring, a moment before the firing started.'

Galatea's adjutant, Sister Reiko, nodded. 'Aye. The baron and his retinue were making for the east terrace.' She was armed only with an ornate dress sword, and chafed at being pinned down by the terrorist weapons, unable to return fire.

The Canoness saw motion as some of Vaun's men dug themselves in behind the ranks of heavy oak pews. The psyker himself was disappearing into a side corridor.

'He must be stopped. Miriya, do you hear me? Vaun is on the loose inside the tower. He may be moving toward the upper tiers!'

As if it were drawn by the sound of her voice, gunfire came her way, clipping at the ancient mosaics in the floor near Galatea's feet.

'QUICKLY, QUICKLY!' SNAPPED Emmel, his hands darting around the folds of his brocade coat. His spindly fingers clutched at a small, fat orb of gold inlaid with ruby studs – a needler pistol from the defunct workshops of the Isher Studio, an antique that dated back to the thirty-ninth millennium. Passed down through the generations, the governor had only killed with it once in his life, when he had accidentally shot a playmate at the age of eleven.

The sense of the object in his hand made clear the understanding of how dangerous his situation was. He barked out more commands to a pair of his elite guardsmen and they in turn shoved forwards past Baron Sherring's gaggle of lackeys, pushing through the people blocking the corridor.

'Please, governor,' said Sherring, an arch lilt to his voice. 'My flyer is just a little further. It will be my honour to convey you away from this fracas.'

'Yes, yes, hurry up.' Privately, Emmel was already entertaining the idea of leaving the ambitious baron on the landing terrace and taking his aircraft to flee to the safety of the impregnable Governmental Citadel. Unless the men sowing chaos throughout Noroc had stoneburners, he would be totally protected there.

'Such luck,' piped one of Sherring's friends, 'such good grace that you thought to bring an aeronef with you, my dear Holt.'

'Indeed,' said the baron. 'Lucky.'

The clanking servitor leading them through the warren of passageways turned a corner and scraped to a juddering halt that sent everyone behind it scattering. There was scarce illumination in these narrow cloisters, but the governor's eyesight was keen enough to see the liquid arc of something thick and oily spurt from the machine-slave's neck. A sound like a sack of wet meal being torn open accompanied it. The servitor gave a peculiar ululating wail and sank to its knees.

'Back!' called Emmel's guardsman. 'Get back, sir.'

New shapes emerged around the corner, jamming the corridor with blades and guns. At their head was the witch.

'Good evening, gentlefolk,' he grinned. 'Ivar's blessing be on you all. I am afraid your flight has been cancelled. An accident with fire has occurred.'

'Kill him!' Emmel shouted, somewhat redundantly as his men were already firing.

There was a horrible moment when the air about Torris Vaun's body bowed and lensed like a heat haze, and fizzing spurts of molten lead spat away from him. Vaun raised a hand in a blasé wave and the two guardsmen began to twitch and scream. Emmel had personally chosen these two from the ranks of his private sentry force for their devotion and fortitude, but that counted for nothing as he watched them die on their feet. Heat radiated from them, along with the burnt-skin smell of over-cooked meat. Thin plumes of fatty smoke streamed from their nostrils and mouths, while the decorative festival ribbons in their hair and beards caught fire in puffs of ignition. Swelling with internal combustion, the guards dropped to the stone floor, burning from the inside out.

Some of Sherring's retinue fled, and they were burned down by the men who followed Vaun. The baron and his closest companion stumbled backwards, bumping into the horror-stricken governor. Emmel was jerked from his shock and fumbled with the orb-gun. It had been so long, he couldn't remember how to use it.

Vaun came closer. 'You don't dare harm me,' Emmel bleated. 'I am a supreme agent of the Emperor's–'

The psyker killed Sherring's pale-faced friend with a needle of yellow flame, the psi-discharge punching the body away down the corridor. He seemed to relish it.

There was a big man at Vaun's back and he nodded at the baron with a strange grin on his face. 'What about this one?'

Sherring blinked and his mouth worked in silence. Vaun leaned in close to the baron and looked him over, as if the noble was a helot on the auction block for purchase. He brought up the still-flaming tips of his fingers and touched them to Sherring's sweaty cheek. The wet skin sizzled and the baron bit back a cry of anger and pain.

'Just a small fish,' Vaun smirked, then with a sudden savage rush, he clubbed Sherring about the head and left him sprawled on the floor.

The big man took the inert gun from Emmel's fingers and tossed it away. 'I am very rich,' pleaded the governor. 'I can pay you a lot of money.'

Vaun nodded. 'I don't doubt it.' He nodded to the other man. 'Rink, take his lordship up to the tier and wait. Raise Ignis on the vox and tell him we're going to pull out. I want the other ships departing in the next ten minutes.'

'And you?'

Vaun glanced back over his shoulder. 'I've come all this way. I can't leave without paying my respects to the lord deacon.'

Emmel tried to resist the big man's iron grip. 'I will not go with you.'

In reply, Rink gave him a careless shove and the governor slammed into the stone wall. He stumbled, dazed and bleeding.

LAHAYN PROPELLED HIMSELF up to the chapel's pulpit. Smoke hung in thick drifts at head height, masking the disorder spreading around the chamber. The priest-lord drew in a deep breath of tainted air and roared into the vox set into the golden angel on the podium's crest.

'Do not have fear. Heed me, my friends. Discord is what these brutes want from us, do not give them their desire!' Some of the speakers secreted in gargoyles on the walls were still functioning, and they carried his words about the chapel like low thunder. 'Rally to the altar here, let the noble guardsmen and the steadfast Sisters of Battle be our shield and sword!'

The aristocrats were a fickle lot, but every one of them had been attending LaHayn's weekly sermons for years, and his words of command were enough to break through their terror and be acted upon. He ignored the grimace that Canoness Galatea shot at him, and from the corner of his eye he saw the Battle Sister snap out orders to the handful of surviving bodyguards, gun servitors and her own Sororitas warriors. A desultory rattle of bolt fire echoed through the chapel from the far nave, lost behind the grey fumes. The attackers had broken off for the moment, probably regrouping.

'All we need do is keep faith and hold, my friends,' he told the congregation. 'Even as I speak, detachments of enforcers and Imperial Guard are on their way here to rescue you.' In fact, Lord LaHayn had no way of knowing if that were true or not – but the Lunar Cathedral represented the greatest concentration of Nevan nobility on the planet, and he expected – he *demanded* – nothing less than the full might of the military to be turned to the matter of their protection.

Beneath his pulpit, the nervous barons and titled aristocrats clustered in his shadow, around the wrecked tables where earlier there had been piles of the finest foods and rarest liquors. Some of the fountains still frothed and bubbled with heady, pungent wines.

'They're coming,' LaHayn caught Galatea's words at the edge of his hearing. 'Stay alert.'

'Have faith in the Golden Throne,' shouted LaHayn. 'The Emperor protects!' From the depths of the smoke, the priest saw shapes moving, and a voice he had hoped never to hear again came with them, mocking and insolent.

'The Emperor protects?' said Vaun. 'Not here, He doesn't. Not *tonight*.'

RINK THREW EMMEL to the floor and placed a large booted foot upon his neck. 'You try to run, and I'm gonna break you.' The governor whimpered something, but Rink didn't care to listen. He raised a small vox transmitter to his lips. 'Ig? Ig, you little firebug, can you hear me?' He glanced around the

Tier of the Greatest Piety, at the dead servitors and smashed machinery. All about the bowl-shaped terrace were glowing threads of smoke from the cathedral below.

After a couple of seconds there came a reply, laden with the crackle of interference. 'Bit busy at the moment. Wait. Wait.' On the night air Rink's ears caught the distant concussion of something very large and very flammable combusting, somewhere in the heart of the city. Over the static-choked channel Ignis gave a wordless sigh of rapture. 'Better. What is it?'

'Playtime is over. Vaun wants us to start heading home.'

'Aw. So soon? I was just warming up.'

Rink sniffed. 'You know what he said. Main event's still to come.'

'Yeah,' Ignis didn't sound happy. 'I'm doing it. We lost one 'copter over the jackyards but that's all. I'll pass word. Hold tight, Rink. I'm coming to you.'

'Don't make me wait.' He flicked off the device and dropped it in a pocket.

Emmel sniffed and tried to move. 'Please, listen to me. Let me speak a language you will understand. Money.'

Rink showed crooked teeth. 'Go on then.'

'I can pay you...'

'How much? A thousand in gold? Ten thousand? A million?'

'Yes.' The governor squirmed.

'Got it on you?' Rink bent low and spoke to Emmel's face. 'Right now?'

'Uh. Well, no, but…'

'Outta luck, then.'

'I don't want to die!' wailed the nobleman.

'And I don't want to be poor,' smirked Rink. 'You can see the nuisance of it.'

'Even gold will turn black in hands as corrupted as yours.'

Rink spun at the shouted words, grasping for his gun. 'Aw, warpshit.'

MIRIYA STEPPED SLOWLY across the terrace, her plasma pistol aimed at the big man. From the corner of her eye she saw Isabel doing the same. Verity hung back in the archway, trying to keep out of sight. 'Listen to me,' said the Celestian. 'You are bound by law to stand down and surrender Governor Emmel. Release him or die.'

'And then what? You'll let me go on my way, like, with a kiss on the cheek?' He dragged Emmel to his feet, using the man like a human shield. 'No, you get lost, doxy, else I ventilate this runt!'

'This is your last chance,' said Isabel. 'Your one opportunity to accept the Emperor's light or die in its shadow.'

Rink's face creased with anger. 'What? What does that mean, eh? I hate you church bitches. But you can't beat Rink now, can ya? Can ya?' With a roar, he threw Emmel at the edge of the tier and fired at Isabel with his laser. Miriya vaulted into a dive, rolling hard on one shoulder. She was dimly aware of her Battle Sister trading fire with the thug, but her attention was on Emmel, sliding across blood-slick stone toward a drop that would smash him against the amphitheatre floor far below. Her gun discarded in her headlong flight, she fell upon the governor as he slipped over the edge and caught a handful of his heavy coat in her hands.

Emmel's jacket ripped but it held enough to keep him hanging there, suspended hundreds of metres above the burning stadium. The muscles in her arms bunching, Miriya dragged him back up. The effort of it dazed her, and she cast around.

Isabel had fallen against a dead servitor. She seemed injured. Miriya could not see Verity anywhere... and the big man...

She rolled on to her back as fresh wreaths of smoke coiled over the terrace, and the criminal was there, leering over her.

He fell on her with a bone-crushing impact, slamming her against the inside of her ceramite armour. Miriya's teeth rattled in her head and she tasted copper in her mouth.

A grinning face, breath stinking of tabac, pressed into hers. She struggled against him. He was twice her size and all of it was hard, packed muscle. The sheer weight of the man was enough to force the breath from her lungs.

'Give Rink a kiss, little Sister,' he hissed, licking her cheek. 'Come on. Don't be shy.'

Her punches to his ribs and groin brought grunts of pain but nothing more. Rink's eyes narrowed and he surrounded her throat with thick hands big enough to crush her skull. She could not pant or gasp. He was going to kill her with her own silence. Miriya tried to dislodge his hands without success.

'Heh,' he smirked. 'No sermons for me now, eh?'

Rink bent forward to lick her again, and with one last effort, the Celestian butted him in the nose. She felt the big man's bone crack and blood spurt, but it seemed to do little more than annoy him. Rink's grip tightened still further and the colour drained from Miriya's vision. Everything changed to a gauzy, charcoal sketch, becoming grey and distorted.

A woolly, indistinct noise like the bark of a dog reached her ears, and then Rink rolled off her. It took a long moment for Miriya to realise that there was sticky, wet matter coating her face and torso. She sat up and unceremoniously used her robes to mop the thick offal away. The Battle Sister shook off her daze and realised that Rink, lying there on the tier next to her, was without his head.

Verity emerged from the haze with Isabel's bolter in her hands, vapour coiling from the barrel. The gun looked wrong in her grip, the shape of it there almost obscene against the virginal white of the Hospitaller's garb.

'Is he…?'

'Dead?' Miriya got to her feet with a wince. 'I should think so.' She staggered a little and Verity put the gun aside to steady her. 'Where is Sister Isabel?'

'Wounded.' Verity did not look away from the headless man.

'Is this the first time you have taken a life, Sister?'

'I…' Her eyes were glassy and hollow, her gaze locked on the corpse. 'I have given the Emperor's

Peace to those who need it many times... But never... I have never...'

'Never killed with a weapon in your hand, in the heat of battle?' Miriya coughed and spat. 'Fortunate for me then that you still remember your training. A little to the left and that shot would have found me, not him.' With gentle force, the Celestian guided her away to where Governor Emmel lay on the stonework.

On more familiar ground, Verity became efficient and quick of hand, using an auspex-like device to divine the man's well-being, touching him to feel a pulse. She frowned. 'We cannot take him from this place, Sister. He has internal injuries that will worsen if we move him.'

'We can't leave him here, it's not safe.'

'You should summon a rescue flyer to recover him and take him to a hospice. Unless a chirurgeon sees to him, he could perish.' The Hospitaller nodded in the direction of the cathedral. 'Go for help. I will remain here. I can keep him stable.'

Dragging her injured leg as she walked, a pale-faced Isabel approached them. 'She is right, Sister Superior. The psyker witch is still loose in the tower. While we tarry here, his every breath is an affront to the God-Emperor.'

'Can you fight?' asked Miriya, eyeing her.

'Need you ask?' Isabel glanced at the bloody laser wound on her thigh. 'A mere flea bite. It appears worse than it is.'

'Then what of you?' Sister Miriya turned back to Verity. 'You won't catch Vaun unawares like his thug here. You can't engage him.'

The Hospitaller gave her a defiant look. 'Then be quick, and I will have no need to.'

Miriya accepted that with a nod, and then recovered the dead thug's lasgun. 'Take this until we can find you a better weapon,' she said, handing it to Verity. 'Use it if you must.'

'But you said I would not be able to fight Vaun.'

The Celestian shook her head. 'There are only two charges left in the weapon. If Vaun comes, I would suggest you use them to grant the Emperor's Peace to the good governor here and yourself.' She gathered up her fallen plasma pistol and walked away. 'It is a better fate than letting that beast lay open your mind.'

THE WITCH MELTED out of the mist choking the chapel with bubbles of burning air dancing about his fingers. He tossed streamers of fire at the aristocrats and swept them around, using them as a Repentia Mistress would a neural whip. Wherever the flames touched skin or cloth, people were instantly flashed into screeching torches. Behind Vaun came his men, spreading further the touch of witchfire.

'Here they come,' Galatea snapped. 'All guns to bear.' She led the Sisters in a quick subvocalised litany, each of them murmuring prayers of blessing to their firearms.

Portia brought up her bolter and Reiko – who had liberated a clumsy ornamental rifle from a dead honour guard – did as she ordered, but the gun servitors and the other men at arms fell apart in a rout. The servitors, too slow of brain to react with anything other than brute reflex, marched into Vaun's firecasts and burnt to death standing up. Internal ammunition magazines cooked off in wailing cracks as limbs and torsos were shattered. The bodyguards and sentries lost their nerve when they were confronted by a psyker of Vaun's deadly prowess, breaking ranks and making themselves perfect targets for his men.

Fire-streaks buzzed past Galatea's head like hoverflies, humming and slow in the melee. The Battle Sisters had come with little to replenish their weapons, and where Vaun's killers fired for effect, the Canoness and her fighters paced their shots. Each had to be certain death for the target. They could not afford to spend more than one precious bolt shell on each attacker.

Vaun's flame-whips guttered out and the psyker dropped low, masking himself and minimising his target silhouette. An eerie glow cast about from the witchkin's eyes. Galatea had seen the like before on those kissed by Chaos or touched by the sign of the mutant.

'By Katherine's heart, what is he doing?' Portia hesitated, trying and failing to get a good firing angle on the crouching man.

From behind her where the liquor fountains gurgled and frothed, Galatea heard the squeal of building pressure and a rush of hot bubbles. Suddenly she understood. 'Get down. Get down!' she shouted, throwing herself into Portia and Reiko.

Vaun released a 'Ha!' of effort and threw a spear of psionic force into the wine drums. Superheated by his mindfire, the volatile alcohols combusted and shattered their wood and iron kegs. With a whoop of air, the atomised liquids turned a pocket of atmosphere into an inferno. A miniature tidal wave of burning Nevan whisky and foaming spice wine threw itself across the cowering nobles. The searing flood boiled them red and screaming, the agony of it so fierce that some of the merchants died instantly.

LaHayn clung to the pulpit as it rocked and sank into the burning tide around it. Before him, striding across the flaming pool without a hint of discomfort, Vaun met his eyes and gave the priest a theatrically contrite bow of the head.

'Forgive me, father, for I have sinned.' The last word was drawn out and sibilant, turning into a harsh smile. 'Hello, Viktor. I'm willing to bet that this isn't how you had imagined things would go when we met again.' With a callous kick, he shoved a wailing noblewoman out of his path. 'It's time for you to reap the whirlwind, old man.'

'You will regret your arrogance, creature,' spat the priest. 'I will see to it!'

Vaun snorted. 'You?' He opened his arms. 'Look around, Viktor. The wastrels you surrounded yourself with are dead or dying. Even your precious Sororitas lie defeated by me.' He pointed at the spot where Galatea and the other women lay wounded and unmoving. 'Meet your end with some decorum, dear teacher. If you ask me nicely, I may even let you spout off some prayers first to your precious god.'

'You dare not speak the name of the Lord of Mankind!' LaHayn's rage rolled across his aspect in a dark thunderhead. 'Pirate. Petty thief and brigand. Your tiny mind lacks even the smallest inkling of my unity with Him!' The ecclesiarch stabbed an accusing finger at the psyker. 'You could have been great, Torris. You could have known glory the likes of which have not been seen in ten thousand years. But now you are fit only to die, remembered only as an anarchist and a criminal!'

Vaun let out a laugh. 'And who will kill me, you decrepit fool?' He drew back his hands and cupped the air between them. The molecules of smoke and haze he held there flickered and condensed, catching fire. 'This ridiculous monument of yours will be your funeral pyre – and once you are ashes I'll plunder your dirty little secrets for myself.'

He was close enough now, reasoned the priest. Close enough to be certain. 'I think not, child,' said LaHayn, and from his voluminous sleeves he produced an ornamental box that ended in a finely tooled argentium muzzle. He squeezed the device and it shrieked, projecting a mid-calibre bolt shell at the witch's chest.

The recoil from the weapon was so strong it almost broke the priest's wrist, but the gun was just the means to deliver the shell to the target. The bolt itself was not the typical carbide-fusion matrix bullet that issued forth from countless Astartes and Sororitas weapons – the very matter of the round was impregnated with psionic energy, culled from the minds of dying heretics. Each molecule of it reeked with mental anguish, pain and psychic terror imprinted on the shell down to the atomic level. These munitions were very rare, but Lord Viktor LaHayn had taken a long time to build up the position he now held, and along the way many such items had come into his possession.

The psycannon bolt struck Torris Vaun in the chest, tearing through the heat-wards that had turned the lesser shots of other men, and spent its massive kinetic energy punching through the flexsteel armour of his battle vest. The impact threw him back into the puddles of burning liquor, ripples of contained psy-force licking around him, fading. He coughed hard and brought up a mist of blood.

'Fool,' growled the priest. 'Did you think I would go about unprepared when I knew that you were on the loose?' He holstered the spent weapon, massaging his throbbing wrist. 'Now I will have the prisoner I promised for this day.' LaHayn glanced down as Miriya and Isabel entered the chamber, guns questing for a target. 'What perfect timing,' he remarked. 'Here, sisters. Here is your witch, ready for the cages–'

A whooshing jet of fire erupted from where Vaun had fallen, pushing the criminal back to his feet. Curls of heat enveloped him and he bared his teeth, chewing on new pain. 'Well played, Viktor,' spat the psyker. 'But I'm not beaten just yet.'

LaHayn's world turned red as the pulpit burst into flames about him.

'Take him!' screamed Miriya, her voice streaming into the concussive blast of noise from her plasma pistol. Isabel fired with her, both of the Battle Sisters throwing their shots at Torris Vaun, knocking him back off his stance.

The psyker stumbled and snarled at them, blood from broken capillaries in his eyes trickling down his face in red tracks. The glowing brand where the psycannon shot had struck him still flickered with desultory glimmers of blue-white energy, and Vaun picked at it with sweat-slick fingers, using his other hand in a warding gesture to banish the incoming bolts. The rounds struck the heat-wall conjured by his mind and deflected, some breaking and melting, others skipping away, but Miriya could see the agony caused by the injury LaHayn had inflicted was taking its toll. Vaun met her gaze for a split second and she knew he realised it too.

'I won't let you run again,' she spat. 'Take the witch!'

Groggy and wounded, Portia dragged herself into the fight alongside her squadmates. Near the wrecked pews, Galatea, a shock of her perfect auburn hair crisped into white ash from the fires, stumbled up from where she lay bearing Reiko on one shoulder.

'You should not have come back,' shouted LaHayn. 'Now you will pay for daring to defy the church.' The priest pointed at the corpses of the raiders where Galatea and the other Battle Sisters had terminated them along the way. 'All your reavers and cutthroats have fled or died, fiend. You are alone and naked before the God-Emperor's righteous vengeance!'

'Always the lectures with you, eh?' Vaun barked out a harsh laugh and shook the sleeve of his coat, revealing a bulbous, ornate device of jewels and metals wrapped about his wrist. 'You make the same mistakes over and over again, Viktor. You never fail to underestimate me.' The psyker squeezed a triangular emerald switch and delicate, century-old microcircuits sent an activation signal.

The Battle Sisters heard a chug of static across their vox channels. Instants later, the shaped charges of detonite that Vaun's men had secreted all about the cathedral exploded. Under cover of the fires and the panic they had gone unnoticed. Still, there were enough in place to do what Vaun wished of them.

The coughing crashes of noise blew out stained glassteel windows and threw doors off their hinges. They cut through support pillars as saws might fell trees, or dashed ancient pews and unlucky people about the place in clouds of vapour.

Stonework from the upper tiers dropped to punch ragged holes through the mosaic floors, and Lord LaHayn threw himself off the pulpit just as a granite angel smashed the thing to matchwood. Blinking through brick dust and pain, the priest cursed the psyker's name as Vaun's mocking laughter echoed back at him.

CHAPTER SEVEN

THE TIER OF Greatest Piety shuddered beneath Verity's feet and she sprawled, falling away from where Governor Emmel lay. His skin was waxy and sallow, and death was close to him. The Hospitaller heard the sounds of rock grinding on rock, and in horror she saw the high spire of the Lunar Cathedral above her twitch and break off, cascading down past the terrace. Growing up on the sturdiness of Ophelia VII, Verity had never experienced earthquakes, and the occurrence of a solid, rooted building shifting around her was new and terrifying. The thunder of explosions from the lower level set the whole church humming, and the woman threw a fearful look to the smoke-choked sky. Where was the rescue ship? If she were here much longer, Emmel would be dead from his injuries or she would perish with him when the great terrace crumbled.

From above, a narrow-beamed spotlight suddenly stabbed down at the tier, probing at the cluttered space. Verity leapt to her feet, the weapon in her hand forgotten, and waved. 'Here. Here!' The sound of ducted rotors reached her ears and in the thick of the haze she saw the dark shape of a coleopter moving against the night sky.

The spotlight passed over her, lingered for a moment and then moved on, tracing towards the entrance arch that led down into the chapel. A figure emerged into the sodium glare, dark coat and tunic spattered with fresh blood, shielding his eyes from the light. The beam faded away and the 'copter swept about for another pass. With a great chill the woman realised that the flyer was one of the ships she had seen strike at the cathedral.

Torris Vaun walked painfully towards the middle of the terrace and halted there, panting hard. For a moment, Verity was struck dumb by the sight of him. The psyker examined the red on his hands and returned to cupping the wound on his chest, sparing her gun a quick look. 'Are you going to use that, nursemaid?'

Verity tried to speak, but no words came. Vaun stepped closer.

'How is the esteemed governor?' He peered at the injured man lying in the shadows. 'Dead, or near enough? Pity. I wanted to use him a little before he died. Oh well.' A rueful smile crossed his lips. 'Plans change.'

The Hospitaller gulped air. Where were Miriya and the others?

'I know what you are thinking–' he began.

'Stay out of my mind,' shouted the woman. More used to handling a boltpistol, she brought up the lasgun in a clumsy stance.

Vaun gave a hollow chuckle and winced in slight pain. 'There's no need for me to exercise my attributes to know your thoughts, Sister. You know what fate befell poor Sister Iona on the *Mercutio*, yes? You are wondering, if he could do that so easily to a hardened warrior like her, what chance does my fragile little mind have?'

'I will kill you.'

He raised an eyebrow, amused. 'You don't have that in you. I think perhaps you wish that you did, but you don't.'

'I killed your man,' she retorted, jerking her head at Rink's remains. 'I can end you too.'

'Oh.' Vaun eyed the dead body. 'Impressive. Perhaps I was wrong about you.' He coughed a little. 'Go on then, shoot me if you dare, little nursemaid.'

Verity took careful aim at the psyker, and she was rewarded by the very slightest twitch of dismay on Vaun's smug face. 'Do not profess to know me when you do not. Your arrogance is sickening. How *dare* you dismiss me, you heartless fiend!' The safety catch flicked off beneath her thumb. 'Any other soul, and perhaps I might have felt distress at taking their life, but you? One look at your face and I am willing to throw away every oath to ethics I have ever sworn!'

The criminal was very still now, watching her carefully. 'Then before you do, I would ask you grant me one thing. Tell me what I have done that has earned such enmity.'

She gasped. 'You… You don't even know? Does killing mean so little to you that you dismiss it from your mind with every murder?'

'For the most part, yes,' Vaun noted. 'Let me see if I can guess. A father? Or a brother, perhaps?'

'My sister,' she snarled. 'Lethe Catena, of the Order of our Martyred Lady, dead by your blade.' A sob caught in her chest. 'You ended her like some common animal!'

'Ah.' He nodded. 'Of course. There's a bit of a family resemblance between you, isn't there?'

His words were enough. '*Die!* In Terra's name, die,' she bellowed, and jerked the trigger of the gun.

'No,' said Vaun, and snapped his fingers at her. Before the lasing crystal in the slender pistol could even energise, the psyker caused the molecules of the emitter matrix to superheat and fracture. Verity knew nothing of this until the gun became red-hot and sizzled against the flesh of her hand. By reflex, the Hospitaller threw the weapon away and cried out. Her shriek was drowned by the thrum of coleopter blades as the flyer banked around and dropped towards the terrace. The Hospitaller fell to her knees, clutching her scarred hand to her chest.

'Keep that as a reminder not to test your betters.' Vaun's voice was an icy whisper in her ears, pushing into her thoughts. 'You are a foolish, maudlin child. I killed your sister because I had to, not because I took pleasure in it. She was an obstacle to me, nothing more than that. Don't complicate matters by making it personal.'

'Emperor curse you…' sobbed the woman.

The psyker reached up to grab a dangling tether as the coleopter dipped low. The noise of it was deafening, but still she heard his words as clear as day. 'This is not about you, Verity. You have no comprehension of what is hidden on this planet, you or that other wench. Your simple minds, stifled by dogma, cannot grasp the notion of anything beyond your experience.'

Verity screamed. '*Get out of my head*!'

'Let me leave you with this. My crimes are legion, of that you may have no doubt, but even in my worst excesses, nothing I have ever done can hold a candle to the sins of Viktor LaHayn.' Hate oozed from the mindspeech. 'You have impeded me tonight, but in the end nothing will stop me from paying back tenfold what that whoreson owes me. *I swear it*.'

Vaun's last words struck her like a physical blow, and she doubled over and vomited.

The coleopter fled into the night, leaving the Sister Hospitaller and the comatose governor for the medicae to find when the aeronefs finally arrived.

DAWN BROUGHT RAIN with it from the sea, a cold and lonely downpour that was grey with spent smoke and powdered stone. The smell of blackened wood was dense in the air.

The eventual arrival of units of Guard and enforcers came too late to save the lives of many a noble, although by the grace of the Golden Throne there were barely a quarter of the city's highly ranked pastors lying dead as the sun rose. Those who had passed away were laid out in the viewing galleries of the central hospice, where their parishioners could file in and out and pay respects to the men and women who had led them to the light of the Emperor.

Miriya found visitors clogging entranceways to the upper floors of the building. She was given to understand that many of the sobbing mourners had also lost family members, but in accordance with Nevan church mandates the funeral rites of priests took precedence over those of all other citizens.

Noroc was as wounded as her people. The stark light of day showed the places where rockets from the air attack had burnt out apartment warrens and gutted hundreds of chapels. In some places, where broken street cables meant the fire engines could not reach, pits of ruined ferrocrete still smouldered. Miriya had seen the same scene repeated on every street corner as she rode to the hospice. Anguish, blank fear, terror on every face.

The Battle Sister's countenance was set in a frown. Twice now, she had laid Torris Vaun beneath her gunsight and twice he had escaped her. The thought of it made her stomach churn, and in darker moments she caught herself feeling the weight of all the turmoil around her. Had she stopped him back there on the *Mercutio*, none of this horror would

have come to pass. Her mood dark as the stormy
sky, Miriya pressed on to find her way to the cubicle
where Sister Verity was being attended.

'OF COURSE YOU understand the deacon's concerns,'
said Dean Venik, looming over the serf boy ministering to the bandage on Verity's forearm. 'I do not
mean to imply that is not so, Sister Hospitaller, but
nevertheless it is important to ensure a full and correct picture of the witch's intentions.'

'How can I know that?' Verity replied. She found
the man to be intimidating, in his arch, unctuous
way.

'What did the criminal say to you?' Venik looked
her in the eye. 'Did he speak of anything... unto-
ward? Did he take the names of Lord LaHayn or the
God-Emperor in vain?'

'It happened very quickly. He... He used his
power...' She held up the livid, inflamed hand, flesh
scabbed with new scarring peeking through the
white gauze. 'I was unable to prevent his escape.'

'A pity.' Venik nodded to himself. 'I imagine you
would have liked to take a part in Vaun's downfall,
after what transpired with your sibling.'

Sister Miriya entered behind the cleric, startling
the man. 'There's still time.' She made the sign of the
aquila. 'Lord dean. If it pleases you, I would speak
to my fellow Sororitas.'

'Sister Superior,' Venik returned the gesture. 'Of
course. I have completed my interview and there are
others with whom I must speak, to gather information for the lord deacon.'

'Sir, a moment,' said Verity. 'What of Governor Emmel? Does he still live?'

The dean flashed a brief, shallow smile. 'By the God-Emperor's grace, he does. It is my understanding that the governor is being attended by ten of the finest medicae in Noroc.'

'Ten?' Miriya eyed him. 'Does one man need so many healers, especially on a day such as this?'

'I am not an apothecary, Sister, I cannot answer to that. I know only that he may never fully regain his faculties after such a brutalisation,' sniffed Venik.

'Who governs Neva now, then?' asked the Hospitaller.

Venik arched an eyebrow. 'His lordship the ecclesiarch, of course. It is only right that in this time of moral outrage the church take the whip hand.' He turned to leave. 'Lord LaHayn's first edict in his new capacity was to reinforce the order for Vaun's capture. The witch is to be taken alive.'

'Dean, perhaps you might furnish us with solutions to another matter.' Verity's nervous voice wavered. 'There are records within the halls of Noroc's Administratum librarium that might assist in tracking the fugitive Vaun. With your permission, I should like to examine them…'

Venik gave a cold smile. 'The enforcers have already performed a thorough check of those documents. All information gleaned will be acted upon.'

'Nevertheless…'

'Attend to your recovery, Sister Verity,' snapped the dean. 'Don't expend energy on pointless endeavours.' He glanced at Miriya. 'I'm sure there are many

avenues of investigation to follow in this affair.'
With a sniff of finality, he manoeuvred past the
other woman and out into the corridor.

The Hospitaller waved away the boy and patted
the bandage on her forearm. The youth bowed as
low as he could without touching his forehead to
the floor and averted his eyes. The Battle Sister in
turn dismissed him with a curt gesture and the
two women were alone.

'You are unhurt,' said Verity. 'And the other
Celestians?'

'As well as can be expected,' Miriya frowned.
'Canoness Galatea was burned, but she bears the
pain with a fortitude typical of her.' She paused. 'I
come to you to apologise for an error, Sister Verity.
I pressed the Canoness to have you remain here
on Neva and in doing so exposed you to a threat
you should never have faced.'

'No,' Verity shook her head. 'You hold no blame.
In some strange way I am pleased that I could look
Vaun in the eye. At least now I can give a form to
the pain in my heart.'

'You should return to the mission of the Order
of Serenity. Last night's attack will change things
here, and I foresee that the bloodshed and turmoil
will only increase.'

'Thank you for your concern, Sister Miriya, but I
refuse. Don't think me a delicate flower just
because I bear no sword or bolter in my duties. My
Order has served on hundreds of hell-worlds and
battlefields. I know the face of horror well
enough.'

The other woman's head bobbed. 'As you wish.' For a moment she was silent, studying the Hospitaller. 'But Vaun... He *did* speak to you, didn't he? Your answer to Venik's question–'

'I was not entirely forthcoming.' Verity looked away. 'Yes. He... He told me Lethe's death was just a matter of course. Nothing personal.'

'A convenient excuse for his kind. How else could he commit such acts of barbarity and continue unfettered by guilt?'

Verity looked up at her, at eyes that were surprisingly gentle in such a hard face. 'But you have killed... And now so have I.'

'And look how keenly we feel it, Sister. This is what separates us from the heretic, the alien. We fight and kill because we must, not for glory or the sport of it. Each death we inflict serves a greater cause.'

The Hospitaller nodded. 'Of course, you are right. Forgive me if I seem irresolute, it is just that... these days have been most testing for me.'

Miriya extended a hand to the younger woman. 'Look to the Emperor, Sister. Whatever clouds your vision, He will be there.'

Verity's gaze turned inward. 'If there was ever a day I needed His guidance, this would be it. There is more that I did not reveal to Dean Venik. Vaun gave me a warning before he fled.'

The Battle Sister sneered. 'His threats hold little sway over me.'

'No, you misunderstand. He spoke of the lord deacon. Vaun said that Lord LaHayn was guilty of crimes far worse than any he had committed.'

'Sedition and lies,' Miriya spat out the denial instantly, although with less conviction than she should have. 'The witch was trying to sow dissent in your thoughts.'

Verity met her gaze. 'I have attended many interrogations in my service and seen many confessions and denials. I know lies when I hear them. What I saw from Torris Vaun was the truth, at least from his point of view. He *believed* it.'

'What a heretic believes counts for nothing,' said the Battle Sister, 'and were you to speak of this to the dean or anyone else, you might find an interrogator turning his skills to you.'

'I have considered that, even entertained the idea that Vaun might have forced some seed of doubt into my mind with his freakish abilities. But all I can think of is that this witch spoke the truth to me while Lord LaHayn did the opposite at the cathedral.'

Her words brought Miriya up short and her eyes narrowed. 'He is a high priest of the Imperial Church, the voice of the Holy Synod. It is within Lord LaHayn's remit to deny us whatever facts or truths he feels are in our best interests.' Despite her reply, Verity could tell that the other woman was not convinced by her own argument.

'Why do that when by his own command he charged us to pursue this man? You heard the dean a moment ago. We are promised help in one breath and denied it in the next. Make no mistake, I want Vaun to pay for his misdeeds – but I cannot escape the fear that there is much more at play in this matter than we know of. There are falsehoods and secrets shrouding us, Miriya. I know you think the same.'

For a long moment, Verity was afraid the Battle Sister would give a sharp denial or censure her for such doubts, but instead the Celestian's head bobbed in regretful agreement. 'Aye. Curse me, but aye, I feel it as well. There are too many questions unanswered here, too many things averted from close scrutiny.'

Verity sighed. 'I am conflicted, Sister. Where does our duty lie?'

'To the church and the God-Emperor, as it always was. But I see the real question you are asking – does Neva's deacon serve Him as well, or is there another agenda at hand?'

She shuddered. 'I dare not even voice such a thing.'

'Then prepare yourself,' Miriya said darkly, 'for a time may come when you must do more than that. Never forget that the price of vigilance requires we watch those who march under our banner as well as those who stand against it.'

'I pray it will not be so.' Verity got to her feet, testing her injured arm. 'What are we to do now?'

'I believe you said something about the Administratum?' The Battle Sister raised an eyebrow.

'But the dean said the enforcers–'

'The enforcers are nothing more than armour-clad night watchmen. The day I accept the second-hand words of their investigators is the day that Sol burns cold in the sky.' She walked away. 'I must attend to the welfare of my squad. In the meantime, I suggest you might use the confusion of the day to visit the halls of records and look for these facts that may help us find our quarry.' Miriya paused on the threshold. 'That is, if you truly do wish to remain here?'

'You ask me to defy the dean.'

Miriya gave her a quizzical look. 'I have done no such thing. The dean merely said that the enforcers have already checked the records. What harm can come from a second examination? Just to be sure?'

Verity threw her a wooden nod. For better or worse, she suddenly understood that a choice had been made in this small room that could damn them both.

WITH A SHARP backhand slap, Vaun sent the medicae scuttling away from him. 'Go on with yourself, now. I've had enough of your fussing.' He tested the places on his face where small cuts were daubed with blobs of healing gel. 'Like a thousand paper cuts,' he grimaced, glancing up as Ignis approached him from the creaking gloom of the barge's hold. 'What now?'

The younger man saw the thought forming in his mind and handed him a lit tabac stick. Ignis had been muted since they returned to the boat, ill at ease over Rink's sudden absence. The two of them had been friends, or close enough. 'He's here,' said the youth, without preamble. 'Brought his aeronef right down on the deck.' He pointed at the steel roof above.

Vaun took a long, hissing drag on the tabac and stood up. 'That was what all the commotion was about, was it?' Here in the barge's makeshift sickbay, Vaun had heard the clatters and shouts of the crewmen. They were all afraid to be carrying the witch and his cohorts but they had been paid very well. He spat, hard. 'Idiot. Why can't he just be a good little snob and play his role?'

Heavy footsteps were descending from the upper deck and Vaun sneered, taking another puff. 'Watch me now,' he told Ignis. 'This is how to handle this kind of man.'

The sickbay hatch came open with difficulty, creaking and moaning. The new arrival was in disarray, his fine robes smeared with soot and a little blood. He found Vaun and shook a fist at him. 'What... What was all that?'

The psyker put on a neutral face. 'All what, milord?'

The other man stamped forward. 'Don't you *milord* me, Torris. You talked to me about speed, about clean kills and surgical attacks. That...' He pointed in the vague direction of Noroc. 'That was nothing short of a military strike!'

Vaun threw Ignis an amused, comradely look. 'What did you expect? A few discreet murders and some swinging from chandeliers in the chapel, perhaps some disquieting deaths for the servants but nothing more?' In a rush, his face darkened and he swept towards the noble, bunching the cigarillo in his fist. 'You wanted power? Power has to be taken. Perhaps if your ridiculous legions of spies and soldiers had an ounce of sense, last night might have gone all the way. The church's stranglehold on Neva broken, LaHayn dead along with Emmel–'

'Emmel lives,' spat the man. 'You couldn't even give me that!'

'Huh.' Vaun paused, considering. 'But he'll be in no state to govern. I don't doubt LaHayn will finish the job for me.' He sighed. 'How amusing.'

'*Amusing?*' The dam holding back the nobleman's rage broke. 'You wreak havoc and leave me exposed, and call it *amusing?* You crooked witchfreak, you have jeopardised everything–'

Vaun crossed the distance between them in a flash, swatting the man to the floor. The noble squealed and clutched at his cheek, where a fresh burn wound lay. 'The only thing in jeopardy is your complacency, baron. For too long you've played your stupid little rivalry with LaHayn like some regicide game, all polite rules and how-do-you-dos.' He stamped out the tabac stick. 'It's not a silly diversion any more, Holt. I've taken it up a notch. Now it's a fistfight, a stabbing. A real feud.'

'I'm not ready,' whimpered the noble. 'There will be killing. War.'

'Yes,' agreed Vaun, 'and when it's done, when Viktor LaHayn is crucified in Judgement Square and you are in the governor's palace signing my pardon for all the good I've done for Neva, on that day you will be thanking me for making it happen.' He leaned closer to Baron Sherring's face. 'For freeing you.' After a moment he stepped back. 'Get to your 'nef and start making plans. It's time to tell the world what a bad man the dear old deacon is.'

The baron got to his feet and shuffled away. 'I... I'll see you in Metis?'

Vaun bowed. 'You can count on it.'

Sherring left them, a shadow of the man who had blasted into the room moments earlier. Ignis tapped his lips with a finger. 'Did you push him there to make him fold? In the brain, like?'

'Not a bit of it. There are easier ways to coerce men than to use a mind-touch on them. I just gave him what he wanted.'

From above, the whir of airship rotors started up. 'And what was that, then?'

'Freedom from blame. Sherring has always dreamed of setting fire to that pious old braggart and his holy churches. I did it for him, and now he's free to step up to the fight without the guilt of being the one who started it.'

Ignis let out a laugh. 'He... He thinks you're doing this all for him? Ha!'

Vaun nodded. 'He'll find out that's not the way of it. Probably just before he dies.'

VERITY COULD SEE little but the long river of illumination that pooled either side of the walkway bisecting the librarium. The edges of shelves vanished into the darkness towards the unseen walls of the long bunker. The morose logistoras who had accompanied her down to this level rattled off a few cursory facts about the place, like a tourist's dataplate. He spoke of how many hundreds of metres

they were below the streets of Noroc, of how many
more levels were below this one. In the middle distance, the Hospitaller could hear the oiled clanking
of huge brass cogs as one of the room's mobile
decks dropped away into the storage tiers. She
stopped to watch the empty space, as big as a scrum-
ball pitch. After a moment, another deck clattered
up to replace it, a piece of a huge library rolling into
position complete with endless racks of papers and
bookish little men working the aisles. Automatically, a flight of tarnished silver servo-skulls dipped
out from the eaves over her head and began
patrolling the canyons of books. Whole floors of the
librarium were moving with ponderous speed, tiles
in a puzzle slate for giant hands.

The logistoras, his ink-stained robe large on his
wiry frame, peered at her through augmented eyes.
'You understand, we don't often see representatives
of your orders in these halls.' He attempted something like a smile. 'The Sisters Dialogous of the
Quill and the Sacred Oath do visit us at times. I cannot recall a Sister Hospitaller in my tenure.' His gaze
turned inward. 'Perhaps I should begin a statistical
check into that datum–'

'Perhaps you should,' Verity broke in, 'but in the
interim, there are the matters of which I spoke to
you?'

'Yes. Crew records for the warship *Mercutio*. I have
not forgotten.' He beckoned. 'Follow.' The clerk-
priest ambled on along the walkway. 'I'm curious as
to why the Order of Serenity would require such
information.'

In the dimness, Verity felt her cheeks go hot. That she had come this far without undue challenge was luck, and with each further step the Sororitas feared her presence here would be found out and declared fraudulent. She floundered for an instant, unsure of how to reply. How would Sister Miriya answer him, she wondered? She'd probably threaten to injure him. *I can do better than that.*

Verity sucked in a breath of parchment-dry air. 'Is it necessary that you know why I require this datum in order to find it for me?' She pitched her voice in the same lecturing tone she'd heard her Palatine use on wayward novices.

'Well, uh, no.' The logistoras blinked brass lashes. 'I was merely–'

'Curious, yes. But forgive me, I was given to understand that curiosity is not a trait that the Adeptus Ministorum wishes to cultivate in its librarians. Is it not an article of faith that you may never read from the books you collate, lest you come into contact with material of an unmutal nature?'

That weak smile again. 'I have never been tempted, Sister.' He threw a nervous look up at the servo-skulls buzzing above them, the thin tubes of lasers hanging from their lipless mouths. 'To do so would incur the ultimate penalty.' He halted at a side gantry and removed a chain-link closing off the section. 'Here we are. The cogitator will provide you with the datum.' He bowed and backed away. 'I hope you will forgive my injudicious use of words earlier. It is just, that with the incident on the night of the Blessing…'

Verity smiled back. 'We are all shaken, priest. Fortunately, the Emperor gives His light to guide us.'

The logistoras bowed again and left her there with the ancient thinking machine, the brassy coils and silver-rope filigree inside it ticking and tocking as it churned out the lives of Midshipman Vorgo and the men who had freed Torris Vaun.

THERE WERE WIDE webs of girders, loops of greasy cable and cogworks everywhere inside the librarium, almost all of them perpetually in the darkness. The meagre glow of the photon candles about the underground hall never reached into the thick ebon shadows that collected at the edges of the corridors. Many of the papers held here were so old that they would wilt beneath hard light, and in some sectors the servitors that ministered to the books operated totally on infrared wavelengths. In such a place, the act of concealment was almost welcoming.

Verity's shadow watched her from the hex-frame supporting part of the ferrocrete roof above the Hospitaller's head. The shadow was molten darkness, merged there into the black with such skill that even the vigilant skulls with their tiny red eyes looked straight at it and passed on, unaware. Verity's shadow watched and listened to her, measuring and considering where the day would take the pretty Sororitas. The certainty began to build in the shadow's thoughts that the woman would not see daylight again and in the interests of preparation, the shadow readied its ghost pistol to kill her.

CHAPTER EIGHT

VERITY PRESSED HER fingers to the place where her brow met her nose and pinched the skin there, trying to massage some sort of life back into her face. She stifled a yawn and blinked eyes that were tired and gritty. On an oaken desk and in neat piles around the cogitator's marble plinth, fan-folds of yellow-brown parchment displayed acres of text in High Gothic, machine dialect and the local Nevaspreche tongue. Many of them sported red tags bearing a tiny rendition of the enforcer shield, along with a text string showing a precinct house number. They represented the places where the investigators had pored over the papers, the point at which they had completed their searches. Verity had read all the same files, up to the red markers and then further back, probing for some connection, some small suspicion of a link between the men who had freed Miriya's prisoner.

She sighed, a heavy dejection threatening to overcome her. There were no timepieces anywhere in sight here inside the librarium, and so she had no idea how long she had been confined in this dark chamber, fingers tracing over page after page beneath the flicker of photon candles. Her lips were dry and she felt a little sick. The libations the medicae had given her after the incident in the cathedral were fading away, and Verity's body was sending her mixed messages for sleep and for sustenance. Her chest felt tight with the dust of old books.

'This is a waste of time...' she murmured, 'all for nothing...'

At the sound of her voice, the cogitator's pewter mask-speaker turned on oiled spindles to face the woman. It was a morose thing, worked out of metal to resemble the aspect of an exalted tech-priest some centuries dead. Bellows and tiny chimes in the throat of the device huffed and rattled, creating a sound that resembled human speech. 'To find clarity, it will be necessary to repeat your request.'

'I wasn't talking to you,' Verity retorted, her frustration and weariness snapping in her voice. 'Be quiet.' For the first few hours, the cogitator had taken to breaking the silence at regular intervals by intoning random church-approved axioms designed to reinforce piety and clarity of thought. The Hospitaller had swiftly tired of repeated assertions that 'A closed mind is never open to heresy' and that 'Death is the currency of traitors'.

'By your command.' The machine clicked and whirred, turning away again. Through the blank gaps of the mask's mouth and eyes, the Sororitas could make out the dim shape of a mottled glass orb and the form of turning grey spools within, pierced by thousands of gold filaments. She understood little of how the cogitators worked, but found her mind wandering to thoughts of the components that formed it. Had they originated inside some ancient scholar-machine on Terra, one so old and learned that it could not be allowed to cease its service?

She shook the thought away and frowned at the ancient apparatus, as if it were to blame for her lack of success. The fatigue she felt was making it difficult for her to concentrate, and she fingered the silver rosary at her neck to focus. The lives of Midshipman Vorgo and a dozen other deckhands from the warship *Mercutio* lay strewn about her on paper and punch card, everything from birth certifications to notices of indenture, stipend accounts and disciplinary warrants.

Verity ran her finger over the raised studs on the index of a man named Priser. It was remarkable how such a small piece of cardboard could so encapsulate the life of a person. She lingered over a blank spot on the index. Just one accidental nick of her fingernail, a dot of spilled ink on the wrong page, and Priser could find himself penniless or declared dead. Such was the monumental inertia of the Imperium's monolithic bureaucracy that the word of these documents was law, and these flawed, impossibly old machines were the custodians of it all. It was a sobering thought to imagine all the things – people, ships, perhaps even entire worlds – that could go missing just for the sake of a wrongly placed decimal point.

Verity realised that she had been staring at the same document for several minutes, reading and re-reading the same line of text in Priser's file without actually taking it in. She sighed, and read it again.

It was a reference code to an incident in the man's service record, some weeks before the *Mercutio* had departed Neva to pick up Miriya's Celestians prior to their rendezvous with the Black Ship. Verity blinked. She had seen this number before.

The woman took up another file and found the same index point. The code was there as well. It was the same in a third, in a fourth. All of them, including Vorgo, sported the same numerical reference, and it lay in place below the red tags placed by the enforcers. A rush of sudden excitement flooded Verity, making her giddy. She tapped the front of the cogitator to attract its attention.

'This code,' she said, showing the eyeless mask the paperwork. 'What does it refer to?'

Clockwork twittered and clicked. 'Your forbearance. Your answer will attend forthwith.' After a few moments, the device made a sucking noise and a vacuum tube in its chest opened, revealing a coiled parchment. 'Sacrifice is the most noble worship.'

She read quickly. The papers were a mimeographed copy of a report from the Naval attaché's office, explaining how a transport tender taking some of the *Mercutio*'s crew on liberty to Noroc had been diverted by a malfunction. The shuttle had been forced to put down in the city-state of Metis and eventually returned to orbit with its passengers intact a day later. There were one or two additional names, but without exception, every man who had a hand in Vaun's escape had been on that transport. Verity looked for the crewmen who had been aboard but hadn't joined Vorgo and the others. None of them were still alive. On a ship as large as the *Mercutio*, deaths by misadventure and accident were a daily occurrence, but the pattern made the Sister's skin crawl. The others had died before the rendezvous.

Gathering up her data-slate, Verity made swift notes with an electroquill. She thought about Vorgo, there in the confinement cell, screaming for a daughter that he never had, and reached for his papers.

Her eyes narrowed. According to the Naval renumary, Vorgo and his shipmates had been given their usual stipend of Imperial scrip to spend during their leave in Noroc – but not a single note of it had been exchanged. That seemed impossible. Metis was notorious for taverns and salacious diversions. Any visiting swabbie with a pocket full of unspent pay would return to ship with nothing to show for it but a hangover and some interesting social diseases.

'What happened in Metis?' Verity asked the question to the air, and suddenly she was very, very awake.

* * *

HER SHADOW COCKED its head and wondered at the words the young woman spoke. It had already noted and logged the paperwork she had been interested in for later evaluation by its master. Verity's body language had changed radically in the last few moments. Before, she seemed to be on the verge of physical exhaustion, but now the shadow could see the spark of adrenaline in her eyes, could almost smell it in the oily air.

The killer weighed this new information carefully, briefly entertaining the idea of terminating the girl now, but years of servitude in Neva's assassin wars had left an indelible mark on the shadow. Haste was the enemy of the invisible murder. It was only certainty that made the single shot, the killing blow perfect. The shadow elected to wait a little longer. Another figure was within the target envelope, and it might become necessary to end more than just the girl's life.

The ghost pistol moved a few degrees. The age and origin of the killer's weapon was unknown. Some had said it was of xenos manufacture, others that it dated back to the black period known as the Dark Age of Technology. The shadow liked it for its silence. Inside the non-reflective matter of the breech, single dart-shaped projectiles nestled and waited. These were made by hand, crafted by sightless tech-priests specially blinded for just that purpose. When fired, they left the ghost pistol with no ejecta, no sound or report of fire. Not even the whispering air about the flying darts could give away their passage, and the material they and the gun were made from was utterly energy-inert. Any senses, from an auspex to a psyker's witchsight, could not see it.

There were many darts in the gun, but one would be enough.

WITH A HEAVY clank, the gantry leading to the main walkway locked into place and the library platform shuddered slightly. Verity looked up to see another logistoras picking his way down towards her. This one was of a lower rank than the adept who had escorted her into the hall, a mere quillan with less than a dozen service buttons. The clerk-priest bowed and pointed a finger at the scattered papers. He seemed rather distressed that the files were displayed in so imprecise a manner.

'I need to revise,' he hissed. 'You have to let me proceed.'

'Revise what?'

The logistoras ambled forward on roller-ball feet and took up the first file that came to hand. Paper looped from a dispenser reel at his hip, a device fashioned to look like a closed book. He shot Verity a glance. 'Certification. After the attack, there's been a lot to do.' A grey tongue drooped from his lips and he licked the paper with it. With a swift motion, the quillan pasted the label to the file and folded it away. He began to repeat the procedure.

Verity took the altered file and studied it. The new addition was a finger's length of black-bordered ticket bearing a date, time and identifier code. In red letters, one word stood out like a livid brand. *Deceased.*

'What is going on?' Verity demanded, turning on the logistoras.

He blinked and recoiled a little. The quillan seemed nervous of her. 'Last night? The attack?' He licked another label and stuck it on Priser's file card. 'Some of the rockets fired struck the reformatory. Many prisoners were killed in the conflagration that ensued.' The clerk paused and gestured around at the files with a metal hand, steel pen nibs for fingers. 'All these men are dead. The files must be revised to reflect the new truth.'

Verity let the logistoras complete his work without interruption. The adept kept stealing sidelong glances at her when he thought she wasn't looking at him, and finally she blew out a breath. 'Do you have something to say to me?'

Another owlish blink. 'I... I know you. Your ident crossed my work queue recently, Sister Verity. I know of your involvement in the Vaun investigation.'

Something in the logistoras's tone gave her pause. 'Yes,' she said carefully. 'I am gathering information on the witch to aide in his capture.'

The clerk-priest paused, his task at an end. 'I have never been commissioned to engage in a criminal investigation.' There was an air of wistful hope in his voice. 'My works are purely administrative. I often wonder what it would be like to–'

Verity took a chance. 'Perhaps you might assist me now?'

The quillan froze. 'It would be my honour. How might I be of help, Sister?'

The Hospitaller's mind whirled. The question danced on her lips. 'I… I want to see the files you have on Torris Vaun.'

'That datum is restricted.' The logistoras eyed her. 'But should I assume you have the requisite sanction from the office of the lord deacon?'

Sister Verity kept all emotion from her face, afraid of giving it away with a simple tell but then the clerk-priests were a sheltered lot not often given to contact with other humans, and she doubted he would be able to spot a lie on her lips. 'You may assume that,' she told him.

The quillan bowed and led her deeper into the librarium.

THEY DESCENDED THROUGH a series of hatches into an iron cupola, which in turn crossed between the slow-turning cogs to another platform, filled with books that were chained to their racks. The logistoras extruded a key mechanism from his palm and granted them entrance. He glanced over his hunched shoulder at Verity.

'It occurs to me, I have not given you my identity. I am Quillan Class Four Unshir, cutter of paper and copy maker.' He bowed a little. 'Pardon me if I seem forward, but if you could see your way to highlight my co-operation in this matter to my savant senioris–'

She threw him a quick, fake smile. 'Of course. Your assistance will be rewarded.' Verity disliked lying, even to a demi-human such as Unshir, but she had committed herself now. 'Emperor forgive me,' she whispered. 'This I do in Your name.'

The quillan glanced at her. 'Did you address me, Sister?'

'No,' she snapped, a little too quickly. 'Vaun's records. Show them to me.'

He bowed. 'Of course.'

Unshir used the keys to unlock a tome sheathed in light-absorbing obsidian, touching a ring of code-spots on the cover to open it. He whispered something that sounded like birdsong into a grille on the book's spine and it obediently opened by itself, pages moving on armatures in a blur. With a snap, the book laid itself flat in Unshir's hands and he turned, presenting it to her. 'The pages are made of a psychoactive papyrus,' he said reverently. 'Don't touch them with naked skin.'

Verity nodded and began to read. These were the books of the tithe kept to record the comings and goings of the Adeptus Telepathica in the Neva system. Whenever a person was found bearing the stigma of a psyker, their name was entered here along with a preliminary record of the abilities they exhibited. In time, when the Black Ships came to claim them, the witchkin would be transferred from the deep cells in Neva's Inquisitorial dungeons to the mysterious vessels, never to be seen again.

And there was Torris Vaun's name. The records were sketchy: apparently sold into slavery as a child, the youth's psychic talents had come to the attention of the Ecclesiarchy's agents – and tellingly, Viktor LaHayn himself, at the time a senior confessor. There were several notes in florid prose on the matter of Vaun's unholy capabilities. He was seen to have committed acts of wilful telepathy, shriving and extreme feats of pyrokene mastery. Verity thought of the fire that burnt in the witch's eyes and gave an involuntary shudder.

'As you can see, the files remain intact.' Unshir nodded to himself. 'Are you satisfied?'

The Hospitaller ignored him. She knew what to look for now, and kept searching the tight scrawl of luminous text for discrepancies. 'The dates…' Verity said at length, marshalling her thoughts aloud. 'The sequence is incorrect.'

The logistoras flinched as if she had struck him. 'You are mistaken. We care for these documents as if they were the words of the God-Emperor Himself. Nothing is wrong.'

'Vaun's detection and capture. There is a gap here, a missing datum.'

'Impossible.' Unshir's pale face flushed red.

'The file jumps from the date he was captured to the notation of his escape from Neva. Where was he during the intervening time? Where was he held? The page says nothing.'

'You are misreading it,' the clerk-priest exclaimed, suddenly irritated.

'See for yourself.'

'No,' Unshir shivered. 'It is forbidden for us to look upon the pages that we write and protect. Our cognitive functions are compartmentalised so that we cannot understand the words which we transcribe.'

'There must be other records of Vaun,' she demanded. 'Where are they?'

'There are no others,' he spluttered, as if the very idea of information residing anywhere but within these walls was a joke. But in the next instant, the logistoras's face clouded. 'Wait. If the lord deacon sent you on an errand, why would you say such a thing? Is this some sort of test? Or perhaps not?'

'I...' Caught unawares, Verity's fragile cloak of deception disintegrated with a single look. 'No, I was sent–'

At last he saw the lie on her face. 'Charlatan. You have *misinformed* me!' Unshir spat the words like a curse. 'You have no right to be here.' Anger and then terror crossed the priest's face as he realised that it was his inattention that had allowed Verity to gain access where she was not meant to. 'Alarm. Alarm!' he called, lurching away towards a control grille on one of the support girders.

From above, the Sororitas heard the keening hum of servo-skulls swooping down from the heights. The quillan's pen-nib fingertips scratched at the security buzzer panel, but then his head ripped open with a noise like tearing cloth and the clattering clerk fell dead to the deck.

Verity thought she saw the shape of something dark moving in among the gantries overhead. Somewhere up there, fizzing sparks of colour cast brief flashes as a trio of servo-skulls were pierced with razored metal darts. The Hospitaller ran, her heart hammering against her chest.

THE SHADOW WAS not in the business of hunting, the assassin did not enjoy the thrill of the chase, the hot rush of pursuit as a target fled in fear of its life. Rather, the shadow's way was one of stealth. The killer strove never to race after a mark, but instead be there when the target was least suspecting, to plant a silent dart in their soft flesh and have them perish never knowing where death had come from. But the Sister Hospitaller had disrupted that plan by deviating from ascribed behaviour patterns. It was unexpected that the woman took the bold step of lying to the hapless quillan, and even more so that she would dare to delve into sealed church records. If there had been an iota of uncertainty that Verity's death was required, it was with that action that she removed any doubt in the assassin's mind.

But then the logistoras buffoon had over-reacted and his murder became necessary, then too the elimination of the servo-skull scouts before they could relay any alarm to the tech-guards on the upper tiers.

The gloom of the librarium was rendered bright by the preysight mechanism within the sealed helm the shadow wore. Ahead, the assassin saw the heat blob that was Sister Verity lurching from one canyon of books to another, directionless and terri- fied. A frown formed behind the faceplate. In her panic, it was making it impossible to draw a bead on the woman, so that a fatal shot might be taken. This was not acceptable.

The killer surveyed the library platform and found a hod of heavy books suspended over one of the wide metal shelves. There were volumes covering matters of decrepit old history, awaiting return to

their rightful place by some minor functionary like
the late Unshir. With care, the shadow aimed at the
cable holding the book carriage up and shot it away.

HUGE BLACK SLABS of the gloom above her detached
from the darkness and crashed down around Verity,
the heavy books striking the mesh decking about
her with ringing impacts. One of the tomes
slammed into her and sent the woman sprawling.
Verity screamed, colliding with the bookshelves and
spinning about. The blow knocked the wind from
her lungs and she felt her precious data-slate fall
from her fingers. She heard a smash of broken plas-
tics as another weighty volume landed squarely on
the little device and crushed it into fragments.

The carriage's load gone, the frame itself dropped
from the cable overhead and fell, tumbling end over
end. Verity tried to get away, but the hems of her
robe snarled about her feet and she came to her
knees. The carriage came down on her, trapping her
legs beneath it.

THROUGH THE VEIL of preysight, Sister Verity's cry of
pain was a bloom of hot orange air in the cool, dry
voids of the librarium. The assassin was aware of
confusion and noise from the other gantries in the
hall. The clerk-priests were becoming aware that
something was amiss, the colours of their bodies
moving and swarming closer. There was little time.
The killing of the Hospitaller had to be now.

Careful, deft fingers dialled the barrel of the ghost
pistol to maximum dilation and the shadow racked

a dart into the breech. A sensor pit on the tip of the gun relayed information to the preysight, highlighting the shape of organs inside Verity's shuddering frame. There was the throbbing orb of her heart, nestled beneath the crosshairs. The assassin's finger tightened on the trigger.

SHE FIRED BLINDLY.

From the connecting gantry, Miriya had seen the book hod fall. She had heard the death scream of Unshir and the pops of detonation as the servo-skulls were obliterated. Her plasma pistol was singing in her hand and she broke into a run, disciplined muscle-memory taking over. In the shade of the towering bookcases she caught a glimpse of flapping robes as Verity fell. The Sister's cry was full of fear.

Miriya fired, releasing a salvo of quick energy bolts up into the steel rafters. She could not see the attacker, but the Celestian's mind operated on an instinctual, instantaneous level. There was some part of her consciousness calculating angles and likely points of attack, aiming at the places where she herself might have hidden in order to kill the girl.

And *there*! For a fraction of a second, backlit by a streak of sun-bright gaseous plasma, a man-shape recoiling in the girders.

The black-suited figure switched targets and shot back at the Battle Sister. Miriya threw herself across the deck in a tuck-and-roll as darts, invisible in the gloom, smashed into supports or punched holes in the covers of rare manuscripts.

Her opponent moved and fired again. The accuracy of the near-hits was punishing, forcing her on the defensive, and it was instantly clear to Miriya that the assassin possessed some form of enhanced senses.

'Preysight,' she reasoned, shaking off her cloak to gain greater freedom of movement. The woman knew of the arcane technology that rendered night into day – the Sabbat helmets of the Adeptus Sororitas had similar capacity – but she also understood its limitations. Miriya aimed low, not at the place where the shadowy killer was lurking, but at the racks of ancient papers beneath. The plasma gun shrieked and cast flares of brilliant white light into the aged, dry tomes. The conflagration was instant, sending a sheet of fire up towards the rafters.

A scream pealed through the air, and there atop the racks was the assassin, framed by orange flames, clutching at its face. Miriya had only a moment. The machine-spirits of the librarium would not stand to let a fire rage for more than a second or two, lest it spread across the entire complex. There were networks of pipes that delivered inert, suffocating gases to such outbreaks – if the flames died, then so would she and Verity.

The Battle Sister's weapon howled.

A FIST OF gaseous matter as hot as the core of a star ripped into the shadow's left arm, just above the elbow. Everything below the joint exploded from the touch of the incredible heat, and the hydrostatic shock of boiling blood sent a hammer blow racing through the killer's body. The assassin tumbled from the bookcases, falling to the decks through wreaths of fire-retardant mist.

Plasma weapons were designed not to target unarmoured forms like the shadow, but to melt their way through ceramite or hull metal. Used on flesh, they were a blowtorch turned upon wax. The pain of the hit was of such intensity that the killer's heart was stopped by it, and in turn, this factor triggered the compact denial charge of hexogen that was implanted beneath the shadow's ribcage. The assassin's patron was not in the business of letting discarded tools fall into the wrong hands.

With a wet crack, the shadow blew apart in mid-air.

FLECKS OF BURNT matter, some of it flesh, some unidentifiable, scattered down around them in a macabre rain. Disgust churned in Miriya's gullet as she batted the burning remains from her cloak. Nearby, Verity extracted herself from beneath the fallen book carriage, favouring her leg. She eyed the black scorch mark, waving away the acrid puffs of extinguisher gas. Nothing recognisable as human remained of the assassin.

Miriya saw the glitter of glass and holstered her gun. There, lost to the shadow when she had taken her kill, was the murderer's arcane weapon. The Battle Sister picked it up and turned it over in her gauntleted hands, running a practiced eye over the deadly lines of the pistol. 'Mark me, what is this?' Her hand found the knurled porcelain butt and the gun fell into her grip by reflex. Through the clear ammunition store drum she could see the wicked barbs of the dart loads.

'You saved my life,' managed Verity.

'Thank the Emperor for placing me here where I was needed most,' said Miriya. 'You have been in here for the better part of a day. I was concerned and so I came to find you. Had I not...'

'Vaun. He must have known,' husked Verity, her throat raw from the vapours of the dead fire. 'Wanted to keep me from finding out...'

Miriya's eyes never left the gun. 'He had ample chance to murder you in the Lunar Cathedral.'

'What are you saying?' The Hospitaller's voice was high with emotion.

'I've never seen the like of this before. I do not think that a corsair like Vaun would be able to field a weapon and an agent such as this.' She weighed the weapon in her hand, gingerly running her thumb over the setting studs. 'The value of this pistol alone could probably buy him the loyalty of a dozen men...'

'Then who–' Verity's words were cut off by a fizzing spit of noise from the ghost pistol's breech. Suddenly the gun went red hot, the structure of it warping and distending.

'Get down!' Miriya drew back her arm and threw the pistol away into the dark with all her might. She heard it clatter against metal walls then in the next moment there was a crash of detonation. The Battle Sister felt, rather than heard, one of the freed darts streak past her face to embed itself in a rack of books. Suspicion sent a cold sensation crawling over her skin. Such an assassin, such weaponry was far beyond the capabilities of a renegade like Vaun. Only someone with influence, with connections that stretched all over Neva and beyond, could have sent the shadow to silence the Hospitaller.

Miriya glanced up and unconsciously traced the silver fleur-de-lys between her armoured breasts.

'THIS IS OUTRAGEOUS!' Venik's voice was almost a scream, his tirade roaring about the Canoness's chambers. 'I do not know where to begin with this litany of misdeeds and insubordination!' He whirled about, his red cloak flaring, to stab a finger at Miriya and Verity. The Hospitaller's head was bowed, but the Battle Sister did little to show any contrition before the furious dean. 'This presumptuous wench dares to go against my explicit orders, against the word of the lord deacon and lie her way into the librarium – and then your Celestian commits an act of horrific vandalism. Hundreds of Neva's most precious manuscripts, the works of a thousand dedicated lexmechanics turned to ashes!'

Standing at the side of Galatea's wide desk, Sister Reiko cleared her throat. 'The term "precious" is an interesting choice of words, Dean Venik. I understand that the papers destroyed were those relating to crop rotations on the Pirin island chain. Considering that archipelago sank into the ocean during the thirty-fourth millennium, one might ask why they might be considered of more value than the life of Sister Verity.'

'The Sister Superior discharged a weapon inside a holy shrine of the Adeptus Ministorum.'

Miriya fixed him with a hard stare. 'Indeed I did, in the defence of a fellow Sororitas, against an intruder who had already murdered an innocent savant. An intruder whom the librarium's guardians failed to detect or apprehend.'

Canoness Galatea steepled her fingers and said nothing, content to watch the interplay with a neutral, measuring expression.

Venik paused, gathering himself. 'Very well. Then, for the sake of argument, let us dismiss the matter of the books and your wanton gunplay, and consider this errant Hospitaller.' He took a step closer to Verity. 'Did I not say to you in no uncertain terms that the enforcers investigation precluded the need for further enquiry? Were my words unclear? Or are the Sisters of the Order of Serenity given to ignoring the commands of their superiors?' The dean was almost shouting again.

Galatea caught Miriya's eye, and the Battle Sister felt the Canoness searching her soul with that level, unflinching stare. At length, she spoke. 'Verity was acting under my command.'

Venik spun to face the older woman, his face tight with anger. 'What did you say?'

'I ordered Verity to proceed to the librarium, despite your words to her. She was there on my authority.'

Unseen by the dean, Verity and Miriya exchanged glances. Galatea had known nothing of the Hospitaller's venture into the hall of records until after the commotion there. *She is vouching for us...*

'Did you?' Venik seemed unconvinced. 'Yet you did not consider informing my office of that fact?'

Galatea gave an off-hand wave. 'I have many duties to attend to in the convent, my honoured dean. I apologise for giving the matter a lower priority.'

Venik glared at Miriya. If he knew the Canoness was providing a way out for the Sisters, there was no way he could challenge her on it. The ranks they held in the church hierarchy were roughly analogous, with neither holding seniority over the other. 'So be it. I hope then, after all that has transpired, that Sister Verity's impromptu venture yielded something of value. Speak, girl,' he snapped. 'Tell us what great revelation you found among the burning books and corpses.'

With a tremor in her voice, Verity explained the datum she had uncovered in the remunery files and the correlation between the mutineers on the *Mercutio*. Venik listened with a sneer on his lips, but Galatea was evaluating every word, and Reiko followed with swift entries on her data-slate.

'This is all you have? Malfunctioning shuttles and unspent money?' snapped Venik. 'Circumstantial hearsay, nothing more.'

'Men have been put to the sword for less,' Miriya said darkly.

'The city-state of Metis is under the governance of Baron Holt Sherring,' noted Sister Reiko. 'The baron's considerable fortune comes from his family's holdings in Neva's transport and shipping guilds. It was a vessel under Sherring's livery that was diverted on that day.'

Galatea nodded. 'And let us not forget, the good baron is a major shareholder in the consortium that controls the orbital commerce station where the witch made his escape.'

Venik's mood changed abruptly. 'You... You are suggesting that a member of Neva's aristocrat caste aided and abetted a known criminal? That he somehow engineered the escape of Torris Vaun?' He snorted. 'These are serious charges.'

'How hard would it be to coerce members of a transport crew or commerce station staff, especially if the pressure came from a noble?' Galatea replied. 'It is well known that Baron Sherring is a ruthless and ambitious man. His numerous contentions with the planetary governor are a matter of record.'

'It is my belief that the mutineers were somehow... *conditioned* by an unknown agency while in Metis,' said Verity. 'I would suggest some form of post-hypnotic suggestion, perhaps keyed to a certain event or stimulus that would trigger a programmed set of behaviour. Such things are medically possible with the correct devices.'

Galatea came to her feet. 'Reiko, prepare my personal Immolator. Dean Venik, you will accompany me to a meeting with the lord deacon. I will demand a warrant to prepare a pogrom against Sherring. If the criminal Vaun has gone to ground in Metis—'

The heavy door to the chambers burst open to admit Sister Cassandra. The woman was flushed with effort. 'Canoness. Forgive my intrusion.'

'I left orders not to be disturbed.'

Cassandra nodded. 'Indeed, but matters require your immediate attention. A communiqué from Lord LaHayn has arrived... There is an incident in Metis...'

'Metis?' Venik repeated, shooting a look at Verity. 'Explain!'

'At five-bell today, the public vox network broadcast a signal from the baron's mansion. Sherring himself has declared secession from Governor Emmel's rule and the law of the Ecclesiarchy. He claims that the lord deacon is guilty of crimes against the Imperium.'

'Impossible,' breathed Venik. 'He has signed his city's death warrant!'

Cassandra continued. 'Lord LaHayn ordered the mobilisation of a reprisal force immediately. We are tasked to march on Metis and censure the baron for his heresy.'

Reiko frowned. 'If Verity is correct and Vaun is hiding out under Sherring's protection, the baron may have more than just some misguided guardsmen at his side.'

'It appears that events have overtaken us,' said the Canoness grimly. 'My orders are revised. Mobilise the Sisterhood. Metis will surrender to us, or we will raze it to ashes.'

CHAPTER NINE

THE ASSAULT FORCE left the highway as the gates of the Staberinde Pass loomed large through the forest. Forward scouts reported that Sherring's Household Cavalry had placed explosive charges on the sheer walls of the cutting, and Canoness Galatea was in no mood to give them cause to use such a crude tactic. With clipped orders, she sent her commands down the line to the Rhinos, Repressors, Exorcists and Immolators. In slow precision, the armoured vehicles proceeded to force their way through the trees. From the brass grilles of a dozen winged speaker horns came the opening cantos of the Fede Imperialis, the battle hymn of the Adepta Sororitas.

Miriya crouched on the roof of the Canoness's transport, the view through her magnoculars bobbing as the tracked tank rode over the dark earth.

They were advancing up a gentle incline, passing through the collar of trees that surrounded Metis City in a thick ring. At first glance, the settlement appeared to be a formidable target: Metis was built into the basalt bowl of a dead volcano, a caldera-city encircled by a natural shield wall. There were few points of entry, and huge gates guarded each one, but on closer inspection, there were myriad weaknesses. In places the stone walls were thinner, thin enough that a sustained missile barrage would be able to crack them.

The Metiser soldiery, although noted for their fine uniforms and skills with ornamental cutlasses, were ill-trained to face armoured assaults and zealous attackers. Baron Sherring's troops were largely local fops with just a handful of Imperial Guardsmen grown fat in a comfortable posting. The Sisters of Battle did not expect to be challenged here.

The Celestian's viewpoint drifted down to the upper edge of the timberline, to where the drum-shaped defence bunkers studded the lower slopes of the city wall. Dean Venik had provided intelligence records showing that the baron's pillboxes were only manned by automated gun servitors. Miriya wondered idly why the church felt the need to keep detailed tactical data on Metis. Clearly Lord LaHayn had long suspected that Sherring might one day secede.

The glassteel dome of the gunnery hatch levered upward to allow an armoured figure to present itself. Canoness Galatea turned in place, sharing watchful, comradely nods to the Sisters marching beside her Immolator. Pooled about her shoulders and cascading down her back was a lustrous cape made from night-black velvet and stark white fur. The Cloak of Saint Aspira was one of the Neva convent's most sacred artefacts, blessed in the great Eccleisarchal Palace on Terra itself. The mantle was fabricated with a strange mesh-like metal beneath the finery, a form of near-weightless armour the creation of which was lost to the ages. It was said that the sanctified cape could turn away a killing shot by the Emperor's will.

The Canoness caught her awed gaze. 'I dislike the pageantry of this,' she said in a low voice, fingering the cloak. 'Such a relic is too holy to be dragged into battle with so unworthy a foe.'

Miriya holstered her magnoculars. 'The power of an artefact is not only in its physical strength, honoured Sister. To see the cloak upon you gives courage to our kinswomen and sows doubt in the mind of our opposition.'

Galatea sniffed. 'It is beneath us. The honour of this mantle is cheapened.'

'Only if we are not victorious.'

The Canoness laid a hand on the twin mutlimelta cannons at the hatch. 'Interesting days, Miriya. You have brought me interesting days, yet again.'

'I could not foresee–'

'That Vaun's escape would spark a revolt?' snapped Galatea. 'Of course not. To you, the mission was simply to take a criminal into your custody. How were you to understand the web of politics and subterfuge that thunders unseen over everything on Neva?' She shook her head. 'I have served the order here for years and still the secret contests of kingdom and society on this world are clouded to me. Sherring, LaHayn, Vaun... All of them are cards in some peculiar tarot.'

Despite herself, Miriya bristled. 'We are Daughters of the Emperor, not tokens on some game board.'

Galatea smiled. 'Exactly, Sister Superior. And that is why this will be an interesting day.'

The column mounted a shallow rise and they were quiet for a moment, the Fede Imperialis sounding about them. At last, Miriya leaned closer to the Canoness and spoke in low, serious tones. 'The issue of Sister Verity. You vouched for her before Dean Venik even though you knew nothing of her venture into the librarium.'

'If you have to ask me why I protected her, then perhaps your understanding of our sisterhood is unclear, Miriya.' She surveyed the horizon. 'Venik has never been a friend to the Adepta Sororitas. He would prefer that men of the Nevan PDF or his frateris militia defend his chapels, soldiers more directly influenced by his will than the word of the God-Emperor. He is like every cleric born under Neva's sky, ambitious and narrow in view. I would not give him opportunity to oppose us.'

Miriya blew out a breath. 'I will speak plainly, Canoness. This artifice, the doubletalk and power play surrounding every word and deed, it chafes at me. I have but one mission and that is to bring Torris Vaun to justice – I have no wish to be come ensnared in politics.' The Celestian's face wrinkled in disgust at the very thought of it.

Galatea gave a rueful smile. 'Then I would advise you, Sister, never to allow yourself to advance beyond your current rank. I have learned to my cost that of all the challenges to the power of His Word, it is the obfuscation of those who claim to serve Him that vexes me the most.' She looked away. 'The rigour of honest battle is a welcome respite.'

'This Sherring… If his sway over Metis is so strong, how was he ever allowed to gain such a position of authority? Surely his tendency to sedition should have been noted?' asked Miriya.

'Neva's nobility have always engaged in skirmishes and duels. Baron Sherring's avarice is no different from others of his kind.'

'Except he has made a pact with a witch.'

'If Sister Verity is correct, so it would seem.'

From below, Miriya caught the crackling hum of an open vox channel then Sister Reiko's voice hissed in her ear bead. 'Canoness, your pardon, but I think you ought to hear this.'

'What concerns you, Reiko?' Galatea looked towards the head of the formation, to where her adjutant rode in a Rhino with the banner bearers.

'A blasphemous broadcast is being sent on the general frequency. I believe it is directed at the defenders of Metis.'

The Canoness gave Miriya a look. 'Let me listen.'

There was a bark of static that shifted into the sound of a man's voice, strong with emotion. '…love for my citizens. And with that ideal, I cannot in good conscience continue to pledge the loyalty of my house and citizenry to a man whose abuse of the Imperial Church knows no bounds. It has been made clear to me that the self-declared Lord Viktor LaHayn is abusing his posting as lord deacon of Neva's diocese. My sources have brought me evidence that he and his corrupt lackeys pay fealty not to Holy Terra, but to a plan of such staggering disloyalty that I dare not utter it aloud. Even now, our sanctuary of Metis is threatened by LaHayn's misguided servants, blinded by their own shortsightedness. We do not wish open war, but that is what has been forced upon us. For our future, for our Emperor, we must reject the twisted rule of the traitor priest. Our city must be a torch of light in this darkness. We must fight and expunge this contagion. *We must fight!*'

Miriya recognised Baron Sherring's voice at once but the arch confidence he had exuded in the Lunar Cathedral was gone now, replaced with a kind of manic intensity. 'He's afraid,' she thought aloud.

'Yes,' agreed Galatea, 'and so he should be.' She tapped the vox tab on her armour's neck ring and silenced the babbling feed from the city. 'Reiko, sound the alert. He's whipping those poor fools into battle frenzy. The battle will not be long in coming.' The Canoness beckoned Miriya. 'Come below, Sister. We should take a moment to bless our ammunition before we engage them.'

VERITY LOOKED UP with a start as the Rhino lurched to a halt, reflexively clutching at the medicus

ministorum case on her lap. As the order had begun
its gathering for the advance on Metis, Reiko had
come to Verity and offered her the sanctuary of the
convent until the matter of Sherring's insurrection
had been dealt with.

Her answer had come swiftly, without conscious
thought. She believed that the baron was conspiring
with Torris Vaun, even more so now that the city-
lord had openly defied the church. In her heart she
knew that if Vaun were anywhere, he would be
behind the black stone walls of the caldera. It
seemed impossible for her to be elsewhere. Verity
had no choice but to see this chain of events
through to its conclusion. Sister Reiko did not challenge her on her choice – instead, she entered the
Hospitaller's name on the roll of battle and found
her a post. One more medicae in the assault force
would be welcome.

Securing her gear, she pushed past the Battle Sisters crowded into the transport with her and pressed
her face to a firing slot in the thick armoured hull.
Her eyes were drawn instantly to a troop of women
who moved in a tight flock, their heads bowed and
hidden beneath makeshift hoods cut from rags of
old battle cloak material, tatters of broken armour
barely covering the pale nakedness of their bodies.

The Hospitaller's heart leapt into her throat; she
had never seen the Sisters Repentia at such close
hand before. They walked like women condemned,
arms folded at their chests to hold their lethal-
looking chainswords as a priest might carry a cross
or totem. She saw the blink of black iron chains

around their limbs and torsos, some with fan-folds of sanctified parchment drooping from their backs like diseased wings. Each of the faceless Repentia bore the marbling of countless scars across her bare flesh, some self-inflicted and others given in ritual before battle. Verity could not help but shudder as her mind connected this sight with the horrors she had witnessed during the Games of Penance.

The vicious, snake-hiss crack of neural whips gave her a start. The Repentia Mistress advanced through the midst of her charges, calling out a litany. 'If I must die,' she snarled. 'I shall welcome death.'

'I shall welcome death as an old friend,' chorussed the Repentia, 'and wrap mine arms about it.'

'Only in death does duty end.' The Mistress crossed her hands and let the neural whips in her hands flick over the exposed skin of her Sisters, kindling the holy hate and righteous zeal within them.

The devotion of the Repentia was at once awe-inspiring and terrible. The Hospitaller could sense the burning need in them for the virtuous glory of unfettered combat. Other Sisters of Battle parted without words and without looking upon them, allowing the Mistress to guide her cadre forward. Even among the Sororitas, the respect the Repentia were shown was rooted as much in fear as it was in esteem. All Sisters in service to the Emperor aspired to the same purity of fervour, but only a few could truly surrender themselves to the terrible power of it as these women had.

One of the Repentia turned her head and from rips in her crimson hood, ice blue eyes in a pale face looked out at Verity. The Hospitaller gasped then the woman turned away again and went on with the rest of the squad.

With a rumble, the Rhino began to move again, following the Repentia towards the battle lines. On the wind, Verity heard war cries and the report of gunfire.

THE METIS HOUSEHOLD Cavalry had laid an ambush for the Order of our Martyred Lady. Just beyond the places where chokepoints had been planted with stands of tough trees to slow any armoured advance, a squad of Salamander scout mobiles was concealed beneath camouflage netting, ranged optics peeking out of the fake leaf-pattern material to spy on the Battle Sisters.

A few officers in Sherring's soldiery had raised questions when told their guns were to turn on the Adepta Sororitas. Those men had been the first casualties of the conflict, quietly killed and replaced with captains who better understood the nature of loyalty to the barony.

As one, the Salamanders discharged their primary armaments, a spread of punishing autocannon fire ripping through their temporary cover to strike at the Battle Sisters' forward line. Women died in streaks of orange fire, and back behind the copse, the scout commander ordered his units to fire up their engines and start the retreat. The cavalry tanks fired again as they moved, lining the perimeter with falling steel.

* * *

'INCOMING FIRE!' REIKO'S voice called from the vox. Aboard Galatea's Immolator, Miriya shook as the driver crashed the gears, splitting from the skirmish line to minimise any splash damage. The Canoness was pressed to a complex device that mingled a periscope scanner with an auspex and targeting cogitator. 'Beyond that thicket,' she grated, 'scouts on the move.' She glanced back over her shoulder at Miriya. 'Exorcists. I want that tree line burnt off. All units, pitch to attack posture and advance!'

The Battle Sister heard the prayers of acknowledgement from the missile-carrying units ranged behind them and she hauled herself up the short ladder and into the vehicle's empty cupola. Miriya was in time to hear the hoots and clarion chimes from the launch tubes of the Exorcist tanks behind them.

Built, like so many of the Imperium's armoured vehicles, upon the standard template construct that formed the basis of the Rhino, Exorcists were among the longest serving tactical units in existence. Almost all of them dated back to the turbulent years of the Age of Apostasy, when they travelled the battle zones of the Wars of Faith as mobile shrines-cum-attack units. Where most of the order's war vehicles were liveried in reds, blacks and whites, many Exorcist units had gold and silver about them in infinite detail. Their planes of ablative armour were worked with inlaid castings, and sprouting from the rear of some were towering organ pipes stained copper in the light of the Nevan sun. From these instruments came not music, but judgement and destruction. With shrieks of fire at their tails, fountains of missiles emerged from the launch tubes, describing an arc up from the launchers, then down upon the Salamanders and the intractable trees. The hardy trees were split apart or felled, clearing the way for Sisters and Retributors to advance. With them came the spike-mawed prows of a dozen Repressors and Immolators.

A second barrage was unnecessary. The surviving Salamanders fled in full retreat, random snaps of laser fire lancing back from men in the cockpits who dared to test the patience of the Sisterhood. Galatea's tank circled about one of the enemy units. The scout car had been flipped on to its side by a near miss, and Miriya caught the vague noise of movement inside as they passed. She paid little mind to it. Her Sisters on foot would deal with any survivors. The Immolator's gun turret turned easily, letting her track the fat-barrelled meltaguns back and forth across the horizon. The Salamanders were quick off the mark, and there was a chance they would get out of range before the Sororitas could find a clear shot.

'They're trying to draw us into the teeth of those emplaced weapons,' Miriya noted. 'Perhaps we might seek a place to breach the shield wall elsewhere?'

'I do not concur,' replied Galatea. 'The West Gate is on this axis. We will collapse it and progress into the city.'

A lasgun beam flew wide of the tank, striking a tree and making it a torch. Miriya cranked the meltas to track the culprit, dialling in the focal length and waiting for the right moment. 'With respect, a breach would be the swifter option. The Exorcists could–'

'My orders are cast, Sister Superior.' The Canoness's tone brooked no argument. 'You are correct, but this is a matter of show as much as it is of tactics. If Baron Sherring's hold over this city is to be broken, we must be seen to penetrate his strongest bulwark, not to enter by guile. The gate will fall, and for that the guns will need to be silenced. Press on.'

'Ave Imperator,' said the Celestian, and squeezed the twin firing bars on the turret. Four lines of shimmering energy burst from the melta cannons and came together, falling like arrows of pure heat. The microwave blasts struck the rear of the trailing Salamander and excited the molecular structure of the scout in nanoseconds. Metal warped and out-gassed, while inside men screamed as searing fumes tore their lungs. The Salamander veered sharply off course and collided with a grove of trees.

Miriya threw a look over her shoulder at the force riding up behind them. At their backs there were dirty clouds of grey smoke coiling into the air. Small blazes started in the woodlands by indirect fire were taking hold.

THE HATCH WAS twisted on its mounts, so it took the driver four attempts to kick the thing open. His limbs were trembling and he couldn't see very well, so touch and a little sight were all he really had to go on. The missile salvos had rocked the Salamander like a dinghy in a storm, and along the way he had planted his head on the metal walls a half-dozen times. He was deaf now. There was nothing but a curious squealing going on inside his skull. Just to make sure he could still speak, the driver let out a couple of curses worthy of a day in the stockade, and picked his way out past the wet paste of remains that was all that was left of his crewmates.

The broken hatch let him out close to the churned dark mud and he scrambled wildly, adding more streaks of soil to the rust-brown, red and oil-black coating the busy heraldry of his cavalryman's uniform. He had lost his stubber pistol somewhere inside the upturned tank, and after finally rolling down a little incline, he came to rest face up.

When the man wiped the blood from his eyes, he saw the circle of women about him, and cried out. They all wore death's head hoods the colour of new blood and were dressed in rags. One of them leaned down to examine him, as a child might consider an insect beneath a magnifying glass.

'Puh-please,' the driver managed to spit out. 'Emperor, please. I am no heretic!'

The woman's lips moved and he struggled to understand what she was saying to him. Finally, the hooded female snatched his hand and pressed it flat to her bare chest so he could feel the vibration as she spoke. He struggled in her grip as he realised she was not speaking, but singing.

'A morte perpetua, domine, libra nos,' intoned Sister Iona. 'That thou wouldst bring them only death, that thou shouldst spare none, that thou shouldst pardon none.'

He saw the glitter of the eviscerator chainsword as she raised it, and then his body lit with pain as she used it to sever the hand pressed to her torso. The driver reeled away and screamed as the rest of the Repentia brought down their blades and cut him apart.

THE TURRET EMPLACEMENTS were hungry for them, and across the open killing zone before the western gate autocannon tracer left purple dashes in the air, chopping at the boots of the Battle Sisters as they used a grounded Salamander for cover. Spent rounds rattled off the armoured scout, clattering like stones in a tin cup.

Glassy cogitator eye-lenses on iron stalks extended from the tops of the flat turrets and there were wires connecting some of them together so that the servitor-minds inside each could share target data. The guns were elderly and ponderous, but still their accuracy was enough to rip apart Sisters who dared to press too far forward, too quickly. The surviving Salamanders retreated behind the lines of the guns, past trenches where heavy stubber cannon were being belt-fed by more of Sherring's overdressed soldiers. The occasional laser bolt showed where Imperial Guard troopers had joined the cavalry in the ill-informed defence of Metis.

Sister Reiko directed the women under her direct command to zero in on the las-fire and kill the guardsmen first. Their training was better than the second-rate locals, whose martial skills turned mostly to parade ground drills and regimented displays. Precise shots on the turncoat guards also had a demoralising effect on the cavalrymen, letting them watch the abrupt and brutal death that they themselves faced if they continued to fight.

Canoness Galatea did not halt the advance. The momentum behind the Sisters of Battle was high, and foolishly Sherring's commanders had staked their tactics on using that against the women, but these were not the common soldiers from other city-states that the Household Cavalry had faced in years past. The Order of our Martyred Lady moved with the speed of passion, divine zeal welling up in all their hearts.

'Light of the Emperor upon us,' cried Reiko. 'Censure the fallen and chastise!' Her flamer shrieked as she leapt from the hatch of her Rhino, and at her side came a banner bearer showing the hallowed standard of Saint Katherine. Rolling through the broken landscape surrounding the gate, a phalanx of Immolators swept in behind Reiko's unit and a squad of Sister Retributors.

The Retributors were faceless valkyries, their helmets sealed against the smoke and fury of the battle. Many of them carried the bulky slabs of heavy bolters and multi-meltas. Reiko urged them on with a sharp gesture from her flamer, writing a sweep of orange fire across the enemy lines. As one, they unleashed the force of their guns, fording the spines of steel tank traps and pouring death into the outer trench lines. Blunt-nosed bullets from the ballistic stubber rifles came off the armour of the Battle Sisters in clatters, falling away like hail. Reiko gave flame in return, torching men too slow to run. Some dropped to their knees and begged. Those she killed as well, her face turned away in disgust as she granted them absolution.

REPRESSORS IN THE front rank nosed into the tank traps and shoved them aside with steady progress. The rusted metal caltrops left gouges in the roadway as they tumbled, rolling into muddy gullies like jacks discarded by a giant child. The Exorcists continued a steady fusillade at the gates, setting the broad metal doors ringing with every solid impact. The Immolators were the edge of the spearhead, fire bolts and microwave energy lances blanketing the ferrocrete until it began to warp and boil.

Miriya heard the clanking of her tank's rear hatch and felt the vehicle rock as the Canoness leapt up on to the dorsal surface. Galatea held in her hand a war-worn volume of *The Rebuke*, one of the many books of sanctified combat doctrine adhered to by the Sisters of Battle. The woman held it high, so that every Sororitas on the field would be able to look up and catch sight of the shimmer-ink illuminations on the open pages. 'We are the reproach of Holy Terra, cut from burning steel,' she roared. 'Show these wastrels the edge that never dulls. The flame's eternal kiss!'

The war cry was old, but it still touched the Celestian as if it were new to her ears, sparking a vicious elation inside her. Her blood singing in her veins, Miriya placed the tank guns on deserving foes and disintegrated them.

The autocannon fire from the turrets hummed through the air as the tanks came into their range, shells punching fists of black earth into slurry.

THE CITY-LORD's residence was based on an ancient royal house from the distant past of Terra. Wide and low, the front of Baron Sherring's home presented a dozen tall windows of armoured glassteel to the ornamental grounds beyond and the shadow of the caldera wall. The baron himself continued as he had for the last few hours, orbiting between the windows and the collection of monitor tubes inset by the bookshelves of his chambers. The door banged open to admit Vaun, who had ignored Sherring's insistence that he don a cavalry uniform and instead remained cloaked in a tunic and trousers of deep midnight blue.

'My lord baron, still pacing? You will wear a trench in that expensive carpet.'

Sherring flushed red with anger and almost threw the monocular in his hand at the psyker. The baron's bodyguards tensed, unwilling to draw weapons against Vaun without a direct command from their employer.

Vaun gave a rude wink to the three figures that followed him into the chambers. Sherring knew the young lad with the unruly ginger hair – Ignis, he was called – but the rat-like woman and the hooded man, these other two were just more nameless hooligans from the corsair's gang of thugs.

'The engagement is not progressing well,' snapped the baron. 'Your estimates of the Sororitas numbers in Noroc was low. You told me they would not commit so much of their order's forces!'

Vaun gave an off-hand nod. 'Yes. The Order of our Martyred Lady has been most devout in its deployment. I understand they sent almost everything they have in this region. The women of the Ermina Mantle have remained to defend Noroc in their stead, so Canoness Galatea might come here and *chastise* you.' A smirk threatened to rise on his face.

'Do you find this amusing?' spat Sherring. 'We are embarking on a battle for the very soul of this planet, against an enemy that you and your cadre are all victims of.' He swept his hand over Ignis and the other two. 'Emperor's blood, there is no more serious a matter!'

Vaun gave a contrite bow. 'Forgive me, baron. I meant no disrespect. It pleases me that I have been able to light the path to bring you to this most important decision.'

Sherring's train of thought faltered for a moment. 'The Sisterhood is more dangerous than I expected. They advance without fear...'

'Yes,' agreed Vaun. 'Zeal is a powerful weapon, isn't it?'

'If only I could show them what lies LaHayn makes them fight for–'

'That would be a mistake,' snapped the psyker. 'As much as it pains us to take the lives of these dedicated servants of the God-Emperor, their misguided faith has blinded them to the truths that we have uncovered. They would never accept your word on the lord deacon's perfidy.' He nodded to himself. 'Take heart in the fact that they will go to the Golden Throne with honour, for their only error is to believe too blindly in the church.'

'This course I have taken...' Sherring's words were leaden with effort. 'I pray that the Ecclesiarchy will see the merit of it, or else we will all be damned as traitors.'

'I am convinced of it, baron. The Ordo Hereticus will call you a hero for the stand you dare to take today.'

Sherring eyed him. 'And you? What of the help that you promised me? Where are the weapons of LaHayn's own creation you said we would turn on him?'

'Here,' smiled Vaun, gesturing at the woman and the man. 'Presenting my comrades Abb the Blinded and the girl Suki.'

It was the baron's turn to be amused. 'Surely you jest? A skinny female and a sightless man? What use are they?'

Vaun inclined his head. 'Show our friend Holt, will you?'

Suki shrank in on herself, and for a moment Sherring thought she might vomit on his rich carpets but then she let out a deep-throated yowl from her mouth and brought a gout of stinking fire along with it. The nearest of his bodyguards was caught in the nimbus of her dragon breath and he died on his feet.

The second guardian had his gun in his hand as the blind man pointed a crooked finger at him. Milky eyes surveyed the room as if they could still see, centring on Sherring's man. Veins on Abb's brow throbbed and the soldier screamed. Smoke plumed from his nostrils and mouth, and he fell to the floor, roasting from within.

'Terra protect me,' whispered the baron. 'Pyrokenes!'

Vaun's smile grew. 'Impressive, yes? I'm granting you the service of these two as a gesture of solidarity.'

'Of... of course...' Sherring recoiled, the smell of burnt human meat sickening in his nostrils.

THEY SENT IN the flyers to strafe the Sisterhood's war machines, the same flight of oval coleopters that Vaun had used to sweep into Noroc during the Blessing of the Wound. That night, the capital's city guard had been slack and paid for its inattention with death, but Galatea's troops were more than ready for an aerial bombardment. Baron Sherring's affection for flyers and aeronefs was well documented, and the Sisters of Battle had come prepared.

The coleopters thrummed through the cowl of smoke growing up about Metis's tall West Gate, lighting up the slow-moving lines of tanks with bolter shells and laser fire. They came in low, counting on surprise, but that tactic had already been exhausted of its value.

Units of Sister Dominions, the special weapons caste of the Sororitas, switched targets from the turret emplacements and gun servitors of the cavalry. Storm bolters and meltaguns converged and brought the first of the disc-shaped aircraft out of the sky, shedding turbine blades and hull metal as it tumbled end over end into the smouldering tree line. The flames outside Metis were spreading now, coiled around the southern and western slopes in a flickering orange torc about the neck of the city.

Two more of the ships collided in panic as their pilots realised too late that the Sisters were not the easy targets they had bombed in Noroc. A third, burning fuel trailing out behind it in a blazing comet tail, turned into the line of armoured Rhinos, and metal met ceramite plate as the two vehicles collided.

THE BLAST MADE the ground ripple and twitch. The shockwave of the explosion fanned up the hillside and tucked under the rear quarter of the Rhino where Sister Verity rode. Her world turned about as the steel box suddenly rotated around her, throwing the women and hardware inside into disarray. Blood streaked her vision as Verity's head rang off the decking and she was whipped about. The clinical, detached part of her mind caught the sound of somebody's neck snapping as one of the Battle Sisters with her was struck by a loose ammunition crate. A warm darkness stole the rest of the dizzying impacts from her and then abruptly, with no apparent dislocation between moments, the young woman found herself lying in the ankle-length grass, her body tight with dozens of new bruises.

Verity moved and took a wave of agony from her joints. A strong set of hands cupped under her armpits and helped her to her feet. She blinked, blurred vision clearing gradually to reveal a flock of red-pink shapes. There was a peculiar noise hereabouts, a tinny insect buzzing.

'Hospitaller, heal thyself,' she mumbled thickly, the words bubbling up with an edge of hysteria. She struggled to make her eyes see properly and when they snapped back into focus, she regretted it. There before her was the wreckage of the Rhino, volatile promethium fuel pooling beneath it amid a paste of Sororitas corpses. Her gut turned over and she gasped.

'The Emperor watches over you,' said a voice close to her ear. 'He has a plan for you, Sister. No other survived from that transport.'

Verity focussed on the speaker, the grogginess in her mind fading with every passing second. She looked down to see a pale, scarred hand holding her up. She followed it to a face beneath a torn red hood and choked out a breath. 'Repentia...'

'By the Emperor's grace,' replied Iona, hefting her idling eviscerator chainblade. 'Your life will be forfeit if you remain here. He did not spare you so that could happen.'

The Mistress, a dark armoured figure with neural whips heavy in her hands, rose into sight and pointed toward the melee. 'The medicae is in our care. Take heed as we press forward. Her life is to be protected!'

Then they were advancing forwards, women in red rags and high rage all about her as the battle swung closer.

CHAPTER TEN

A BACKWASH OF raw heat seared Sister Miriya's cheek and she leaned into the firing controls, bringing the turret ring of the Immolator about in a hard arc. In the lee of the closest autocannon emplacement, a cavalryman with more bravery than intellect worked at a portable mortar, jamming a fresh shell into the breech. The Battle Sister lit up the meltas and drew a line of wavering heat across the ferrocrete and mud to where he stood, burning him down in a flashing scar of detonation.

Attracted by the activity, the cogitator brain in the turret began a ponderous turn to bear on the tank. Miriya kicked at a control switch by her feet and spoke a quick prayer to the God-Emperor and His tech-priests. The switch brought the blessing of power to a single-shot tube launcher that clung to the flank of the Immolator. Words of consecration wrapped about it on streams of parchment and the shapes of holy seals in red and white wax sheathed its exhaust vents.

Miriya pointed at the gun emplacement and glanced at the Canoness. 'With your permission, honoured Sister?'

'You may remove the obstacle,' nodded Galatea. 'The hunter is yours to command.'

'Aye.' Miriya needed no more encouragement, turning an ornate brass key inset on the turret's dashboard.

The tube chugged out a fat flower of white smoke, and from the middle of that bloom came a wicked projectile, the tip saw-toothed and barbed. Through a means that was beyond Sister Miriya's understanding, the hunter-killer missile spoke directly to the machine spirit of the Immolator and its auspex, there in the few seconds between leaving its birth chamber and turning to its target. The rocket went up into the grey air as a salmon leaps from a river, then turned about its own axis and penetrated the top of the autocannon turret.

The gun emplacement burst open in a black and red flash, unspent shells ripping the air as they ignited in the inferno. Along the line of enemy turrets, a ripple of electric shock streaked through the cables connecting the servitor-brains inside each, and the maws of guns twitched in confusion.

'Press the attack,' screamed Galatea, vox microphones in her armour taking her words and amplifying them through the loud hailers of her tank.

'Faith unfailing.' Every sister on the field replied in kind, backing up their war cry with bolt shell, fire and fury. The Exorcists and Immolators angled and fired upon the mechanical gun bunkers one by one, opening them so that the butchered masses of once-human brains within were boiled into the air.

The echo of multiple detonations sank into the smoke, falling at the feet of the charging Adepta Sororitas. In their trenches and boltholes beyond the towers of the West Gate, soldiers broke and ran at the sight of the women. Red cloaks snapped at the backs of the Battle Sisters and what faint sunlight made it through the war mist flashed off their black power armour. Those who were unhooded showed faces of wrath framed by tresses in ashen or jet. The passion of the God-Emperor was among them, the spirit of Katherine the Martyr their shield and their sword.

The defenders of Metis gave return fire but on came the women, a force of nature made manifest.

THE REPENTIA CARRIED Verity with them as a wave might have carried a piece of driftwood out to sea. She was beyond her own control, guided and pushed by the hands of the red hoods and their Mistress, inside but isolated from their small band. The Hospitaller pulled her own robes around her, better to cover her face from the roaring madness of the battle. There was nowhere she could look that the bloody ruin of war was not laid out for her to see.

Here, the illustration from a medicae script made
real, where the shattered glass egg of a servitor was
spread about the ferrocrete; there, a man cored like
an apple, bones white in a red mass of singed meats.
Verity had come across wounds as savage as these
and more so, but those had always been at a distance. She had seen the dead and the dying once
removed from the field of conflict, the thought of
where those wounds had originated some abstract,
dislocated concept. Now, she watched the inflicting
of those damages, she smelled the familiar burnt-
copper aroma made new and horrible by those
sights.

Verity staggered and the Mistress caught her arm
and stopped her from falling. The Sisters Repentia
stormed on before them, throwing themselves
heedlessly over barbed wire bales and into the
depths of trenches behind. Lesions covering them
across every centimetre of skin, the Repentia called
down death in banshee wails. Their heavy eviscerator chainswords made short work of the men,
spinning razors of teeth shredding flesh, bone and
cloth on the down stroke, the blunt iron edge on
the weapon's other face caving in skulls and
ribcages on the upswing.

The one called Iona, the woman that had
invoked the Catechism of the Penitent after failing
to save Lethe from death, worked at the craft of
killing with blank frenzy. Verity watched her drive
her sword through the sternum of a screaming
cavalry officer, and found the most terrible thing to
behold was the empty, doll-like glaze in Iona's

eyes. The Hospitaller felt the conflict of emotions returning, the same hurricane of anger, sorrow and regret that had taken her the day she arrived on Neva. Had Iona felt the same? Had she been so scarred by Lethe's brutal killing, that all she could do was throw herself to the mercy of a blood-spattered redemption? Verity was troubled to realise that on some level, she could empathise with the pale woman.

'Advance!' screamed the Mistress. 'Take only sins, not prisoners. Leave only flesh, not corruption. Onward. *Onward*!'

Verity was taken with them, into the trenches and tunnels that led to the city.

LOCAL LEGENDS SAID that the West Gate of Metis had been forged from the hull metal of the first human colony ship to arrive on Neva, back in the time of expansion when the stars were new to mankind's touch. They were, in their own way, relics of great import to the people of this planet, but the gate dared to bar the way of the God-Emperor's chosen agents. The steel which had travelled a million light years from the place of its forging was shattered by a hundred Sororitas guns, and with a sound like the collapse of heaven, the four-storey gate was felled.

The razor-prowed Repressors bit into the debris scattered across the highway, tracks spinning as they fought to gain purchase on the ferrocrete. Dead men and killed machines were forced into gutters as the Daughters of the Emperor marched in skirmish lines behind an armoured fist of tanks. Their blood was up, and down the streets before them the wind carried their hymnals.

The last line of defence left by panicked officers, laser-armed snipers in the outer buildings stitched crimson threads into the Sisters. Miriya and the other women in the tank turrets paid them back tenfold with plasma and rockets, tearing the upper floors from stone tenements and razing the wood and tile of others. At their backs, the fires from the forest advanced in with them, the curling smoke and flames hissing over the bloody trenches.

Metis was a city of riches. Like so many conurbations on Neva, the scars of poverty and lawlessness that touched the faces of many hive worlds and colonies were absent, or, at least they were *elsewhere*, shifted to the factory moons where the poor and the desperate could be corralled. The most down-market districts were veritable palaces compared to the rat-warren hovels that Sister Miriya had seen on some rim worlds. Still, they burned just as well. A bow wave of civilians, new refugees made this day by the arrival of the Sororitas, raced from their homes as the Immolators tore past them. Those that dared to stand in defiance to the Sisters of Battle were given the ritual censure of holy shot. Those that made proper obeisance were left by the roadside.

The Canoness rode tall atop her tank at the head of the castigation legion, the cloak of Saint Aspira billowing out behind her and snapping in the breeze. She coiled her book in one hand, directing the Dominions in the forward lines to places where errant cavalrymen challenged their procession. Some of the baron's soldiers threw down their arms and prayed for mercy when they saw the Sororitas coming. Men twice Miriya's age mewled like children as they met her gaze, finally understanding what crime they had committed. Some of them laid eyes on Galatea's cloak and knew it for what it was, a holy relic touched by the aura of their Eternal Lord. The Canoness was the Emperor's avatar, swift and terrible with her justice.

Miriya could read the questions they asked of themselves in their faces – How could we ever have thought to defy the church? What will become of us? Will we be forgiven? The staccato cracks of bolt pistols answered for her. Those in Sherring's brocade and brass-button finery were being culled for their disloyalty.

'From the lightning and the tempest, our Emperor, deliver us.' Galatea quoted the verse from the battle prayer by rote. 'From plague, deceit, temptation and war, our Emperor, deliver us.'

Sister Miriya tasted cordite and burnt wood in the air and turned away to run her gaze over the Sororitas lines surrounding the slow-moving tank. On foot, Reiko caught her eye and gave her a grave nod. The veteran Superior walked with Isabel and Portia at her side and a wounded banner bearer behind. Among the red robes, Miriya realised that she saw no sign of the Hospitaller Verity, and on reflex she made the sign of the aquila. 'Terra protects the faithful,' she whispered, watching the newly dead roll by beneath the Immolator's treads.

'TORRIS!' IGNIS'S STRIDENT voice carried along the marble corridors and stopped the psyker dead in his tracks. Vaun turned on his heel, clasping a pict-slate in his hand.

'Calm down, boy, you'll catch something alight. What's the panic?'

The ginger-haired youth gulped air. 'The baron is coming apart at the seams in there.' He jerked a thumb at the door to the chambers. 'He sent me to find you.'

Vaun tapped his lips with a forefinger. 'It's my estimation that our welcome is about to be worn out for good. It's time to take steps.' He glanced around. There were no guards in earshot, as one of Sherring's first frantic orders had been to send all available men to fortify the mansion house gates. 'Where are those bloody nuns?'

'West Gate's been breached, all vox traffic from that quarter is nothing but dead air or weeping. Fires are spreading, too.'

'This isn't a raid of punishment, then,' the criminal replied. 'The Sisterhood won't leave a stick unburnt here. Our dear pal Holt is going to be made an example of.'

Ignis's fingers crawled over his shirt and plucked nervously at his collar. 'I don't want to be here when they arrive.'

Vaun shrugged. 'Who does? Don't worry, we'll be long gone by then. In my capacity as the baron's "special consultant" I'm going to have his racing 'nef fuelled and put on the roof pad. Once we see the tanks rolling up the mall we'll kite out of here and go for the keep.'

The youth's eyes went wide with surprise. 'The keep? You found it?'

The psyker waved the pict-slate at him. 'Not me, boy. Sherring did. All part of the agreement I made with him. This is his price for my good company.'

'But how? That old bastard LaHayn kept it hid–'

'Doesn't matter how, Ig, just matters that we know where it is. The honourable lord deacon's dirty little secret is ours now, and it's ripe to be plundered. Sherring was busy while we were off planet – sure, he's an oily little tick, but he's connected on Neva. Must have cost him big to get this.' He weighed the slate in his hand. It seemed such a small thing to be so important, and yet inside the primitive bio-cell memory of the device were strings of numbers that meant more to Torris Vaun than any other prize he had taken.

'Sherring won't just let us go.' Ignis frowned. 'We're supposed to help him win this battle.'

'Yes. How sad.' Vaun pocketed the slate. 'That just shows how big a fool he really is. Beneath all the braggadocio, the airs and graces, Sherring doesn't see past the end of his own nose. So while his back is turned, while he's making enough noise to wake the dead, we take what we want from him and slip away real quiet, like.'

A smirk flickered on Ignis's face. 'You set him and LaHayn at each other like dogs. All this kicking and screaming, Metis seceding and all, this is just your smokescreen!'

'You're learning, that's good. Best way to get men to work for you is to have them think the job is their idea.' Vaun patted him on the shoulder. 'It's all about weakness. You find it in your mark, then you break them with it.' The sound of distant shellfire reached them, rumbling through the walls and setting the molycrystal chandeliers above their heads twittering with vibration. 'This little bloodbath is going to cover our tracks nicely. By the time the confessors and the cardinals are through sifting the ashes of Metis, we'll be kings of the Null Keep and everything in it. And then... then, Ig, we'll cut our names into the galaxy.'

'Do you think... Could we destroy a planet, maybe?'

The psyker smiled. 'You know, I've always wondered how that would feel. It's going to be interesting to find out.' Vaun gestured down the corridor. 'Go keep the baron busy. You'll know when it's time to go.' He was two steps away when the younger man's question came after him.

'What about the others? They're still out there in the thick of it. Abb and Suki, I mean.'

'I know who you mean.' Vaun said, without turning around. 'There are always sacrifices to be made, Ignis. You know that.'

'But we lost Rink already. If there's just us two–'

'There'll be plenty of new recruits in the keep,' he snapped, 'more than enough.' He threw a hard look over his shoulder. 'Do as I said. I can't afford to play favourites, not this late in the game.'

Vaun stalked away, leaving Ignis rubbing gingerly at the scarring behind his ear, and remembering.

THE CENTRAL AVENUE from the breached gate guided the Sisterhood to Metis's grand plaza, within the confines of which stood the fenced grounds of the baron's stately mansion. The circular city was arranged like a wheel, with spokes radiating out from the centre and concentric rings of boulevards growing ever smaller as they contracted inwards. At some of the crossroads along the line of the advance, the armoured vehicles and the Battle Sisters met makeshift barricades that were stormed by concentrated attacks, or hastily emplaced Leman Russ tanks drawn from the token Imperial Guard garrison. The line soldiers who had agreed to stand against the Sisterhood were ritually burnt alive, denied even the mercy of a bolter shell. They moved on, ever on, leaving the tanks afire or in fragments.

From giant speaker horns hung from the city's boxy buildings, Baron Sherring's hysterical speeches played in loops, his words nearly shrieks. Galatea ordered each one of them destroyed with rocket or laser, and in turn made the loud hailers on the Sororitas vehicles broadcast songs of penitence and admonishment. Panic warred with the Battle Sisters for mastery of the streets as they moved ever closer to the core of Metis, like a slow arrow toward its heart. The edges of the caldera were enveloped in fire now, and to observers on ships in orbit the plume of smoke appeared as if the dead volcano had returned to life.

CROSSING INTO THE outer gardens of the plaza, Miriya saw flashes of red in the near distance and caught the whirring of eviscerators. The Repentia had pressed on and taken the first kills of Sherring's personal guard, the golden sashes and ribbons the men wore soaking up their blood as the tireless blades took them. Galatea leapt down from the back of the Immolator, and Miriya dropped back through the turret hatch to follow her out into the battle. *I've ridden long enough*, she told herself, *it is time to face the traitors close at hand.*

Desultory laser fire and bolt shots hissed through the air around them, missing cleanly as the baron's men tried to beat the women back. Galatea was snapping out orders. 'Sister Reiko, take the Retributors and assault the southern flank. Sister Miriya, have your Celestians come together and follow in the path cut by our Repentia.'

'Aye,' chorused Reiko and Miriya, saluting with a balled fist to the fleur-de-lys on their chest armour.

A jerk of motion from Portia caught Miriya's eye. The Battle Sister was looking skyward, and she pointed with her gun, her tawny face split in a grimace. 'Dominica's Eyes. What is *that*?'

There was a shape coming towards them, swooping low through the drifts of haze. It was a woman, arms open to them, buoyed up on thin sheets of orange fire. Portia did not wait for an answer to her question and fired at the apparition. The flying woman brought her hands close to her chest and forced a gaseous breath from her lungs. She spat choking flames down at the Sisters with a rattling crackle of noise.

Miriya reeled away, the stench of burning bile washing over her. She felt acid mist prickle her eyes and ground the heels of her hands into them, throwing herself as far as she could from the blast.

Portia and Reiko fired, lancing shots after the woman. 'Witchkin,' spat the veteran Battle Sister. 'A psyker freak!'

Blinking the stinging miasma away, Miriya drew her plasma pistol and threaded hot flares of white light at the dragon-breath woman. The psy-witch described a lazy loop in the misty air and dropped to the ground in a crouch, rolling to avoid bolt fire. Miriya saw a second figure now, a portly little man, advancing with purposeful steps from the smoke. He raised stubby fingers in a claw-like gesture, humming to himself. 'Careful, Reiko!'

Her warning had scarcely left her lips when the veteran superior turned her bolter on the fat man. The air about him wavered and the shots deflected away. It was the same trick that Vaun had used to protect himself during the attack on the Lunar Cathedral.

Around the man's feet, circles of coloured ornamental grass and flowerbeds crisped and wilted. His face turned florid with hard effort and sweat beaded on his broad brow. All in the space of moments, the

psyker who called himself Abb used his preternatural talent to excite the molecules inside the sickle
magazine of Sister Reiko's boltgun. In a throaty roar
of detonation, every shell in Reiko's weapon
exploded at once. The crash of flame took off her
gun arm and ripped away most of her breastplate
and the flesh beneath. The woman was punched
back into Miriya and the Celestian was thrown
against a stone plinth.

The aromas of ash and cooked flesh filled Miriya's
senses. She pushed Reiko off her and the woman's
head lolled to one side, a ruined face in mute shock.
In that moment, as she clutched at her Sister, the
light faded from Reiko's eyes and she went slack.
Cursing, Miriya let the body slip away and stepped
forward, leading with her plasma gun.

Abb saw her coming and marshalled his power
again, drawing from the pool of inhuman energies
at the heart of his psyche. For Miriya, it was as if she
had suddenly stepped into an oven, the dreary,
moist warmth of the day crushed under a punishing
heat. The Celestian had a moment of old sense-
memory from a battle in the deserts of Ariyo, as if a
pitiless sun had turned its full might upon her in
that single instant.

The plasma pistol sang in her mailed grip, the
bright blue-white emitter coils along the breech
sparking wildly with eager power. Plasmatic energy
weapons were infamous for inopportune failures
and catastrophic overheats, but in all the years that
Miriya had used this handgun, she had never once
had cause to regret it. It was a daily ritual of hers to

pray over the firearm and ask the Emperor's forbearance in its use, so that she might employ it to
exercise His displeasure.

'With this flame, I purify,' she murmured through
dry lips.

Abb screamed as he forced the charge of burning
energy from his mind, turning the power on the Battle Sister. Miriya's finger twitched on the trigger plate
and the plasma pistol obeyed her. Psy-force and
superheated, sun-hot plasma crossed in the air and
split the day with thunder. The Sororitas reeled
back, burnt and snarling. Abb became a thing of
smouldering black meat, dying as the energy shot
enveloped him.

The stench of the psyker-woman's coarse exhala-
tions turned on the wind and Miriya followed her
Sisters as they engaged Vaun's pyrokene killer in
combat. Portia, Isabel and a dozen other line Sroro-
itas stitched bolt shells in the air as the witch threw
herself here and there, bobbing and weaving on
pinions of fire. A fresh gushing spew of loathsome,
steaming bile splattered among them. Miriya marvelled that so dainty a frame could continue to emit
tides of flaming vomit. The foetid dragon-breath
claimed the life of another Sister as she watched,
cutting off her screams as it melted away the meat of
her throat.

'Converge,' cried Portia. 'All guns to bear on the psy-
whore!'

It was difficult to predict where the sylph-like girl
was going to go next, the glowing flex of her fire wings
confusing the eye of the shooters. For a moment,

Miriya wondered if the venerable Sister Seraphim would be needed to down her, but the order's swift attack cadre was elsewhere in the battle, engaging the few remaining flyers still circling high above. Taking heed of Portia's cry, the Battle Sisters turned on the psyker, and in seconds she ran out of places to fly. Shots from Isabel's gun, Galatea's inferno pistol and the bolters of a dozen keen women crossed at a point where the witch's flight took her, and ripped her open in mid-air. The fiery toxins in her chest ignited and she blew apart, raining down gobbets of torn flesh.

Miriya averted her eyes and shielded her face. She had no desire to become dirtied by the fallout from the death of such a creature.

'Suffer not the witch to live,' Isabel spoke the words with grim finality.

'Aye,' said the Canoness, 'but there are more than these two to bring to their end. My orders have been given. Advance and take the mansion.'

'Are we free to kill Vaun?' Miriya asked, a little too eagerly.

'The lord deacon's commands were clear. Torris Vaun is to be taken alive.' She turned away. 'Baron Sherring and any other conspirators are to share the fate of these mutant freaks.'

ALL THE WATCHTOWERS of Metis had been cut down or torched, and the overcomplicated pipeworks that controlled the city's rainbirds – the water nozzles for damping down the dry season – were severed. There remained nothing but wells and water buckets left to quench the encroaching fires, and those too were soon abandoned when the people understood that the conflagration would not be beaten. Sherring's subjects fled, choking the main avenues to the gates, but they streamed out into the woodlands only to find the trees ablaze there as well, the crackling necklace of heat beating at them with heavy hands. The Sisters of Our Martyred Lady had come to bring fire to the faithless, and they would only quit this blighted place when every building in Metis was ash. The flames reached high into the darkening sky, fingers of orange and black rising like hands in supplication and prayer. The city cried out for forgiveness, begging the Throne on distant Terra for respite that would never come.

Deep in the centre of the caldera, the Sisterhood heard the calls and closed their ears to them. Baron Holt Sherring had disobeyed the Nevan diocese, and so by order of Lord LaHayn, he was declared excommunicatus. The Ecclesiarchy had signed the warrant at dawn, charging that Sherring had turned his face from the Imperial Church and made a myriad of false accusations. No matter how strong his belief might be, no matter how misguided, Sherring was a traitor and a heretic in the eyes of the Sisterhood – and in the object lesson that would be his death, LaHayn had ordered that the baron's citizens share in his punishment.

Metis burned, the city slowly surrendering to the unstoppable flames as street after street turned to hell.

SISTER MIRIYA LED with Cassandra, Portia and Isabel at her side, moving low and swift across the gentle rise of the ornamental lawns. The rattle of shots came from somewhere ahead of them, and the

Celestian saw puffs of exhaust gas lick out from arrow slots in the walls of the mansion house. She surveyed the structure, looking for a means of approach, for a place where a breach might be made.

Cassandra was turning over the same thought, her eyes pressed to her magnoculars. 'There, the two ornate doors. Do you see them?'

Miriya nodded. 'Heavily guarded, though. I see stubbers. We'll need to take those down before we can enter the building.'

Further up the rise shapes in red and black emerged from the smoke and charged at the cavalrymen's barricade. 'What in the name of Celestine is that?' Isabel pointed a finger. 'Look there, do you see them?'

Cassandra gasped. 'The Repentia. By my blood, they're attacking them with just their blades!'

Miriya sprang to her feet. 'We'll not let them throw their lives away. To arms. Follow them!'

The Battle Sisters scrambled to take up the slack behind the red-hooded fighters, adding bolter and plasma gun to the chorus of strident death that came from the chainswords. Ahead of them, Miriya saw streaks of firepower from the stubbers hammer into the Repentia women. Some of them were killed instantly, others wounded mortally, but only those who died faltered. Their Mistress cracked her whips at their backs or turned the punishing neural lash on the enemy.

Isabel and Portia took up a flanking position while Miriya and Cassandra fell in behind the Mistress. The Sister Superior marvelled once more at the righteous fury the Repentia exhibited, the masked women beheading and gutting any one of Sherring's soldiers too slow to avoid their ceremonial eviscerators. Backing them with gunfire, the two units quickly made short work of the barricade's defenders. The cavalrymen were wheat before the scythe of their holy vengeance.

Stepping over the broken barrier, Miriya saw a Repentia drenched in blood as she struggled to get to her feet, the stuttering blade of her chainsword still buried in the skull of a turncoat officer. By reflex she extended a hand and helped the woman stand. The face shadowed by the red hood turned to hers and she saw pale skin dotted with scarlet, shaved straw-blonde hair fine against a scarred scalp. 'Iona?'

'Sister Miriya…'

The harsh sting of a neural whip darted at Iona's back and she stiffened, but did not cry out. 'You will not speak,' shouted the Repentia Mistress. 'The edicts forbid communion with those of your life before the oath!'

Miriya's hand shot out and caught the end of the whip, the barbed tip spitting out pain through her armoured glove. She jerked it, hard. 'What say you?'

The Mistress tore her lash from the Sister Superior's grip. 'You know the lore as well as any of us, Miriya. She may not speak to you!'

The Celestian opened her mouth to spit out some rebuke, but one look from Iona's hollow gaze silenced it. 'Yes. Of course.' She turned away and let the Mistress reassemble her women.

Cassandra was speaking into the vox pickup on her armour. 'Canoness. The way into the mansion lies open at the doors beside the gardens.' She flinched; there was a livid laser wound along her forearm.

'Sweep and clear,' Galatea's voice crackled through a dozen ear beads. 'Find Vaun. No survivors.'

Miriya acknowledged the command with a nod and glanced at her second's injury. 'Can you fight with that?'

'I will compensate–' began Cassandra.

'Let me help,' the new voice brought the Celestians to a halt, and Sister Verity emerged from her conceal-ment in the lee of an overturned half-track. Miriya was without words for a moment. Verity's eyes were haunted, and there was blood of many hues across her robes even though she appeared to be unhurt.

'You should not be here,' snapped Portia.

'They brought me,' said the Hospitaller, indicating the Repentia.

'A miracle she lives still,' said Isabel in a low voice.

'Yes,' agreed Miriya, 'a miracle.' She stooped and found a boltgun close to the slashed corpse of a Sister man who had once owned it. She offered it to Verity. 'We shall not test the whims of the fates further. Defend yourself.'

The Hospitaller shook her head. 'I'm not a com-batant.' She clasped the scentwood case of her medicus ministorum to her chest to make more of the point.

'It was not a request,' said Miriya, an edge in her tone. 'Take the gun. I cannot have a Sister at my side who will not fight.'

'In the God-Emperor's name, my remit is to save life, not destroy it.' Verity's voice was quiet but it was as steady as a rock.

'Even traitors such as these?' The Sister Superior swept her hands about at the dead men. 'Their lives are forfeit. The Emperor's church has declared it so.'

The other woman nodded. 'That is true. But still, I am not an instrument to bring death.' She met Miriya's gaze. 'That is your job.'

Miriya's eyes narrowed. 'It is. But perhaps you have been spending too much time carrying out more secular duties. You forget yourself. Vaun and his traitors will not make so keen a definition between a Sister Hospitaller and a Sister Militant.'

'That is why the Emperor has you walk with me,' replied the nurse.

'Take the gun,' repeated the other woman.

For a moment, it seemed as if Verity would deny her again, but instead, she took the boltgun and tucked it into her habit.

The Repentia Mistress's call to arms stopped the Celestian from answering. 'A spiritu dominatus. Domine, libra nos. Death to the heretic and witchkin!'

Miriya held her plasma gun high and pointed after the raging Repentia. She could think of no battle cry, no stirring quote at that moment. In silence, the Battle Sisters followed their hooded kin into the echoing halls.

CHAPTER ELEVEN

THE WORDS PRESSED into Ignis's brain like burning darts. *Now's the time, lad. We're casting off. Get to the roof pad, fast.*

The youth clutched at his head and staggered, a thin trickle of blood leaking out of his nose. He bumped into the chart table that dominated the centre of the baron's chambers, setting the confusion of markers and tiny flags upon it tumbling.

'What are you doing?' snapped Sherring, pushing past one of his soldiers. 'Answer me. What is going on?' His expression was taut with anxiety.

Ignis waved a vague hand at the nobleman. 'I... I have to go...' He shook his head to rid it of the after-effect of Vaun's telepathic touch. Bile rose in his throat and he coughed.

Sherring grabbed his arm as the youth tried to make for the door. 'Stop where you are!' He pulled Ignis around to face him, pinched and furious. 'Where is Vaun? He's abandoned me. Tell me where he is!'

'I'll go look for him–'

Quick! came the mind-speech, and a fresh wash of nausea washed over Ignis. *The Sororitas are here! We can't tarry!*

'Can't tarry...' Ignis echoed the words under his breath.

The baron saw the moment of glazing in the young man's eyes and understood what was unfolding. 'You hear him, don't you? Damned witchkin can know each other's thoughts, eh? Where is he? What is he doing?' He shook Ignis violently. 'Tell me now, you worthless gutter rat.'

'Get off me,' Ignis retorted, fighting to free himself from Sherring's frantic grip. 'I'll bring him to you–'

'Liar,' roared the baron. 'He used me. You did this to me, made me ruin my beautiful city!' Sherring's free hand came up with an ornamental dagger in it. 'I'll kill you!'

'No!' Ignis shouted, and the word hammered at the air in the room. In the echo of his cry, every photon candle and view-tube spat sparks and burst into flames.

Sherring shrank backwards in shock, still brandishing the gold blade. 'You... You can't defy me. I am your better!'

'Shut up, you pathetic lackwit,' Ignis spat back at him. 'All the money in the galaxy isn't going to save you now. You were played. You're just a mark!' With each word, the sputtering electrical fires pulsed with flashes of heat.

The baron shot imploring looks at his men. 'Slay the witch. Destroy him. I order you.'

The cavalrymen had their guns in their hands, but they were pointed at the floor. The officers exchanged glances: all of them had seen Sherring's rapid deterioration over the past hours, and none had the desire to cross the psyker on the baron's word. Outside, beyond the tall glass windows, Metis was hidden beneath a curtain of smoke, and through the walls came the sounds of gunfire and men dying. The soldiers watched in silence, waiting for the battle to end. In their eyes was the mute knowledge that they had already lost.

'We are leaving, baron,' sneered Ignis, 'and there's nothing you can do to stop us.' The youth turned and strode towards the doors.

'You will not.' Sherring threw himself at the boy and buried the knife in his back. Ignis was caught unawares and collapsed to the floor. He tried to drag himself away, the little fires around the room throbbing with his heartbeat. 'You will not,' shrieked the baron again, his lips trembling with agitation.

Something hissed and spat outside the sealed security doors to the chamber, then in the next second a flat report of sound tore through the air and the heavy wooden portal crashed open.

Wreathed in smoke, Sister Miriya and her cohorts strode into the room. Sherring baulked as he caught sight of the remaining Repentia, scarred and soaked in the blood of his men.

'Too late...' whispered Ignis, reaching with trembling fingers towards the knife in his back.

'Baron Holt Sherring, city-lord of Metis and its territories, you are bound by Imperial law.' The Battle Sister advanced, her plasma gun aimed at his chest. 'Your crime is heresy, declared and made known by the Lord Deacon Viktor LaHayn.'

Sherring raised his hands in a halting motion. They were wet with the youth's blood. 'Wait. Please. You don't understand, it's LaHayn who is the heretic. You don't know what he has been doing. He wants to usurp the Golden–'

'The sentence is death, to be carried out with all due alacrity.' Miriya raised the pistol to come level with his face.

The baron threw Ignis a pleading look. 'Please!'

Verity caught the gesture and her heart went cold. 'Miriya, the boy–'

Ignis was as quick as lightning. His eyes flashed and the guttering fires about the room erupted like blowtorches. In a split-second the chamber's walls were yellow with streaks of conjured flame, licking up at the opulent tiles and scrollwork of the mansion's ceiling.

Bedlam broke out among the cavalrymen, some of them diving for cover beneath the chart table, others turning their guns on the Battle Sisters. Isabel and Portia shot back, but the blaze funnelled out under the psyker youth's control, ripping into a burning tornado. Verity was shouldered to the floor by Iona as the flames spiralled past her. Ignis sent the column of fire into the Repentia Mistress and the other hooded woman, setting them alight. Their death screams were piercing, the flames carrying them out into the open as the back draft shattered the chamber's armoured windows.

A tail of trailing heat slammed into Miriya and sent her flying across the room, smashing her into a cogitator bank and spinning her about like a top. A streak of energy from her pistol went wide, knocking down one of the cavalry officers with the force of its plasma nimbus.

Iona pushed away and threw herself at Ignis, brandishing her eviscerator, the ragged red hood flying from her shoulders. The psyker was on his feet, marshalling the fire into a spinning shield of flames, burning the chart table and the heavy brocade curtains. A wordless cry of vengeance on her lips, Iona charged him and thrust herself through the heart of the firewall. Her clothing and armour combusted about her, the incredible heat controlled by the boy burning off layers of her skin as she cut through it. Streamers of blackened flesh curled off her as she fell on him.

Ignis raised his arms to ward her off, but the chainsword came down upon him with an executioner's hand upon the hilt. The spinning tungsten-carbide teeth ripped into the bone and matter of his shoulder and cut into the youth's chest. Rendered nerves firing for the last time, the boy grabbed at the Repentia as she buried her blade in him, and took her in a burning embrace. Ignis perished drawing his witch-fire into himself, and his blackened corpse crashed through the chart table with Iona in a fatal grip. The Repentia wailed as she followed the psyker into death. They were a monstrous parody of two lovers, melded as one in a halo of orange flames.

Without the psyker to keep the inferno alive with his unholy power, the guttering fires shrank and spat, crawling like fat insects over the walls. It took a monumental effort for Verity to turn her face from the carnage. She attended to Miriya, pulling barbed injectors from the depths of her medicus ministorum.

Nearby, Cassandra spoke a few words of the Oath of Katherine over the dead Repentia. 'You are redeemed,' she told the corpses. 'Go to the next life free of your burden.' With a flick of her wrist, the Battle Sister salted the body of the psyker with drops from a vial of holy water. The liquid hissed into steam where it met the heated bones.

The Hospitaller frowned and applied a brass syrette to Miriya's jugular vein, forcing the injector rod into her skin. The Celestian twitched with shock as the chemical philtre charged her bloodstream, fighting off the hydrostatic shock from Ignis's psy-strike. After a long moment, Miriya blinked and opened her eyes.

'What… did you give to me?' she demanded.

'A restorative,' said Verity. 'A blend of witch-bane and tetraporfaline, blessed by the apothecarium. You should rest a moment, you are bleeding.'

Miriya pushed her aside and dragged herself to her feet. 'I have no time to shed blood for traitors.' The Celestian found Sherring on his knees, cowering by his desk. 'Where were we?' she asked him. The drug in her system made the pain of her wounds seem distant and unimportant.

'I am not the enemy,' whispered the baron. 'The deacon is the devil.'

'If that is true,' she told him in a low voice, 'then when the time comes I will judge him as harshly as I have judged you.' Miriya pulled the trigger and vaporised the upper torso of the kneeling man with a single shot. Bolter fire joined her from the guns of the other Battle Sisters as they executed the remaining men in Sherring's chambers.

VAUN FELT IGNIS die like a light going out in his mind, and he swore violently. In the control cupola of the aeronef, the baron's tech-priest gave him a worried look. The psyker had already killed the two comrades of the adept as a show of force and the priest was fearful he would be next if he displeased the criminal in the slightest.

'Don't stare at me,' growled Vaun. 'You have a job to do. Get this thing airborne.'

The tech-priest blinked tin eyelids with a clicking noise. 'But, there was another to come? You said we should wait.'

Vaun tugged the escape ladder and the metal frame folded up into the belly of the sleek airship racer. 'I changed my mind. We're going now.' He strode over to the cowering adept and thrust a data-slate under his nose. 'You know where these co-ordinates are?'

Cogs inside the tech-priest's elongated skull case clicked and whirred as he stored the numbers on the slate in a datum buffer. 'Yes, but that zone is restricted. It is a geologically unstable region, dangerous volcanic flows and sulphur swamps–'

'Take me to it,' Vaun stabbed a finger at the smoke-filled sky. 'Now.'

'It's a toxic wasteland,' the adept twittered. 'We will die there!'

Vaun gripped the tech-priest's robes and squeezed. 'You'll die here unless you get this 'nef moving, understand?'

The adept nodded and began to work the controls. With clanks of oiled steel, Baron Sherring's personal flyer detached from the tethers holding it to the roof and unfurled its sails. The powerful thermals blooming up from the burning city took hold of the craft and guided it skyward.

'HONOURED CANONESS, THIS is Sister Miriya.' The Celestian spoke into her vox. 'I have bestowed the Emperor's justice upon Baron Sherring.'

'I understand,' Galatea's voice crackled through her ear bead. 'We are delayed. A pocket of the turncoat Guard has decided to make a stand in the glasshouses. Secure the mansion and find Vaun.'

'Your will.' Miriya cut the communication and glanced at Verity. The Hospitaller was bent over the burnt remains of the psyker and poor Iona. 'Stand away,' the Celestian snapped, suddenly angered by the woman's lack of respect for the dead.

Verity did not obey, and instead crouched close to the blackened skull of Ignis. 'There is something here.'

'It is not your place to interfere with the departed–' began Cassandra, but Miriya waved her to silence and crossed the chamber, laying a heavy hand on Verity's shoulder.

'Desist.'

'I do no dishonour to Iona,' retorted the Hospitaller. 'I imagine each of you owes her a debt from her time in your squad. Know then that she saved my life today as well. It is the witch that interests me.' She used a stylus to point at something in among the bones and charred meat of the dead man. 'Look here. Do you see?'

Miriya studied the object. It was a pewter half-orb, as small as a tikkerbird egg, fused to the curve of Ignis's skull. Wires as thin as human hairs spooled out from it along the inside of the bone. 'A bionic implant? I've never seen the like.' She ran a finger behind her right ear, touching the place where the device had been rooted in the psyker's body.

'Curious,' said Verity. 'The bone has partly covered the metal. This was grafted to him several years ago. It appears to be Imperial technology, not xenos or traitor-made. As to the purpose, I cannot fathom it.'

'Perhaps some device to conjure his witch-fire?' Portia made a disgusted face.

'Very advanced,' added the Hospitaller, and she looked up at Miriya. 'Far beyond the acumen of a thug like Vaun.'

A silent communication went between them, the recollection of the shadowy assassin in the Noroc librarium.

AT THE BROKEN windows, Isabel reacted with a start. 'Listen. Do you hear that?'

'Just shelling–' began Cassandra.

'No. Rotors!' Isabel pointed as a silhouette moved over the glass. 'There!'

The wind changed then all the women heard it, the thrumming chop of propeller blades slicing through the thick air. Miriya sprinted to the windows in time to see the sleek bullet-shape of Sherring's gaudy aeronef passing over the mansion. The prow of the airship dipped and then rose, angling away from them.

'It's *him*,' spat the Celestian, and she threw herself out of the oval of shattered glass, landing heavily in the torn gardens below. The flyer cast a dark pool of shadow beneath it, and Miriya ran to keep below it. Her training took over from her conscious mind, compartmentalising the pain from her injuries and the adrenaline rush in her bloodstream. Her vision caught on a trailing tether dragging down the ornamental steps where it hung from the aeronef's underside. With every passing second the cable was drawing shorter as the craft gained height.

Ignoring the gunfire that lanced past her, Miriya leapt at the tether and caught it in the grip of her armoured gauntlets. No sooner had she done so than the aeronef's props pitched up in tone and the airship pushed away at great speed. Suddenly, the

Battle Sister was hanging suspended beneath the vessel as the mansion grounds flashed by beneath her feet. With dogged and relentless determination, Miriya pulled herself up, hand over hand, towards the passenger cupola beneath the gas envelope.

'Is this the best speed you can muster from this craft?' demanded Vaun, menacing the adept. 'It's supposed to be a racer.'

With visible effort, the tech-priest found his voice. 'The weight distribution is in error.'

Vaun prodded him with a finger. 'Perhaps I should lighten the load, then? I'll start with your corpse.'

'No,' screeched the adept. 'The correct prayers must be offered to the machine-soul. I will compensate.'

'Bah!' The psyker shoved him back at the console and turned away, steadying himself on the listing deck as the priest mumbled and made symbols in the air over the navigational console. 'Get us some more altitude, at least. I don't want to be in range of those Exorcist tanks.'

The front quarter of the aeronef's cupola was made from a skeleton of girders and a cowl of transparent glassteel, so that the late baron and his cronies could view the landscape below the aerial yacht. Now all that lay beneath the flyer was streets choked with dead or dying, burning buildings and the debris of a murdered city.

A fitting epitaph for a braggart and a fool like Sherring, considered the psyker. He was sure that the baron, with his overblown sense of grandeur, would have enjoyed the idea that his precious Metis would not endure without him. Playing Sherring had been easy. Like every one of these idiot nobles, he had thought that his little world, his tiny games of empire, were the only things that were of any import. It mattered nothing to the rich men of Neva that on other planets there were creatures of such alien nature that they would devour whole worlds, or that there were places where the raw stuff of Chaos itself came to life. The universe began and ended at the edge of the Nevan solar system, and they cared nothing for the greater galaxy beyond, as long as it didn't interfere with them and their asinine festivals.

Vaun thought differently. It was ironic, really. There was only one other man he knew who was native-born to this pretentious and grandiose planet, but who saw the wider view as he did, and Torris Vaun hated Viktor LaHayn with every fibre of his being.

It was that hate that had first brought Sherring into the psyker's orbit. Vaun had seen the avaricious desire in the baron's eyes, the need for power in the man that overwhelmed everything else. Vaun had aided the baron in strengthening his position and in turn Sherring had helped Vaun break the chains that bound him to the deacon. But while the nobleman had craved position and title, Vaun played – and was *still* playing – a far longer game. And now, at last, after Vaun had been forced to spend years on the run here and in deep space, the loathsome prig had finally made good on his promises.

'And for that, I pay you in immortality,' whispered the psyker, catching sight of a hobbled statue of the baron as the aeronef passed over the city. 'No one on Neva will ever forget the name of Holt Sherring,' he told the effigy. 'You'll go down in history as a traitor and a fool.' Vaun spat at the statue and turned away, his resentment kindling.

The data-slate was there in his pocket, heavy with the price he had paid to get it. Oh, of course he had never intended to keep those wastrels Abb and Suki around. Had they survived, he would have just found another way for them to serve as fodder for the cannon. After all, their talents were hard to control and unpredictable. Vaun had only recruited them because they were all he could find.

But the boy... That made him angry. Ignis was a sharp lad, and he had real potential. Vaun had seen in him someone worthy to be his protégé, a psyker with ability, but nicely untroubled by such clutter as ethics or morality. It annoyed him to have to lose so promising a tool before he could bring its potential to bear.

With a snort, he dismissed the thought. At the keep he'd find all the raw material he needed to start afresh, and then maybe he would blow Neva apart, just like the lad had wanted.

A creaking noise in the deck plates drew his eyes from the window and set the killer's nerves on edge. They were not alone. Vaun spun, calling fire to him.

A SHAPE IN black armour and red robes threw itself into the cupola from the rearward compartment, crashing through the hatchway. The psyker's face twisted in a grimace as he recognised the woman.

'You again,' he said, with loathing. 'This is becoming tiresome.'

'How did she get aboard?' asked the tech-adept, cowering at the helm.

'Be silent,' Miriya broke in. 'You'll have time to speak for your crimes soon enough.'

'Crimes?' bleated the priest. 'He forced me. He killed my brethren.'

'You should have died with them. That would have shown dedication. Now you are guilty of collusion with a criminal.'

Vaun smiled, amused by her. 'Don't be so hard on the poor wretch, Sister. I can be very persuasive, if I've a mind to be.'

'Your co-conspirator Baron Sherring is dead,' Miriya told him. 'This vessel is being tracked by units of the Order of our Martyred Lady. You have no way to escape the church's reprisal.'

'Oh,' sniffed the psyker, his voice taking on an arch tone. 'Perhaps I should bow down and surrender? Yes, should I do that and beg for a swift and merciful death?' He gave a derisive snort. 'You dare not fire that weapon inside this vessel. One misplaced shot could sever a fuel line or puncture the gasbag. You'd kill us all.'

'You do not understand my devotion to the God-Emperor, witch. My life counts for nought if you still draw breath. If the price I must pay to have you dead is my own blood, then I do so willingly.' She fired, the plasma gun cutting hot light across the cabin.

Vaun threw himself away from the stanchion where he had been standing, the haze of rippling heat from the discharge searing his face. He cried out in pain and threw back a trio of flaming darts. The bolts missed the Sororitas and blew out an ornate windowpane. 'You mad, blinkered bitch,' he swore. 'Stupid little wind-up toy. You have no idea what is really going on here, do you? LaHayn is the worst traitor of them all.'

'When I read your crimes to the quill servitors, I will be sure to add defamation to the list.' Miriya stroked an indent on the plasma gun's breech and dialled the weapon's emitter nozzle to a narrow beam setting. Ducking from behind a support pillar, she fired again, slashing through a tertiary cogitator console.

A sudden thermal made the aeronef lurch to starboard and both the combatants were knocked off balance. The tech-priest wailed, his voice like a warning siren.

Vaun's next flurry of psi-fire hit home close to the woman, one glancing dart of burning air searing her shoulder plate and carving a scar across the wood panelling behind her. Miriya snarled and fired again. The plasma weapon turned a steel stanchion to hot slag and sent flame licking up to the ceiling of the compartment.

'I should have known better than to expect intelligence from a servant of your corrupt religion!' Vaun called out to her from behind cover. 'I may be a thief and a killer, but at least I am true to myself. I don't do the bidding of ancient, crooked clerics!' He gave a harsh, mocking laugh. 'Tell me, Sister, have you never questioned? Have you always been the same trained mongrel, just a dog on some priest's leash?'

Miriya said nothing, moving carefully towards the sound of his voice. She placed each footfall with absolute care, keeping herself steady as the airship listed. The walls of the caldera drifted by below them, hazed by the smoke from the burning forest.

'If only you knew what I know,' continued Vaun. 'If only you could see the horrors that Viktor LaHayn has perpetrated over the years. You think I am a threat to your precious law and order? *Ha*. My plans are just for money and mayhem. The deacon intends nothing less than the unseating of your god!' His voice was thick with hate. 'My crimes are a child's compared to his madness.'

The Celestian hardened her heart against the psyker's words, forcing herself to put aside her doubts. He was very close now, a few hand spans away, crouched behind a recliner couch in rich grox-blood leather. Miriya took careful aim.

'I know you don't trust him. You and the nurse-maid both, there's something that gnaws at your thoughts. If you kill me, by the time you understand it will be too late. LaHayn will take the Imperium for himself. I'm the only one who can stop him. That's why he's so desperate to capture me.' The psyker seemed to be struggling with the effort of speaking. 'He needs me to complete his plan.'

The woman cared nothing for that order now, she would finish this wastrel and weather the ire of the deacon later. 'In the God-Emperor's name—' Miriya threw herself around the couch and levelled the gun – at *nothing*. 'Vaun? Where?'

'Here.' From behind her, the hot claws of his burning hand pressed into the flesh of the Battle Sister's neck.

'How…?'

Vaun chuckled. 'It's not just a matter of throwing balls of fire and the like, Sororitas. Being a witch brings certain other talents to the table. Misdirection, among others.' He blinked sweat from his eyes. 'Quite tasking, though.'

'Kill me then, if you dare,' she growled. 'For my death there will be ten Sisters to take my place.'

Contempt dripped from Vaun's words. 'You foolish women are so predictable. So desperate to throw your life away in service to the church, you practically beg to be killed. It's what you want, isn't it? To become a tragic martyr like your beloved Saint Katherine, to perish on a heretic's blade and earn your place in the pathetic annals of some forgotten convent?'

Miriya's gaze remained locked forwards. Ahead of her she could see the adept cowering at the helm, his spidery brass limbs working the tiller.

The criminal pressed harder. 'Would you like to die now, Sister? Would it assuage the guilt you carry like a millstone about your neck? Far easier to end your life in a futile gesture than to live on in pain, isn't it?'

'Vaun,' said the woman, gently turning her hand to aim her pistol, 'you talk too much.' Miriya pulled the trigger and the plasma gun spat flame across the cabin. The gaseous plume melted the helm into runnels of liquid metal and sent the tech-priest screaming away, his robes on fire and his augmetics twisted by the heat surge.

The aeronef's deck pitched hard, throwing the two combatants apart and slamming them into the wall. The Battle Sister tasted blood as her head rebounded off a support girder. She heard Vaun shouting a string of inventive curses and her vision blurred for a second.

When she blinked it clear, Miriya saw the blackened forest rising up to fill the airship's windscreen, fire-stripped trees reaching up to snatch at the flyer.

NIGHT HAD FALLEN by the time they located the crash site in the woodlands south of Metis. Sister Verity had expected to find a field of wreckage, but Baron Sherring's aeronef was intact for the most part. The elegant bullet shape of the airship's gas envelope was dirty and discoloured, some of the cells torn open and flaccid. The craft had cut through a burnt copse and landed at a tilt toward its starboard side, exposing the passenger cupola to the air. The front of the compartment was a mess of broken glassteel and twisted girders.

At her side, Sister Portia consulted an auspex and frowned. 'The device's machine-ghost speaks of lives still inside, but the glyphs are contradictory.'

'Heat from the fires,' said Cassandra, approaching the downed ship with her bolter held ready. 'The warmth radiates up from the ground. It confuses the sense-taker.'

Verity picked her way through a trail of shredded hull plates and bits of ornate furniture that had been ejected during the landing. Her boots crunched crystal droplets from a chandelier into the ashen earth, and she stepped around a stool detailed in red leather, that had landed intact and incongruous in this black setting.

From the corner of her vision she saw Isabel stoop and recover something from the dirt. 'The Sister Superior's weapon.' She held up the plasma pistol by its barrel. 'If it fell from her grasp...' The unspoken words curdled in her throat.

Cassandra shot her a look. 'Keep searching.'

Verity saw a flicker of motion among the disorder of wreckage and called out. 'Here. Someone alive!' The other women were at her side in an instant, working together to lift away a metal panel the size of a dining table. It was still warm to the touch, and had they not been wearing gauntlets, their hands would have been scorched raw.

From under the panel emerged a crooked man, almost strangling under the weight of his own robes. Brassy claw-hands, hooked and spindly where they were half-melted, snapped and clicked. 'Hello?' His voice was laden with static, like a poorly tuned vox.

'Tech-priest,' said Isabel with more than a little disappointment. 'Where are Vaun and Sister Miriya?'

'Thank you.' The adept pointed back at the grounded airship. 'Inside, I believe. Thank you. Believe.' He gave a metallic cough and tapped the vocoder implant in his throat. Verity remained a moment to examine him as Cassandra led the other women on in a steady, weapons-high approach.

She glanced around, taking in the desert of burnt land and skeletal trees, the towering plume of smoke issuing from the caldera-city dark against the night sky. Verity felt leaden and heavy with disgust at the sight. How many thousands had died today in order to punish Baron Sherring's stupidity? The unfettered carnage sickened her, and the Hospitaller found herself entertaining an almost treasonable anger toward the lord deacon. LaHayn had shown callous disregard for the people of Metis, not all of whom were to blame for their city-lord's foolish choices. With effort, she forced the thoughts away.

A sudden commotion near the wreck snapped her back from her reverie. Cassandra had a man by the scruff of the neck, dragging him out of the cupola. *Vaun.*

The Sister of Battle applied a vicious kick to the back of the psyker's legs and sent him sprawling to the ground. As Verity gingerly approached, she could see he was badly wounded, his face cross-hatched with new scars caused by flying fragments of glass. He managed a bloody smile.

'Ah. Nursemaid. Kind of you to come and minister to me.'

Without a word of command between them, Cassandra, Isabel and Portia all pointed their guns at his head.

Vaun blinked. 'Oh. Viktor has changed his mind, then? I'm to die now?'

Verity strained to master her loathing of the man. 'Your execution will be at the lord deacon's pleasure.'

His smile widened. 'Lucky me. How frustrated you must all be, little sisters, to find me alive and your harlot Miriya not. Worse still, that you must keep me so.'

Verity looked at Cassandra. 'Miriya is dead?'

'There was no sign of her body in the aeronef.'

Vaun's head bobbed. 'Dead. She fell. So sad.'

Skin met skin with a loud smack and before she even realised it, Verity was looking at her hand, at the red mark where she had slapped him.

Real anger flashed in Vaun's eyes.

'Careful,' he said, in a voice low and rich with menace. 'You mustn't damage me further.'

'To hell...' The words were a ragged gasp. 'To hell with that.' Verity turned with a start as Miriya approached from the tree line, carrying herself awkwardly. The Hospitaller instantly recognised the signs of broken ribs, contusions and minor wounds. The Sister Superior marched as best she could into the circle of women, taking her pistol from the hand of a stunned Isabel.

'In Terra's name, how did you survive?' whispered the Battle Sister.

'As the witch said,' Miriya nodded at the psyker, making signs over her gun, 'I fell. By the grace of the Golden Throne, I did not die.'

Even Vaun was lost for words in that moment, but then Miriya thumbed the activation stud on her plasma weapon and he knew what she was going to do next. 'No, no,' he blurted. 'You can't kill me here. On the 'nef, no one would know, but here, these ones will see you. You can't disobey the deacon in front of them.'

'The deacon be damned.' Those words alone were enough to earn Miriya a thousand lashes. 'Die, witch.'

'Miriya…' There was a warning in Verity's tone. 'Our orders…'

The Sister Superior didn't seem to hear her. Miriya's entire world had collapsed to the space between the muzzle of her gun and Vaun's head. 'You are trying to marshal your witchfire, but the pain hobbles you. You know that I hold your life in my grip, Vaun. How does it feel to be the victim? Can you taste it?'

Then, slowly and inexorably, the psyker's eyes went cold. 'The deacon be damned,' he repeated. 'My own thoughts, Sister. Shall I tell you why? If my death is but a heartbeat away, then let me give you a gift before I go. Let me tell you why Viktor LaHayn deserves damnation, more than I, more than any sinner you have ever sent to his grave. Let me do this small thing.'

Verity saw Miriya's finger tighten on the trigger – but not enough. As she watched, the Hospitaller heard her own voice rise in the silence.

'Let him speak.'

CHAPTER TWELVE

VAUN WAS NOT smiling now. 'Your curiosity is all that keeps me breathing, isn't it?' He moved his head slightly to look at Sister Verity. 'I thank you for these additional moments of life.'

'He has nothing to give us,' Cassandra murmured irritably. 'Sister Superior, if you will break the lord deacon's edict to keep this witch alive, then do it now, before he tries to talk us to death.'

Vaun blinked at Miriya, and she searched his face for truth and lies. The psyker's aspect was one she had never seen on him before, without masks or artifice. In his way, he was naked to her. 'Is it absolution you want?' she asked him. 'Will you confess your sins to me?'

'Oh, there shall be a confession,' he nodded, 'but not mine. I'll give you LaHayn's in proxy. Tell you the secrets.' Vaun raised a bloodied hand and tapped a spot at the base of his skull. 'Show you things.'

Miriya's eyes narrowed as she remembered the strange device Verity had found implanted in the head of Vaun's cohort Ignis. With a quick motion, she holstered her plasma pistol.

A moment of relief crossed Vaun's face. 'You've seen the value in my words.'

The Sororitas shook her head. 'I have learnt that every sentence you utter is just one more gambit in the strategies you spin.' She looked at the other women. 'Hold him down.'

Before Vaun could struggle, Cassandra and Isabel took Vaun's wrists and pressed him against a slab of hull metal. Portia kept her gun on him. The psyker blinked, trying to muster his powers, but his injuries had made him weak and tired.

Salvaging a turn of ragged, sharp-edged wire from the wreck, Miriya fashioned a makeshift binding to hold the criminal's wrists together. She glanced at Verity. 'You have a sanguinator in your medicus kit, and neuropathic drugs. Show them to me.'

The Hospitaller did as she was asked. 'What do you want me to do?'

'Sedate him.' There was a long moment before Verity understood that Miriya was not telling her but ordering her to do it.

Vaun struggled. 'I told you, I will freely explain everything!'

The Sister Superior gave him a measuring stare. 'I must be convinced.' She pointed at his arm, and

Verity reluctantly discharged the glass injector into the psyker's clammy skin.

The rush of chemicals struck his bloodstream. He let out moans and the occasional coughing yelp, the sounds rolling about the burnt landscape. Now and then, small fires puffed into life around the clearing as Vaun's pain exhibited itself through his witchery. The whites of his eyes showed. Like the fluids that had contained him in the glass prison capsule on the Black Ship, the potent philtre robbed him of the will to create his mindfire. He became groggy and pallid.

Finally, when she was sure he was quietened and unable to attack them, Miriya allowed him to answer questions. 'You have your audience,' she told him, 'now enlighten us.'

Verity gently cleaned the dirtied sanguinator. 'How did you escape custody?'

Vaun sniffed wetly. 'Unimportant. You know the answer to that already.'

'You were in league with Sherring. He brought the men of the *Mercutio* to Metis and coerced them.'

'Clever, clever Holt. Too clever for his own good. Yes, a simple task, really. With the reach his clan gave him, to the shipping guilds and the commerce station, he found it easy. A man's mind can be moulded quite quickly, if one has the right tools and is untroubled by morals. Those that did not take to the imprinting… They were allowed to die. The others he made my erstwhile saviours, although they would never know it, seeds of my control sleeping in their heads.' The psyker coughed and spat. 'The one who came to the cargo bay…? He carried the order in his unconscious, then spoke it to all the others.'

Cassandra's lip curled. 'You expect us to believe that you allowed yourself to be captured on Groombridge? Just so you could be brought to Neva?' She snorted. 'There must be simpler ways to come home.'

The ghost of a smile emerged. 'Indeed. But I am such a slave to my sense of drama.' His self-amusement faded. 'I wanted to make sure Viktor would let his guard down. I knew his arrogance would make him complacent and careless, but for that to happen, he had to believe he had beaten me.' Vaun's teeth flashed. 'All to give him a greater height to fall from!'

'Your hate for him must consume you,' said Verity, pity in her words.

He glared at her. '*Hate*? There's not a word strong enough to describe my loathing for your precious deacon. A million deaths won't pay back the years he took from me, the life he stole.'

'Explain, witch,' demanded Miriya. 'I grow weary of your obtuseness.'

'Ask yourself this, Sister. If my talents were so deadly, then why was I not surrendered to Black Ships whilst I was still a mere child? Why was I not put down? What happened to me between then and now?'

'The datum,' said Verity quietly. 'The records of the librarium. There were missing pieces…'

'Years!' spat Vaun. 'Made into an experiment for him, a tool, a *plaything*! He took only those he could conceal, only those with the strongest potential. Broke us like animals, used us!' With a savage yank, Vaun tore a clutch of hair from the back of his head to reveal the distortion where a metal implant lay under his skin. 'This was just one of his gifts!'

'Like the pyrokene in Sherring's mansion,' said Isabel.

'Yes. We were all his playthings, doctored and neutered by LaHayn's secret scheming.' His eyes were wide and manic. 'Do you see now, Sister? Can you begin to understand? His agenda is not that of your church – it is not even that of your god. With his puppet governor and willing slaves in one hand, and those blind and hidebound to your dogma in the other, LaHayn does as he wishes. He plays his long game–'

'Must we listen to any more of this?' Portia growled. 'We have dallied long enough with this wastrel. Canoness Galatea must be informed of his capture, and the witch must be processed.'

'Aye,' added Cassandra. 'Can any of these creature's ramblings be corroborated? Is there more evidence than his treasonable spewing?'

'There is,' said Verity, after a long moment. 'In the deeps of Noroc's librarium, I found facts that back up what he has told us. I am certain there would be more to find, if only we could search deeper.'

'Facts? Enough to take the word of a witch over that of a High Ecclesiarch?' demanded Portia. 'I imagine not.'

'But there is doubt, yes?' Vaun broke in. 'You must have seen the edges of LaHayn's grand falsehood, you felt it out there. I know you have, else your

Sister Superior would have executed me the moment I was pulled from the airship. You want to know, don't you? You have to be sure!'

'Doubt is the cancer in the minds of the unrighteous,' said Portia, quoting a dictum from the *Cardinae Noctum*.

'Only the certain can know faith. Only they are fit to judge,' countered Miriya.

'Whose words are those?' asked Verity.

'The great Sebastian Thor's, from his speech at New Hera during the Age of Apostasy.' She turned a penetrating stare on Portia. 'Are *you* sure, Sister? Beyond all shadow of uncertainty?' Portia's silence was answer enough.

'Heh,' managed the psyker. 'As entertaining as it is to listen to you cite your turgid scripture at one another, may I continue?' Vaun blinked. 'By your own admission, the Canoness knows nothing of my survival as yet. Keep that silence for me and in return I will open the doors of the deacon's duplicity to you. Better than that, I will take you to the site of his blackest and most mendacious secret.' He took a breath, his eyes glittering. 'I will take you to the Null Keep, and you will see for yourself.'

'A covenant with a witch?' Miriya made a disgusted face. 'You would dare to utter such a suggestion to a Sister of Battle?'

The man gave a sigh of false contrition. 'It is your choice, Sister Superior. But you know as well as I do that the moment I leave your sight, it will be my death and you shall never have the answers you want. You will never know why I came here, or what it was that the Hospitaller's sibling perished for.' He ignored Verity's sharp intake of breath and focussed all his attention on Miriya. 'By the time you realise that I speak the truth, all the scripture in the galaxy won't be able to stop Viktor LaHayn from ripping your precious Imperium apart.'

'And what would you gain from this selfless act?' demanded the Battle Sister.

'The satisfaction of watching you realise that I do not lie. It will be sweet to see you recognise the betrayal of your own priest-lord.'

None of the women spoke, and the moment seemed to stretch out into hours. Only the crackle of distant fires on the wind crossed between them. Then at last, Sister Miriya cast a glance at the tech-priest, where the adept stumbled around the damaged aeronef.

She called out to him. 'You, cleric. Will the flyer be able to make sky again?'

The priest gave a jerky nod. 'Many systems were damaged, but the machine-ghost is well. It will fly once more, although without such grace as before.'

'Make it ready to lift.' She turned on Vaun. 'This Null Keep of which you speak, this place of secrets. Where does it lie?'

'A few hours by 'nef. I was on my way there myself when you, uh, joined me.'

'You will take us to it.'

A chorus of disbelief erupted from the other Battle Sisters, but Miriya silenced them with a stern gesture.

'Galatea will not allow this,' said Cassandra. 'Her orders were most emphatic.'

'I know what her orders were,' Miriya replied, 'but I also know that since we arrived on Neva, at all turns we have been confounded by a bodyguard of lies. I want the truth, and if it takes this blasphemy to lead us to it, so he will.' She beckoned the psyker up from where he lay. 'No word of Vaun's capture will go beyond the five of us. We shall not return to Noroc, nor surrender our prisoner to the church. These are my orders, and you will obey them, if not for me then to honour the sacrifices of Lethe and Iona.' She cast her gaze upon them all, and one by one the women returned nods of agreement. Portia was the last, but finally she bowed her head.

'You shall not regret this,' said Vaun, a razor behind his smile.

'You know nothing of regret,' she told him, and shoved the witch towards the damaged aeronef.

GALATEA STEPPED OVER the debris of a broken window and surveyed Sherring's chambers with a cold eye. The baron's centre of operations was a poor attempt at a war room, something that an armchair warrior might create in order to play the role of general. A group of Battle Sisters had already been detailed to isolate and attend to the corpses, placing strips of sanctified parchment over the dead men that bore warnings not to approach the bodies of the traitors.

The heavy stink of cooked meat still hung about them, mingled with the omnipresent musk of burnt wood from the city. It occurred to the Canoness that she had not taken a single breath of clear air for hours, since the advance into Metis had begun. With sadness, she watched two women carefully wrap a dead Repentia in a funerary cloth.

'My lady.' A veteran of the Seraphim corps entered the room and gave a short bow.

'Sister Chloe? What is it?'

'We have completed our sweep of the mansion house grounds and put the disloyal to the sword.' The powerful Seraph-pattern jump pack on Chloe's back made her seem taller and broader across the shoulders than the rest of the women in the room. Galatea knew her from campaigns of old, where the arrow-faced warrior had led her unit on pillars of orange jet flame through throngs of heretics. 'Evidence of the baron's treachery is being gathered as we speak.'

The Canoness nudged Sherring's corpse with her boot. The fact that Chloe had not told her the news she wanted to hear was confirmation enough, but she asked the next question anyway. 'And the witch Torris Vaun?'

'No trace. The baron's personal aircraft was seen departing the mansion's grounds. It is likely the witchkin fled, my lady. A unit of Sisters went in pursuit.'

'Whose?' she demanded.

'Unverified at present. Several units have yet to respond to status queries.'

'Miriya…' said the Canoness, under her breath. She waved Chloe away. 'Keep me apprised. You are dismissed.'

The Sister Seraphim rocked on her heels, self-consciously. 'With respect, Canoness, there is another matter. I also bear a message from one of the adepts in the command vehicles. The lord deacon's office has been attempting to contact you for the last hour. They seem most vexed.'

Galatea concealed a wan smirk. 'Of course. I would imagine so.' The Battle Sister had purposely tuned her vox frequencies to take in only local signals immediate to the engagement at hand, not the high channel communiqué links that would connect Lord LaHayn to her ear. She wanted little distraction, reasoning that anything of great import would be relayed to her eventually. Galatea hooked her fingers over indents in the neck ring of her Sororitas power armour and was rewarded by an answering chime in her ear bead relay. 'Canoness Galatea, returning to network,' she announced.

Within seconds, the even voice of the PDF officer Colonel Braun came to her. 'Honoured Sororitas,' he began, an edge of irritation creeping into his words, 'at last. Stand ready. I have the Governmental Palace for you.' No doubt the soldier chafed at being ordered to sit by a vox and wait for Galatea to come back on stream.

A message from the Governmental Palace? The Canoness pursed her lips in thought. Had Emmel recovered enough to resume his duties already?

The next voice she heard answered that question immediately. 'Canoness, this is Dean Venik. Thank you for your attention. We have been observing the confrontation via scrye-scans from the *Mercutio* in orbit. Lord LaHayn demands a report on the situation there.'

'Put him on,' she replied, walking out into the halls and atria of the mansion. 'I'll brief him myself.'

There was a miniscule pause. 'The lord deacon is… indisposed. You may brief me in his stead.'

'Indisposed? I had thought he would wish to hear of the witch's fate first-hand.' She frowned. 'No matter. My honoured dean, please let the deacon know that by his decree, Metis is burning and all who stood against the rule of the Emperor have been made to show due contrition… or they have died. Baron Holt Sherring and his city cabinet have been terminated, as have a number of pyrokenes that we encountered acting in his employ.'

'Vaun?' demanded Venik impatiently.

Galatea thought it curious that Venik showed no concern over her mention of the other fire-witches they had dispatched. 'Status unknown, presumed at large. The Sisterhood is engaged in a search for him.'

Fury erupted from the dean. 'You burn a city and still you cannot cage this creature? Lord LaHayn's disappointment will be great.'

'I will explain it to him–'

'I told you, Sororitas, he is unavailable.'

'And why might that be?' snapped Galatea, the tension from the day's fight and her dislike of the dean breaking the veneer of her civility. 'What is of such import that he cannot speak to me himself? Is he even there in the palace with you?'

She could almost hear Venik's look of shock at her retort. 'The… The deacon does not have to justify his movements to you, Sister Galatea.'

The woman waved her hand, as if she were dismissing a nagging insect. 'Yes, of course. Permit me then to inquire after the health of the noble Governor Emmel. Is he recovering?'

Venik's voice changed in a moment, from irksome to disingenuous. 'Ah, yes, but of course. You would not have heard. It saddens me to report that the governor passed away a few hours ago. The deacon was there at the time to administer last rites and the Emperor's blessing.'

'Dead?' Galatea weighed this in her mind. 'Then who presides over the government now?' She racked her brain for the name of Neva's sub-viceroy and Emmel's second, a large fellow and the scion of a family of Imperial Guardsmen. 'Baron Preed, is it not?'

'It is not,' replied Venik with more than a little swagger. 'The lord deacon determined that for the best of the Nevan people in this time of great moral and spiritual crisis, the Imperial Church should take a more direct role in the management of the planet. Until further notice, I have taken on the honour of assuming the governorship.'

The Canoness fell silent. Such a decision was unprecedented in the modern Imperium. Since the Age of Apostasy, when the High Ecclesiarch Goge Vandire had tried to turn the galaxy to his rule, the separation of church and state in the ruling of human worlds had become an unbreakable dictum;

a dictum that LaHayn had swept away while the Sisters of Battle were deep in the thick of the fighting. Galatea frowned. While she believed utterly in the church's rightness in all things, this was a development that did not sit well with her, but it would do her no good to let Venik know her mind. Finally she spoke. 'My congratulations to you on your new duties, honoured dean. May they bring you what you deserve.' She turned back to the burnt-out chambers. 'I will contact you again once Vaun is ours.' Before Venik could speak further, she deactivated the link studs on her vox control and walked away, brooding.

ONCE THE AERONEF had reached its optimal altitude, the ship's nature as a racing yacht came to bear. Even with the damage it had suffered, even with only the lone, twitchy tech-priest at its controls, Sherring's airship cut through the clouds of Neva's skies with the swiftness of a raptor, at times riding on the rapid jet streams of the planet's upper atmosphere as fast as a cruising Thunderhawk.

Verity watched the landscape below alter as they travelled further north. The habitable zones of countryside gave way to valleys choked with dense grey snows and these to chains of black, basalt hills. In among them, stubby volcanic peaks spat desultory chugs of ash, and in many places there were thin streams of lava. Neva was at its most geologically active in this region, riven with small earthquakes and outgassings of fumes. Nothing lived here beyond the hardiest plant life and a few dogged invertebrate life forms. So the mythology of the planet said, the toxic lands would have one day expanded to engulf the entire world if not for the arrival of the Emperor of Mankind, who, with a gesture to His magnificent technologies, halted the march of the volcanoes and reined them in. The blighted landscape remained now as a reminder of the planet's turbulent core and one more example of Neva's unanswerable debt to the God-Emperor.

Behind her, Cassandra was in hushed discussion with Miriya. 'This is a pointless voyage,' she growled. 'We've been travelling all night and for nothing. Vaun is lying to us.'

'That much is certain,' replied Miriya, 'but we must know for sure. We shall give him enough rope to hang himself.'

'I can hear every word you are saying,' said the psyker from across the cupola. 'And it makes me sad. Is there not even the smallest iota of trust in you? In anyone?' He looked directly at Verity. 'Even the nursemaid?'

'It would be easier to give you some credence if you could reveal this mystery destination of yours,' said the Hospitaller. 'Come now, Vaun. How much further do you expect us to go?'

The man threw her a weak smile and glanced at a chronograph on the 'nef's bulkhead. 'No further,' said Vaun. 'We're here.' He nodded to the tech-priest. 'Take us down, cogboy, nice and easy. And douse the lumes. They'll be watching.'

'Who will be watching?' asked Miriya, striding forwards to where the naked sky peeked into the wrecked cabin.

'LaHayn's dogs.' He pointed into the darkness. 'What do you see?'

Verity squinted. 'Only the volcanoes.'

Vaun nodded. 'As you are meant to. That is the outermost lie.' The aeronef dropped quickly, just a few metres from the ground now. With his bound hands, the psyker took the adept's claw and turned it so the flyer's tiller moved. In return, the ship wavered sideways. 'The battlements are cloaked with clever designs, the points of entry disguised. Look now. Do you see?'

The Sister Hospitaller did and she gasped as a string of casements seemed to appear from nowhere along the surface of the tallest ashen crag.

'The Null Keep,' smiled Vaun. 'I've been away too long.'

FROM AFAR, NO human eye or auspex scan would ever have considered the towering structure to be anything other than what it first appeared to be: one more huge volcanic tor, seething with roils of dirty steam and clogged rivulets of sluggish lava. Yet the closer one came to the mount, the more it changed to resemble a citadel rather than a natural form. At one time, centuries, perhaps millennia ago, the craggy basalt peak had been untouched by the devices of human technology, but now it was a masterpiece of clandestine engineering, a castle made by stealth that stood undetected in this barren arroyo. Shafts had been bored into the thick walls of the rock face, connecting the magma voids in the same manner as ants and termites lived within their earthen colonies. These open chambers had been emptied of molten stone, sealed seamlessly with a science that was lost to humans in this age, and made habitable. Some of the voids were small things, perhaps the size of a few rooms. Others were large enough to accommodate an Imperial Navy corvette, layered with decking, corridors and internal crawlways.

The slumbering volcanic shaft at the axis of the citadel provided tireless reserves of geothermal energy from mechanisms sunk into the liquid mantle of Neva, venting excess gouts of superheated steam from conduits about the surface of the tower.

Battlements and window slits looked out on the approaches. Cunningly fashioned from the cut of the rock itself, these openings appeared to be natural formations. Only on closer examination could the dim glow of biolumes be seen behind them. Spines of obsidian glass and petrified trees masked clusters of armoured sensor vanes and vox antennae. There were even dock platforms, planes of flat stone that extended out far enough to accommodate something the size of a coleopter or a land speeder.

Every shadowed hollow in the sheer face of the mountainside could be home to a watching sense-engine or a concealed weapon emplacement. It was an oppressive edifice, black and leaking menace into the hot, sulphurous air. The endeavour to create such a structure, the will to hide a secret tower in this barren landscape, dwarfed the palaces and temples of Noroc. The construction's original purpose was lost to antiquity, but whatever it had been made for, it had been born in secrecy. The walls of the inner chambers masked everything that took place within, patterned with exotic ores that defied the study of the few tech-adepts allowed to survey them. Nothing, no wavelength of radiation, not even the warped energy of the human psyche, could escape the walls of the tower. The silence of the Null Keep was deeper than the vacuum of space.

THEY LEFT THE aeronef in a steep-walled chasm, the nervous and shifty Mechanicus priest chained to the landing skid in case his curiosity got the better of him. When the Battle Sisters had secured the adept, Miriya's intent look at Verity sparked a pre-emptive denial from the Hospitaller.

'Do not ask me to remain here, Sister Superior. I have no intention of staying in this lightless cabin while you venture out.'

'I have only your safety in mind,' began Miriya, but Verity shook her head.

'I have come this far. I will see this road to its end.'

Vaun snorted. 'Ah, bravo, nursemaid. You have such tenacity.'

Miriya turned her ire on the psyker, barely moderating the tremor in her gun hand. 'We are here, witch. Now tell us, what is this place?'

'You cannot simply be told what the Null Keep is,' Vaun said darkly. 'You must see it for yourself.'

Portia snorted. 'For Katherine's sake. For all we know, this could be some elaborate trap. We'll venture inside and find a horde of mutant psykers baying for our blood!'

'If I wanted to kill you, Sister, it would have been simple to reduce this aircraft to ashes,' Sweat beaded his brow and with an effort Vaun managed to make a puff of flame snap from his fingertip. 'No, I *want* you to see this. It will please me no end to watch the truth barge its way into your shuttered minds. Even if you gun me down then and there, you'll never escape the fact that I was right... and your precious church is wrong!'

The woman pulled her bolter, but Miriya held up a warning hand. 'You know better than to let a witch goad you, Portia. Recite the Saint's Lament and reflect upon it.'

Her face soured, but the dark-skinned Battle Sister did as she was asked, turning away to mumble the prayer under her breath. Miriya looked to Vaun once more. She could see the neuropathic drugs were beginning to wear off, and she knew that Verity had no more.

'She has a valid point. Why should I trust you, witch?'

'Nothing I have ever said to you has been a lie, Sister Miriya,' he replied. 'I see no need to change that now.' He paused. 'The keep is the covert domain of Lord LaHayn. It is here that I spent those lost years of my life-' Vaun threw a look at Verity, '-here that your precious deacon's schemes are incubating. As the nursemaid said, this place is the end of the road. For all of us.'

Miriya accepted this with a nod, then with her hands she made a couple of sharp sign-gestures, battle language directives that the other Sisters instantly reacted to. The woman took her plasma gun from its holster and spoke the Litany of

Activation to it. She approached Vaun and gave him a level stare. 'You will have heard this from me before, but it bears repeating before we go forward. If you betray us, your life will be forfeit. All that keeps air in your lungs is my desire for the truth. Give me cause to doubt you, and I will give you the screaming, bloody end that you so richly deserve.'

'Such a compelling argument,' he teased, 'and pray tell, if I do indeed give you the truths you seek, what then? What gift do I get?'

'A chance to repent and a quick end.'

'Well,' Vaun smirked mockingly. 'I'm convinced. Shall we go?'

THERE WERE ENTRANCES to the Null Keep, but none of them were less than four hundred metres above the level of the valley floor. Instead, Vaun led them to a place where the oval mouths of steam tunnels opened to the cloudy sky. 'This is the manner in which I exited the citadel on the day I escaped. Many had attempted it before me and all had been brought back for us to see, their bodies bloated by scalding and their skin falling off in sheets.'

'You speak of this place as if it were a prison,' said Cassandra.

'It is that, and it is other things as well. A honeycomb of cells exists within these walls, dungeons cut in the solidified magma bubbles, rooms impossible to gain purchase upon...' He shuddered at the memory.

Isabel gingerly peered over the lip of the tunnel and ducked back with a start, blinking furiously. 'Ach. The heat. It will roast any exposed flesh!'

Miriya traced the fleur-de-lys on her chest plate. 'Don your helmets. Our power armour will protect us.'

Isabel pointed at Vaun. 'What about him? What about the Hospitaller?'

The psyker shook his head. 'There is a routine to the outgassing from the core. The temperature falls and rises in a precise rhythm, which I can predict. Keep close to me and I will guide you through, but do not dally. Hesitate in the wrong place and you'll be cooked.' Like a suitor asking for a courtly dance, Vaun offered his hand to Verity. 'Stay by my side, dear nursemaid.' He ended the sentence with a leer.

'Verity,' Miriya nodded. It was as much an order as she was going to give.

Loathing rose on the Hospitaller's face as she gingerly approached him. 'Have no fear, Sister,' said Vaun in a silky voice. 'I promise I will be the consummate gentleman.'

The girl closed her eyes, fighting down the disgust that she felt, and Miriya gave Vaun one final look of warning. 'Portia, with me. Cassandra, the rear. Isabel, you will keep our erstwhile guide honest. If you so much as suspect he is leading us astray or performing a foul act upon Sister Verity's mind, you have my consent to kill him where he stands.'

IN A RAGGED line, they entered the tunnel and ventured inside. Boiling hot streams of scorching air rumbled past them, fogging the visors of their Sabbat-pattern helms with condensation. Miriya toyed with the preysight setting, but the colours were a riot of tumbling reds, whites and oranges, and she quickly became disoriented.

Blinking sweat from her lashes, she pushed on, conscious of the suit's internal mechanisms labouring to keep her body cool. The tiny fusion core apparatus in her power armour's backpack showed warning glyphs at the corner of her vision, the temperature gauge rising quickly toward the red line.

The Battle Sister kneaded the grip of her gun and pondered Portia's words again. For all she knew, Vaun was leading them into a pit of boiling lava – but to have brought them this far only to take them to certain death? It was not his way. In the days since his escape aboard the *Mercutio*, Sister Miriya found she was coming ever closer to understanding the mind of the aberrant. Vaun's ego was his driving force, and to merely end her life and that of her squad would not be satisfactory for him. He wanted them to admit *he* was in the right before they died.

In the back of her mind, a small voice asked the question: *and what if he is?* Miriya shook the thought away and kept moving.

AFTER WHAT SEEMED like hours of walking in a doubled-over crouch, they reached an intersection festooned with service walkways. Vaun sagged a little, but directed them on to a service hatch. Portia ventured through and beckoned them into a maintenance room. Relief welled up in each of them as the Battle Sisters took a moment to remove their helmets. Verity was pale and her habit was drenched with sweat. She drained most of her water bottle before she administered a potion to each of them that would restore the balance of their bodies.

There was another door in the room and Vaun walked across to it, peering through a barred slit. The strength that had been missing from his gait was starting to return. 'Here we are,' he said, a curious sadness in his tone that Miriya had not heard before.

The Sister Superior took a look herself, and gasped.

CHAPTER THIRTEEN

It was a gallery of obscenities.

The window slit looked out across the inside of a wide-open chamber, criss-crossed with the webwork of a hundred catwalks and pipeways. Complex loops of cabling went this way and that, similar to those in the streets of Noroc but far more sophisticated. Dangling from them were hooked arms, some empty, some bearing the weight of platforms or aged metal cubes as big as a tank. Many hung suspended, while others moved in trains towards unknown destinations. Among the constant rumble of activity there were odd sounds that might have been screams or electric discharges – it was hard to be sure. As far as Sister Miriya could see, the outer walls of the decks that dropped away into the depths were ringed with cell after cell of greenish, murky glass, the same sort of capsule that Vaun had been sealed in when he was brought to the *Mercutio*. An irritable sensation crawled over her skin and she tasted an indefinable tang on the air, a thick, greasy aroma. She wrinkled her face in a grimace.

'You can sense it, can't you?' Vaun asked in a low voice. 'The despair and pain of a thousand psychics, living and dead. The walls of the citadel are imprinted with it, stained by their anguish.' He shook his head. 'Imagine how it feels to me.'

'My heart bleeds for your suffering, witchkin,' she said with disdain.

Human shapes moved on some of the levels. Sister Miriya craned her neck to get a better look, but she was too high up for proper scrutiny. She could make out the doddering metal-meat amalgams of servitor drones, blinded men in what might have been Mechanicus robes, but most of the figures wore habits of drab grey, loose garb that swaddled them and became a blank moon-faced mask over their heads.

Vaun saw where her attention was directed. 'The tenders. Such a horrible joke, a soft and compassionate appellation perverted by these heartless cretins.'

The Sororitas considered the witch at her side. Now was the time to be the most watchful of him. By his own admission he had wanted to gain entry to this place, and she had facilitated that for him. Vaun's need to remain in her company was likely waning by the moment, and when the opportunity presented itself, she had no doubt that he would attempt to flee.

The other women had taken water and a brief moment for prayer. Cassandra approached, her face conflicted. 'Sister Superior, is there any sign of alarm? I am concerned, even though Portia found nothing to indicate any sense-engines that might alert the... the inhabitants.'

'Delicate machines do not last long in the humidity of the tunnels,' answered the psyker, 'and besides, the Null Keep's lines of defence are designed to keep people from leaving, not entering. Unless you decide to clatter about on the lower levels or deliver a sermon, we should remain undetected.'

Miriya gestured to her Sisters to ready themselves. 'We are intruders in this place, so be wary. Until we are sure of what practices are at hand within these walls, we must conceal ourselves.' She holstered her pistol. 'If the need comes, silent weapons only, clear?'

'Ave Imperator,' chorussed the women.

The Sister Superior shoved Vaun in the back, towards the door. 'Come, then, heretic. Let us see what spectacle you were so eager to lay your eyes upon.'

The psyker gave her a venomous snarl in return. 'My pleasure. I'm sure you'll find it most educational.'

VERITY LET HERSELF be shepherded between Isabel and Cassandra, moving with all the care she could muster through the myriad pools of shadow on the upper tiers of the chamber. Her mind flashed back to Iona and the Sisters Repentia at Metis: they had done the same, protecting her with calm and flawless skill. But Iona was dead, a torched skeleton, and the rest of the Repentia had fallen alongside her. The Hospitaller felt a hard stab of guilt in her chest. She did not want the same fate to befall these women.

Part of her railed at herself from within. Why could she not have simply remained behind on the aeronef? Or back in Noroc? Better still, why had she not paid her respects to Lethe and then returned to her order's works on the outer moons? Verity felt empty and incomplete, grasping for some intangible form of closure that would heal the wound left by her sibling's death, but as events continued to unfold around her, more and more she was beginning to realise that nothing, not even the contrition and execution of Torris Vaun, would close that void. *Emperor, grant me guidance*, she prayed silently, *I beg of you, deliver me from this*.

'Observe,' Isabel said, pointing. 'The open area below. It appears to be an exercise yard...'

An actinic green flash blinked down in the enclosure and Verity shuddered as a thin screech filtered up a moment later. 'They killed someone.'

Miriya brought them to a halt and observed the area through her magnoculars. She was silent for a while, as if she were trying to make sense of what she was seeing. Verity strained to look with the naked eye, but all she could determine were antsized dots moving and swarming – and once in a while the blink of a lasgun discharge.

'A training squad,' said Miriya at length. 'There are… helots, perhaps? They are being used as targets for the ones in chains. Those robed in grey are directing the proceedings.'

'The chains are made of phase-iron,' said Vaun, his hand straying to his opposite wrist, rubbing at the site of an old injury in recollection. 'It sears the skin when psychic energies are used.'

Verity nodded. 'I have heard of this material. It is a rarity, a relic from the Dark Age of Technology.'

Vaun sniffed. 'It is not a rarity here, nursemaid. LaHayn has it in abundance.' He gestured around at the walls. 'Imagine acid boring into you every time you tried to speak, or breathe, or eat. That's what that damned metal feels like.'

The Sister Superior put away her scope and drew back from the edge of the deck. 'We move on.'

'What is going on down there?'

'A live fire exercise. The captive witches are being taught to kill with their minds.' The thought of such a thing clearly disgusted her.

Deeper in the shadows, Vaun pointed towards a section of the chamber walled off into compartments. 'This way. There used to be laboratories and chirurgeries on this level, before the fire.'

'Fire?' echoed Cassandra.

Vaun just smiled and kept walking.

On they went, trailing behind the amoral corsair in a wary line. Verity fingered her silver rosary chain, tracing the careworn letters etched into the surface of the bright metal. She ducked to step through a distorted hatch that had been warped by a massive discharge of heat. The carved black stone and steel plate of the outer chamber gave way to the same kind of design the Hospitaller had seen in dozens of space vessels and Imperial buildings. The crenellated columns and arched, rivet-dotted beams would have been just as home on a Navy starship as they were here.

She caught glimpses of disused laboratories, some with patches of dark colour spattered about the walls and the moribund air of decay within. Weaves of gauzy spider webs coated many of the objects inside, sealing them in the past. Other doors were of heavier gauge metal than the hatchways and set with oculus slits and heavy, ponderous gates: confinement cells. The woman found herself unwilling to peer inside, for fear of what she might see.

Ahead of her, Isabel's body language altered slightly. The Battle Sister was on more familiar ground, the shape of the corridors known to her. Verity had no doubt that Isabel, Portia and the others had been trained to fight inside such confines. Parts of the floor were uneven, deformed by the same heat-blast as the hatch, and her arm shot out to grab a stanchion to stop her from tripping over. The Hospitaller's hand came back to her coated with a thick layer of slimy ash. She knew at once that it was organic residue from an immolated body. With exaggerated care, she wiped the matter away and shot Vaun a disgusted glare. If he sensed it, he gave no indication.

Portia held a small beam lantern in her fist like a club, using the stark yellow ray it cast to probe into places where the overhead biolumes could not reach. Some of the side compartments of the corridor were pitch dark. The light glittered off things made of glass, sometimes across sluggish pools of stagnant liquid. Verity's impression was one of neglect, of abandonment.

'The witch spoke truthfully,' said Portia. 'I see operating tables and medicae devices. Perhaps the Hospitaller could tell us more?'

Verity bobbed her head in acknowledgment and stepped forward. 'If you could bring your lamp–' A scrape of metal on metal silenced her with a start, and the Battle Sisters froze.

'Someone there,' murmured Vaun in faint anticipation.

Portia pressed the lantern into Verity's trembling fingers and gave Miriya a questioning look. The Sister Superior returned a nod and the other woman slid out of the corona of light and into the darkness. There was another noise, and this time it was unmistakable: the sound of human footsteps, a dithering, unsure movement.

An indistinct outline, no more than the Hospitaller's height, wavered at the corner of Verity's eye, there in the gloom of the chirurgery chamber. Her automatic reaction was to turn the torch beam upon it. A blank, doll-like face blinked into solidity before her, with black circles for eyes and a slot for a mouth. The white mask merged into the figure's shabby grey over-robes. Caught in the light, the tender threw itself across the room at a panel on the far side of the chamber.

Startled by the apparition, Verity could do little but track the robed shape. One hand was within a finger's length of touching the console when Portia faded out of the dark and caught the tender. It happened so quickly the Hospitaller had only flashes: the wet snap of bone as the tender's arm was ruined; a rustle of clothing and the glint of a weapon; glossy black Sororitas armour glittering like an insect's carapace; the ripping crack of a neck breaking, a coughing gasp and a falling body.

'Forgive me,' said Portia to the Sister Superior. 'He was attempting to reach this vox lectern. I reacted to stop him raising an alert.'

'You acted properly,' noted Miriya.

Verity swallowed hard. The moment of death had taken hardly a blink.

Portia took the beam lantern back from her rigid grip and turned it on the dead man, using her free hand to peel back the blank mask. A rather ordinary face looked back up at them, the expression of faint surprise still there.

'Hmph. Nobody I know,' Vaun interjected. 'Good kill, though. Very nice technique.'

Portia did not look up from her examination of her victim. 'It would be my pleasure to demonstrate it to you at close quarters, maleficent.' She pulled at a line of buttons and the over-robes fell open. 'This mantle is lined with a ceramite weave.'

'Body armour,' offered Cassandra, 'in case their charges get too boisterous.'

'The clothing beneath...' Portia fingered a garment in rich red material. 'This is the attire of a cleric.' She found the dead man's necklace: it was a string of onyx beads ending in a golden aquila, an affectation of the Nevan branch of the Imperial Cult.

Vaun laughed softly. 'How troubling. Now, what would a pious servant of the God-Emperor be doing here, I wonder?'

Miriya rounded on the criminal. 'You knew. You knew and yet you let her end the life of a priest and said nothing,' she spat. 'His blood is on your hands!'

'Along with hundreds of others,' retorted Vaun, his amusement gone in an instant, 'not that I care.'

'You'll be made to,' vowed the Celestian. 'You have my word on it.'

The man made an annoyed snarl. 'Ach, look beyond that, woman,' he snapped, pointing at the corpse. 'Don't you understand what it means?'

Isabel was examining the consoles in the chamber. 'I am no tech-adept, but I believe he appeared to be attempting to perform a prayer-diagnostic on these devices.' She ran her hands over a set of tarnished brass dials and a wavering hololithic screen hummed to life. The image was leached of colour, but it clearly showed the activities of a group of similarly dressed figures working at a body on an operating dais. Verity watched for a moment before realising two things: the body was a person still alive, conscious and unanaesthetised, and the display was a visual record of something that had taken place in this very room.

The screen threw more light about the chamber, illuminating the white porcelain dais and the dark stains of dried vitae about the blood gutters.

Vaun craned his neck to get a better look at the activity on the hololith. 'Now, her I *do* know,' he noted, 'or rather, I did. Kipsel, her name was.' He looked away. 'She died of that.'

'Of what?' Verity asked, in a dull voice.

Vaun tapped the lump behind his ear. 'Of this.'

Isabel scrutinised a ticking display rotor in High Gothic. 'Kipsel. That name is here in the recording. Dates, as well.'

The Hospitaller looked over her shoulder. The dates fell squarely in the time period where Vaun's librarium files were empty. She looked up at the screen and her eyes widened. 'Can you halt the progress of the image?'

The Battle Sister turned a control and the recording slowed down to a stop. 'What is it, girl?'

Verity pointed at the corner of the hololith, her finger breaking the surface of the ghost image. 'It's him. It's both of them.'

'Holy Terra... Yes, I see it.' Isabel worked the controls again, making the image shift to bring that section of the picture forward.

Verity and the other women saw several men, garbed in the same robes as the dead priest, but with their hoods down. Two men in particular were at the core of the group, the others around them showing obvious deference. Their profiles were unmistakable, even though time and the poor recording marred the likenesses.

Vaun indicated the men with a theatrical sweep of his hand. 'Honoured Sisters, may I present his most loathsome self, the Lord Viktor LaHayn and his lick-spittle Venik.'

MIRIYA ORDERED HER Celestians to sweep the operating theatre and the anterooms that spread off from it. It appeared that the dead priest had been in the process of surveying the contents – perhaps in preparation to return them to use, she wondered – and one of the rooms contained a wheeled cargo lighter, stacked with spools of glittering wire. Verity identified it as a variety of datum storage media, the same as the hololithic screen used to replay the images of LaHayn and the ill-fated Kipsel. There were uncountable hours of footage here, and Emperor-knew how many recordings of witches undergoing the same brutal violations.

The Sister Superior considered the spools with dispassion. She had no sympathy for the psykers, but the eager, almost wanton manner in which the woman Kipsel had been desecrated struck a chord in her mind. The church did not torture and maim without good cause, and it gnawed at her that she did not know what Lord LaHayn's motives were.

'This must have been going on for decades,' murmured Cassandra, 'and yet I have never heard of the like.'

Miriya wondered if the Imperial Inquisition might have had a hand here, but there was nothing to indicate the presence of the Ordo Malleus or any other branch of the God-Emperor's inquest. In her experience, inquisitors were only too pleased to trumpet their deeds to the church. No, the studied and careful concealment of what was taking place in the Null Keep made her seasoned warrior's mind taut with suspicion.

Verity examined the operating dais. There were tools, now rusted and dull, still stored in drawers set into the cracked porcelain frame. From a tray connected by a corroded servitor-arm, she plucked out a silvery orb and held it up to the torchlight. Miriya exchanged a look with the Hospitaller as they both recognised the same design of implant device from the inside of Ignis's skull.

In another anteroom there were objects that were undeniably of inhuman origin. Suspended in tanks of thin oil, Portia turned her torch to illuminate steely constructs mated with rods of green-hued glass, all long lines and right angles. Next to this, a curved hollow of yellowed bone marked with purple eldar runes, its purpose unguessable, and finally a grotesque hydrocelaphic ork skull, bloated beyond normal size by the touch of mutation.

'Viktor always had eclectic tastes,' noted Vaun archly. 'There's no avenue of investigation he won't venture down.'

Something inside Miriya's iron-hard resolve snapped and she backhanded the psyker with a savage, lightning-fast blow. Vaun stumbled away, clutching at a bleeding cut on his cheek as she drew her plasma pistol. 'I have reached my limit with your games, creature. I want no more of your half-truths and obfuscations!'

Vaun spat blood on the tiled floor. 'You pull that trigger, wench, and the whole keep will know it. You'll never get out of here alive!'

'I'll take that chance.' The collimator coils atop the gun hummed and glowed. 'No more games, no more wordplay, no more circumlocution. You'll tell me the truth now, or else I will gun you down and tear it from these black walls myself!'

The psyker dabbed at the wound on his face, measuring the moment. 'Very well. It seems I have no choice.' He sighed. 'It's an interesting story.'

TORRIS VAUN HAD been no more than a youth when he discovered that the cleric in his settlement had contacted the capital and told them of his 'talents'. In a fit of directionless anger, the boy had burned the church to the ground with the humming, electric potency that lurked behind his eyes. The cleric, his dirty habit smouldering, had made it into the graveyard before he set him alight too, and Vaun had stood and listened to the crisping crackle of flaming human meat.

Not a single soul in the town would come near him as he waited by the chapel arch, watching his handiwork. They were too scared to approach for fear he would do the same to them. As he listened to the townspeople point and whisper, Vaun decided that he would have to leave this place and strike for bigger, greater things. Of late, the settlement had grown stifling, the challenge of terrorising the little township ever less interesting.

Presently a man arrived, a swift coleopter depositing him on the hill. Another priest, Vaun noted. He began to muster his powers in preparation to kill again. But when the newcomer came close enough, Torris could see he was laughing. The black humour was infectious, soon the youth was laughing too. And there, in the glow of the burning church, the new arrival offered him his hand and a chance for fortune and glory the likes of which Vaun had only dreamed.

'YOU KNOW THE story of the Wound, of Saint Celestine and the Passing of her Glory?' Vaun waved his hand. 'Of course you do. But Neva's past holds more to it than that, or the ridiculous games fought by the nobles with assassins and cat's-paws. You just have to look deeper. Much deeper.' The psyker righted a fallen chair and sat upon it, warming to his subject. 'Celestine's coming cleared the warpstorm that had shrouded this planet and for that she was duly enshrined in its miserable annals. But that occurrence was not the first time the clouds of the empyrean had converged on Neva. You see, such a thing has happened here dozens of times, as far back as the Age of Strife.' He paused, fishing a battered tin box from his pocket. 'May I take a cigarillo?' Vaun asked Miriya. 'It's been a while–'

Cassandra reached down and slapped the box from his hand, sending it skittering away into the shadows.

'Ah. That would be a no, then?'

'Keep talking,' growled Miriya.

'Very well. The storms. While some worlds that felt the touch of the warp were destroyed or worse, fell bodily into the realm of Chaos, Neva was not one of them. No, instead the caress of the immaterium was subtler, more insidious. Like a taint upstream flowing down a river, the warp left a mark on this world. It turned the bloodlines of every living soul upon it, just a little.' The man held up his thumb and forefinger a few centimetres apart. 'But just enough. Tell me, Sister Superior, how many psykers are there for every normal human in the Imperium?'

'One or two in every hundred thousand births, perhaps less.'

Vaun nodded. 'On Neva the number would probably be closer to five times that.' He ignored the looks of incredulity on the women's faces. 'Neva's brush with warp space means that its people are more attuned to the psychic realm. Most of them never know it, they just get "feelings" or have strange dreams. But many of us exhibit the more, shall I say, *unique* properties.'

'Impossible,' snapped Portia.

'Short-sighted as ever,' retorted Vaun. 'Think, dullard. Neva is not the only world to have such a blessing. What of Magog, or Prospero, the holdfast of the Thousand Sons? Those planets were rich in preternatural power.'

'Magog obliterated itself,' said Verity, 'and the Space Marines of the Thousand Sons turned to Chaos. Prospero vanished into the Eye of Terror.'

Vaun dismissed her words with a wave of the hand. 'Details, mere details. The fact remains. The bloodlines of Neva are laced with metapsychic potential. I am living proof.'

'What does this mad theory have to do with LaHayn and this place?' demanded Miriya.

'Everything.'

THE CLERIC – HE was an arch-confessor then, of high rank among the diocese and not yet the *Lord* Viktor LaHayn – took him to a dark castle and made him play with his ability. Vaun excelled, untroubled by moral concerns and other petty things, and LaHayn saw potential in him for greatness. He hadn't known it at the time, but now Vaun understood: LaHayn, a normal, pathetic dead-mind like all the others, was jealous of him. He craved the power that came so easily to Torris, and when he couldn't engender it in himself, he worked to make himself master of those who had it.

LaHayn had had his pet adepts place things inside Vaun, opening up his brain and doctoring it. The agonies were fierce, worse than any thing a non-psyker could ever have imagined, but they also opened the floodgates to stronger wells of burning power within him. Vaun's mindfire blossomed, and in the service of his new master, he was compelled to fight in the secret wars that raged beneath the placid surface of Neva's society. But as Vaun's ability and prowess grew, so did his resentment.

The day came when Vaun crossed paths with an avaricious baron named Holt Sherring. The baron had only fragments of the story of the Null Keep and Neva's dark secret, but it was enough to make him a player in LaHayn's game. When Vaun was sent to kill him, Sherring offered the psyker a way to smash his enforced habituation and set himself free. There was no hesitation in Vaun's agreement – but he no more wanted to be a pawn of the baron than the deacon, and as soon as he was able to break free, Vaun fled to the stars to carve a reputation for himself, and brood on a reprisal.

'THE NULL KEEP was created in the deep past as a bulwark against the daemons of the warp, and LaHayn took it for himself. It was an ideal location for his works, isolated, invisible. He kept his dark machinations concealed so they could not taint his public image, just as Neva's people moved their polluting industry to the outer moons.' Vaun tapped his knuckles on the wall, remembering. 'This was my home, my prison, my torture-house. All of us, the pieces in the lord deacon's games. After I broke free, I swore I would come back to obliterate this place. And bless poor, stupid Holt, but he found it for me.'

'I do not understand,' said Isabel. 'If you were held here for so long, why did you need Baron Sherring to find the location for you?'

He pointed at the implant. 'Viktor's adepts are very talented. The implants they created place blocks on the mind. I can no more hold the location of this place in my head than I can count the number of stars in the galaxy.' He snorted. 'It's all blurs. A clever way to stop any escapees from returning to plague him. Or so he thought.'

'You learned to break your conditioning?'

A nod. 'You see, LaHayn learned the secret of Neva as an initiate, from a secret sect of Gethsemenite monks. He told me that it was a revelation for him.' Vaun smiled coldly. 'Years later, he had me hunt down and kill every one of them, burn their monastery, destroy their manuscripts.'

'You were his weapon...' said Miriya.

'I was his slave.' The brittle ice of his smile shattered. 'He compelled me, made me kill for him, all so that he could cement his position in the hierarchy. I helped keep this secret, you see. If an inquisitor got too close, or some cleric who knew too much grew a conscience, it was I that barred the way. The burned dead in the name of LaHayn's grand scheme grew large in number.' He looked at the floor. 'For a time I liked it. I was his red right hand, his sly agent of menace. But I knew that one day I would outlive my usefulness to him.'

Vaun took a long breath. 'While I guarded his secrets, LaHayn worked diligently at his endeavours. He gathered those with the psychic gift and made sure that the tithes to the Black Ships were just as they should be. He threw them the weak ones, the lesser and broken minds, all the while skimming off the cream for his own private cadre here at the keep. Slowly and surely, he has been experimenting on my kind, peeling back the secrets of the mind with ancient technology and callous resolve. All the while, building an army, keeping them asleep until he needs them. For when his invasion begins.'

'Invasion?' echoed Cassandra. 'What do you speak of, criminal?'

'The invasion of Terra, of course. The lord deacon intends nothing less than to destroy the Golden Throne of Earth.'

THE AQUILA-CLASS shuttle carved a supersonic path through the roiling black clouds of the wastelands, tipping up on the edge of a wing to skirt about the plumes of toxic gas issuing from the muttering chains of volcanoes. Designed to resemble the Imperial eagle with its wings outstretched, the craft was swift and capable: an icon of the Emperor's will made manifest in steel and ceramite. There were only a few of the ships in service on Neva, and only one dedicated exclusively to the use of a single man. In the passenger compartment, Lord LaHayn ignored the buffeting of the flight and replaced his empty amasec glass in a receptacle before him. An enunciator on the bulkhead shaped like a choral mask gave a peep of sound. 'Great Ecclesiarch,' came the voice of the pilot servitor. 'We are approaching the keep. Please prepare yourself for landing.'

'Good,' replied the deacon with a nod, and he pressed himself back into his sumptuous acceleration chair. His outwardly calm demeanour masked the churn of his inner thoughts. The course of events was in serious danger of spiralling out of control, and LaHayn feared that the tighter he made his grip, the more threads would slip through his fingers. It was imperative for the Great Work that he personally took command of things – and there was no place better suited than his sanctum sanctorum, his perfect retreat and workshop here in the Null

Keep. The lord deacon had left Venik behind, preening at his new role as Neva's interim governor. The haughty dean would give the nobles and the people something to focus on while LaHayn worked behind the scenes. With luck, he would have everything on an even keel in time for the state funeral of poor, stupid Emmel.

At the edges of his thoughts, a doubt unfurled. Who was to blame for this turn of events? In the cold light of truth, the blame could easily lie at his feet. Had he not been so rigid in his orders, had he been willing to let the Battle Sisters terminate Vaun on sight, then none of his carefully wrought schemes would be so close to discovery. He dismissed the thought with a grimace. This was not the place for uncertainty. No, the woman Miriya, it was with her that the blame rested. Her stupidity in letting the witch escape to wreak havoc… The priest glanced out of the viewport as the keep hove into view and smiled thinly. Still, some good had come of this comedy of errors. Vaun's covert contact with Sherring had become obvious and that had allowed him to eradicate a rival. Now all that remained was to complete the circle with Vaun himself.

The shuttle dipped towards the peak of the towering volcanic cone, passing through dark, ashen smoke, and LaHayn pondered on the matter of his former protégé. Vaun would come to the keep, of that he had no doubt. From the moment he had heard of the escape and flight to Neva, he had known what destination Torris sought. It was only a matter of time until teacher and student faced each other again.

'And this time, there will be an end to it,' he said aloud.

A CLOISTER BELL tolled through the decks of the Null Keep and reached to the upper tiers where the Sisters concealed themselves.

'Perfect timing,' grinned Vaun. 'Viktor does have an excellent sense of theatre. I've always admired that about him.'

At the hololithic lectern, Isabel manipulated the controls to gain some sense of what was transpiring. 'A general alert, Sister Miriya,' she said reading the glyphs. 'A ship is landing at one of the docking platforms.'

'I could show you,' offered Vaun. 'The screens link into a central nexus web. The tenders used them to broadcast those dreary hymns. With your permission, of course.'

'Do it,' ordered Miriya.

'Excuse me…' The psyker moved around Isabel and altered the setting of the device. The image changed to become an exterior view of a flat, glassy landing pad. After a moment, an honour guard of robed tenders marched up in a line as a shuttle dropped into view. There was no sound. The aircraft's wings folded upwards and claw-like landing skids deployed before it settled to the ground. Miriya looked closer. The man descending the ramp from the shuttle was unmistakably Viktor LaHayn.

'Now do you accept the veracity of what I told you?' demanded Vaun. He drifted away from the console, moving slowly out of the nimbus of light.

'There may be some truth in it.' Cassandra's admission was grudging.

Miriya glanced at the witch, then back at the hololith. It was the moment that the man had been watching for, the single instant when all the Sisters had turned their attention from him. Finding such a point in time was the mark of a true genius, Viktor had always told him. 'The key to greatness,' he had pontificated, 'is to know patience, to know when the tipping point is before you. Strike then, and you will leave your adversary in disarray.'

Just so. Vaun had let them push him about, abuse him and deride him since the moment they had found him in the wreckage, and all of it had been a play leading to this instant. Even the watchful, shrewd Sisters of Our Martyred Lady were not infallible, and it would be his pleasure to show them that fact.

Two things happened at once. The mindfire that Vaun had been carefully marshalling for the last few hours erupted into the room, the air igniting. The women were punched down by the back draft. At the same time, he was at the vox lectern, slamming home the punch-switch that sounded the alert klaxon.

Shot and shell came snapping at his heels as he threw himself out of the derelict operating theatre and into the ruined corridors. Vaun ran and found his old hiding places, laughing silently as the tenders came swarming upward.

CHAPTER FOURTEEN

MIRIYA'S RAGE KNEW no limit. Howling like a wild-cat, she stood in the throat of the oncoming firestorm and sent streaks of killing fire back towards the aggressors. Her fury was a terrible thing to see unleashed, and her anger – directed at herself as much as at the enemy – lit the corridor around her with plasma flames.

The Battle Sisters left the decrepit medicae lab behind as the tenders came to suppress them. The initial group deposited by the cable-lifts fired first, unwilling to do anything but attack the group of intruders. They were easily dispatched, no match for the Sisters of Katherine when their blood was up. But these were only the first. More men in grey robes came, and this time they brought blood-hounds. The brains of the bound psy-slaves had been reduced to animalistic levels, and they scuttled on all fours, howling as they threw wild darts of psychokinetic force about them.

The tenders were well armed for priests. What they lacked in the cold application of soldiery exhibited by the Sisters, they made up for with their rare bolter-crossbow weapons, glittering with artificer filigree. Humming electro-stakes as long as Miriya's arm rained down the open hallway, rebounding off the steel walls in sparks of searing blue light. The Celestian heard an irate curse behind her as Isabel took a stake in the shoulder, spinning her around like a top. The priest-troopers and their cohorts came on, pressing the attack, pushing the women deeper into the iron compartments.

Portia was at her side, snarling over the noise of her bolter. 'What now, Sister Superior?' she demanded, placing a scathing emphasis on Miriya's rank. 'Our means of entry is cut off, and these clerics outnumber us more and more with each passing moment!'

Miriya ducked behind a burning console to collect her thoughts. The plasma weapon in her hand was glowing cherry red with discharge, and she could feel the heat of it through her gloves. *Damn Vaun.* she railed at herself. *Damn the witch and his lies. My foolish curiosity has led my cohort to ruin!*

'Sister,' snapped Portia. 'What are your orders?' The smell of hot metal issued from the breech of her gun as she retreated into the lee of a stanchion to reload a spent sickle magazine.

Miriya glared at her. 'We quit this place. A higher authority must intervene here. I will contact the Canoness!'

Another electro-stake whistled through the air above them. 'Vox signals. Blocked,' came Isabel's voice, each word tight with pain. 'I can't get a message out.'

'Even if we could get a communication through the walls of this blighted tower, Galatea will execute us for disobeying her orders,' retorted Portia.

'There will be a transceiver array in this place. We will find it and sound a clarion.' Miriya stared at her gun, metering her rage. 'I will take whatever punishment the Canoness decrees – but she will see my transgressions as miniscule when she understands what we have discovered here!'

'Aye, providing she's willing to take the testimony of a corsair over the lord deacon. We have only Vaun's word–'

'You saw the same as I,' snapped Miriya. 'LaHayn has a secret agenda in this place, and that cannot be denied.'

'*Mercutio* should blast this crag from orbit,' spat Isabel, returning fire with her uninjured arm. 'Accursed pastors. You dare attack the Daughters of the Emperor?'

Shot and stake crossed each other in the enclosed space. The stink of spent cordite and scorched steel cut the women's throats with every breath. Miriya glanced back at Isabel, and saw Verity tending to her injury even as the Battle Sister worked at her bolter, reloading the weapon one-handed. Behind them,

Cassandra stabbed a finger into the melee. 'Something's coming...'

The words had barely left her mouth before the deck plates beneath their feet began to shudder with dozens of heavy footfalls. Miriya turned back to see the tenders and their hound-psykers parting to allow a trio of heavy gun servitors to approach the firing line. Almost the size of dreadnoughts, the flesh-metal amalgams stomped dead clerics into slime beneath their clawed feet as they shouldered forward. Meltaguns whined up to full capacity and oily snaps of sound announced the unlocking of multi-barrelled stubber cannon. 'Fall back,' she shouted, hurling herself from her cover just as the machine slaves filled the passageway with a screaming riot of gunfire.

She saw Cassandra grab a handful of Verity's cloak and bodily throw the slighter-framed girl back down the corridor. Portia tossed a krak grenade at the servitors and then joined Isabel in shooting. Miriya paced shots into the stumbling, inexorable man-shapes, her plasma pistol cooking off a drum of battery acids in an acrid slam of concussion that doubled with the blast of the grenade. One of the servitors tripped and fell, making the deck plates twitch again with the force of its collapse, but there were more than just these three. The Celestian saw four more piston-legged monstrosities lurching out of the gun smoke.

'Back. Back. Find a branch corridor, a vent grille, anything!'

'Nothing!' came Verity's panicked voice. 'This is a dead end. We are boxed in.'

Isabel growled with every step she took, the stake still embedded in her arm clearly grinding against the bone as she moved. Miriya felt a sting of pride as her Sister did not let it slow her chastisement of the enemy. Isabel had always been one of the keenest shots in the Celestians, an elite among the elite. As if in acknowledgement of this, there came a death cry from one of the grey robes as a careful bolt shell stove in a tender's ribcage. The Sister Superior stepped past Portia, firing again and again at the marching servitors.

'Ah,' Portia cried in desperation. 'If only I had a storm bolter!'

Despite the onrushing threat, a peculiar amusement rippled out among the women, the charged emotions so close to death turning to black humour. 'Offer it to the servitors,' retorted Cassandra. 'It would kill them quicker than any gunshot.'

Miriya's face split in a fierce grin. If this were to be the end of them, then in the name of Katherine, Celestine and the Thousand-Numbered Saints, the Sisters of Battle would make the end a costly one for LaHayn's lackeys.

Something in the walls shifted and banged against flat plates of metal, and without warning the floor lurched to one side. Iron clasps as big as her head snapped open on the walls and ceiling. The gun servitors shrank back as the women lost their footing.

'What in the saint's name...?' cried Cassandra, grabbing at an iron pillar.

Suddenly the corridor down which they had been forced was drifting away from them, a gap widening with each passing second. Miriya's perception was confused for a moment before she realised that the dead-end corridor was nothing of the kind – it was a trap, an open-ended box at the end of a conduit, suspended on chains like the cells they had seen from the maintenance gantries. There was little to gain purchase on and the Sororitas skidded on the sheer metal deck as a crane arm pulled the captive chamber away, swinging it over the wide open void between the keep's inner tiers.

Portia teetered close to the edge and her boot slipped out from under her. Isabel was near and she tried to grab her, but habit made her offer her bloody, numbed arm and the limb refused to obey. Portia fell backwards out of the lurching box and plummeted down. Isabel turned away as a sickening crack of bone and shattered ceramite briefly joined the tide of clamour inside the keep.

Another Sister lost. Miriya allowed herself one tiny moment of anguish at Portia's ending and then sealed it away inside her heart. There would be time to mourn later, when candles could be lit and canticles to the fallen recited. 'On your guard,' she snapped. 'Be ready!'

With a swift jerk, the motion of the container was arrested and the box hung for long seconds in midair. The women could see nothing outside except the glitter of lights on the far tier and coils of dark vapour, then the chains above squealed and the metal box went into freefall. Miriya was slammed against the side of the container and clung to it, watching the levels of the keep flash by, watching the flat expanse of the lowermost tier rise up to meet them at a frightening speed. She screwed her eyes shut and called the God-Emperor's name.

When the impact came, she feared her neck would be snapped. Instead she was thrown into Cassandra and the women collapsed in a heap, tossed around inside the box like gambler's dice in a cup. The headlong fall of the container had been halted a metre or so from the ground, deliberately to shock and disorient them. Blood gummed her right eye shut as Miriya struggled to get to her feet and failed. Every joint in her body sang with pain. She made out the blurry forms of robed men advancing on the box, shock-staves in their hands. Like the power mauls of the enforcers, the weapons delivered punishing electrostatic discharges that could cripple and maim. Miriya managed only to croak out a denial before the tenders swarmed into the container and beat the Sisters into senselessness.

CONSCIOUSNESS, WHEN IT returned, did not come in a slow trickle or gentle awakening. It forced itself into Verity's perception like a violent intruder, hammering jagged chunks of painful wakefulness into her. She felt sick and gasped as she failed to prevent her stomach from ejecting thin, watery bile. There was the coppery metallic taste of blood in her mouth, and the acrid taste of raw ozone. The stink of air ripped open by electricity filled Verity's nostrils and she suppressed another gag reflex. The action made her head loll, her neck rubbery and loose. The Hospitaller blinked, and tried to take stock. The cool, clinical portion of her mind ran through a checklist of injuries, finding contusions and cuts, but thankfully nothing that would indicate broken bones or internal bleeding.

How long? How long was I unconscious? Labouring, she drew in a breath of tainted air and attempted to look about her. There were iron manacles circling her wrists and ankles, linked by chains to a strange pulley device above. More chains and more pulleys were connected to the slumped forms of Sister Miriya and the other Sororitas.

'Miriya?' she managed, pushing the slurred word out of her mouth, her tongue like a lump of old leather. 'Cassandra? Do you hear me?'

When no reply came, she tried to turn in place, but the exertion was like shifting a sack of wet sand. Verity let herself sink to the chilly black flagstones beneath her feet and massaged the painful places in her arms and legs. Looking about, she could see that the chamber they had been placed in was not a holding cell, but a large workshop. Banks of benches with quiet tech-adepts and servitors surrounded them, hard at work on unfathomable tasks beneath the sickly light of ancient biolumes. There were tall, indistinct objects at the edge of her perception, but the Hospitaller couldn't begin to grasp their purpose.

A groan drew her attention back to Sister Miriya. The Battle Sister righted herself. 'My weapons... equipment. Taken?'

'It appears so,' said Verity, her voice croaky. 'My medicus ministorum has been removed from my person, even my holy tome.'

'Mine as well,' replied the Sororitas, searching the pockets in her robes. The Hospitaller had heard it said that the copies of the sacred texts carried by Sisters of Battle held kill-needles and memory-metal knives concealed in their pages along with the God-Emperor's wisdom. The women glanced up as footsteps approached.

Verity followed Miriya's gaze and felt ice form in the pit of her stomach as Lord LaHayn emerged from the shadows. A group of tenders followed him in tight escort, and one marched with his hood back, a device in his hand trailing cables behind it. The deacon wore a peculiar aspect. He seemed distressed, in the manner of a parent disappointed with a misbehaving child.

'Sister Verity, Sister Miriya. You cannot know how unhappy it makes me to find you here.'

The furious Sister Superior was suddenly on her feet. 'What in Holy Terra's name are you doing in this foul place, cleric?'

LaHayn threw a nod to priest at his side, and the man turned a dial on his control unit. The pulley over Miriya's head ground its cogs and she was hauled upward with a jerk, just enough to take her a couple of centimetres off her feet. She hung there like a puppet painted in black enamel, cursing the deacon.

'Show some respect for my rank, Sister. Now, tell me, how did you get here?' he asked calmly, his voice carrying. 'Tell me how you found the Null Keep.'

'Go to hell, traitor,' barked Cassandra, and for daring to speak she too was hoisted upward with a painful wrench.

'Traitor...' LaHayn rolled the word around his mouth, as if it were some rare delicacy to be sampled. 'Perhaps in the eyes of a fool. A true servant of the God-Emperor would understand I am anything but seditious.' He studied Verity. 'Will you answer me, Hospitaller? I know I could put these Sororitas to the question for days and nights before they broke – but you? I think you would not be so strong.'

'T-test me, if you will,' Verity managed, fighting down her fear.

LaHayn nodded. 'Perhaps another query then, something easier. Torris Vaun. Where is my errant witch?'

'Don't answer him,' snapped Cassandra. 'He knows where his lackey is. He's playing games with you.'

Cold amusement bubbled up in a frosty chuckle. 'My lackey? Ah, perhaps Vaun was that once upon a time, but those days are long gone, more's the pity. Perhaps if I had not allowed my attention to wander...' LaHayn snapped his fingers, putting an end to his reverie. 'No matter. What's done is done.' He watched Verity's face, thinking. 'Yes. I think I can answer my own questions. He brought you here, didn't he? Vaun found his way back and he used you to get here.' Another nod. 'Cunning. He's lost nothing of his skill.'

The unhooded tender spoke for the first time. 'There was no sign of the pyrokene on the upper tiers, ecclesiarch. If he is indeed within the perimeter of the keep–'

LaHayn snapped out orders. 'Triple the guards at the engine hall. Draw weapons for all adherents. Vaun is to be captured intact.'

The priest frowned. 'My lord, that will deplete numbers in the dungeon tiers.'

'I am well aware of that, Ojis,' retorted the deacon. 'Now do as I say. He'll try to breach the chamber. We'll take him there.' Ojis turned to relay the commands to the other tenders as LaHayn brought his attention back to the women. 'I suppose I should thank you. In your own muddling way, you have fulfilled the decree I set you: to bring me Torris Vaun alive.'

'That creature should have been terminated when the Argent Shroud found him on Groombridge,' snapped Isabel, nursing her injured arm.

LaHayn sneered. 'Do you know how rare he is? You can't begin to comprehend the investment he represents, the effort I have spent. His value is a thousand times that of your lives.' He looked away. 'I want him to live, woman. He is the last piece in a puzzle I have spent a lifetime assembling.'

'So it is you we should blame for Vaun's rampage, then?' Verity asked, finding a reserve of defiance inside her. 'All this leads back to you, lord deacon.

You sent the killer to the librarium. You're the spider in the web, not that witch.'

'Your fortitude against my shadow was quite unexpected, I admit. As for Vaun, his time runs thin. I might say the same about you,' he frowned.

'You would spill the blood of the Daughters of the Emperor?' spat Cassandra. 'You would be dead at Vaun's hands if not for us. We saved your life at the Lunar Cathedral.'

'You did,' nodded LaHayn, 'and that is the only reason why I have not executed you out of hand. Sisters, you present me with a conundrum: what am I to do with you? I do so object to the waste of material with such promise.'

'If you will end us, then do it now,' demanded Miriya. 'The stink of the witch about you fills me with repugnance.'

He approached her. 'You are mistaken if you believe that this is a matter of collaboration, Sister Miriya. No, this is about *control*. My Great Work is dedicated to the harnessing of the psyker gene, just as the magos biologis craft germs for a virus bomb or the Mechanicus construct a cogitator.' Verity could see the deacon warming to his subject, the same arrogant poise he showed when he addressed the people during the Games of Penance moulding his manner. All he lacked was a pulpit from which to hold forth.

LaHayn gestured to Ojis and the tenders. 'Many have been brought into my fold, Sisters. Dedicated adherents to the God-Emperor, one and all. If only you understood my vision, you would see the perfection of it.'

Verity saw the opportunity and seized it before the others could take a breath to decry him. 'Then tell us, lord deacon. Explain what possible prospect could compel you to craft a secret opus, hidden from the eyes of the Imperium.'

He laughed. 'Oh, how arch. Do you think me so venal that an ill-worded taunt would make me spill my secrets to you?'

'But you will,' growled Miriya, 'because you crave an audience. You and Vaun are alike in many ways, deacon. Your egos drive you, you're compelled by the belief in your own rightness. You both live to prove that those who deny you are wrong.' Miriya's eyes narrowed. 'So do it. Attest to us how right you are.'

THE ANCIENT MAN-MADE halls of the Null Keep were just as he remembered them. The floors of old black basalt slid past and recollections crowded in on him. Sense-memory of his youth came forth, still dull at the edges with the lingering effect of the neuropathic philtre. The feeling of the cold stone against the slaps of his bare feet, the tenders watching the young prospects as they made them play hunt-and-seek in the service tunnels.

He halted in the half-dark, licking his dry lips, working the wire binding off his wrists. The psyker felt a peculiar sense of elation, perhaps even a little fear. He let himself toy with it for a few moments, before purging it from his mind. This place – it had been the site of his awakening, but also of his greatest betrayal.

Vaun's face twisted in anger. He hated himself for the way that he had admired LaHayn in the early days, the way that he had been only too happy to do the priest's bidding. But then, he had been immature and unschooled. Now he knew far better, and so he nurtured his hate of the man who had betrayed him.

He wondered how he could have missed something in his former mentor that seemed so obvious to him now. Like all the others LaHayn had covertly recruited from the tithes destined for the Black Ships, Vaun had only been a means to an end – a wager against the deacon's grand plan for glory. He reflected on this, and sensed there in the stone around him the faint traces of despair. So much had been done, so many horrors turned upon the minds and bodies of psykers in this place. Their collective misery stained the walls, it leaked like glutinous oil into the mentality of any who had the preternatural sense to feel it. Vaun shored up the opaque thought-walls inside him and blotted it out. It took much of his will to bring silence once more.

Gingerly, for the first time in months, the psyker allowed himself to think of the engine. He saw the device in vague, ghostly sketches, half-glimpsed, and faintly remembered flashes. The thought of the machine and its impossible geometries threatened pain. Conjuring it in his head was like probing a newly scabbed wound, and yet, it was the end goal for everything that transpired here. As much as Vaun feared it, he wanted it, but to lay his hands upon the device would not be an easy task. He drew himself into an inky pool of shadow as two tenders raced past him. To get what he wanted, Vaun thought, he would need to do that which he did best: engender anarchy and disorder.

As MIRIYA SPOKE, Verity watched the deacon carefully. 'Vaun showed us evidence of your experimentation on the witchkin. Tell us why you are marshalling an army of freaks!'

LaHayn's face darkened with anger. 'Not freaks, you insolent woman. Enhancements. Improvements. My subjects are stepping stones on the road to the Emperor's destiny!'

'You dare to speak his name in this temple of horrors?' spat Isabel.

'Be quiet, girl,' he sneered. 'Your dogmatic order understands nothing of the Lord of Mankind's machinations.' LaHayn took a breath. 'I will indulge you, because it will amuse me to see your minds struggle to comprehend the awesome reality.' He dragged Verity to her feet. 'You know the story of the Heresy, of how the God-Emperor was felled by the archtraitor Horus and confined forever to the stasis of the Golden Throne.'

Reflexively, Verity made the sign of the aquila, the still-loose chains on her manacles clanking as she did so. 'And from there, the God-Emperor watches over us.'

'Yes...' LaHayn looked away. He seemed genuinely moved by the scale of the sacrifice made by the Master of Mankind. 'But what you do not know, what is recorded only in the most secret and arcane places, is the nature of the Great Work that He was about when Horus's perfidy drew him away.' The deacon's voice dropped to a low, reverent whisper. 'I have dedicated my life to that knowledge. I have found scraps of datum from across the galaxy, collated and sifted them, and drawn together a piecemeal vision of what I believe to be the Emperor's lost labour. That is what I continue here, His works.'

'By cutting up psykers and stuffing them in bottles?' mocked Cassandra through gritted teeth. 'You'll have to do better than that.'

The deacon stalked away in annoyance, his voice rising to echo about the stone chamber. 'With each passing century, more and more psykers are born within the Imperium, far more than the Adeptus Ministorum will admit to. These are not mutant throwbacks, they are the hand of human evolution struggling to exert itself. The fools of the Ordo Malleus try to stem the tide but they are blind to the truth: the progression of mankind's psychic potential is inevitable, that it was the will of the Emperor to shepherd it, not destroy it.'

'Madness,' retorted Miriya. 'How can you claim to know the God-Emperor's mind? His intentions are beyond those of normal men. You've made some patchwork ideal from half-truths and rumour, then trumpeted it as fact. This is delusion, priest, *delusion*.'

He shook his head fiercely. 'Don't you see?' LaHayn hissed. 'He knew that one day all mankind would develop the power of the mind. It is our destiny. Think of it, imagine a time when every man is a god himself, a subject in an Imperium that spans the universe. Can you even begin to comprehend the glory of it?' The deacon's eyes glittered. 'Had He not been wounded so grievously by Horus, that destiny is where we would be now. He would have led us there. Instead He lies trapped on the Golden Throne, hobbled and frozen.'

Cassandra went pale. 'All humans, to become psykers? It sickens me to contemplate such a thing.'

'Bah!' roared LaHayn. 'If the psyker is such a canker, then why do we rely on them to light the way for our starships, to carry our communications, to fight on our battlefields? Where is your answer to that dichotomy? The Empire of Man would be in ruins without their kind, and if we could become them, we would know no boundaries.'

'The witch opens the gates to the Ruinous Powers–' began Verity.

'Only those who are weak,' insisted the deacon. 'The Ruinous Powers would be shattered if every human being could match them on their own ground.' He let out a sigh, suddenly spent with the effort of his argument.

Verity broke the silence that followed, her mind still whirling with the echo of the ecclesiarch's tirade. 'There are no words to contain the scale of heresy that you have uttered, lord deacon. This is... It is madness beyond all reason.'

'The colour of Chaos is on him,' spat Isabel. 'He must be tainted to believe such lies.'

LaHayn looked at her sadly. 'So limited in vision. So afraid to go beyond your rigid canon. If it is not written in your books of rules, then you cannot comprehend it happening, can you? You are afraid of anything that challenges your narrow views. It is easier for you to call me a heretic and claim I am loyal to the warp gods, than to accept I might be right.' He sneered at her. 'I pity you.' The priest-lord beckoned Ojis forward. 'I see now my breath has been wasted. I had hoped to offer you a place at my side, but none of you have the scope of vision I require.'

'If you kill us, more Battle Sisters will come,' blurted Verity. 'If we found the Null Keep, then so will Galatea.'

'If you are thinking of your little Mechanicus friend and that battered aeronef of Sherring's, don't waste your time,' said Ojis. 'Both were obliterated by our pyrokenes but an hour ago.'

'I will not kill you out of hand,' LaHayn turned away. 'The tenders are always short of fresh test subjects, psychic and latent. You'll serve them.'

Ojis worked the control in his hands and each of the chained women was hoisted up, a train of pulleys dragging them toward a cable lift.

'Even if you are right,' cried Verity, 'even if you are following the work of the Emperor, what can you possibly do? He lies in state on the Golden Throne, millions of light years from here. Will you make a militia of witches and have them tear His body from the heart of the Imperial Palace?'

'Terra was not the only place where He performed His experiments, child.' The deacon's voice faded as he wandered into the shadows of the workshop. 'Neva's connection to the warp was no happenstance. It was His doing. This planet is an experiment, and before He fell, the Emperor left something here.' LaHayn looked up to watch them vanish through a slit in the chamber wall. 'I'm close to unlocking the last secrets, and when I do, I will remake mankind in His image.'

THE ROUGH CONDUITS of the mountain's lava tubes pre-dated the arcane constructions within the confines of the Null Keep. Many of the tubes still connected to the murmuring, quiescent core of the volcano, funnelling hot air and steam throughout the ashen cone. There were others, like this one, choked with collapsed stone and forgotten. Vaun used his hands and feet to ease himself down the angled tunnel, pressing his weight to the walls to drop metre by metre. It pleased him to see that the map he kept in his head had changed little. There was a kind of secret amusement that came to wandering freely within the very heart of LaHayn's castle.

Alone, the psyker could admit to himself that his scheme had not unfolded in the manner he had expected, but then his greatest skill had always been his ability to improvise. That was why LaHayn had selected him as his personal pyrokene assassin, it was the reason why Vaun had only ever been sent on the most dangerous, most problematic missions for his teacher. The irony that this was also the factor that had led to Vaun's ultimate rebellion was not lost on the psyker.

He dropped onto a shallow ledge. In the stone wall nearby there was a shuttered grille and beyond it – if his memory served him correctly – the uppermost tiers of the place the tenders called 'the sty'. Heavy bolts held the vent in place, but they were nothing more than simple steel. With care, Vaun applied his fingers to the first of them and concentrated. In moments, the metal was glowing cherry red. Gradually, the bolts began to sag and distend.

THEY WERE NOT cells, not in the sense that Miriya would have described them. Rather, the confinement that the gun servitors had forced them into were square pits sliced out of the volcanic rock, sheer-walled with iron grates closing off any means of escape. The Battle Sister peered up and made out the shape of a monorail line crossing the ceiling far above. No doubt sustenance was lowered in and cradles were used to hoist out the luckless when the tenders had need of them.

They had been kicked into a pit two at a time, Cassandra and Isabel in one, and Miriya here with the Hospitaller in another. After the machine-slaves had retreated, the Sister Superior called out to her comrades and was rewarded by a faint reply. Cassandra seemed angry and determined by the sound of her voice. Her strength by example would bolster poor injured Isabel.

Miriya completed a circuit of the chamber, probing each corner for anything of use, and at last sat heavily upon a rusted bedstead. Bruises were already forming in the places where her flesh had been slammed against the inside of her armour, first in the fall of the trap container, and now again from being tossed into this room.

'Any bones broken?' ventured Verity. Her face was dim in the gloom. 'Are you in pain?'

'Constantly,' frowned the Battle Sister. 'My trigger finger aches from lack of use.' She probed gingerly at her neck where the flesh was visible. 'Curious. I expected them to strip us naked.'

Verity coughed. 'Thank the God-Emperor for small mercies.'

Miriya shrugged. 'Merely an oversight on the part of that priest, Ojis. You know servitors, they will do only what they are told to do. He bade them bring us to the dungeons, and so....' She gestured around at the black walls.

The Hospitaller came a little closer. When she spoke again, her voice was low, so as not to carry to the next cell. 'I am concerned for Sister Isabel's welfare. The wound upon her was quite severe. She may not last more than a day, perhaps two.'

'The Sisters of Katherine are resilient,' said Miriya. 'Isabel has known far worse than that. Mark me, she once took a glancing blow from the plague knife of a Death Guard and lived to tell of it. A week of fevers and delirium, but still she returned to the battle and gained honours.'

'I will pray for her, then. It is all I can do if I cannot minister to her injury.'

'I am sure she will thank you for that.'

Verity gave her a sideways glance. 'Truly? I am not so sure. In these days past in the company of you and your Battle Sisters, I have felt like an impediment. I fear Isabel, Cassandra and their like measure piety by martial prowess alone.'

'Then you are mistaken,' insisted the other woman. 'None of us doubt your dedication to the church, not after the strength of character you have shown, Sister. We are blessed to have you in our company. You may bear no weapon, but you have the soul of a Celestian.'

'Thank you.' Verity looked away. 'You have my sorrows on the passing of Portia. First Lethe, then Iona…'

'Each died in Terra's service,' said Miriya. 'We should all pray for an end so noble.'

'You have fought many battles together?'

A nod. 'On countless worlds. Insurrections and Wars of Faith. Witch hunts and castigations. We have spent much blood and ammunition together since our novitiate days at the Convent Sanctorum.'

Memory clouded Verity's eyes. 'My order also draws from the schola on Ophelia VII.' She gave a wan smile. 'I recall the day that Lethe was chosen for the Order of our Martyred Lady. She was alight with joy.'

'Lethe was a good friend and a steadfast sister-in-arms. Know that I do not exaggerate when I say the squad felt her loss as keenly as you did.'

Verity nodded. 'I understand that now. To be Adepta Sororitas… No matter which order we give fealty to, we are all defenders of the faith in our own way.'

'And your Sister, and Portia, and Iona are worthy to be named among them.' Miriya leaned close and placed a hand on Verity's shoulder. 'You understand that after what we have heard, we cannot suffer LaHayn to live a moment longer?'

Verity nodded again, the cold truth of the words lying heavy upon her. 'What must we do?'

'Purge him, Sister, or perish in the attempt.'

CHAPTER FIFTEEN

IT WAS A dungeon, and the designs of such places had not changed in tens of millennia, since the very first days that men caged men and tortured them to gain secrets and superiority. Robbing their prisoners of even the dignity of that name, the tenders considered the tiers of cells in the Null Keep as a paddock for things they thought to be less than human. The clerics who had pledged loyalty to LaHayn's project kept his secret well. One glimpse at the men with eyes sewn shut and lips fused together in the test chambers was enough to instil that kind of devotion. There was always a need for more experimental subjects, whether it was for the psyker-slaves to practise on or for LaHayn's pet biologis adepts to doctor. The tech-priests liked to toy with the brains of the operant and the latent, trying to enhance the powers of the former and engender spontaneous psychic phenomena in the latter. These experiments were designed to induce 'breakouts' – artificially generated telepaths and psychokinetics – but more often than not, their end results were corpses or things that had to immediately be put down. Vaun stole past the testing rooms, the humming psychic landscape of silent screams prickling at the edges of his mind. His quarry lay elsewhere, deeper inside the prison levels.

There were only a few tenders in the main chamber, busying themselves with hushed discussion at a cogitator pulpit or ministering to the gaggle of gun servitors ambling about the perimeter of the room. The machine-helots were constantly in motion, never tiring of their endless patrols of the lava tube corridors.

Vaun recalled from his youth the way the oncemen clanked about the stone floors, the mouths of their guns forever questing for something out of place, so that they might kill it. He had heard that the blanked minds of the servitors were festooned with implanted triggers, devices that would stir pleasure impulses in them whenever a runaway was brought down. The psyker used a maintenance ladder to convey him to the ceiling where the overhead cargo rail was fixed. Light did not reach up here, but his abhuman senses were more than enough to let him navigate his way, metre by careful metre.

Presently he came to a pulley and chain arrangement, dangling close to the guard station in the middle of the elliptical chamber. Vaun turned himself so that his feet were flat against the ceiling and his body pointed downward along the line of the chain. Below him, he could see the tenders in conversation, utterly unaware of the killer that hung silently above them.

'I've secured the new intake as you requested,' said the first, 'but there are not enough guards for the chamber.'

A nod from the second priest in grey. 'Ojis had them transferred to the engine room. The orders came directly from the deacon himself.'

'Is he here? Did you actually *see* Lord LaHayn?'

'I was not so blessed.'

Vaun sneered at the sanctimonious tone and gathered his power, cupping it in his mind like a hand shielding a candle flame. With a sudden shove, he pushed off and the heavy chain unravelled with a clanking rush.

The two tenders looked up in surprise, and their upturned faces met a rain of fire coming down. Streaks of unnaturally heated air ripped into them like laser bolts. Vaun spun about on the chain, letting the action whip him around. He spread the fingers of his free hand and let witchfire streak out from it in a wide red fan. The psionic flames lashed the priests who tried to flee and the slow-reacting servitor drones.

He dropped from the chain into a ready stance and moved to a tender who was beating madly at his burning robes. Ignoring the fire and the man's cries, Vaun hoisted the cleric off the floor and ripped a ring of heavy keys from his belt. The tender tried to say something, but Vaun threw him hard against the wall and he fell away. Flame licked about the ebon stonework, pooling in runnels of molten liquid.

Stubber rounds cracked past the killer and Vaun ignored them. At the back of his mind, he could feel the gaze of other psykers upon him, and in the half-dark it was possible to glimpse dulled eyes peering out from barred slots in cell doors. *Be ready, cousins.* He broadcast the thought to all of them. *Freedom is close at hand.*

The slow gun-slaves were gathering themselves and formulating plans of engagement. Vaun could hear them clicking orders to one another in the metallic prattle of machine code. He had to be quick. Stepping over a smoking body he found the second tender on his hands and knees, feeling his way toward an escape tunnel. Vaun took a handful of his robes and spun him over. Grotesque burns covered the pink-black mass of the priest's face and his hands were swollen claws. This one also had a hoop of keys, which went into Vaun's grip with the others. The tender tried to say something, but his heat-ravaged throat could manage nothing more than a mew. Vaun broke his neck with a savage kick and left him to choke.

Gun servitors advanced on him as he reached the wide cogitator pulpit. Vaun rammed the keys home in twin slots. Normally, two tenders would have been needed to perform the action at either end of the long console, but Vaun's psychic reach had none of the limits of his flesh and blood limbs. The keys turned, one by hand and the other by telekinesis, and a hooting tocsin warned of the opening of the cell doors. The servitors hesitated, weapons deflecting from the single target at the pulpit to the dozens of new ones boiling out of their confinement. Vaun tipped back his head and laughed as the ponderous machine-slaves were beaten down and torn apart by angry psykers.

He watched his erstwhile brethren fight like beasts. These were a poor lot, he realised, and barely one of them with the skills or brains of those he had recruited before Groombridge. The late, dull-witted Rink and disagreeable Abb had been the model of genius in comparison. These ones had no discipline, not an iota of the self-control that Vaun demanded from his men, and in such low numbers they would not last long against a concerted effort by the deacon's forces. The poor fools all bore scarring where the phase-iron of their cells had burnt them time and time again, but they would do. Even an army of rats would be better than no army at all.

'Cousins,' he called, the word cutting through the acrid, smoky air. 'There's more of those tinplate clockworks down here, and plenty of tender tenders to boot.' The escapees replied with lusty cheers. 'The time has come to pay back that old whoreson LaHayn in kind. Who among you would join me in handing out some reprisal?'

'*Aye,*' they called, tearing guns from flesh-mounts and surging into the tunnels. Vaun laughed again, his amusement lost in the clamour.

* * *

THIN DROOLS OF meat smoke dropped into the prison pit, pooling around the ankles of the women. With quick gestures, Miriya directed Verity back against the black stone walls, concealing her in the shadows. Gunfire, the crackling of flames and shouts of pain filtered down to them. The metal grille over the cell was sent clanging with noise as a troop of gun servitors stamped across it, weapons letting out chugs of stubber fire.

'It's him, all right,' growled Miriya. 'I know that voice. The witch clings to life like some kind of parasite.'

'I don't understand,' replied the Hospitaller. 'What could he want down here in the dungeons?'

The Sororitas kept her eyes fixed on the bars above, coiling the beads of her chaplet ecclesiasticus in her hand. From one end of the rosary of black pearls dangled a sliver insignum in the shape of the letter 'I', dressed with a stern skull imprint: the sigil of the Witch Hunters. 'You heard his words. He is rallying them, inciting them. Like a lit torch to a drum of promethium.'

As if to give weight to her words, a flash of flames licked over the ceiling above, and a tender ran past, his robes burning.

Verity blanched at the strangled sounds of the priest's death screams.

'It appears we may not have the luxury of a considered escape,' added the Sister Superior dryly.

The popping of weapons died off and soon they heard the scramble of footsteps overhead. Faces, dirty with soot and grime peered down at the women with mixtures of avarice and hatred. A familiar, insouciant aspect soon joined them. 'Well, well. What an interesting reversal of fortunes this is,' said Vaun, savouring his amusement. 'How does it feel to be the prisoner now, Sisters?'

Miriya seemed to lack the words to convey her cold, hard anger at that moment, and so she simply turned her head and spat into the darkness.

Vaun's smile waned. 'I had thought Viktor would have killed you for me. I see that he couldn't even get that right.' The psyker sighed, and some of the other escapees about him giggled in amusement. 'Enjoy your new accommodations, ladies. I'm sure you'll find them just as disgusting as I once did.'

'You can't leave us here,' Verity blurted.

'Of course I can. You let me live when you had the chance to kill me, Sister Miriya. Now I have the opportunity to return the favour!' Vaun mocked, and he turned to go. 'While I go on to lay waste to this planet, you'll still be here, trapped and helpless, waiting for a rescue that will never come. Perhaps you'll die from starvation or infection. You might find a trickle of water from the upper tiers, which will sustain you for a time. Eventually, though, you'll need to find food.' He leered at the Hospitaller. 'But with nobody to feed you, there's only one source of meat down there.' With a callous laugh, he moved off, his new cohorts trickling away after him.

'Bastard.' The word slipped from Verity's lips before she realised it, and her cheeks reddened. 'Sister, forgive my profanity. It was unseemly of me...'

Miriya watched the grille carefully to be sure that Vaun had gone. 'On the contrary, Sister, I concur. He *is* a bastard, of the most loathsome order.' The Celestian turned her attention back to her chaplet. For a moment, Verity thought the woman was going to commence a prayer, but instead she gripped the skull icon adorning the insignum and turned it counter-clockwise. Workings inside the chaplet clicked and whirred, and with an oiled hiss a shaft of razored metal emerged from the device. Miriya saw her watching. 'Case-hardened argentium-carbide steel,' she explained, 'so that a Battle Sister may grant herself the Emperor's Peace if she is captured.'

Verity's face blanched. 'You don't intend to…?'

Miriya shook her head. 'It is not yet time for either of us to kneel before the Golden Throne. Not while there is work to be done.' The Battle Sister wrapped her fingers around the silver fleur-de-lys on her breastplate and twisted it, yanking the metal decoration off its rivet. She turned it in her other hand and held it like a push-dagger.

The Hospitaller's eyes widened as she began to understand the other woman's goal. 'How can I help?'

Miriya shrugged off her battle cloak and tensed. 'Pray for divine intervention.' The Battle Sister drew back and then ran at the wall. At the last second she used the rusted bedstead like a springboard and threw herself at the stone facia. Sparks flew as the chaplet blade and the steel flower bit into black rock. Impossibly, Miriya hung there, clinging to her improvised pitons. With slow, unbending will, Verity watched her push upward, grinding the knifepoints against the sheer basalt for leverage.

The younger woman did as she was asked, and began a whispered litany.

THE PRIEST OJIS bowed so low that LaHayn thought the man's hooked nose would touch the stone tiles. 'Your grace, there has been an incident on the dungeon tiers…'

'Elucidate.'

'A failure of containment in the cell blocks.' The deacon thought for a moment he detected a measure of reproach in the priest's voice, but he let it go. 'It appears the locking mechanisms were released. Several test subjects and aberrants scheduled for exploratory execution have escaped. There are not enough gun servitors to police the entire level…'

'How did this happen?' he snapped. 'Whose failure is this, Ojis? Answer me.'

'My lord, I did warn you about depleting the numbers of–'

LaHayn advanced on the man. 'You dare lay the blame at *my* feet?'

Ojis paled. 'No, no, my lord.' He backed away a step. 'I was merely making an observation.'

The deacon snarled and looked away. 'This is not coincidence, Confessor Ojis. The witch Vaun is at work here. I know his methods. This is a smokescreen.' He tapped his lips. 'You are to take direct control of the frateris militia inside the keep. Get below into the dungeon tiers and bottle up those freaks. Terminate them all.' LaHayn began to walk away.

'But, your holiness,' piped Ojis. 'I am not a warrior.'

'We are all soldiers in the Emperor's war,' the deacon replied. 'Never forget that.' He threw Ojis a last look. 'I am relocating to the engine chamber. I do not want any more disruptions.'

'But what about Vaun?'

LaHayn grimaced. 'He'll come to me of his own accord, mark my words.'

'EMPEROR, HEAR ME, give me strength,' the Celestian prayed, her arms tight with tension and effort. 'Grant this mortal shell a grain of wisdom, a teardrop of Your might…' With the last word, she pushed herself up to the very lip of the prison pit. Miriya did not look down. If she fell now, it could break bones or worse, snap her neck. As she had told the Hospitaller, she did not have the luxury of death while the witchkin was still loose. 'Channel Thyself to me, make Your will known through this vessel.'

Grasping the metal grate over the pit, the Battle Sister turned herself about and found the place where a throw-bolt secured it in place. She ground her boots into the walls, pressed the ceramite curve of her armour's spine to the iron grille and steadied herself. 'I am Your wrath,' intoned Miriya, completing the catechism. 'Your fury and resolve. Give me strength, I am the Hand of the Emperor.' The words released a flush of adrenaline into her body and the Celestian threw her full weight against the bolt. The metal clanged and bent, but did not give way.

She let out a snarl of anger and effort. Her boots slipped on the stone, then found purchase again; she would not get another chance at this. 'Give me strength,' spat Miriya, drawing concentration from the acts of faith performed by the living saints. *'I am the Hand of the Emperor!'* New energy coursed through her, fuelled by her devotion, and she slammed herself against the metal. With a screech of breaking steel, the bolt snapped in two. Suddenly she was on the floor of the dungeon, the iron grille hanging open behind her.

A ragged figure – shorn of all hair it was impossible to know it if were male or female – gawped at the sight of the Sororitas, and ran away down the stone corridors, calling out in strangled yelps. Miriya ignored it and set to work dragging a pulley cradle into place on the overhead rail. Within a few minutes, Verity had joined her and soon they were hoisting Cassandra and Isabel out of the other pit. The Hospitaller went to the injured woman's side and began to minister to her. Broken slats of wood discarded in the melee went into a makeshift splint.

Miriya surveyed the corridor. All along the walls, cell doors lay hanging open, some discoloured by flames or pocked with bullet impacts. There were dead servitors in heaps, some distinguishable only because their brass and steel bionics were visible among the blackened meat and bones of their corpses. The bodies of tenders lay about in corners, and in some places the remains of what were likely the prisoners of the Null Keep, malnourished and shabby humans still fresh with operation scars.

Cassandra approached her squad commander and gave her a hollow-eyed, determined look. 'What say you, Sister Superior?'

'This indignity will not stand, Cassandra. We must see this place wiped from existence, as quickly as His spirit will let us.'

'Aye,' nodded the veteran Battle Sister. 'My thoughts still reel with the enormity of this madness. It beggars my belief to comprehend it all... To think that at the start of this we were chagrined at such an assignment.' She looked away. 'With each step we take on Neva, we spiral closer to insanity!'

Verity broke in with a sharp cry. 'Someone's coming.'

The ragged figure had returned, and this time with company. There were six of them, all in the shapeless coveralls of the keep's inmates. Miriya raised an eyebrow as she realised that some of them were carrying Godwyn-De'az pattern bolters. The largest of them, a scarred female, had the Sister Superior's plasma gun tucked in her waistband. The psyker prisoners were wary: they knew that these women would be far more difficult prey than the slow-brained servitors.

Cassandra broke the watchful silence. 'Those weapons are icons of the Imperial Church, and they do not belong to you. Put them down, now.'

The large woman grunted like an animal. 'These toys not yours no more. Mine.' She prodded herself in the chest.

'Where is Vaun?' demanded Miriya. 'Where is your leader?'

The woman spat. 'Ain't my leader, ya painted chapel harlot. He's taken those who'd follow and gone.'

From the corner of her eye, Miriya saw Cassandra fingering her rosary. 'You are in charge here, then?'

The woman nodded. 'Got something to say 'bout it?'

Cassandra frowned. 'I find myself wondering. How could your mother have given birth to an ork with pink skin?'

It took a second for the insult to register, but then the hulking female was swearing and grabbing at the gun. The Battle Sisters moved as one. Miriya tossed the broken fleur-de-lys like a throwing star and used it to open the neck of a witch balling ticks of lightning around his fingers. Cassandra's chaplet, with its hidden blade revealed, crossed the space between the Sororitas and the prisoners, burying itself between the beady eyes of the ringleader. The other four were still reacting as the Battle Sisters engaged them hand-to-hand, breaking necks and snapping bones with deft motions and kicks from their boots. The last of them skittered away, pressing fingertips to his head. A wall of hard air rolled forward and battered the two of them back. Miriya felt a rush of panic as she was shoved toward the dark maw of the open prison-pit.

A gunshot rang out and the last errant psyker fell screaming, clutching his stomach, the invisible force dissipating instantly. The Celestian turned to see Isabel with her recovered bolter wobbling in an unsteady, off-hand grip.

'A fine shot,' she managed.

Isabel's face was sallow and clammy. 'Not so much. I was aiming for his head.'

Cassandra handed Miriya her plasma gun. 'They must have found our wargear.'

'Perhaps it was in a storage cell nearby?' opined Verity. 'I should search for my medicus case. I doubt these commoners would have known what to do with it.'

'Be quick,' ordered Miriya. 'Vaun has sown havoc here for his own reasons, and we should take advantage of it while we can. We must contact the Canoness.'

ABOVE THE GLOOM of the dungeon tiers, the Null Keep's inner chambers spread open into honeycombs of interlocking voids. In the past these spaces had been formed around great reservoirs of magma flowing from the core of Neva, but in the thousands of years since they had become cool and dank, turned over to the works of man.

Like all the spaces within the volcano-citadel, the air was forever heavy with a dry, stone-baked heat that took the moisture from a man's lungs. Vaun moved up one of the broad spiral ramps that led to the upper levels, patting sweat off his brow. The arid, claustrophobic air welled up unpleasant memories of his youth, and he damped them down with a determined snarl. At his heels, the loose gang of escapees followed. Their initial bellicose manner had softened somewhat as they left the dungeons behind. The smarter ones among them were starting to think beyond the next five minutes, wondering what good the breakout would do them if they had no plan, no escape route, and no direction. Predictably, they looked to their rescuer for guidance.

Vaun hesitated in the shadow of an ascent ramp and held up his hand, halting the others. The open chamber ranged above them was a maintenance bay for the landing pads high on the peak of the volcanic mount. Cranes as tall as watchtowers cradled a handful of coleopters and the pregnant shapes of cargo blimps.

'Skyships,' said a lisping voice behind him. 'We should take one and fly for it.'

Vaun looked back at them, not bothering to single out the speaker. 'Are any of you pilots?' Silence greeted him. 'Do any of you know where the deacon hides his bolter turrets on the outside of the keep? No? Then by all means, be my guest.'

'We might be able to do it…' ventured another, a gangly female. She pointed upward. 'Skinny up the cranes, maybe.'

'You'd be dead before you tasted sky,' growled the psyker. 'Stick with me and you might live to see daylight.' He pointed towards the cable-car train lying unattended at a nearby dock platform. 'We'll take that to the upper tiers. If we do it quietly, they'll never know it until we're knocking at the door.'

'The upside?' hissed the bucktoothed lisper. 'You wanna go deeper into the keep?' He rolled his eyes. 'The tenders keep us outta those decks for a reason, mate. It's runnin' alive with warp-poison up yonder!'

'Perhaps,' admitted Vaun, 'but not in the way that you can understand it.' He gave them a cold smile. 'Trust me, cousins, the only way out is to go through the deacon.'

'So you say,' retorted the man. 'We're grateful for you throwing the switches an' all, but I reckon from here on in, we'll take our chances.'

The psyker took a threatening step closer to the escapee. 'I didn't bust you out as a kindness, little fellow. You're all in my debt now. You can repay it by doing what I tell you.'

The lisping man twitched. Vaun sensed the twinkle in his aura as the escapee coiled up whatever witch-mark power he had in preparation to strike. 'You're not the boss o' me–'

Vaun did it so quickly that the prisoner had no time to scream, there was just a flash of yellow across everyone's retinas as the fireball flew from his hand and burnt its way into the lisping man's chest. Flames sizzled and popped, the corpse turning about in a wild pirouette before collapsing in a heap. The other ex-prisoners staggered backwards, the brutality of the quick murder had taken every one of them off-guard. The psyker gave his charges a level look, reeling in the enjoyment he felt. 'LaHayn's up there,' he said, jerking a thumb at the roof, 'and he's holding on to a prize bigger than anything you wastrels have dreamed of. I'm going to take it, and you're going to help me.'

'The train, right?' said the gangly woman, nervously. 'What're we dallyin' for, then?'

Within moments the cable carriages had cast off and began their slow ascent of the funicular rails. A warm anticipation buzzed in Vaun's hindbrain. He couldn't be sure if it was some side-effect of proximity to LaHayn's engine chamber or the rush of his own excitement, but the further they climbed, the more he failed to hold back a predatory grin on his face.

THERE WERE FUMES everywhere, and the air tasted like sour meat on Ojis's tongue. His trembling fingers searched forward over the metal grid of the elevator cage's floor, tracing through expanding puddles of oily fluid and wet spongy masses of what could only have been spilled brain matter. The confessor's legs did not appear to be working, and so with the dignity of his exalted station left far behind, he did his best to haul himself out of the lift. His mind reeled, the chaos that had erupted around him fuzzing his recollection of events.

He had been in the cage, descending into the dungeon tiers with his adjutants and the handful of servitors he had been able to divert away from the deacon's blockade. The chimes sounded as the elevator arrived in the staging atrium, and then…

Then there had been gunfire and screaming, the detonation of something large and pulpy spattering all over his hood and robes. Black-clad shapes, glittering like sword beetles, brandishing weapons. *An ambush.*

'This one is still alive,' the voice rattled in his ears, as if something had been knocked loose and broken inside his skull.

Strong, gaunt fingers took him by the arms and hoisted him up. The priest's vision swam with pain as his legs turned uselessly beneath him. Bone was poking wetly from his right knee joint. He managed a gasp as his mask was pulled off.

A face gained definition before him. A woman, after a fashion, sun-toned skin marred with grime and lines of blood. She had eyes like blue diamonds and the set of her jaw was cruel. With a start, Ojis recognised her. She saw it too.

'I am Sister Miriya, of the Order of our Martyred Lady, and you are my captive. Answer my questions and you will be granted mercy.'

Ojis blinked. His eyes were gummed with gluey fluids. He managed to nod woodenly.

'He has the sigils of a confessor on his rosary,' said the first voice again, from somewhere behind him. 'This one was with LaHayn before.'

'Yes,' said Miriya, studying him carefully. 'Ojis, wasn't it?'

The priest paled. She knew his name as well! This was going very badly. 'Please…'

'What are you doing here?' she demanded. 'Where's the deacon?'

'I was sent to suppress… escape.' His cranium ached as he tried to look around. Ojis could make out more dead bodies in the corridor. Whatever had happened down here, they had arrived to late to do anything about it. 'His holiness… in the engine chamber, at the central deep.'

'Engine chamber?' repeated a new voice. He saw another woman, clad in white robes, her golden hair in distress. 'The Null Keep has an engine? But this place is a building, not some kind of vessel.'

Ojis felt woozy as he shook his head. 'Not… Not that kind of engine.' He licked his lips. 'Please… Help me.'

Miriya drew him closer. 'Where is the keep's communicatory? Speak, heretic!'

'Above,' he wheezed out the word. 'Can't get there without me.' He raised a hand. A fat gold ring glittered on one finger. 'I… I have the command signet.'

'Confirmed,' said the other Battle Sister. 'There is a governance mechanism preventing access to the uppermost levels of the citadel.'

Miriya's face soured and she let the cleric drop in a heap. He cried out in pain, but she ignored him. 'There is nothing so low as a false priest, Confessor Ojis. The God-Emperor keeps a singular hell reserved for your kind.'

Ojis looked up at her. 'But… the ecclesiarch is enlightened. He knows the way…' He broke off, coughing.

'The way to damnation,' Miriya replied, pressing a plasma pistol to his forehead. The gun hummed to life.

'No… No. Please. I recant!' burbled Ojis. 'Please, Sister Miriya. You and I, we are both the kindred of the cloth. I beg you!'

Miriya paused. 'You have betrayed the Imperial Church and the God-Emperor of Mankind. What could you possibly hope to beg from me, heretic?'

In a small voice he said: 'Forgiveness?'

The chilling look in her eyes was all the answer he received. Her finger tightened on the trigger.

'Sister, wait,' called one of the other women. 'You cannot shoot him.'

Ojis sagged, relief flooding him. *I'm saved!*

'Why?' demanded Miriya.

The other Battle Sister indicated the lock panel on the elevator controls. 'This device not only requires the key of his signet ring, but also an optic scan.' She pointed at the confessor's face with a combat blade. 'Had you shot him with a plasmatic burst, his eyes would have been destroyed.' She offered the knife to Miriya. 'You should use this instead.'

Miriya accepted the weapon with a gracious nod. 'Thank you, Cassandra. Please, hold him down for me.'

THE CONFESSOR'S BODY performed one last service for the church: as the lift cage arrived at the top of the ascent channel, she threw it into the elevator bay. The still-warm mass of corpse-flesh set off the servo-skulls in the guardian niches at the door to the communicatory, drawing their laser fire. Cassandra and Isabel used the distraction to shoot down the machines and move in. Inside the cramped chambers, blinded vox-adepts cowered in corners, too terrified to react against the intruders, constantly mumbling the message hymns burned into their neural tissues. Thin slivers of watery daylight peered in through observation ports, showing the Nevan sun as it climbed over the rocky crags beyond.

Miriya made the sign of the aquila and addressed the central vox terminal, speaking directly into a bronze mask that turned to present a mouth grille to her. In a clear but fatigued voice, she said a string of hallowed code phrases, prayer lines seemingly chosen at random from the Books of Alicia. The machine knew the cipher, as every communications device in the Imperium did: an emergency Sororitas contact protocol, known only to those of high Celestian rank and above.

'Hear me,' she began, 'I seek audience with the honoured Canoness Galatea of the Order of our–'

'Miriya.' Galatea's voice crackled back at them through the mask-speaker. She turned the Battle Sister's name into a curse. 'If you wish to confess, the time for that has passed. You should consider yourself deserter extremis.'

Isabel choked back a rebuke. 'How… How could she answer so quickly? Such a message should take hours–'

'Silence your Sister, Miriya,' retorted the Canoness. 'Look to the west. Your censure comes on swift wings, errant one.'

Verity pressed her face to one of the window slits. 'I think I see something. Bright glitters in the dawn sky.' She looked back at Miriya. 'Aircraft?'

'A reprisal force is inbound to your position, Sister Superior,' continued Galatea. 'Once I understood your wilful denial of my orders, I had the captain of the *Mercutio* scry the area about Metis City from orbit. His sense servitors tracked that aeronef you stole all the way to the wastelands.'

'There is an explanation for my every action,' insisted Miriya. 'I initiated this very communication to inform you of my location–'

'*You disobeyed me,*' raged the Canoness. 'You took this world's most wanted man into your own custody. What possible explanation could you have for that?'

'I have uncovered a conspiracy of which Torris Vaun is only one facet, my lady,' Miriya said cautiously. 'Within this fortress, the lord deacon is engaged in a dire plan of the highest heresy. I shall willingly give myself to any punishment you will ask of me, but I must insist you first hear this!'

The vox channel crackled for a moment, then Galatea's voice returned, resigned and grim. 'The transports will be within strike range in less than five minutes, Miriya. You have until then to convince me not to kill you.'

The Battle Sister began to speak, explaining all that had transpired since the assault on Baron Sherring's mansion.

CHAPTER SIXTEEN

EACH TIME HE entered the chamber, there was a moment when Viktor LaHayn recalled the very first time he had done so. He remembered the rough hessian blindfold being pulled from his eyes, the strange, directionless green-blue light impinging on his vision. He remembered the hand of the Gethsemenite abbot on his wrist, tight with anticipation, but it was the giddy rush of vertigo that came when he laid eyes on the engine that had always stuck with him.

The abbot was dead now, murdered along with the rest of his sect by Vaun, but the great device rumbled on unchanged, the two great spinning rings of black steel forever turning about the construct's central axis like spun coins. LaHayn had to stop to look at the thing. The motion of the rings, the slow orbit of the metallic rods within them; their movement made him light-headed. It was a marvel of ancient and lost technology, the way that the disparate components worked without touching one another or apparently connecting in any way. The engine was as large as a house, yet it floated above the floor of the chamber effortlessly, steady as a rock. Nothing held it up but the azure glow. The tech-adepts had once tried to explain the method of the sciences behind it, but LaHayn had dismissed them. It was enough for him to know that the engine was the creation of the God-Emperor.

He approached it. A low fence of brass bars kept the unwary from getting too close, but the deacon ignored it, scattering a couple of cowering Mechanicus enginseers as he stepped into the nimbus of the machine's energy field. The adepts clicked and whirred at one another in urgent data streams. Like his tenders, they too were garbed in featureless grey robes.

Once, as with every other tech-priest in his service, they had been loyal members of the Cult of the Machine God, sworn servants of Mars. But that had been before LaHayn's agents had recruited them, by kidnapping, subornment or by acts of piracy. To a man, they had all protested and struggled against the demands he had made on them – *until* he showed them the engine. It was pitiful, in a way. Every single Mechanicus he took had willingly broken their oath and pledged themselves to his service the moment they laid eyes on the device. They knew it for what it was: a physical connection to the great works of the Emperor. They had many names for it: the Psymagnus Apparat, Anulus Rex, the God-Hand… But LaHayn preferred the designation the Gethsemenites had given the device. They simply called it the engine, a fitting name for a device that held the power to remake the stars.

The last days of the God-Emperor were a mystery to many. His actions in the dark time before the betrayal of the Warmaster Horus were shrouded in mythology and layers of obfuscation ten thousand years thick, but in all the holy tomes that spoke of His final actions before the enshrinement on the Golden Throne, there were mentions of His Works, of the secret machinations He was about in the laboratoria beneath the Holy Palace on Earth.

In forbidden tomes, LaHayn had discovered scraps of old creed that the current generation of the Ministorum had declared apocryphal. He collected references to things that flew in the face of the current beliefs, names that none dared to speak, talk of star-children and the births of new gods. The deacon courted death a hundred times over just for daring to possess such knowledge.

Through all his gathered secrets, he traced one thread, unravelling it from the tapestry of the God-Emperor's clouded legacy. That strand of causality spanned the light years that stretched from Terra to Neva, undeniable proof that this distant world was touched by His hand, just as it was coloured by the passage of the warp. It was plain to see once the pieces were assembled, and the priest-lord saw it with shining eyes. The engine was the Emperor's bequest to humanity, to Viktor LaHayn himself. Like a sentinel, it had waited here beneath the stone walls of the Null Keep, waiting for one with the breadth of vision to know its purpose and awaken it. There was absolutely no doubt in Viktor's mind that he was that man.

The deacon came as close as he dared to the spinning rings and held out a hand, letting his fingertips enter their aurora. Trickles of force shifted through him, and he became a prism for their light. It was a gentle caress, the merest fraction of the true energy inside. He could feel the primitive matter of his brain struggling to comprehend the power of it, and always, the same fleeting sense of something magnificent just beyond his reach. *If only...*

Not for the first time, LaHayn let himself drift and dream about what it would be like to know such capability. *To have the power to become one with the machine... To touch the distant mind of my god...* The enormity of that idea struck the breath from him.

'Soon.' The words fell from his lips. 'It will come to pass.'

He retreated beyond the cordon and found a tender on his knees, the cleric's face flat against the floor so he would not lay eyes upon the holy workings of the engine. 'My lord deacon,' said the priest, 'word from the high crags. A force of strike craft approach in skirmish formation. The sensor servitors read them as bearing the mark of the Sororitas.'

His lips thinned. 'How many?'

'Ten, perhaps more. Their silhouettes match the configurations of troop transports and armour carriers.'

LaHayn swore an oath so base that the tender flinched. 'My hand has been forced. The Sisters of Battle are too narrow-minded to accept any explanations of our mission here.' He sighed. 'They cannot be allowed to interfere. You are to decant the pyrokenes. Deploy them in defence of the keep.'

The tender dared to look up. 'How many, my lord?'

'All of them. The time for half-measures is over.'

ORDERS WERE RELAYED; commands became deeds. In the primary chambers where the ebon basalt vaults held ranges of glass cubicles, the hanging cable guides and open crane claws turned to the work of unlocking the psyker pods from their mountings. Ferrying them in the same steady, patient manner as burrowing insects would convey precious eggs within a colony mound, the machines took the huge fluid-filled beakers to exit chambers and tipped the contents upon the dark rock floor. One by one, LaHayn's slumbering army of witches was being rudely awakened, and in the depths of their doctored minds, anger lit fires that the tenders directed towards the oncoming enemy.

Within the motion of this activity, in among all the moving carriages and turning cogs of the keep's cableways, a single train of cargo trailers moved against the flow, passing upward unseen toward the closed tiers.

THE PILOTS BROUGHT their craft through the treacherous rocky straits surrounding the Null Keep, keeping low to avoid the desultory puffballs of anti-aircraft fire from bolter emplacements on the upper battlements. Canoness Galatea had not considered opening a channel to the citadel with any request for surrender, those within could clearly see the black and silver livery of the transport flyers and they knew who it was that approached. If the denizens in the keep had wanted to sue for peace, they had ample opportunity to ask for it – not that it would have been granted.

The razor-cliffed valleys leading to the tower of black stone were narrow and forbidding. Galatea had consulted with the Seraphim commander Sister Chloe during the flight from the staging area, and via hololithic conference with the sensors officer aboard the *Mercutio*, a rough and ready plan of assault had been drawn up for the attack on the keep. Stealth, it seemed, was the key strength of the location – but once that advantage had been squandered, it was no more or less defensible than the dozen other castles and strongpoints that her order had broken in the past. She hid it well, but there was a small fraction of the Canoness that was thrilled by the prospect of battle. Too long in the high realms of Neva's moneyed society classes had made her feel distant and removed from the true purpose of the Sisterhood, and the glory that was to be taken in punishing the disloyal.

Her intention was not to lay waste to the tower, but to break the lines of defence and take those within as prisoners of the church. She numbered the lord deacon and the errant Sisters of Miriya's unit among her quarry – it would be easier for her troops to gather everyone and return them to Noroc for a full Inquisitorial inquest rather than attempt to sort through the web of accusations here. Whatever the outcome today, it would mean that Neva's church and state would be forever changed in the aftermath.

It was difficult for the Canoness to countenance the idea of a senior ecclesiarch in league with psykers, but worse treacheries had been known to happen.

The flyers split from formation and began a rapid deployment, dropping to skate their landing gear across the black sand without slowing to a hover. Drop ramps yawned open and Battle Sisters threw themselves out, trailing descent tethers that would slow them and prevent the women from breaking their necks on landing. Other ships disgorged the flat ingots of tanks. Galatea saw the bulldozer blades of Repressors grinding forwards and the black shapes of Immolators bearing down on the keep's outer perimeter. Units of Sister Retributors and Sister Seraphim went with them, the lightening sky making their armour glitter.

Chloe's voice crackled in her ear. 'My lady, we are about to deploy. Engagement commences on your mark.'

'Begin,' she said into her vox pick-up. At that word of command, her flyer dipped towards the ground and the Celestians in her personal guard made ready to disembark. It happened quickly: the ship scraped dirt with a hollow howl and Galatea threw herself out of the gaping hatchway. Then in a flood of hot downwash from the thrusters, the angular shape was powering away and the Canoness came to her feet surrounded by walls of black stone and women hungry for battle. 'Press forward,' she began, but a thunderous salvo of fireballs cut into the air ahead of the tanks, drowning out her voice with their passage.

'Flamers?' said one of the Celestians. 'Inferno guns, perhaps?'

There was a familiar taint in the air, a greasy thickness that made her gut coil. 'Not flamers,' she growled, 'witchfire.'

Close to the keep, hidden gates were rolling open and out of them streamed figures in mad, violent disorder. To a man, they were all ablaze, pulling streams and spheres of unnatural flame from their bodies to hurl at the Sisters.

Galatea crossed herself with the sign of the aquila and began firing.

THE WAY DOWN from the communicatory was nowhere near as swift or as simple as their ascent had been. The elevator cradle steadfastly refused to operate at Verity's increasingly frustrated commands, and finally the Sisters were forced to descend to the lower tiers of the keep by the zigzags of steel staircase that ran alongside the lift shaft. They moved in near-silence, never speaking, with only the occasional grunt of pain from Isabel to punctuate their passage. They went down and down for what seemed like uncountable numbers of steps.

At random, clatters of moving metal or distant explosions would find their way into the shaft and filter to their ears. The sounds seemed vague and second-hand, the dim echoes of a battle being fought by others.

Eventually, the stairs spread out to a shallow deck of corrugated metal and bare, open grids. Verity made the mistake of glancing down at her feet and her stomach knotted tight inside her belly. In the ruddy gloom, it appeared as if she were standing on thin air, the access shaft dropping away into abyssal depths below her boots. She looked away, taking care from that moment to keep her gaze steady at head height.

There was a balcony at the edge of the deck; saw-tooth bays along one side allowed small cable cars festooned with guide-lines and metallic cogs to dock there. They resembled smaller versions of the omnibus-carriages from Noroc, even down to the protruding runner board at the rear and the handle-operated switching gear. Other docks were empty, home only to gently twitching bunches of cable.

Cassandra studied the bronze dials set into the nearest of the cable cars. 'The tenders must utilise these carts to travel around the keep's interior.' She plucked at a row of rocker switches, each labelled with a string of text in High Gothic. 'Destinations within the tower are listed here. Some are locked off.'

'Show me,' Verity watched Miriya drift closer. Cassandra pointed out switches with fine brass cages over them and lock-imprints where a signet was to be placed. The Battle Sister fished Ojis's severed finger from a compartment at her belt and tested it in the locks – the switches obediently opened.

'This one…' said the Celestian, picking a cable car. 'The late confessor has kindly provided us with passage to the restricted tiers of the citadel.'

Isabel's voice wavered with suppressed pain and reflexively Verity went to her to check her dressings. 'Were not the Canoness's directives clear, Sister Superior? Forgive me, but did she not say we should attempt to link up with the landing force outside?'

Miriya nodded. 'That is fully my intention.' With a clicking of oiled gears, the concertina-mesh gate on the cable car opened. 'But only after we have completed our immediate mission.'

'To find Vaun?' asked Verity, absently dabbing a counter-infective philtre on Isabel's bandages.

The Celestian shook her head. 'To kill him.'

THE PYROKENES MOVED forward against the Sororitas skirmish lines in a tidal wave of unholy fire, the coiling stink of rotten, burning meat advancing ahead of them on the dry wind. Jets of orange promethium from heavy flamers on the front ranks arced outward to meet them, but the burning liquid splashed harmlessly about the witch-soldiers, lapping at their heels like breaking surf.

From her vantage point, Canoness Galatea saw the failure of the guns and barked an order into her vox. 'Bolters, forward! Projectile and energy weapons only.' With unerring precision, the Battle Sisters with flamer weapons dropped back to let their comrades with boltguns and meltaguns take their places. The oncoming pyrokenes met a spread of heavy shells and microwave beams as they boiled over the pass.

To Galatea's fury, the fusillade did not break their advance. Those hit by the incoming fire stumbled, some fell, but barely enough to make a difference. The swarming, burning figures overwhelmed a troop of Retributors and scorched the earth about them, then the fire-psykers ran over a silver and black Repressor tank, attacking it with their bare hands.

Abhuman fingers, clawed and shrouded by a nimbus of flames, dug into the metal of the armoured vehicle's flanks and bulldozer blade. The psychic heat softened the plating, riddling the Repressor with gouges where the pyrokenes dug into its surface like hot pokers pressing into wax. The tank crew were firing in all directions, but the creatures seemed oblivious to the shredding barks of the guns. Galatea saw one of the burning men rip the hatch from the tank and throw it away, then seconds later a shriek of sound came from inside the vehicle as witchfire flooded into it.

The Canoness shouted a battle prayer at the top of her lungs and urged her troops into the melee. Overhead, she heard the throaty roar of jet packs as Sister Chloe led the Seraphim, each woman borne up on streaks of white, each with a gun in either hand stitching tracer fire across the advancing foe.

The speed of the witch-fiends was frightening: they moved like an insect swarm, tumbling and scrambling over obstacles and each other, setting alight to everything around them that could combust. Galatea's bolter howled on full automatic, the sickle magazine clip emptying into the closest pyrokenes she could target. The psykers danced and twitched beneath her fire but failed to fall. She saw great fat chunks of flaming meat being ripped from them and blown away, and still they came on. Whatever devilish force of will drove them, it was incredible.

At her side, a Battle Sister with hair the colour of granite joined the Canoness with her storm bolter. It was enough: the psykers exploded in concussive bursts of noise, detonating hot, fleshy fragments and needles of bone.

'Emperor's blood, these creatures take a lot of killing...' growled the Battle Sister.

Galatea shot her a look. 'Fortunate, then, that we have much of that art to provide.'

'Aye,' snapped the woman, pivoting in place to engage more of the enemy line. Her gun flashed orange-red and more death screams filled the smoke-clogged air.

THE CABLE CAR continued to rise through the deck of the keep, passing through levels where tenders ran back and forth like frightened birds or darkened tiers that showed flashes of workings as old as the heavens. They moved too quickly to determine much, passing into narrow channels wide enough that only two cars could fit within them, then suddenly back out again into open voids strewn with curves of decking. The thin glow of aged biolumes gave the Battle Sisters little chance to see much more of their surroundings than glimpses, but they could hear the distant thrum of great machinery, and the faraway noise of gunfire.

Verity stayed close to Sister Isabel. The woman steadfastly refused to allow the Hospitaller to give her wounded arm anything more than the most cursory of examinations, or even to let her change the bandages that had become rust-brown with clotted blood. She had accepted nothing from Verity but a few dermal pads, small adhesive discs impregnated with pain nullifying agents. A trio of the white gauze circles ringed the neck of the injured Sororitas like a collar of dull jewels. Isabel's face was tight with denied agony, her skin pale and sallow.

Verity drew an injector carousel from the scent-wood box at her hip and dialled a dose of powerful restorative from the glass tubes inside it.

Isabel eyed her warily. 'What are you doing?'

'You require medication,' replied Verity. 'It is my duty to give it to you.'

'I refuse,' the Battle Sister responded. 'My wits must be sharp, now more than ever.'

'Do as the Hospitaller says,' Sister Miriya said gruffly. 'Pain is a distraction. I need you focussed.'

Isabel grumbled under her breath, but let Verity give her the dosage. The woman glanced up as she withdrew the injector. A high-pitched humming tickled the edge of her hearing. 'That noise…'

There was little room inside the cable car, and the iron box rocked on its guide wires as Miriya came up with her plasma gun in her hand. She had heard it too.

'Look sharp–'

Lasers, thread-thin and red as hate, lanced out of the darkness and cut across the carriage. Verity yelped as a beam took a finger's length of hair from the end of her hair, but nobody was injured.

Miriya and Cassandra fired back into the black void and something exploded with a shattering crash, but the humming did not cease.

'Servo-skulls,' explained Isabel, using Verity's shoulder to prop herself up. 'Guardians. We're getting close to the sealed levels.' Two more of the grinning silver orbs dogged the cable car as they ascended, moving between support stanchions as they kept pace.

Isabel fired, missed, and cursed. Cassandra's aim was true, and she clipped one of the skulls squarely in its anti-gravity drive mechanism. The automaton spun out of control and collided with its partner, destroying both of them.

Verity tried to peer out of the open cradle, but without warning Isabel dragged her down with a handful of her robes. There was a fleeting impression of something huge and metallic dropping from the upper levels, and the cable car rang like a bell as a brass-clad gun servitor landed amid the Sororitas. The quarters were too close for the armed women to shoot at the machine-slave, and Verity choked in fear as the thing swung a multi-barrelled stubber gun at her head. Something clicked and whined inside the gun mechanism but it failed to engage.

This close to the servitor, Verity could see its one human eye glaring down at her and the ropes of spittle coating the helot's lips. It moved, trying to crush her against Isabel.

She struck out at the hybrid with the only weapon she had to hand – the injector – burying the needle in the wet jelly of its organic eye. The device discharged a massive quantity of stimulant potion, and the gun servitor went rigid with shock. It gave a rattling gasp and sagged against its own leg pistons.

'Did you kill it?' ventured Isabel.

Verity swallowed hard to rid her mouth of the taste of bile. 'A heart attack.' She glanced at the empty injector in her hand.

Cassandra frowned, examining the dead mechanism's casing. 'See here. It was already damaged. Looks like a glancing hit from a flamer.'

Miriya cradled her pistol, peering into the dark as they ascended through it. 'There should be more of them out there. Why aren't there more?'

'Thank the Throne for small mercies,' said Verity, as the cradle bounced over a set of points and began to slow. They turned, the carriage lurching from side to side, as a flat docking platform hove into view. The console ticking off the distance markers clicked to zero and without further surprises, they arrived at the secure deck.

The women disembarked in quick order. It was Cassandra who found the corpses of two more dead gun servitors and with them, a dark-skinned man in the grimy coverall of a prisoner. There was no flesh on the man's hands, just the burnt sticks of his fingers. His clothes were crosshatched with lines of scorching.

'What does this portend?' demanded Isabel, irritably.

Miriya glanced at a train of cargo carriages locked to one of the other docking rigs, her expression grim. 'It means we are not the first to arrive.'

THE LOUD HAILERS bellowed out the words of Katherine's Lament, and Galatea felt the passion swell in her veins. Unbidden, a savage grin broke out on her face. Yes, there was death and destruction about her, yes, her Sisters were fighting and dying in conflict with a mass of the most dire witches, but by the eyes of the Emperor, she felt alive with divine strength.

The Canoness waded into the sea of flames and dispatched any tainted souls that dared to stand against her. At her back, her bodyguard of elite Celestians marched with the battle hymn on their lips and bloody vengeance falling wherever they turned their guns.

A pyrokene freak scrambled from the basalt rocks, howling murder. The witch had been shredded by the near-hit of a frag grenade detonation, ripping the psyker's legs from his waist, and yet still the mutant came on, shouting through the aura of gold fire surrounding it, projecting itself forward on the spindly pins of its arms. It threw itself at Galatea, mouth yawning to present a throat full of fiery bile.

The Canoness reacted with preternatural speed, the adrenaline racing through her veins in a flood of holy quickening. Her bolter's breech clacked open, the gun empty, and she took a chain at her belt and whipped it upward. At the end of the pewter links was a golden ball the size of a man's fist: a censer, still fuming with a potion of consecrated oils and sacred herbs. Galatea brought it up and used the device as a mace, batting the pyrokene away with a single stroke. The solution within the censer spilled across the pathetic creature's face and sent it screaming into the dirt. There it lay, clawing and dying as the potent oils ate into it like acid.

Galatea reloaded and moved on, her Celestians shooting in controlled hurricanes of bolt fire. There had been a moment when the pyrokene attack had begun, when the momentum of the Adepta Sororitas advance reeled, but the Canoness had turned them through it and now the psykers were in disarray. Broken from their wall of murderous fire, they were easier to kill in isolated clumps.

The constant rattle of heavy bolters and the ear-splitting hiss of meltas overwhelmed the rumble of unchained witchfire. Brute, ungoverned power was no match for the ruthless, unstoppable fervour of the Battle Sisters. To a woman, they felt the hand of the Emperor at their backs, the spirit of the martyr swelling in their hearts. There was no such crime as the dark horror of the witch in the eyes of an Adepta Sororitas, nothing so base and so vile as a mind that had eschewed the warmth of His light and turned their face away – toward avarice, toward godlessness and the anarchy of Chaos. Their unbreakable faith shielded them against the malice of these foes, such forces of inner will that the weaker of the witchkin would find their foul cantrips ineffectual, but what they faced today was of a very different order. If Sister Miriya were to be believed, these were mutants fashioned by the hand of man, and worse, the hand of one who wore the garb of the High Church.

The tanks had been staggered by the enemy, but now they rode high and with steady pace, crushing the blackened bones of fallen witches into the volcanic sands that coated the narrow valley approach. Hot tongues of energy from multi-meltas flashed, ripping into the battlements of the towering Null Keep.

Sister Chloe's voice called on the general vox channel, her words taut and urgent. 'Hear me below. The witches are drawing back. Be wary!'

'It's a trap.' The words came from her lips before Galatea was even aware she had spoken them, some deep-rooted battle sense drawing the conclusion before her conscious mind was even aware of it. 'All tanks, converge fire upon the entrance cavern to the keep. Ignore all other targets.'

'What other targets?' began the grey-haired Battle Sister with the storm bolter, again at her side. Her words died in her throat as the last few witches came together and began to hurl fire in their direction.

At the same instant, pockets of black sand about their feet bubbled and churned. Sooty pyrokenes, aglow with hate, dragged themselves from burrows beneath the ground, emerging behind the advancing Sisters. Galatea whirled and cut them down before they could get free of the basalt dirt. The

Celestians fell into a combat wheel and released bolt fire to all points of the compass.

'Too little, too late,' snarled Galatea to her enemies. 'Tactics first, force second,' she lectured. 'Whoever commands these wastrels is no soldier.'

The tanks drowned out the sound of the rout of the psykers as they fired in one destructive salvo. Beyond the thinning ranks of the witches, the guns of the Immolators found their mark. Dark obsidian stone and heavy iron split asunder as spheres of explosive force tore their way into the Null Keep. The holdfast was breached, and the Sororitas onslaught came on.

'THE DOOR'S LOCKED,' said the gangly woman, throwing Vaun a look over her shoulder. 'The old creep ain't gonna open it just 'cos you ask nicely…' She flicked at her fingers where streaks of greenish fire clung across the rows of her knuckles, and spat at the black gates of phase-iron.

Vaun glanced around at the scattered corpses of the gun servitors, the broken pieces of the machine-slave force that the tenders had left to perish defending the engine chamber. He frowned, unable to find something suitable. The psyker turned his attention to the escapees. At last his eyes fell on a fat male, balding and sweating hard in the humid caverns. A line of acid drool lapped from his flabby lips, spattering at his feet.

'Flame-spitter, aren't you?' Vaun approached him, measuring the man's size. He seemed close enough for what was needed.

The fat man nodded once and more drool left his mouth as he spoke. 'Sometimes, I just can't keep it in.' He had a highborn accent, proof that it wasn't just Nevan commoners that LaHayn preyed upon. The other prisoners backed away, sensing danger. 'What's wrong?'

Vaun smiled warmly. 'Nothing. You'll do fine.' The psyker closed his eyes and turned a hammer of psychic force inside his mind which released itself in a thud of displaced air. The fat man went squealing away and slammed into the heavy doors.

'What...?' The shock robbed the drooling witch of any other words. He tried to get up, but the force of the push had broken both his legs.

Vaun pictured the churning roil of psionic ectoplasm simmering in the fat man's ample gut. His kind of pyrokene was a peculiar breed, manifesting their ability like mythic dragons spewing fire from an endless reservoir of incendiary bile. The fat man and his sort were walking flamethrowers.

The psyker let his mind create the reality. He projected a boiling heat inside the wailing man, watching him twitch and moan. Chemical reactions made his body expand, the grey fleshy wattles on his neck stretching tight. Vaun's errant minions went for cover just as the fat man exploded. The wet concussion hammered at the phase-iron doors, chewing a ragged hole in them. The gates tilted and sagged off their huge hinges.

Vaun strode into the engine chamber with his head held high, and rough laughter in his chest.

* * *

THE STINKING WAVE of putrid concussion knocked LaHayn against the ornate gold control podium, and he reflexively snatched at the argentium pepperbox gun connected to his wrist by an onyx rosary. Lasers keened at the far end of the chamber as tenders and servitors alike fired on the new arrivals; but through the noise, the grating, hateful sound of one man's amusement told him immediately who had dared to breach the sanctified hall.

The tech-adepts in the sub-pulpit beneath him tried to disengage themselves from their cogitators and flee, but the priest-lord struck out at them with savage blows. 'Cowardly fools. This is no time to abandon the work. Proceed as I command you and begin the commencement!'

They reluctantly followed his orders, and while the firefight raged on, a crackle of ancient cogs echoed about the chamber. LaHayn watched as one vast wall of the engine room grew a vertical fissure along its length, opening with ponderous speed to emit a cherry-red glow. The metres-thick doors drew back to allow a heavy tide of dry heat to roll in; beyond them was the open throat of the volcanic chimney at the Null Keep's heart, and just in sight the slow tides of the mountain's magma core.

The rings of the ancient device basked in the ruddy glow, picking up speed as the power from the geothermal tap increased. For a moment, LaHayn forgot the battle raging nearby and felt a childlike excitement blossom inside him. 'Dear God-Emperor, it is working!' Eyes shining, the deacon made the sign of the aquila and anointed the controls at his podium with a vial of sacred unguent. He looked up, barely able to hold back the tears of joy, as the shifting metal planes inside the spinning rings shifted and merged. They turned about and coalesced into something that could only have been a throne. LaHayn worked the controls, moving his fingers over them in complex patterns that he had made into personal rituals. 'Yes,' he cried, 'at last, the conjunction of events comes to pass. As it was foretold, *as it should be!'*

The iron throne extended out of the spinning glow on a rod of brilliant white, cracking the black stone with the wash of its energy. The priest threw himself down and bounded towards it, the blessed radiation engulfing him in warm, soft clouds.

He was only an arm's length away when the fire-streak lashed into him. The burning thread of psy-force entered LaHayn's body from behind, just below his ribcage. It cut straight through him in a fountain of bloody steam, melting bone and organ meat. The deacon crashed to the basalt floor, the dull reflection of his agonised face staring back up at him.

Vaun made a tutting noise as he approached. 'Your problem has always been that you leave everything to the last moment, Viktor.' The psyker waved his hand and let another salvo of flame lines hiss from his fingertips, savaging the closest tech-adept. He paused over the priest as LaHayn struggled to drag himself across the stone. 'No, no. Too late now. You had your chance.'

'Not… ready…' the deacon groaned. 'Until… now…'

'That's just what I wanted to know,' grinned Vaun. He glanced up, licking his lips. 'This is it, then? The Psi-Engine of Neva? The machine that will make me a god?'

'No…'

'Oh yes,' retorted Vaun, 'and because I'm feeling so generous, I'm going to let you live long enough to see it happen.' He left LaHayn behind and marched into the glowing aurora. 'Goodbye, Viktor. And thank you.' He settled into the steel throne, shuddering with power.

The priest rolled on to his side and propped himself up. 'Ah. No, dear boy. It… It is I who should thank *you.*'

For the first time, uncertainty formed on the psyker's face. He opened his mouth to say something, but the throne folded about him, wrapping him in flat planes of burning metal.

Vaun cried out, but it was Viktor LaHayn's laughter that filled his ears.

CHAPTER SEVENTEEN

THE SOUND OF gunfire drew them in, the last pointless defences of the engine chamber echoing down
the hellish corridor to the cable car dock. Grim-
faced, Miriya led her Sisters over the ugly wreckage
of the iron doors. It was only then, when they were
inside the cavernous hall itself, that they saw where
the blood-coloured illumination was coming from.
Rising above the torn remains of the dead tenders,
of the butchered prisoner pyrokenes and the golden
stump of the command pulpit, the great circling
rings of the engine hurtled around one another in
defiance of gravity. Miriya and the other women
were struck silent by the sight of the machine. The
thunderous roars of white energy crackling about it
were mesmerising. In coils of actinic blue, strings of
text in High Gothic emerged along the faces of the

rings, detaching themselves to float in the air like windblown leaves. A rumbling pulse throbbed from the shifting planes of metal at the core of the impossible construction, and with every falling beat the Sororitas could hear the wailing, plaintive cries of a man.

Vaun. The sound of his voice chilled her to the bone. It was not the arrogant, brutal confidence she had come to expect from the psyker, but a horrific cry of terror, as if his very soul were being stripped from his body.

The open flue of the volcano seared the air with great wavering sheets of heat, beating at their bare skin and sluicing sweat from their bodies. Miriya shook her head to break the spell of the fantastic machine and shouted commands to her Sisters. They reacted unhurriedly, blinking with lizard slowness.

'Verity, Isabel, remain here. Cassandra, you and I will approach the… the device…' Miriya checked the charge of her plasma pistol and frowned. The weapon was close to exhaustion.

'With respect,' ventured Cassandra, 'we need every able hand.' She gestured at the dead strewn about them. 'In smaller numbers, we guarantee we will share their fate.'

'Aye,' Isabel added. 'I'll not stand back and watch. The Hospitaller can see to me if I falter.'

Miriya glanced at Verity. 'What say you, Hospitaller?'

But the sight of the machine entranced the golden-haired woman. 'Look,' she said, raising her hand to point. 'The deacon…'

The Sister Superior heard the resonance of LaHayn's voice carry to her and her face paled. 'God-Emperor, no... Please, no. He has already begun.' She was ashen. *'We are too late!'*

'RELEASE ME!' SCREAMED the psyker, every cell in his body alive with crackling energy that poured into him from the warp. 'The power...'

'Power?' mocked LaHayn, dragging himself to the top of his podium. 'But that's what you wanted, isn't it, Torris? Power beyond all avarice, power to rape, murder and pillage across the galaxy? Now you can taste it all.'

Vaun cried out in agony, slamming himself against the seamless cowl of metal holding him inside the spinning rings.

'Tell me how it feels, little man,' demanded the deacon, his eyes locked on the pain-wracked face of his former apprentice. 'What is it like to be a vessel too small to hold the magnificent potential of the empyrean?' He laughed. 'The suffering must be unspeakable.' He moved levers and dials that had not been touched in over ten millennia, shifting the huge mass of the engine in place. In turn, the throbbing hum of power drawn from the raging magma lake below them increased, feeding the ancient mechanism's needs.

'You are such a fool, Torris,' said the priest-lord. 'I am almost saddened by the way I was able to draw you to me. How strange to think that on some level, I actually hoped you might be able to best me. I suppose that is the forlorn hope of every teacher, is it not? That their prize student will one day exceed them?'

'Hate you,' spat Vaun. 'Heartless.' He tried to muster the fire in his mind, but every ounce of raw flame he could call upon was instantly sucked away into the raging white discharges about him.

'Oh, you wound me,' retorted LaHayn, clutching at the very real injury in his gut. 'But never again. Like the errant son you are, you came back to have your revenge on the father figure in your pathetic, wasted life. Blinded by your greed, your mindless desire for anarchy. Never once did you suspect that it was because I wished it!' He shouted the words. 'You are here because I let you come, boy. I stayed the hand of the Sororitas on Groombridge, I allowed you to come here and play your foolish games with Sherring!'

Vaun shook his head. 'Liar.' His fists balled in helpless anger.

'Hard to accept, isn't it?' LaHayn coughed and dabbed blood from his lips. 'But it is the truth. I knew I would never bring you home by capture or coercion. I had to make you think it was all *your* idea!' He propped himself up on the lip of the podium. 'Who do you think it was that ensured Sherring discovered the location of the keep? Who was it that let him get away with his corruption of the *Mercutio*'s crew and the secret arming of his forces in Metis? I did, you dupe. You gave me the excuse to destroy my most troublesome rival into the bargain!' The priest smiled, showing blood-flecked teeth. 'I want you to understand this, my boy. Every freedom you have ever enjoyed, every liberty and choice you think you had, all of it has been by my permission. Each day of your pathetic life, from the moment you took my hand outside that burning church, you have travelled only as far as my leash about your neck would permit–' LaHayn's words cascaded into a hacking, painful cough. When he looked up again, a steely hate coiled in his eyes. 'You were my greatest triumph, Torris. The strongest, the most powerful psychic killer I had ever fostered – but you are *nothing* compared to what I will become. You have outgrown your usefulness, and it is time for the tool to perform its final task.' He threw open his hands. ' The engine is ready, after a hundred thousand lifetimes – and you are the spark that will ignite it.'

'Never,' screamed Vaun, reaching into himself to pull every last iota of destructive energy from within. 'Never, *never*, NEVER!'

The engine howled with sympathetic feedback, and to the deacon's shock, the rings released immense hammers of flaming psy-fire to the four corners of the black stone chamber.

EACH PLANET HAS its legends of the apocalypse, the roots of superstition stretching back through time to the cradle of mankind. Some speak of murderous solar explosions, others of eternal winters or heavenly raptures that would scour worlds clean; on Neva the myth of destruction was one of fire and brimstone. The parables left behind by the long-dead first colonists foretold of a horrific day when the magma core of the planet would rage out of control and shatter continents with eruptions of molten rock.

Torris Vaun's mind held onto those visions of catastrophe as his towering rage boiled inside him. The tight confines of the machine throne coiled about his body, tightening around his skin and pressing invisible forces into his brain – but at the same time, the resonating engine was filling him with impossible power, charging his crude flesh with reserves of psychic potential beyond anything he could comprehend.

His mind was drowning in a screaming sea of churning, raw emotion, the spinning rings slowly forming a conduit through him into the soul-shattering madness of warp space. Vaun's thoughts were slipping away from him, the matter of his skin and bone becoming less and less defined as the machine absorbed him. In moments, he would become a shade, a ghost of the man he was. With sudden, blinding clarity he understood what was happening to him, what it was that LaHayn had conspired to do. In the crudest, most basic sense the ancient psionic device was no different from any other engine. To fully bring itself to optimal capacity, it required a spark of ignition – a scrap of human kindling to set it running to full power.

You are the spark. The priest-lord's words echoed in the blazing halls of his mind. It was inconceivable for Vaun to contemplate that the energy surging about him was only the primer for the engine's true millionfold capacity. He tried in vain to hold the thought in his mind but the conception of it slipped away, leaking out. The psyker was drowning in sunfire, dying by degrees as the killing light subsumed him. The fear and terror at his predicament were burning out of Vaun, leaving nothing in their place but raging anger, at LaHayn, at himself, at the Battle Sisters and at his hated homeworld. The murderous loathing rose up like a black tide as he accepted the brutal truth – he had been used, played like an instrument by that unspeakable old monster, turned to do the deacon's mad bidding even when he believed that his life was his own. And now he was going to die for his mentor, he would vanish and disintegrate into pure psychic energy so that LaHayn could take the power of the engine for himself.

Vaun allowed himself one last moment of regret: he had forged such great plans from the day he had learned of the psi-engine's existence. The psyker pirate wanted to turn it to his own cause, to make himself unstoppable against the Inquisition or any other foe that would stand against him. He did not care about the wars between LaHayn's precious Emperor and the mad beasts of the Chaos Gods – all he wanted was to aggrandise himself, to plunder any world he cared to and shatter those that displeased him. All that was ashes now, and in moments he would be too.

He thought of the boy Ignis, dead now, his face lit with callous glee at the thought of a planet's death. *I'll give you that, lad,* he told the ghost-memory. *We'll have revenge yet.*

Below on the pulpit, LaHayn wheezed and shouted something angry and incoherent. The damnable priest could see Vaun's refusal to go quietly reflected in the flashing dials of his arcane console. The psyker forced a laugh out of the necrotic flesh of his throat and drew inward, gathering in the very last mental embers of his own violent identity. The spinning rings clattered against each other with showers of sparks; the engine was not designed to hold an unwilling sacrifice.

Vaun let the memories of those ancient death-myths fill him and with one final effort, he plunged his raging spirit into the thundering magma core and let it loose.

WITHOUT WARNING, THE black earth around them rang like a struck gong. The Canoness stumbled and barely regained her footing, one of her Celestians snapping out a hand to steady her. In annoyance she shook off the woman's grip and barked out a command. 'Report.'

Her words barely carried over the sullen, grinding rumble of rock on rock, and high over their heads loose basalt pebbles flickered and shifted.

'Seismic activity,' came the voice from the command vehicle. 'Auspex detects energy surges inside the keep.'

The cracking of stone broke around them and Galatea threw herself aside as fissures cleaved the ground around her. She watched in mute horror as a shallow pinnacle of black rock detached itself from the sheer valley wall and dropped into the midst of a Dominion squad. The Battle Sisters were not given enough time to scream. Others threw themselves from the path of tumbling boulders and avalanches of dark sand. Those too slow to react paid with their lives.

Ahead of them, the open maw where the keep's broad iron portcullis had been breached ground against itself, shedding a rain of dusty particles. For a moment it seemed as if the tremors were falling, but then they rose again, twice as powerful.

'It's getting worse,' said the Celestian at her side, voicing the Canoness's thoughts for her.

Galatea tabbed the control stud that changed the vox channel and broke into the frequency used by the transport flyers. They were still close by, orbiting on station. 'Heed me,' she snapped, 'pilots report, what do you see up there?' She turned her face to the sallow sky and frowned. Something seemed wrong about the clouds around the citadel. They were moving even though there was little wind, spinning into odd, ring-like formations.

'Eruptions in all quadrants.' The flat voice of a flight servitor informed her without emotion or inflection. 'Pyroclastic flows sighted in several areas. Volcanic disturbance increasing exponentially.'

'Impossible,' snarled the Sororitas. 'This zone is seeded with magma stabilisers. There hasn't been an eruption on Neva for a thousand years.'

'It appears we are overdue, then,' Galatea's eyes narrowed. She could see it now, hazy gossamer waves in the air as plumes of heat might rise from a campfire. They radiated out from the tower to all points, and with each new pulse the rasping earth twitched again. A distant crash of noise reached them in the black arroyo as another peak some kilometres distant blew itself apart, the upper quarter of the jagged stone tooth disappearing into a vast blot of grey ash. Sulphurous fumes turned her, coughing, from the fractures in the ground. Within them she saw the dim glow of lava marching inexorably upward.

'What is happening in there?' She asked the question aloud, not just of herself but also of the shuddering mass of the stony fortress.

'Your grace?' The Celestian gave her a searching look. 'Shall we go on?'

Galatea's order was on the tip of her tongue when a fresh shudder ran through the stone and earth. With a sound that drove nails of pressure into their ears, the rock beneath the treads of a fully loaded Rhino troop carrier gave way. The slab-like armoured vehicle skidded against the tilting plane of ground it lay upon, jets of smoke blasting from the exhaust pipes as the driver tried to fight the sudden incline. Women threw themselves off the roof and leapt as best they could from open hatches, but in grotesque slow motion the tank sank backward into the crevice with a howl of tortured steel. Half a dozen Battle Sisters, dead in the blink of an eye.

The earth's torment did not lessen. Now it moved like something alive, trembling and shaking. Galatea staggered again as she shouted into the general command channel. 'All who hear, heed me. Fall back from the keep. All Sisters are to withdraw in

skirmish lines, no delays, fleet of foot!' She threw a
nod to her guardians and the Celestians drew close
to her. 'Pilots, execute recovery operation immediately!'

There was a dull reply from one of the coleopters.
'Landing zone is unstable. We may not be able to
make a touch-down–'

'You'll do it, or by Katherine's eyes I'll see you
whipped.' The retort ripped at her throat with each
breath of tainted, hellish air. 'I'll sacrifice no more
Sisters to this blighted place.' Galatea panted and
coughed. Her troops were already donning their
helmets and she did the same, sealing out the foul
atmosphere. Inside her armour, a blessed draught of
recycled air came to her and she swallowed it with a
wheeze. Her optics caught sight of a flyer dropping
low, thrusters flaring through the spreading drab
haze. She waved a squad bearing injured women
past her, once again shifting her vox frequency to
the select channel used by the Imperial Navy. '*Mercutio*, respond. This is Canoness Galatea, notae
gravis.'

'*Mercutio*,' came the cool tones of the warship's
commander. 'We are monitoring your situation
from our orbit at high anchor, milady. Is there business for us?'

'Aye,' she replied. 'The church has need of you.'

'WHAT ARE YOU doing?' bellowed the deacon. 'You
cannot defy me. This is the will of your god!' He
spat with bilious anger, blood flecking his lips, pain
knifing him in the stomach. The gold and brass

frame of the pulpit shuddered with every humming pulse of misdirected power that flashed from the clashing rings. Furious with frustration, LaHayn slammed his fists against the ornate panel before him. This was not supposed to happen. The subject was supposed to die quietly, willingly, giving up his mind-essence to set the engine to speed!

'Curse you, Vaun, you arrogant insect!' About the chamber, stone pillars fell into rubble and elaborate obsidian statues ten millennia old were dashed to pieces. Through the open gates to the keep's volcanic core, the leaden lake of magma was alive with crashes of escaping gas and heavy, torpid waves.

'No,' the psyker's words were distorted and lengthened, pulled like tallow into a dull drone. 'Curse *you.*'

LaHayn could make him out in the depths of the energy nimbus, a pale and paper-thin shade of the insolent rebel that had faced him in the Lunar Cathedral, and yet still Vaun resisted him. From the corner of his eye, the priest-lord saw movement on the floor of the engine chamber, but disregarded it. The last of Vaun's pathetic band of escapees or some surviving member of his own servant cadre? It mattered nothing to him now. He pulled at a nest of bronze levers and the pulpit lurched forward, a coiled armature unfolding beneath it. The golden podium came up and into the edge of the aura field, setting showers of sparks glowing in the air.

'Destroy it all,' moaned Vaun. 'Revenge. *Beaten you.*'

'Never,' snarled the deacon, coiling the line of an onyx rosary in his hand. It was difficult: his blood slicked his fingers and made the links slippery. 'Not by a wastrel... witch like you. You're just the ember to prime the pump!' At last he pulled the box-shaped holdout gun into his grip, clasping the ornate surface. With infinite care, he aimed the ornamental weapon at his old pupil's face. 'No escape this time.' LaHayn's thumb pressed down on a bejewelled trigger button and the little gun released a hollow thunderclap.

LaHayn heard the crackle as Vaun desperately tried to thicken the air between the muzzle and his skull. He saw the recognition of failure dawn on those pallid features, and with a grating shout of victory, he basked in the glorious moment of the kill. The psycannon bolt lanced through Vaun's fading mental shields as if they were nothing more than cloth. It entered his skull through the nasal cavity and travelled into the meat of his brain, shedding needles as it did. The penetration core ruptured inside him, imploding. With nothing to animate his flesh any more, Torris Vaun, the corsair of Neva, hated criminal and witchkin lawbreaker, died with a feeble gasp. His final release of mental energy melted into the psi-engine and the machine glowed white.

The deacon let the spent gun and rosary drop from his fingers, clattering away to the floor below him. He rocked with shallow, pained laughter, clutching at the edges of the pulpit. He had left ruddy fingerprints everywhere his hands touched the shining metal. 'It is done,' he told himself. 'Every great endeavour requires a sacrifice.' Taking a shaky step, LaHayn moved towards the edge of the podium. The spinning rings were within arm's reach, throwing rays of warmth across him each time they passed. He was smiling, tears shining on his face even though every movement was like fire in his belly. But no, he had come too far, struggled too long to die on the very cusp of his destiny. He felt the hand of the God-Emperor upon him, beckoning him forward.

'I will do it, master,' he said aloud. 'I will do it for your glory.'

Something heavy and dangerous thrummed past his head and set him off-balance. The priest-lord cried out and grabbed at the ivory relief carving of the Imperial eagle on the crest of the pulpit, a single heartbeat away from falling short. He turned his gaze downward and saw, like ants crawling around the foot of a giant, the figures of Sister Miriya and her damnable companions. The woman raised a pistol and he knew that she had drawn a bead between his eyes.

'Viktor LaHayn,' she intoned. 'You are bound by the law of the Imperial Church. Stand down and submit to chastisement or you will be executed for your heresy against our God.'

He could do nothing else but laugh at her.

MIRIYA IGNORED CASSANDRA'S muttered cursing. She could see how easy it had been to miss with her bolter shot – the air danced around the high metal pulpit in shimmering waves and cascades of glowing blue symbols tumbled silently about them like falling snow. For the moment, the rolling havoc of the volcano had subsided, but the lava flow still rumbled at their backs, ready to turn violent again at a moment's notice. All of them had witnessed Vaun's murder. The peculiar disintegration of his body set them aghast, but Miriya ordered them closer. The witch was dead, and that was one less deed for them to fulfil. Just LaHayn remained, mad and wounded and commanding this insane mechanism that only the Emperor Himself could master – if the heretic was to be believed.

He looked down at them, a bloody horror in ruined robes. The Celestian had seen men and women live far longer than they should have with stomach wounds such as his, weeping and praying that death would take them and spare them the agony. LaHayn's face was a mass of conflicts: rapture, pain, hate and elation. 'B-bear witness,' he croaked. 'think yourselves as lucky as Alicia and the Brides of the Emperor when they were brought before Him after the Apostasy... You will see. *You will see!*'

'Kill him,' hissed Isabel. 'Before it is too late, kill the damned heretic!'

But there was something, some tiny fragment of Miriya's soul that could not break the awe she felt before the spinning rings of the engine. She could not give voice to the manner in which she knew, but with a certainty that was as solid as the stars in the sky, she *knew* that LaHayn was correct about one thing. This machine was not the creation of man, but of her God-Emperor. The truth of that froze her blood in her veins.

LaHayn stabbed a finger at her. 'You see it. You know it is real. Understand me, girl, once I embrace the engine I will be remade. That is its ultimate purpose, to rewrite the book of life. I want this gift, I am destined for it!'

Verity shook her head, desperate to deny him. 'You cannot interfere with the work of our Master…'

The cleric tipped back his head and revealed the base of his skull. The familiar bolus of the silver sphere implant was visible beneath his skin. 'Oh, but I can.'

'You are no psyker,' retorted Cassandra.

'In moments, I *will* be. The greatest of them.'

'No…' murmured Miriya. The concept of such a thing was too much for her to take in.

'*Yes!*' he roared, spitting blood. 'Oh yes! I shall fulfil our god's will. I shall travel to Terra and awaken Him, and we will transform mankind in His image…' His voice cracked. 'Listen to me. All the pieces are in place. The keys found, the codes broken, the assumption is upon me. Consecrate it with your faith, dear sisters. Watch me take up the mantle lost by blessed Malcador and become the Second Sigillite!'

Miriya's breath caught in her throat and her hand wavered. LaHayn invoked the name of the Emperor's first-chosen adjutant, the secretive administrator-priest selected in the days of the Great Crusade, the man who – so the legends said – had been the first human being to bear the mark of the soul-binding ritual that forever connected him to the Father of Mankind.

Malcador had perished thousands of years ago and no man had ever dared to try and take his title. It was written that the Sigillite was one of the most powerful psykers in creation, second only to the mental might of the Emperor. That the deacon believed he might stand in Malcador's place was either blasphemy of the highest order or the folly of lunacy.

Her aim steadied and her finger tightened on the plasma gun's trigger. 'Viktor LaHayn, in the name of Holy Terra, consider your life forfeit.'

The priest-lord threw his body from the podium as she fired. There was the shriek of clashing energies and then the chamber turned white with pain.

THE BURNING LIGHT sent Verity to the floor, pressing her face to the stone to stop her from being blinded. Isabel was not as swift and she fell to her knees with an animal howl on her lips. The white flash rolled away and Verity resisted the urge to claw at her eyes, blinking furiously. Every glowing ember in the chamber felt like a needle through her skull. She staggered, off-balance, almost falling over the prone Battle Sister. Her gaze travelled upwards even though some inner voice screamed not to do so.

The motion of the spinning rings had changed. Slower now, more languid, they turned and dropped close to the ground, coming about one another, crossing and re-crossing. As they moved, their orbit was tethered by lines of invisible force to a glittering shape at the hub of motion. Suspended there in a rack of red-gold light, the Lord High

Deacon Viktor LaHayn was screaming in silence. His face reflected a merging of two polar opposites – utter, inchoate fear and rapturous joy. By turns his aspect showed one and then the other, waxing and waning through each emotion. White particles gathered about the places in his stomach and torso where he had been injured – Miriya's shot having hit its mark, for all the good it had done – and gradually tapes of flesh and new muscle were gathered out of the air to repair him.

Verity sensed the Sister Superior stumbling to her feet. A flash of plasma from her gun darted into the nimbus of the engine, but once within it slowed to a crawl, the white fury of the sun-hot gas dissipating. Cassandra fired too, her bolt shells puffing into powder where they struck. The Hospitaller sniffed. The air was growing colder by the second, patches of frost blossoming on the stone floor in defiance of the fact that a live volcano rumbled only a few metres distant. Icicles crackled as they formed on the walls and the podiums about the chamber. Her breath emerged in pops of vapour, and the chill crept into their bones.

Miriya grimaced. 'Hard to kill, this priest....'

'He's drawing energy from the air itself!' Verity suddenly understood. 'Preparing...'

'That shall not come to pass,' growled the Sororitas. 'Sisters. Curb the witch!'

Cassandra drew the gunmetal ingot of a snub bolter pistol from a holster in the folds of her robes and pressed it into Verity's hand. 'Take this, and use it. No oaths or excuses now.'

Verity swallowed a gulp of frosty air and nodded, holding up the weapon. At her side, Isabel aimed through bloodshot, blurry eyes. All of them opened fire at once, shells and plasma bolts flaring darkly against the nimbus of the rings.

LaHayn's head jerked, as if he noticed them for the first time. The Hospitaller could see where his thin mane of silver hair was leaving him, the shape of the implant clearly visible as it pulsed beneath his skin. Her stomach knotted in pure loathing. The man had done it, with deliberate intent he had turned himself from a pure-strain human being into a psychic aberration. Just like the crawling wisps of frost vapour about their ankles, Verity sensed the deacon's burgeoning powers reaching out, tracing tendrils of insubstantial mind-stuff. There was a pressure behind the bridge of her nose, as if an iron rod was being forced into her brain. She kept firing, the bolt pistol making her bones jar with every discharge.

Insects.

The word tolled through the four women and made each of them cry out in pain. Verity's eyes flooded with tears and she blinked as they chilled upon her icy cheeks.

'Don't falter,' shouted Miriya, her throat catching. 'For the God-Emperor–'

I Am Your God Now. The impact of the voice was a physical blow, cracking the newly formed ice sheets. *You Will Be The Last To Defy Me.*

'Have faith!' The Sister Superior was weeping brokenly as she said it.

There were still shots in the gun, but for all the effort Verity put into squeezing the trigger, nothing happened. Hopelessness, sharp as a razor, cut across her soul.

From the rings came a hoop of perfect gold light, crackling with dark spheres of exotic radiation. The ephemeral circle radiated out across the engine chamber and struck the four Sisters, violating their minds with terrifying ease. It was the manifestation of the priest-lord's will to break them.

Verity felt as if her bones had turned to water. She sagged, struggling just to stay on her feet, abruptly weighted down with a dreadful, heartbreaking despair. Suddenly everything seemed meaningless, her every thought and deed for nothing, her life a waste of breath and blood. She was dimly aware of Isabel behind her, crying like a child and lamenting. Cassandra, always tall and strong, as hard as steel, she too slipped to her knees on the rimes of hoarfrost and folded in on herself, becoming small and pathetic inside the hollows of her armour.

'Throne, no.' The Hospitaller couldn't be sure who it was that cried out, but she saw Miriya blurring, coming closer. She felt like she was drowning in misery, every pore of her body clogged with grey desolation, each breath hollow and leaden. *It was him*, she raged inside, *LaHayn is doing this to us, turning our dark fears upon us!*

'We must resist,' wept Miriya, shaking Verity by her shoulders. 'We cannot let him stop us.'

Try as she might, the Hospitaller only saw a blurry dark shape in Sororitas battle armour, and the face of her poor, dead sibling looking back at her.

'Lethe, Lethe,' she sobbed. 'Don't leave me. Please. I'm lost without you.'

Inside her heart, the cavern of sorrows she had held at bay after her sister's death yawned wide and swallowed her whole.

MIRIYA SHOOK HER head, struggling to break the priest-lord's telepathic hex, but the force of his mind clung on and coiled about her psyche. Everywhere she turned she saw the faces of the dead, the marching regretful corpses whose lives had been entwined with hers on the field of duty. Lethe and Iona, Portia and Reiko, they stalked her with mournful aspects and empty souls, crying her name, accusing her with sorrowful whispers. And there were more beyond them, ranks of those she had fought alongside in the past and survived: Sister Rachel in the bombed out ruins at Starleaf, killed by a Traitor Guard laser sniper, Nikita and Madeline lost in the catacombs of Pars Unus, and more and more. Her Battle Sisters and her victims surrounding her, beating her down with each deathly wail. Her mind reeled, on the verge of shattering.

She fell to the icy floor and cried out in pain as something sharp lanced into her palm. The agony snapped her thoughts into clear focus for a second. There, buried in the heel of her hand was a golden aquila charm on a broken onyx chain. *A sign!*

She whirled about, pulling on her last reserves of devotion, brandishing her pistol and snarling. 'I deny you. You are false, priest. I name thee traitor!'

So Be It. LaHayn's dark eyes flashed as he gathered up a coil of killing psychic power. Miriya found Verity at her side. The Hospitaller gripped the careworn sliver of her votive rosary in one hand and pressed it into the Battle Sister's grip.

'Must not... suffer the witch... to live...' she managed, every word a monumental effort.

'Aye,' said Miriya, drawing her Sister to her. 'In the God-Emperor's name, we shall not bow before you, LaHayn!'

Die, Then, he said, unleashing unhallowed flames upon the two of them, witchfire shrieking across the chamber.

'Faith,' cried the women in one voice. 'Faith unfailing!'

CHAPTER EIGHTEEN

A SPIRITU DOMINATUS, *Domine, libra nos.*
The sacred words of the Fede Imperialis, the hallowed battle-prayer of the Adepta Sororitas, formed in the minds and hearts of Verity and Miriya. *From the lightning and the tempest, Our Emperor, deliver us. From plague, deceit, temptation and war, Our Emperor, deliver us. From the scourge of the Kraken, Our Emperor, deliver us.* The two women clung to one another, eyes averted from the hell unfolding about them, each clasping the silver rosary chain. The tiny thread of beads was a mere token, such a small thing, an icon of personal devotion with none of the pomp and glory of the church's great artefacts, and yet it was no less a key to the faith of Sister Verity, no less a symbol of fidelity to Sister Miriya. The witchfire thundered across the icy stone and engulfed them

in blue lightning, but still they prayed. *From the blasphemy of the Fallen, Our Emperor, deliver us. From the begetting of daemons, Our Emperor, deliver us. From the curse of the mutant, Our Emperor, deliver us.*

Legend had it that the faith of the Adepta Sororitas was so strong that no psyker could ever break their conviction, that only the most monstrous of the witchkin could threaten their purity. It was said that when a Sister was at her most pious, when she was at the moment of most virtuous sacrifice to the God-Emperor's spirit, the shield of faith that surrounded her could turn any blow from the mind of the aberrant and unholy. Only when her faith was tested to the breaking point could a Sororitas truly know the power of her own zeal.

Miriya gripped the silver rosary and shouted the words of the invocation to the skies. 'A morte perpetua!'

Verity's voice carried the final line over the crash of psychic flames. 'Domine, libra nos.'

As suddenly as it came, the searing, murderous heat faded away, back into the bone-chilling cold. Verity's eyes snapped open and she saw Miriya before her, holding on to her rosary for dear life. 'We… We are unharmed… By the Throne, we turned the killing blow. By faith alone we set our souls as armour!'

Miriya's eyes shone and she turned, raising her plasma gun in her mailed grip. 'Yes… Katherine preserve us, dear Sister, yes. We resisted!'

NO! LaHayn's rage made the chamber shake. *This cannot be. You should be dead, you pestilent whores!*

The Battle Sister released her grip on the rosary and faced their enemy. 'I will die when the God-Emperor calls me to His side, not at the whim of a crooked, insane freak.' She sent a salvo of plasma bolts hissing into the priest-lord's aura. 'You failed to break us, LaHayn. Now the turn is yours!'

To Verity's shock, the Celestian threw herself into the glowing nimbus of energy, her black ceramite gauntlets sparking as they took purchase on the surface of one of the spinning rings. She called her name, but it was too late to stop her. With a sudden hot flash of bright lightning, Miriya was drawn into the deacon's psi-sphere by the motion of the loop. Inside the orbit of the halo, the woman seemed to shimmer, as if time moved at a different speed within the radius of the engine.

THERE WAS AN abrupt and terrible awareness of dislocation. It was at once alien and familiar, bringing back the memory of an unnatural sensation each time she had been aboard a starship plunging into the miasma of warp space. Miriya's senses rebelled for a split-second and she forced bile down from her throat as the world about her *shifted*.

Inside the corona of the ancient device, she drifted as if in zero gravity, held fast only where she could cling to the turning hoops of phase-iron. It was like looking out through a sphere of frosted glass, the shapes and colours of the chamber beyond visible but clouded into distorted blurs. There were strident, strange sounds in here with her, drawn-out shrieks and muttering cries, thoughts bleeding over from the minds of every other living being within the keep. For a moment, she thought she heard Torris Vaun, yelling in agony, but then the echo faded.

LaHayn drifted above her, eyes aglow with hate as he stared down at her. 'How dare you approach me. You soil this holy construct with your presence!'

'Heretic,' she retorted. 'You have no right to speak of what is holy. You sacrificed the privilege of the church and your own humanity, the day you decided to revive this artefact!'

The priest threw up his hands and his anger fluttered in red sparks. 'How can you be so wilfully blind, you arrogant wench? It is you who seeks to block the path of the Emperor, not I. You who cannot see the glory of this device!' He drifted closer to her, radiating power. 'I will *know* Him. I will peel back the veil of time and grasp the mind of the God-Emperor as no human has for ten thousand years!' LaHayn smiled. 'And when I do, when He shakes off the dust of eons and opens His eyes, it will be my face before Him. It will be my reward that is granted!'

Miriya levelled her gun. 'There are no words to plumb the depths to which you disgust me, priest. This madness ends here.' She fired.

The deacon scrambled to throw up planes of force, dragging sheets of flickering radiation from the inner surfaces of the rings to block each shimmering plasma bolt. The Sororitas saw blinks of panic in his eyes. With her outside the spinning rings he had been able to marshal his power more easily, but with an adversary this close to him, he was finding it a challenge to maintain the upper hand. That this newborn witch had power beyond any she had encountered before was not in question, but LaHayn was new to the command of such abilities and he wielded them with clumsy application. He was on the defensive, reacting to her instead of fighting back. She moved and fired, moved and fired, harrying him.

LaHayn spat with fury and did something with his free hand. Miriya felt another vertiginous shift in the depths of her gut as the entire engine began to move across the chamber, the walls passing slowly by beyond the glassy aura field.

'More,' he growled beneath his breath, 'more power to me...'

Inexorably, the engine drifted out across the throat of the volcanic chimney, ascending to where geothermal power conduits snaked up the inside of the basalt flue. The thick adamantium channels extended into the fluid core of Neva, to energy-exchange mechanisms of such advancement and age that their science was unknown to all but the most learned mechanicus adepts on Mars. LaHayn hissed and exercised his new strengths, drawing raw energy straight from the grids.

Miriya's shots pealed harmlessly off the shields he placed in their way, every bolt melting. The Celestian felt the pressure within the engine sphere as the priest-lord engorged himself, his body resonating with potential. LaHayn's wiry, whipcord frame was changing, gaining mass and presence by the moment. He was taking on the aspect of the god that he believed himself to be.

She kept firing, the plasma pistol growing hotter and hotter in her hands as the red rage of boiling magma churned beneath their feet. The emitter coils atop the breech of the weapon were glowing blue-white with discharge and the heat of the labouring gun touched her flesh through the flexsteel and ceramic plates of her gauntlet. Overload warning glyphs were blinking on the grip. But still she kept firing.

'Why do you reject me?' shouted LaHayn. 'Don't you understand what I am doing? Do you want our Master to exist forever in stasis, frozen in eternal death, starved of life, the chance to complete His greatest work denied?'

'You are only a man,' she shot back, 'and no man can dare to command the destiny of the Emperor!'

He leered at her through the haze of spent plasmatic gases. 'Put aside the weapon, Miriya. Your heart is pure, you have proven that. The God-Emperor will need souls as pious as yours when He awakens, you can become part of this new beginning... Think of it,' cried the deacon. 'You will be the new Alicia Dominica, greater than any of the living saints!'

His invocation staggered her; the name of the greatest Sister of Battle, the hallowed Mother of Every Order, echoed in her mind. To be spoken of in the same breath as she... It was an incredible thing to consider.

'You can be that woman,' LaHayn pressed, sensing her hesitation, 'all your errors undone, all your failures reversed, every death made a life – if only you stop resisting the truth.'

Lethe and Iona. Portia and Reiko. She saw them all and more in her mind's eye, the imploring looks on their faces, and she had her answer. To give any other would have been to deny them the creed for which they had died, and to deny the truth that lay within her heart. 'In Katherine's name,' she screamed. 'Death to the witch!'

Sparks stung her as the gun's delicate mechanisms began to boil, the heat radiating off it in waves and melting the ceramite on her fingertips. The plasma bolts, usually collimated and regular in form, spat from the pistol now in screeching ejections of fury, lengths of heat lightning crackling off the weapon. LaHayn snarled and fought away the attacks, enraged at her refusal to capitulate. The gun was seconds from a critical failure, and with a hissing snap the casing cracked along its length. The warning glyphs were a virulent red. At the last moment, Miriya let her muscles take over and she hurled the weapon at the priest-lord as hard as she could.

LaHayn's mistake was that he reacted as a man, not as a psyker. His nascent powers could have deflected the thrown gun in an eye blink, but he was too new to them for it to be a reflex. The deacon caught the weapon in his hands and howled as the scorching heat of it burned him, and in that instant the overloaded plasma pistol detonated in a fireball.

The blast ripped great strips of molten flesh from Viktor LaHayn, flashing the soft tissues of his eyes to cinders, carving him open with daggers of flame as hot as a sun. His bone and marrow turned to molten slag, the opulent ministerial robes and golden icons he wore becoming blackened ashes in less than a second. Miriya's armour went slick and flowed like oil as she turned away. The ignition threw a bow wave of air compressed into a hazy white ring, slamming her out of the dying energy nimbus and against the sheer walls of the volcano's flue. She fell, clawing at black stone and adamantium decking.

With their organic component abruptly immolated, the spinning rings lost all synchronisation and clashed with an ear-shattering cacophony. Metals that had been forged in the hearts of long-dead neutron stars and etched with the blood of artisans from a thousand planets came apart. The rings fractured, dashed against one another, and lost all coherence. The aura field popped like a bubble and the machinery of the Emperor's lost engine fell the rest of the distance to the waiting deeps of the magma core. Somewhere down there, what remained of the High Ecclesiarch Lord Viktor LaHayn of Noroc boiled away into greasy vapours.

THERE WAS VERY, very much pain. The invisible knife rattling between her ribs was quite likely a broken bone piercing her lungs. The blood that bubbled out of her mouth with each exhalation virtually confirmed that. Her right eye was gummed shut with fluid weeping from a gash on her scalp and when Miriya attempted to run a hand through her hair it came away daubed with crimson. The power pack on her back had shut down, forcing her to move the weight of her battle armour without assistance from the synthetic myomer muscles beneath the ceramite sheath. In turn, some joints in the armour had become fused together by the brief, intense heat.

She took a ragged breath laced with sulphur fumes and looked down from the metal ledge where her headlong fall had finally ended. Her vision swam, but she swallowed the moment of disorientation. Far below she could see the vast doors that opened on to the engine chamber, where Verity and the others Sisters still remained, but the fall of the machine had torn the conduits away; she had no way to descend to them. Miriya tapped her vox, but her reward was an earful of static. Reluctantly, she began to push her way upwards, towards the beckoning oval of sky above. Each movement was like torture, but she was resolute.

THE CLATTERING RUIN of the falling machine brought silence in its wake among the three Sisters. Verity, Isabel and Cassandra knew that the destruction of the engine marked the execution of the heretic deacon, but with it a dark fate for Miriya. Ash falls and coils of volcanic haze were thick about them, and rumbling tremors did their best to knock them off their feet.

Cassandra spat and threw a grimace at the entrance to the chamber. 'Rockfall,' she said in a weary voice. 'The way is not clear to us.'

Isabel was on her haunches, her eyes lost beneath a makeshift bandage. 'Sister, speak plainly. Is there any way out of this lightforsaken cavern?'

'Not for us,' came the reply. She glanced at the Hospitaller. 'Sister? What say you?'

Verity's attention was elsewhere. At the far corners of the chamber there seemed to be constellations of light gathering, small soundless flickers of colour that moved and flowed like mercury. 'Do you see that?' she asked.

As she spoke, a large cluster of the light-wisps fused and crackled. The sound sent a shiver through the air, splintering the walls with its passage. 'What was that?' demanded Isabel, instinctively grabbing her gun.

Cassandra paled. 'Oh, Throne.' She pointed. There were more pinpricks appearing by the moment, some of them hanging in the air like hovering insects. 'It's the warp. It's leaking through.'

Verity found herself nodding. She had once been on a transport ship bound for a relief effort on behalf of the Ministorum where the vessel's Geller Field had suffered a dangerous fluctuation on entering the empyrean. On the lower decks, where the field had been at its thinnest, similar phenomena had occurred. Ghost lights, dancing dots of colour that were the tiniest pinpricks of warp matter impinging on the real world. They were the probes of the intelligences that swarmed in warp space, hungry to taste souls. 'The engine,' she said. 'LaHayn's machine… It must have softened the barrier with the immaterium. Things… will break in.'

'There!' Cassandra aimed and fired. For a split second Verity had the impression of something disc-shaped and trailing filaments emerging from a coruscating shadow, then the bolter ripped it apart. The Battle Sister quickly reloaded, frowning. 'Back to back, quickly. There will be more of them.'

THE CLIMB TOOK agonising hours, or so it seemed. With blood pooling in her boots, Miriya pushed herself over the lip of the volcanic vent and staggered down the sharp incline. A few hundred metres away she saw the artificial rock shelf where the oval landing pads sat. An aeronef laboured into the air as she approached, dangerously overloaded. It began to sink almost as soon as it took off. She estimated it would get no more than a kilometre away before it fell back into the wasteland.

An insistent droning circled her head and the Celestian tried to swat away whatever insect was causing it. She concentrated for a moment and realised that what she was hearing was the feed from her vox. Fumbling at her ear bead, she listened again. The citadel's arcane jamming systems did not operate beyond the inside of the keep. It was a chorus of overlapping channels and commands – her vox had obviously been damaged in the fall – but she recognised the orders being flashed back and forth.

'Retreat?' she said aloud. To hear it said after all they had fought through clouded her expression with annoyance. She spoke into her pickup. 'Say again,' Miriya demanded. 'Whose gutless orders are these?

The reply buzzed in her ear. 'Miriya. For Katherine's sake, where are you?' The Canoness was furious.

'Atop the keep,' she replied. 'Who gave that order?'

'I did. The target zone is clear. You should be long gone!' Miriya could almost see the snarl on Galatea's face. 'You were ordered to rendezvous with the attack force. You were told to leave the keep!'

'I… intended to carry out that command in due time–'

'You have contravened orders once more,' shouted the distant voice, 'and now you'll pay the price for it.'

'I chose to… chose to interpret your orders differently, Canoness. I beg your forgiveness…' Miriya was close to the landing pads now. She saw two robed men working with frantic pace at an idling coleopter.

'Do you hear me?' spat Galatea. 'Let there be absolutely no room in your mind to interpret *this* command. Sister Superior Miriya, you are to desist in all combat activities immediately and evacuate the Null Keep to our rally point in the southern valley, where you will submit yourself for arrest. You have less than eleven standard minutes to comply!'

'Eleven minutes?' she repeated. 'Until what?'

'Until the orbital bombardment from the *Mercutio* reaches your co-ordinates. Pray tell, Sister, do I have your full and undivided attention now?'

Miriya choked on the words. 'A lance strike will reduce the entire citadel to rubble.'

'And whatever remains of LaHayn and his heretic army,' replied her commander. 'Unless you wish to join them, I advise you to find transport, and quickly. Ten minutes and twenty-two seconds.'

'My squad is still down there,' she snapped.

She heard a sigh. 'Regrettable. They will be honoured for their service to the church.'

Miriya cut off the vox link and swore a gutter oath. 'I'll not throw any more lives away for nothing,' she told herself, 'never again.'

With care, she approached the coleopter, letting the whine of the engine cover her footsteps. The tender didn't know she was there until he took a fist-sized lump of volcanic rock in the temple. He went sprawling and she used the motion to divest him of the long-barrelled lasgun he carried. The second man reacted with shock as he walked into view around the curve of the fuselage.

'You,' she snapped. 'Can you fly this aircraft?'

He gave a wary nod.

'Good.' She aimed the lasgun and took the prone man's head off with one shot. 'You'll be next unless you do exactly, precisely what I tell you. Understand?'

Another nod, this time wooden and nervous.

She followed him into the cockpit pod and pressed the still-warm muzzle to the back of his head. 'Take us down the throat of the mountain, quickly.'

The man jerked in the chair and started to speak, but Miriya swatted him with the gun barrel. 'Remember your associate? Remember what I told you? Now do as I say!'

The coleopter's motors chattered up to full speed, and with a bump they left the landing pad, the blunt nose turning towards the steaming maw of the volcano.

* * *

THE THINGS THAT came through the holes in the air were horrors the like of which Verity had never dreamed: skinless things with hundreds of yellow-toothed mouths, screeching furies and spidery forms with too many clacking legs. These were the common predators of the warp, the mindless monstrosities that infested the immaterium beyond human consciousness. The sounds they made as they died were terrible, the liquids spilling from them in garish colours that matched nothing in creation. The gun Cassandra gave her spent the last of its bolt rounds all too quickly, and half in fright, half in fury, the Hospitaller threw it at the creatures.

Step by step, the encroaching fiends pushed the Sisters back to the very edge of the chamber, where the steep drop-off plunged hundreds of metres to the lava lake below. Torturous heat at their backs, and a massing wall of Chaos beasts at their front. Verity, Cassandra and Isabel measured their lives by each breath of air.

The injured Sororitas snarled in despair as her bolter's breech snapped open, the last of her ammunition expended. 'I'm spent,' she told them.

The hordes hesitated. They seemed to understand that the prey was at the point of no return, and they giggled and snapped at one another in anticipation.

Cassandra glanced at the sickle magazine in her bolter and blew out a breath. 'I have three rounds remaining,' she said carefully. Her eyes tracked to Isabel and the wounded Battle Sister returned a weary nod. Then Cassandra looked at Verity with a hollow sadness on her face that the Hospitaller had never seen before. 'Sister? Do not fear. I'll make it quick.'

'No,' Verity shook her head, realising that tears were on her face. 'It is not us I feel sorry for, but our Sisters. They are the ones who will have to shoulder the pain of our loss.'

Cassandra nodded. 'You are brave, girl. I would not have thought it of you. I am glad you proved me wrong.'

'And I,' said Isabel. 'Lethe was proud of you. Now I understand why.'

'The honour was mine.' Verity bowed her head and whispered a prayer, waiting for the Emperor's Peace, but in a roar of downwash, an entirely different saviour arrived.

ENCOURAGED BY A series of colourful threats and a shot through the canopy, Miriya forced the pilot to bring the coleopter into a hover by the open gates into the engine room. The situation imprinted on her refined tactical mind in an instant, the Sisters against the edge, the line of shapeless, hooting forms. There was a control board at her right hand and she stabbed the glyphs to activate the stubber guns in the flyer's nose. Rigged with cogitator sense engines, the weapon cupolas saw where she aimed them and busied themselves by automatically opening fire on anything that moved. The pilot dutifully turned the coleopter to present its flank to the women below, and Miriya felt the aircraft pitch as they scrambled aboard.

'Here,' she heard Verity call from the cramped rear compartment.

'Go,' Miriya prodded the pilot with the lasgun, but he needed no more goading. More things were leaking through the expanding warp rifts and these new ones had wings and claws. At maximum thrust, the spindly flyer rose through the ash-fogged air and out into clear sky, turning southwards.

Cassandra came into the cockpit and started to speak but Miriya held up a hand to silence her and pointed at the sky. Dozens of quick, twinkling stars were falling down towards the Null Keep.

By the time the shockwave of the first impacts reached them, they were safe in the canyons, and leaving LaHayn's mad dream further behind with every passing second.

THROUGH THE CHAPEL window, Verity could see the tower of the Lunar Cathedral, clad in flapping tarpaulins where the work crews were busy putting the hallowed church back to the state it had been in before the attack. On the streets, the newly appointed governor, Baron Preed, had softened the news of his predecessor's death by declaring a national holiday, and a bloodless one at that, lacking in any enforced tithes. In part this was due to the hasty installation of a new deacon at Noroc's church, the moderate cleric-teacher Lord Kidsley. In the days that followed the obliteration of the Null Keep, news spread quickly about the perfidy of Lord LaHayn. His name was anathema now, icons of his face taken down and torched by the hundreds.

Privately, Verity held the opinion that only one death would never be enough to pay back such a base and self-serving man. Sister Miriya's thoughts on the subject had been predictably harsh, involving more profanity than was mannerly for a woman of the cloth.

As if the thought of her brought her into existence, the door opened to admit the Battle Sister. She was without armour, still limping from her recent injuries, and yet she seemed no less imposing than the day Verity had first met her. They exchanged nods.

'I was not aware that Galatea had summoned you as well.'

'She did not,' said Verity. 'I came of my own volition.'

Miriya frowned. 'Why?'

'I could do nothing less.'

The Celestian was about to say more, but the chapel door opened once more to admit the Canoness, and with her Sister Chloe, her acting adjutant.

Galatea threw Verity a hard look. 'I had thought you would be off-world by now, Hospitaller.'

'Soon, Canoness. However, before I left, I felt my expertise might be needed here.'

'No one is sick here, girl.'

'I speak of matters of truth, not illness. I am well versed in both.'

Galatea took up a place at the altar. 'Neva rebuilds,' she said at length. 'I have begun a series of purges among the ruling cadres to expunge any lingering traces of LaHayn's sacrilege. This sorry episode will resonate through this world's history for centuries to come… if indeed the planet survives that long.' She gave Miriya a steady, unflinching stare. 'You proved me right, Sister. You brought me trouble… So much trouble.'

'That was never my intention.'

She snorted. 'It never is.' The Canoness pointed to the distant cathedral. 'The Synod want you executed, Miriya. Despite the part you played in terminating the heretic and the witch, your wayward disobedience colours everything!' She banged her fist on the altar. 'Twice you openly defied me, and by extension, the Imperial Church!'

'I did what I thought was right,' said the Celestian.

'Right?' snarled Galatea. 'You invite a death sentence. You place me in a very difficult position, Sister. What am I to do with a woman who blatantly flouted the orders of her superiors?'

'Let her live,' said Verity. 'Let her serve the church with the same honour and courage she showed at the keep.'

'Those things are meaningless without order,' Chloe broke in. 'Each Sister serves as part of a whole. None of us are a law unto ourselves.'

'I will accept whatever outcome the church decrees.' Miriya murmured.

'You would die?' snapped the Hospitaller. 'Even though you did what any loyal Sister would have done?' Verity faced Galatea. 'This is how our faith tests us. Not by rigidly adhering to books of ancient canon without care or thought, but by placing us in harm's way and trying our resolve with challenges beyond our experience. If we are forever rigid and unbending, if we never dare to take a chance against our enemies, then what good are we to our Emperor?' Her passion was sudden and heartfelt. 'We become nothing but mindless zealots locked on a course, blinkered and bound... like Viktor LaHayn.'

There was a long silence before the Canoness addressed Chloe. 'She's quite eloquent, this Hospitaller.'

'Yes, I thought so,' agreed the Sister Seraphim.

She sighed. 'I do not wish to see you perish, Sister. But nevertheless, insubordination cannot go unpunished.' Galatea's gaze rested on Miriya, and in a moment of cold familiarity, she repeated the words of LaHayn. 'There must be reciprocity.'

The woman nodded. 'I understand.'

The Canoness approached her. 'Sister Miriya, it is my judgement that you be stripped of all your honours within the order and your status as a Celestian elite, henceforth reduced to the line rank of Battle Sister.' She took the chaplet ecclesiasticus from Miriya's belt loop and broke it, tearing off a handful of beads from the length before handing the mutilated rosary back to her. 'You will continue to serve the God-Emperor in the church's mission. Perhaps in time, if you temper your bouts of non-compliance, He may grant you the chance to regain these privileges. If not, then at least you may fight and die in His name.'

Miriya bowed. 'Thank you for your mercy, honoured Canoness.'

Galatea turned away. 'The *Mercutio* breaks orbit at ten-bell, Miriya. I want you aboard it when it does.

I will have enough to deal with in the coming days without you to concern me. Go now.'

Verity could see the rejection wounded her, but she hid it well. 'As you wish. Ave Imperator.'

'Ave Imperator,' chorussed the other women, as Miriya hobbled from the chapel.

MERCUTIO DETACHED FROM the commerce station with elephantine slowness, the broad prow of the frigate turning away from the orbital complex to the open seas of space. In the observatorium, Miriya was alone with her thoughts.

She felt conflicted: part of her was relieved that at last the debt she owed to Lethe and the others was paid in full, just as part of her felt isolated and morose at her dismissal and censure. The Sororitas was to take the *Mercutio's* journey to the port on Paramar and there submit herself to the local convent for a new tasking.

Something in the ebon sky caught her eye. There were shapes moving out there, dark as the volcanic glass of the Null Keep. She crossed to the transparent dome to get a better view.

Black Ships. There were two of them, approaching Neva in a silent formation. The sight made her shudder, it was almost unheard of for more than one of them to be seen at a single time.

'They have come to pore over the materials and research left behind by LaHayn,' said a voice. Miriya turned to see Verity, clad once more in her travelling robes, as she entered. 'They will take what they want and sanitise the rest.'

The Sororitas did not question the Hospitaller's presence; she felt comforted by it. 'I find myself wondering, Sister. What if LaHayn did have some flawed insight into the Emperor's works?'

'Perhaps he did,' admitted Verity, 'perhaps not. It is not our place to know such things. At least, not yet. One day, when He rises from the Golden Throne, all questions will be answered.'

'Yes.' Miriya made the sign of the aquila, watching the dark vessels pass them by.

'You have other questions,' noted the younger woman.

'My destiny is clouded, Sister. For the first time in my life, I know not what my destination will be.' She closed her eyes for a moment. 'I am unsettled.'

Verity drew closer. 'Then, if you wish, I might offer a path to you. My duties in this system are at an end, just as yours are. I have already been given orders to join the mission of Canoness Sepherina, who journeys from Terra to perform a rite of reconsecration on the planet Sanctuary. You would be welcome to join me.'

'I would appreciate that.' She extended her hand. 'Thank you, Verity.'

'I owe you my life, Miriya. I do it gladly.' The Hospitaller took her hand and smiled.

Mercutio sailed on, amid stars as constant as their faith.

About the Author

James Swallow's stories from the dark worlds of Warhammer 40,000 feature the *Blood Angels* books *Deus Encarmine* and *Deus Sanguinius*, as well as short fiction for *Inferno!* magazine. His other works include the *Sundowners* series of 'steampunk' Westerns, the *Judge Dredd* novels *Eclipse* and *Whiteout*, *Rogue Trooper: Blood Relative* and *The Butterfly Effect*. His non-fiction features *Dark Eye: The Films of David Fincher* and books on genre television and animation; Swallow's other credits include writing for *Star Trek Voyager*, *Doctor Who*, scripts for videogames and audio dramas.

WARHAMMER
40,000

The outrageous adventures of Ciaphas Cain continue!

DEATH OR GLORY

A CIAPHAS CAIN NOVEL BY SANDY MITCHELL

More Warhammer 40,000 from the Black Library.

*The Imperium needs a hero, whether he wants
the job or not...*

DEATH OR GLORY

by Sandy Mitchell

'THIS WAY.' KARRIE led us through a maintenance
hatch I'd barely noticed before, gaining access with a
short catechism to a speaker grille beside it which
seemed to recognise her voice.[1] As it swung closed
behind us, cutting off the tumult in the corridor, I
found myself in a dimly lit passageway, considerably
narrower than the one we'd just left, its walls lined
with colour-coded pipes shrouded for the most part
in dust.

'Where are we?' Divas asked.

'Conduit twenty-three,' Karrie told him, as though
that meant anything to any of us, and led the way at
a rapid trot which set up interesting oscillations in
her uniform. 'We'll make better time in here.' She was
evidently looking for something, because after a couple of minutes she stopped abruptly and I collided

with her, taken by surprise, but not so much so that I didn't enjoy the experience.

'What are we waiting for?' Divas asked, looking almost as confused as Jurgen. By way of an answer, Karrie picked up the handset of a vox line and punched out a code on its numeral pad.

'I'm trying to find out what's going on,' Karrie said. As she spoke I felt a faint tremor through the deck plates under my feet, and if anything the expression of concern on her face intensified. 'That doesn't sound good.'

'Commissar?' Jurgen directed my attention to a small data lectern standing in a nearby niche, beneath an icon of the Omnissiah, no doubt for the use of any enginseers carrying out routine maintenance on whatever vital systems were currently surrounding us. 'Could you find out anything from that?'

'Maybe,' I said. I'm no tech-priest, of course, but like anyone else I'd been taught the basic rituals of data retrieval at the schola, so it seemed worth a try. While Karrie began a hushed and urgent conversation with whoever was on the other end of the vox line, I muttered the catechism of activation and slapped the power rune. The hololith came to life, projecting a rotating image of the Adeptus Mechanicus cogwheel, and I entered my commissarial override code, hoping that it would prove as effective with naval equipment as it did with its Imperial Guard equivalent.

'It seems to be working,' Divas observed, just quietly enough to disrupt my concentration. 'What are you looking for?'

'Frakked if I know,' I snapped, shutting him up, and turning back to the keypad.

Jurgen pointed to one of the icons encrusting the cogwheel.'That looks like a picture of the ship,' he offered helpfully, underlining the point with a waft of halitosis. None of the others looked remotely familiar, so I selected it, and a three-dimensional image of the *Hand of Vengeance* appeared, rotating slowly, flickering slightly in the fashion of all such devices. A couple of points on its hull were coloured red, stark crimson blemishes, which penetrated a deck or two beneath the skin like ugly wounds. As we stared at it, trying to understand the information we were getting, another appeared, and almost simultaneously I felt that faint vibration through the deck plates once more.

'What does that mean?' Divas asked. The palms of my hands tingled again. Nothing good, of that I was sure.

'We're taking damage.' Karrie replaced the voxline, her expression strained. 'The ork fleet was waiting for us.'

'How could they know?' Divas asked. 'We made the transit by accident, didn't we?'

'Apparently not.' Karrie's voice was clipped and decisive. 'The Navigator's down, due to some massive psychic shock, and ours isn't the only one. Nearly half the flotilla's been knocked back into the materium well outside the deployment zone, and the greenies are using us for target practice. Luckily some of the warships came through too, or we'd be floating scrap by now.'

'How could they do that?' Divas asked, his face white. Karrie shrugged.

'Who cares?' I said, my mind already racing. 'We have to rejoin the regiment, and get the shuttles away.' I reached for my commbead, hoping Mostrue would have had the common sense to begin embarking the gunners. 'If we can't get the artillery planetside we might just as well have stayed on Keffia.' The guns were the least of my worries, of course, but seeing them safe would be the best excuse for getting off the ship as quickly as possible. With any luck the greenskins would be so busy blowing up the starships they wouldn't have much attention or ammunition to spare for the relatively miniscule shuttles. A moment later my hand fell away again. The commbead, along with practically everything else that might have been useful to us in this unexpected crisis, was sitting back in my quarters.

'You're right, of course.' Divas nodded, apparently taking fresh heart from my words. 'What's the quickest way back to the hangar bay?'

'Down here.' Karrie indicated the route we should follow, and switched off the lectern, no doubt hoping we'd memorised it. Having grown up in a hive, the three-dimensional maze had imprinted itself on my subconscious almost as soon as I'd glanced at it, so I was sure my innate sense of direction would be enough to see me safe to our destination if we lost contact with our guide. Divas looked a little more dubious, but tagged along, keeping as far away from Jurgen as he reasonably could. 'I'll take you as far as the portside access corridor, after that you're on your own. I've got to get to my post.'

'Understood,' I said, breaking into a run again as she began to lead us through the belly of the ship. In truth we could only have been moving for a handful of minutes, but the jolt of adrenaline and the uncomfortable sensation of waiting for the next tremor in the deck plating, wondering if the enemy weapons would strike close enough to kill us next time, seemed to stretch the moment interminably. At length, however, Karrie pointed to another hatch apparently identical to the one by which we'd entered this strange, hidden realm behind the corridors we'd become so familiar with over the past few weeks.

'Through here,' she said, pressing a rune beside the portal, and it hissed open. Once again, a babble of agitated voices and the clanging of boot soles against deckplates assailed my ears. The volume was noticeably lower, however, so presumably most of the Guardsmen aboard had managed to rejoin their units, and the vast majority of the crew was at their posts.

As we emerged into the corridor itself I hesitated for a second, Jurgen at my side, in an attempt to orientate myself. I had a pretty good idea of where we were, and a moment later I recognised a landmark, the vivid scarlet icon of an emergency lifepod, one of hundreds placed at strategic positions around the hull. The identification number told me we were on deck seventy-four, section twelve, only a few hundred metres from the hold where our Earthshakers had been stored.

'You should find your way from here easily enough,' Karrie said as a couple of Guardsmen hurried past, Catachans without a doubt, their heavily muscled torsos betraying their world of origin as clearly as their uniforms. I was about to reply when the deck seemed to twist beneath my feet, with a shriek of rending metal, and the ceiling suddenly became a great deal closer. The lights went out abruptly, to be replaced a moment later by dull red luminators which strobed like a panicked heartbeat. Sirens began to wail, sounding curiously attenuated.

'What the hell was that?' Divas shouted, over a dull roaring sound which reminded me of a distant wastefall[1] echoing though the underhive. I shook my head, momentarily dazed, and tried to clamber up again. Somehow the task seemed harder than it should, as though I was fighting against a strong wind. As I regained my feet I began to realise that this was precisely what was happening.

'Hull breach!' Karrie was running down the corridor even as she flung the words back over her shoulder, the wind tugging at her as she did so, making her unfastened jacket and long, dark hair flutter like banners. 'Hurry, before the deck seals!'

The rest of us needed no further urging, you can be sure, stumbling after her as fast as we could. Some tens of metres away, to my horrified dismay, heavy steel doors began to slide across the passageway, sealing it off, and condemning us all to an agonising death. It was like running in a dream, where the more effort you put into forcing your limbs to move, the slower they become, the object you're striving to reach receding with every step.

'Come on, sir! Nearly there!' Jurgen held out a grime-encrusted hand, which I took gratefully, lagging as I was further and further behind the others. My commissarial greatcoat was catching the rush of air like a sail, slowing me down even more. I began to curse the impulse to arm myself before leaving my stateroom, although I was to be grateful enough for it before too long, since the tightly buckled weapon belt prevented me from shrugging the encumbering garment off. We weren't going to make it, I could tell, the thick slabs of metal moving closer and closer together as I watched…

Abruptly their progress halted, and I caught a glimpse of the two Catachan troopers straining to keep them apart, their overdeveloped muscles bulging with the effort. No ordinary men could have managed it, but the natives of that hellish jungle world are made of unusually stern stuff, and to my delighted astonishment they seemed to be prevailing. Faces contorted with stress, they shouted encouragement as our battered quartet neared safety at last.

'Cai!' Divas hesitated on the threshold, turning back to stretch out a hand towards Jurgen and myself, urging us on, and incidentally blocking the gap as he did so. Karrie slipped past him, her slight frame a distinct advantage under the circumstances. 'Come on!'

'Get in there!' I shouted in return, barging him through, desperate to get to safety. Knocked off balance by my frantic charge, he stumbled into the Catachans.

Slight as the impact of that collision was, it was enough. Among the strongest specimens of humanity they may have been, but even their mighty muscles couldn't tolerate the strain of keeping that heavy portal open for long. As their concentration wavered they were finally overwhelmed, the frantically whining servos gaining the upper hand at last. I had a final glimpse of Karrie's horrified face as the slabs of metal clashed together, then Jurgen and I were hopelessly trapped, seconds away from death.

The story continues in

DEATH OR GLORY
by Sandy Mitchell
Available now from www.blacklibrary.com